DEC   2020

HIDDEN

TREASURE

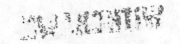

ALSO BY JANE K. CLELAND

Antique Blues

Glow of Death

Ornaments of Death

Blood Rubies

Lethal Treasure

Dolled Up for Murder

Deadly Threads

Silent Auction

Killer Keepsakes

Antiques to Die For

Deadly Appraisal

Consigned to Death

HIDDEN

TREASURE

A JOSIE PRESCOTT ANTIQUES MYSTERY

JANE K. CLELAND

MINOTAUR BOOKS
NEW YORK

First published in the United States by Minotaur Books, an imprint of St. Martin's Publishing Group

www.minotaurbooks.com

Library of Congress Cataloging-in-Publication Data

Names: Cleland, Jane K., author.
Title: Hidden treasure : a Josie Prescott antiques mystery / Jane K. Cleland.
Identifiers: LCCN 2020030036 | ISBN 9781250242778 (hardcover) | ISBN 9781250242785 (ebook)
Subjects: GSAFD: Mystery fiction.
Classification: LCC PS3603.L4555 H53 2020 | DDC 813/.6—dc23
LC record available at https://lccn.loc.gov/2020030036

First Edition: 2020

10 9 8 7 6 5 4 3 2 1

This is for all the people who've given me second chances. Thank you.

And of course, for Joe.

AUTHOR'S NOTE

This is a work of fiction. While there is a Seacoast Region in New Hampshire, there is no town called Rocky Point, and many other geographic liberties have been taken.

HIDDEN

TREASURE

CHAPTER ONE

I was feeling fine, better than fine. I was riding high. My TV show, *Josie's Antiques*, had been renewed for a fifth season, and Ty and I had just closed on the house of my dreams. What a way to start a Monday.

I was back in my office after seeing Ty off for a can't-change-the-date, hush-hush training exercise in Vermont, part of his job for Homeland Security. I was itchy to be up and doing. I couldn't stop smiling.

My phone buzzed. It was Cara, Prescott's newly promoted office manager. "A Celia Akins is here, Josie. She insists on seeing you right away." Cara lowered her voice. "She's the niece of the person you and Ty bought the house from. She says there's a problem."

We'd only owned the house for an hour—how could there be a problem? "What kind of problem?"

"She didn't say."

I could hear the tension in Cara's voice.

"All right. Bring her up."

When I heard footsteps on the spiral staircase that led to my private office on the mezzanine level, I dislodged Hank, Prescott's Maine Coon cat, from my lap so I could stand. He made a frustrated, guttural whine. Hank had attitude. I reached down to pat his furry little head, and he sauntered away.

Celia Akins was short and stocky with curly dirt-brown hair, a double chin, and thin lips. At a guess, she was around forty.

I thanked Cara and said hello to Celia as I walked toward the seating area. I stood in front of a yellow brocade Queen Anne wing chair.

Celia murmured hello as she sank onto the matching love seat. Her ruddy cheeks were flushed, and she seemed to have trouble meeting my eyes.

"Thank you for seeing me without an appointment."

"I'm glad I was here."

"I feel terrible talking about family matters to a stranger, but we need your help. My sister, Stacy, and I. For our Aunt Maudie." She lowered her eyes to her hands gripped tightly together in her lap, then raised them to look me dead in the eye. "You bought my Aunt Maudie's house."

"My husband and I did, yes."

"Stacy and I are Aunt Maudie's only living relatives. We're protective of her. We love her."

She seemed to expect a response. "She's a lucky woman."

She licked her lips, then lowered her eyes again. Her discomfort was making me uncomfortable.

She raised her eyes. "I made a mistake. This is all my fault."

"I'm sorry, but I don't understand."

"I didn't check everything before the movers came. Stacy lives in New York, so naturally it was my responsibility because I'm local. I didn't do a good enough job, and now Aunt Maudie is missing a trunk."

"A trunk?"

"She doesn't remember when she saw it last." Celia paused again, pressing her lips together. She was in the throes of some strong emotion, but I couldn't tell what. "It's perfectly understandable that she's confused and forgetful. She lived in that house for forty-five years, ever since she married Uncle Eli, and Uncle Eli was born there. The house had been in the Wilson family for more than a hundred and fifty years. After all those years, and alone . . ."

"Moving can be a nightmare."

"Exactly, and it's extra awful for someone forced to sort through generations of accumulation not their own. Aunt Maudie can't remember seeing the movers load it. The movers say they took everything they were supposed to and delivered it all as instructed, some furniture to me and all the rest to Aunt Maudie. Stacy thinks it got thrown out by mistake when Aunt Maudie brought in the junk removal company, but there's no way to tell. They track loads by weight, not items. Our only hope is that it was somehow missed during the move."

"I wish I could help, but I don't think I can. I did a walk-through this morning before the closing. The house is empty."

"I know losing a trunk isn't like losing a deck of cards, but it's possible. The attic is big and dark. So is the cellar. Maybe it's behind the boiler, and just got missed. I was hoping you'd let me take a look."

I felt a twinge of hesitation, an innate territorial objection, but only a twinge. I knew how wrenching it was to lose cherished objects.

I swallowed my qualms. "Of course."

Celia stood. "Can we go now?"

I agreed, and she called her husband, Doug, and asked him to meet us there.

Fifteen minutes later, I rolled to a stop on the sandy shoulder behind Celia's silver Toyota RAV4. Doug, she said, should arrive in a minute or two.

I led the way through the black metal gate and along the flagstone walkway to the porch, then leaned against one of the round columns and settled in to wait for Doug. Tall tiger lilies and white heirloom bearded irises lined the walkway. I could hear the waves breaking as they rolled to shore, but I couldn't see them. They landed with a soothing, hypnotic rhythm, not a crash or a roar, more like a rumble. The briny scent of the ocean glided in on a soft breeze. The sky was bright blue and cloudless. It was a picture-perfect day, a day for new beginnings, one of God's days, my mother would have said.

"Thank you for this," Celia said. "I know it's an inconvenience."

Given her somber mood, I didn't want to tell her that despite my slight hesitation, I was thrilled to have an excuse to walk through my new house, my home, again.

Doug drove up in an old green Subaru Outback. He looked to be around the same age as his wife, early forties. He was tall and skinny with big ears that stuck out from his head and graying hair cut close. He wore a short-sleeved blue shirt with too-big jeans and work boots.

When he reached the porch, he patted Celia's arm, then turned toward me. "We appreciate this."

"Of course."

I used my key, and the three of us stepped into the entryway. The house, which was located on a secluded triple lot abutting the north end of Rocky Point Beach, featured a wraparound porch, hexagonal rooms, and fanciful detailing. In our coastal New Hampshire community, it was called the Gingerbread House. I knew from our real estate broker that Mrs. Wilson had moved to the independent wing of Belle Vista, an assisted living facility, three months earlier, which explained the dank odor. Sunlight dappled the old oak flooring and flecked the mahogany doors and window frames with golden glints. On the walls, squares and rectangles in a darker shade than the rest of the paint, ochre instead of tan, indicated where artwork had hung.

"You mentioned that the trunk might be in the attic or the cellar," I said. "Shall we begin at the top?"

We climbed the main staircase, a grand affair that included a spacious landing halfway up. I paused for a moment at the oversized windows to look out over the Atlantic. Sun-sparked glitter danced along the midnight-blue surface. From the landing, we trooped up the rest of the stairs to the third floor. The attic, located on what was the equivalent of the fourth floor, was accessed through a bedroom at the front.

It was stuffy under the eaves. Three dangling low-watt lightbulbs provided the bulk of the light, helped along by sunlight that trickled in from porthole-like windows mounted high on the north and south walls. I stood in the center watching Doug and Celia search the entire area. With Doug holding an old flashlight he'd brought along, Celia squatted to peer behind joists and crossbeams. Other than dust motes, the place was bare.

"The cellar next?" I asked.

We walked back down, this time using the back stairs. We passed through the butler's pantry and took the last flight down.

The basement was about ten degrees cooler than the ground floor. Its concrete walls and floor had been painted industrial gray a long time ago. Except for three rows of empty wooden shelving, a small apartment built into the back corner, and a separate room for the boiler, the space was wide open.

Celia walked directly to the boiler room. I stood at the threshold, watching Doug aim his flashlight while Celia examined the space between the boiler and the wall.

"Nothing," she said. She walked back into the open area, stopped in the center, and turned around. Her lower lip quivered. "The trunk's not here."

Doug put his arm around her. "It's all right."

"No, it's not," she whispered, "and it's all my fault."

"No, no," Doug said.

"I knew Aunt Maudie was getting forgetful. I should have done more."

"You did the best you could."

After a few seconds, I asked, "Did you want to walk through the rest of the house?"

"There's no point," Celia said. "There's no place left to look."

Celia walked out, her feet dragging. Doug thanked me again and handed me a slip of paper with his and Celia's phone numbers written in a spidery scrawl. I stood on the porch watching as they trudged down the path. They disappeared behind the screen of sumac and scrub oak that shielded our property from Ocean Avenue.

I leaned against the column, breathing in the salt-steeped air.

I hoped Celia would come to realize that anyone can lose anything, whether it's a pack of cards or an entire trunk. Maybe then she could forgive herself.

CHAPTER TWO

T he next morning, Tuesday, I arrived at the Gingerbread House just before eight to supervise two of my employees packing up the crystal chandelier from the dining room. Ty and I planned on putting it back after the renovation, and I was champing at the bit to appraise it and learn its history. The removal was a delicate and exacting process, and when the chandelier was safely crated and in the van, I breathed a to-my-toes sigh of relief.

During our early morning phone call, Ty told me that his training exercise had not met expectations, probably a euphemism for a complete bust, so he had to revamp the procedure. If there was another misstep, he'd need to go to Washington to discuss ways and means with his boss.

The demolition-planning phase of our house renovation was scheduled to begin tomorrow afternoon, and Ty was concerned that he wouldn't be there for our last-look and measuring session. I knew I could measure the rooms and sketch out the various nooks and juts on my own, but I'd been looking forward to planning paint colors and furniture purchases with Ty as we walked the house for the last time before the reno began. I swallowed a pang of disappointment and assured him that I would be fine. But four eyes were always better than two, and measuring is far easier when someone else holds the other end of the tape measure, so I called Tom Hill, who'd been Mrs. Wilson's live-in handyman-cum-gardener, and who'd agreed to continue maintaining the grounds for us through the renovation. Luckily, Tom was available, and glad for the work.

While I waited for him, I got a step stool and toolbox from my car trunk and brought them inside, then straddled the porch railing, enjoying the warmth. Tom appeared at the gate. He was tall and fit, close to thirty, with short sandy hair and regular features. He'd spent eight years in the army, and it showed in his posture and demeanor. He waved to me, a half-salute, then turned back to the road and said something I couldn't hear to someone I couldn't see. When he finished, he strode down the path toward me, smiling.

"Top of the mornin' to ya," he said.

"And to you. Thanks for helping me out on such short notice."

"Your timing was perfect. Julie's car died last night, so she's using my pickup. You called just as she was getting ready to head to school, so she was able to drop me on her way."

I'd met Tom's girlfriend, Julie Simond, a couple of times when Ty and I stopped by the Gingerbread House. We'd found Tom fussing around the garden and Julie fussing around Tom. She was twenty-three, hailed from Plainview, a blue-collar town close to the interstate, and was studying nursing at Hitchens University.

"Bummer."

"It comes at a bad time, that's for sure."

"I can give you a ride home when we're done here."

"Thanks. Julie only has one class today, and her shift at the diner isn't until later, so we should be okay."

I led the way inside. "We can leave the toolbox here. I'll bring the step stool with me—I'm short."

"You're petite."

"Ha! A rose by any other name . . ." I picked up the step stool. "I think dividing up to check the rooms, then measuring together will be the fastest approach."

"Sounds good. Should we skip the attic and cellar?" Tom asked. "Celia said they were completely empty."

"You spoke to her?"

"This morning. I was installing some track lighting for one of Celia's neighbors—she was nice enough to recommend me. Anyway, Celia's pretty bummed the trunk is missing, and from what I hear, this trunk contains some valuable stuff."

"It's horrible to lose things. You feel so powerless."

"Like I told her, you do what you can, and that's all you can do. So, what's our plan?"

"I think skipping the attic and basement makes sense. You can start on the north end of the third floor and I'll start on the south end, and we'll meet in the middle." I explained that my walk-through with Ty before closing had been just a quick look-see, and now I wanted us to look inside each drawer and cubbyhole of the bedroom's built-in wardrobes and deep closets, under anything that wasn't flush to the floor, and on or over anywhere else where something might be found.

Forty-five minutes later, having examined every inch of every flat surface in three rooms, about the halfway mark, I walked to the middle of the corridor that ran the length of the house. I let my eyes wander to the ornate crown molding, the wainscoting, and the large scrolled leaf-edged ceiling rose, fine details Ty and I wanted to keep, along with the wide oak plank flooring, which had been burnished to a luxuriant red-gold through more than a century of care and polish. The silence was omnipresent, broken only by an occasional creak as the old house settled and a hushed sense of the ocean's movement. The serenity was relaxing, like nestling into a reading nook with a favorite book. After a moment, I called for Tom.

He stepped over the threshold of the bedroom nearest me, holding a rusty wrench in front of him like a conductor holding a baton. "Guess what I found?"

I tapped my chin with an index finger, pretending to think. "A rusty wrench."

Tom grinned. "How'd you guess?"

"I'm known for my sharp-as-a-tack deductive reasoning. Where did you find it?"

"Under the radiator."

"I bet whatever plumber did the repair still wonders what happened to his wrench."

"He probably blamed his apprentice for stealing it."

"Oh, I hope not." I laughed. "I bet the plumber is the sort of fellow who is terrific at his job, focused and intuitive, but when he's not working, he's a little scatterbrained. He blames himself." I smiled. "You can tell a lot about people by how they fill in the blanks."

"I'm cynical. You're optimistic."

"I don't think of you as cynical."

"Of course you don't. An optimist wouldn't."

I laughed again.

"This rusty wrench is my total take. How about you?"

"Not even a rusty wrench." I told him where I left off and asked him to finish up. "When you're done, how about if you take the second floor? I'll start in on the ground floor."

"Sounds good."

Downstairs, I made my way to the music room, so named because of the vignette-style classical musical notations on the wallpaper. A built-in bookcase was bare. So was the firewood storage cubbyhole next to the fireplace in the living room. The dining room was huge, perfect for big get-togethers, a thought that always made me smile.

As the only child of only children, I had the tiniest of families—only one cousin, and she lived in England. Ty was also an only child, and his parents hadn't been close to their siblings, so while he had a decent-sized extended family, he barely knew them. Thanksgiving dinner for two at a table designed to seat twenty would be fine, but I thought it would be more fun to fill it up. I began preparing a mental list of who we could invite to join us.

All the bookcases in the study were open and empty. The powder room didn't even have a medicine cabinet I could look in. I used my step stool in the kitchen to confirm that all the upper cabinets were empty. So were the bottom cabinets and drawers. The last space to check was the butler's pantry, one of my favorite parts of the house.

At twelve by fifteen feet, it was bigger than most bedrooms and featured a wealth of storage and fifteen-foot ceilings, like the rest of the house. In addition to the two back stairway doors—one leading up to the second floor and the other leading down to the basement—a swinging door accessed the kitchen, and a side door opened onto a flagstone pathway and a kitchen garden. There was a big window in the side door, but not much sunlight made it inside because of a deep overhang, a nice feature when collecting herbs in the rain, but of limited help on a sunny day when you're trying to see into corners. Floor-to-ceiling custom-built storage units covered all available wall space.

As I reached to open a drawer in the built-in closest to the outside door, I heard a steady, repetitive click-clack. Someone wearing high heels was walking purposefully toward me. Startled, I gasped.

"Hello?" a woman called. "Ms. Prescott? Are you here?"

I took a few seconds to regain my composure, then pushed through the swinging kitchen door. Three paces in, I could see the entryway. An attractive woman I'd never seen stood five feet from the front door.

"I'm Josie Prescott," I said.

She smiled. "I recognize you from your TV show. I'm a huge fan. I'm Stacy Collins, Maudie Wilson's niece, Celia's sister."

She must have read the astonishment on my face as I glanced at the front door because she said, "Apparently, the bell is broken." She smiled. "I used my key."

"Your key."

"I went to your office, and they told me you weren't in. I thought maybe you were here, and you are! I'm hoping you have a moment to talk."

Stacy was a few years younger than Celia, thirty-five or thirty-six, perhaps, and cut from entirely different cloth. Whereas Celia was comfortably proportioned and dressed with country simplicity, Stacy was svelte, every inch a city girl who dressed to impress. Her salmon sleeveless raw silk sheath fit her as if it had been made for her, and maybe it had. Her blond hair was cut in a striking wedge. She wore ivory open-toed pumps with three-inch heels, two inches higher than most women in Rocky Point wore.

I slipped past her to the front door and opened it. "Why don't we step onto the porch?"

She hesitated, probably worried I was giving her the bum's rush, then walked outside. I patted my back pocket to confirm I had my key before following her out and shutting the door.

I leaned against the porch railing. "What can I do for you?"

She tried to smile, realized it wasn't working, and let it go. "This is painful for me to talk about. I wish it wasn't necessary, but I guess there's no way around it." She paused for a moment. "As you may know, I live in New York City. I came up for a few days to see how Aunt Maudie is adjusting to Belle Vista. I'm really very fond of her." She paused again. "Celia told you that Aunt Maudie's trunk is missing. Thank you for letting her look for it. It turns out that a cat statue and fancy box are MIA, too."

"I'm sorry."

"Aunt Maudie admits she can't remember moving them, just like the trunk."

I wasn't warming to Stacy. She didn't say that Aunt Maudie *reported* that the objects were missing or that Aunt Maudie *told* her about it, or even that Aunt Maudie *confided* in her. Stacy chose the word *admit*. It made me feel sorry for Mrs. Wilson, who, it seemed, had been *interrogated* by her nieces until she *confessed*.

Stacy laughed. "Of course, she has no memory of *not* moving them, either. She doesn't even remember when she saw them last." Her phone vibrated. She took it from her purse and glanced at the display, then said, "Excuse me a moment." She stepped aside two paces and turned her back.

"Alyson, how are you?" she asked, her voice suddenly silken. She listened for a moment. "I'm so pleased! Did you decide on the zebrawood or the padauk? . . . Oh, I agree. Zebrawood is perfect . . . Thank you . . . Yes, that's right . . . Good . . . Fine . . . If you send me the purchase order, I can get the team started right away."

She finished the call, then turned back to face me, her eyes alight. I sensed she was in her milieu and on her game, and loving every minute of it. I found it hard to respect people who reserved their best behavior for special circumstances like meeting a celebrity or interviewing for a job or, as in Stacy's case, talking to a customer, but I certainly recognized her look, a private moment of celebration for a hard-won achievement. I felt it every time Prescott's competed against larger antiques auction houses for an important consignment deal and won.

"Sorry about that," she said. "I've just launched a new furniture line."

"And you just landed a good order!"

"Twenty-seven three-legged oval waterfall tables with tricolor resin for a boutique hotel in Philadelphia." Her smile broadened. "Needless to say, I'm excited."

"Tricolor?" I asked, intrigued.

Stacy smiled. "If you ask a new mother about her baby, she'll show you a thousand photos. This style of table is my baby. May I show you a photo?"

I'd seen river tables, with a central meandering blue or turquoise resin "river" running through the wood surface, and waterfall tables, where the resin "waterfall" runs down a mitered side, but I was unfamiliar with multi-colored resin.

"Sure."

She brought up a picture on her phone and handed it over.

The photo showed a rosy wood table with a gently curving river that seemed to undulate, and water that seemed to fall over the sides in torrents. The three-dimensional depth was evident.

I looked up and smiled. "It's magnificent."

"Thanks."

"Is that rosewood?"

"Yes, with aqua, royal-blue, and white resin."

"Most resin tables I've seen are one-dimensional. How did you get the effect of the water actually moving and falling?"

"That's the secret sauce. I invented a new tool—it's patent pending—that allows the craftsman to generate drapes, folds, and ripples of resin, resulting in a feeling of motion, both in the river and in the waterfall. My favorite part is the white froth." She smiled with a sassy gleam in her eye. "I offer ten options based on combinations of wood type and resin color. Want to see them all?"

I laughed, my initial negative impression shifting. "Some other time. Do you always use exotic wood?"

"Always and only. That's another part of the secret sauce. I'm working with a botanist to create a sustainable model—I've started a tree farm in Louisiana, just outside of New Orleans."

"Congratulations. I'm dazzled."

"Coming from you, that means a lot. Which brings us back to the issue at hand. When it comes to the missing trunk, Celia just rubs her hands together, oh, woe is me. The bottom line is that the ball is in my court and I can't flinch from what is obviously a difficult duty. You need grit and guts to launch a furniture line, and I've got plenty of both, to say nothing of gumption. You've started a business, so you know what I'm talking about."

"I'm sorry," I interjected, "but I don't see what—"

"The point is that I'm working on a thousand details at once," she said, breaking in, "including dealing with a myriad of legal issues. I was on the phone with my attorney today, and I mentioned Aunt Maudie's forgetfulness, not asking for an opinion even, just chatting. She told me that if you found the trunk or the box and cat, you might have a viable claim. It seems that 'finders keepers' is an actual thing." She smiled, but this time it didn't reach her eyes. "We're not looking for trouble, none of us is. All I'm asking for is the truth. If you found them, please tell me."

"The legal issue isn't relevant," I said, trying not to bristle. Stacy didn't know me, so her suggesting that I might have questionable ethics said more about her than me. "If I found anything, I'd return it."

Stacy turned toward the street, her hands gripping the railing, a self-anointed savior grappling with defeat. After a moment, she turned back toward me and lifted her chin. "Let me give you my card." She extracted one from an inside pocket in her purse and handed it over.

Stacy's company was called Tables by Collins. Positioned just below the name, a tagline read HEIRLOOM-QUALITY, ONE-OF-A-KIND, CUSTOM-CREATED EXOTIC WOOD AND RESIN TABLES INSPIRED BY NATURE AND CRAFTED IN AMERICA. Her showroom was in SoHo, in Manhattan. The off-white cardstock was thick, the lettering engraved.

"If you find anything," she said, "please call."

"Good luck with your company."

She met my eyes, accepting my brush-off with good grace. "Thank you for your time."

The minute I heard her car engine turn over, I called our locksmith.

CHAPTER THREE

I considered calling Ty to tell him about Stacy's visit, but I knew he was in the middle of fixing his training glitch, so I decided to save it for later. Instead, I returned to the butler's pantry and resumed my search for forgotten items. I heard the faint patter of footsteps overhead as Tom continued his work on the second floor.

My total take after an hour of searching included a black plastic teaspoon, a small-gauge scratched-up metallic-blue crochet hook, and a Chinese take-away pack of hot mustard. Add in Tom's rusty wrench, and we had a lot of nothing.

Last-looks are time-consuming, tedious, and painstaking, and worse, they rarely turn up anything of value, but like the arduous process of digging out weed taproots before winter sets in, if you don't want to welcome spring with a carpet of pigweed choking your tulips, they have to be done, and you'd better be thorough. I stood in the center of the pantry, taking one last, careful look. I approached the center unit on the wall the pantry shared with the kitchen. The top cabinet didn't open. In fact, it didn't even have a handle. Every other top cupboard featured double doors with simple wooden pulls, and they all opened easily. Maybe this single door wasn't a door at all but a false front, installed to cover up an old eyesore—a falling-down baker's chimney, for instance. I ran my flashlight over every inch and discovered a hair-thin horizontal seam, just above the counter, and two chest-high round wood putty patches.

I swung through the connecting door into the kitchen. The size and layout of the cabinets on the kitchen side of the shared wall exactly matched the ones in the pantry. I used my flashlight, and sure enough, there was a whisper-thin horizontal seam directly above the counter, a match to the one on the pantry side, and two holes of some sort, both imperfectly patched with wood putty, painted white to match the cupboards. Evidently, door handles had been installed at some point and later removed.

I ran to the toolbox and rummaged through until I found a pick, a slender hooked probe, the kind of tool used to remove O-rings and seals.

Back in the pantry, I gripped the rubberized handle and slid the probe into one of the wood-putty-covered openings, twisting it to penetrate the rubbery putty and gain purchase. When I had a solid grasp, I tugged. Nothing budged. I tugged again. Nothing. Instead of pulling, I pushed gently, then, when nothing happened, with more force. I felt no movement, not even the slightest shift.

I left the probe in place and stepped back, trying to figure out why my pick wasn't working. Given there had been a handle, the door must have opened somehow, at some point. Maybe it was sealed. I shook my head. No, not if I could see a seam. Maybe, I thought with a flash of excitement, it wasn't a door but a panel that lifted, slipping into a groove in the ceiling. I looked up. In the weak light, it was impossible to see whether there was an opening. I could get a ladder to examine it or simply try to raise the panel.

I lifted, and as if by magic, a six-inch-wide slot in the ceiling appeared and the panel rose swiftly, smoothly, and silently, disappearing into the opening within seconds, stopping when the pick ran into the ceiling. I was staring into a three-foot-high aperture. Between the effortless way the panel slid into the ceiling cavity and the dangling ropes, I knew I was looking at a dumbwaiter, an old-fashioned elevator designed to move objects, not people, via a pulley system. More astonishing was what was inside—a tin and wood-slat dome-topped trunk about four feet wide.

"Holy cow!" Tom exclaimed.

I spun toward his voice. He stood at the foot of the back stairs, the rusty wrench in his hand, his attention riveted on the trunk.

"What the . . . ? Is that a secret compartment?"

Before I could explain, a firm knock sounded on glass, and Tom and I looked over our shoulders. Julie stood under the overhang. She was cute, with strawberry-blond hair cut short and a smattering of freckles across her nose, but she looked exhausted, with bowed shoulders and dark smudges under her eyes.

I looked at Tom. "Talk about timing."

"That's why I came down. Julie just texted that she was here. The front bell doesn't work, so I told her to come to the side door and took the back stairs to let her in."

He placed the rusty wrench on the counter and opened the door.

"Hi," Julie said. She stepped inside and pointed at the trunk. "You found it."

"Just now, yes," I said.

"Mrs. Wilson had a hidey-hole?"

"You're close. This is a dumbwaiter." From their blank expressions I could tell they'd never heard the term. "A dumbwaiter allowed staff to transport food, cleaning supplies, and so on between floors." I touched one of the loose rope pieces, sending it swaying. "It's not automated; it's mechanical, like a window shade. Tug on this section of rope and the elevator goes up. Tug on the other part and it goes down. This one is broken."

"So Mrs. Wilson used it for storage," Tom said.

"Not simply storage, I should think. More like a private hiding place. I'm going to call my company to send a van, then videotape it in place. First, though, I want to call Mrs. Wilson and relieve her mind. Do you have her number?"

He did, but my call went straight to voicemail. I left her a brief message saying I'd found her trunk and asking her to call me to arrange delivery.

"She doesn't check her cell phone much," Tom said. "Sometimes I have better luck calling the main Belle Vista number."

"Good idea."

The phone was answered by a young woman named Lainy who told me Maudie Wilson was out.

"Oh," I said, disappointed. "Do you know when she'll be back? I have some good news I'd love to deliver as soon as possible."

"I'm sorry, but I'm not allowed to discuss residents' whereabouts."

"I understand. I just need to know when she'll be back."

"I guess it can't do any harm . . ."

Lainy lowered her voice as if she were revealing a secret to a girlfriend.

"Maudie is on a Rocky Point Women's Club–sponsored tour of the Museum of Fine Arts in Boston. We don't expect her until dinnertime."

"Fun! Would you ask her to call me about her trunk?" I gave my contact numbers. "She can reach me on my cell phone or at Prescott's in the morning." I thanked her and ended the call.

"I can drive the trunk to Maudie, if you want," Tom offered.

"Thanks, but I might as well use a Prescott's van. That way we can wrap it in furniture blankets and crate it up properly."

I stepped outside onto the concrete stoop to call Cara and was immediately struck by the rich scent of thyme, sage, chives, mint, and sea. Cara said she'd dispatch someone. I slipped the phone into my back pocket and turned in time to see Julie reach into the dumbwaiter, evidently planning to lift the trunk lid.

"Please don't touch it," I said, and she stepped back, her guilt and embarrassment apparent.

"Sorry."

"No problem." I smiled. "It's just that I want to record it first. My company has a policy—we video-record everything before we touch it." I laughed. "Except rusty wrenches and packets of Chinese mustard."

Julie smiled. Tom laughed.

"Even though this isn't Prescott business," I continued, "I'll feel better knowing I've documented where I found it and what's inside." To say nothing of preempting Stacy. With her seemingly litigious attitude, I could see her trying to stir up trouble.

"Is there enough light?" Julie asked.

"We're not looking for publishable photos or anything like that, so . . . yes." I handed Tom the measuring tape. "I'll record everything, describing what I see. You do the measurements." I opened the small iPhone tripod I carried in my tote for just this use, set my iPhone's camera to video, and tapped the START button. "I discovered what seems to be an inoperable dumbwaiter. Inside was this trunk."

Tom called out the measurements as he took them, forty-four inches wide, twenty-seven inches deep, and twenty-three inches tall.

"Give it a lift, Tom, and tell me how much you think it weighs."

He used the two side handles to hoist it, held it in place for a few seconds, then lowered it. "More than fifty pounds, less than a hundred."

"Based on my knowledge of trunks of this type, the trunk itself probably weighs thirty pounds, so that means there's something with some heft inside."

Together, Tom and I wiggled the trunk to the edge of the dumbwaiter, then eased it to the floor.

"More than fifty pounds, for sure," I said. An escutcheon plate covered a skeleton keyhole. "There's no key in the lock, but maybe we'll get lucky. Tom, would you see if you can lift the lid?"

Tom unlatched two side hasps. "Here goes nothing." He tried the lid, and it opened with a faint squeak, releasing a woodsy aroma—fresh, not mossy.

"Thank you, Tom." I continued my annotations: "From the appearance of the wood slats lining the trunk and the scent, I suspect the material is red cedar." I stepped closer and peered inside. "Approximately a foot down, there's a large black book with the word 'Bible' stamped on the front in gold and a pile of envelopes tied together with baby-blue satin ribbon. Something shiny is visible below those items. Tom, would you please lift out the Bible and letters?"

He placed them on the counter.

I flipped through the stack of letters, fifty or more. I raised the top one to face the camera. "From a quick examination, every letter appears to be addressed to Maudie Collins, postmarked in the late 1960s. The return address indicates they were sent from a military address by Sergeant Eli Wilson."

"Love letters," Julie said. "So romantic."

I lifted the Bible, gauging its weight.

"The Bible is heavy," I said as I recorded it, "a quarto volume, bound in black leather with gilt lettering." I fanned the pages. "The leather is worn and rubbed, the pages heavily foxed." I opened it. "There are two family-tree graphics printed on the inside front cover, both completed in ink. One is labeled 'Collins,' the other 'Wilson.'" I set the Bible aside. "Let's see what else is in the trunk." I leaned in to see. "Wow." I stared at what seemed to be a jewel- or faux-gem-encrusted silver-colored box featuring a black cat design with extensive gold metal inlays.

I strained to lift it out. Tom hurried over to help. Together we placed it on the counter next to the Bible.

The red and green stones winked as they caught the light, and Julie inhaled sharply.

"Whoa," Tom said in the kind of hushed tone you use in church. "Are those real?"

I leaned closer, assessing the glints and prisms refracting under the dim light. The stones were embedded next to thin lines of what looked like gold, forming a complex squared-off geometric pattern, a kind of maze or labyrinth. In the center was a black cat about eighteen inches tall, embellished with gold earrings. It had cerulean eyebrows, glittering green eyes, and brick-red lips. It sat in profile, sleek and proud, its chin raised. Certainly the motif evoked ancient Egypt, but reproductions and counterfeits were common, and reflected light glinted off faux jewels, gold plate, and nickel in much the same way as it did on genuine jewels, 18- or 24-karat gold, and sterling silver.

"Maybe," I said.

"It must be worth a fortune."

"Only if it's real. Let's continue. Tom, please measure the box."

"Twenty-four ... by twelve ... by twelve."

"Thank you. I'm pegging the box and contents at around thirty pounds, the same as the trunk."

"What do you think is inside?" Julie asked.

"Let's see."

I adjusted the view so the camera took in the entire box.

As I reached for the latch, Julie stepped closer, her eyes fixed on it as if she were certain she'd find the fountain of youth. I raised the lid.

The three of us leaned in, staring at a supine statue of a seated cat snuggled on a cushy black velvet pillow. The cat appeared to be made of basalt-colored metal with what looked like silver inlays and a gold nose ring. I lifted it out and set it next to the box.

"It's a cat," Tom said in the tone a teenager uses when he discovers his birthday present is a boring educational toy, not the shoot-'em-up video game he'd requested.

Julie touched his arm. "That's what Stacy said ... a pretty box and an ugly cat."

"It looks scaggy," Tom agreed.

He called out the measurements: eighteen inches high, eight inches wide, and ten inches long.

I turned the box so it rested on its side and used my flashlight to seek out a maker's mark or stamp on the bottom, but it was unembellished. I recorded all sides of the box and cat, then set the box right-ways up and placed the cat back on its pillow.

I took the phone off the tripod and stepped closer to the trunk to capture images of the inside. "Inside the trunk, running the length of all four sides, is a series of thin ridges, which I presume were intended to support shelves. The shelves appear to be missing."

I stopped recording. "That's it," I said. I replaced everything in the trunk and closed the lid. I turned to Tom. "Did you finish upstairs?"

"Yeah, there's nothing."

"No surprise, but it had to be done. Now we measure."

Julie insisted she wanted to help, which speeded up the process. She and Tom worked the tape measure. I took notes and sketched out floor plans. Ty and I had already recorded videos, but from past experience, I knew my drawings would tickle my memory about the many quirky elements that gave the house its charm more than a video. Midway through, two of my employees arrived, packed up the trunk, and wheeled it away.

When we finished the measuring, I walked Tom and Julie out.

Tom paused halfway down the porch steps. "I just can't believe Maudie forgot the trunk. She must be in worse shape than I realized."

Tom had a point, a sad one. No woman would desert a family Bible, a sheaf of love letters, or a cherished box. But I also knew how overwhelming moving could be even during the best of times.

"Don't underrate how disorienting the whole process has been," I said. "Moving out of a house this size that had been in the family for a hundred and fifty years, well, I'm amazed she didn't forget more things."

"True . . . still . . . this trunk . . . that's a heck of a thing to forget."

He was right. If the cat was an original Egyptian artifact, the jewels adorning the presentation box were genuine, and the objects had clear provenance, documenting the box's ownership from creation in ancient Egypt to the present, it might be worth a king's ransom. Of course, the odds that we could locate such records were almost nil, even if they had ever existed, which in itself was a long shot.

I worked at harnessing the power of optimism, but the truth was that when it came to understanding the dark side of human interactions, I was fully as cynical as Tom, so I couldn't help but wonder whether Celia and Stacy were determined to get their hands on the trunk because they wanted to help their aunt, as they said, or because they wanted to help themselves.

CHAPTER FOUR

N ed Murphy, Prescott's go-to locksmith for new hardware and vintage skeleton keys, and our primary source for antique fittings, didn't arrive until after two. By the time he was done outfitting the five doors—front, back, side, shed, and Bilco—with new locks, and I'd followed him to his store, Murphy's Hardware, to have copies made, it was nearly four.

Before driving back to my office, I indulged myself with a little daydream, picturing Mrs. Wilson's expression when she saw that everything inside her trunk was safe and sound. I smiled all the way back to work. I love being the bearer of good news.

In summer, dusk doesn't settle over New Hampshire until after eight, and the sun was still high above the trees that ringed my property as I turned into the parking lot around five.

I stepped out of my car, my mind a million miles away, thinking about Ty, hoping his work was going well, considering whether I felt like making Dijon maple chicken for dinner, and brooding about my best friend, Zoë. Her daughter, Emma, was gung ho for the marines, eager to sign up. Zoë, terrified at the prospect of her being deployed to a war zone, was doing everything she could to stop her, causing Emma to feel diminished and disrespected. I understood both sides, which didn't help anyone. Communication had gotten so rocky, I was worried there would be a breach, which was the last thing either one of them wanted. I wished there was something I could do to help.

"Josie!"

I froze, wrenched out of my reverie, then looked every which way, trying to see who'd called my name.

It was Celia. She popped up from the bench over by the willow tree where she and Doug had been sitting and walked quickly toward me. Doug followed more slowly.

"Hello!" I called.

"You found Aunt Maudie's trunk," she said, smiling.

I was taken aback. Had Tom spilled the beans? Or Lainy, the receptionist at Belle Vista? It didn't matter, I supposed, since I hadn't asked anyone to keep the find secret because this wasn't business. Still, I was disappointed. The good news was mine to share, or should have been.

"Yes, it's true!" I told Celia. "I'm excited! I already have a call in to your aunt."

"Tom said you brought it here."

"That's right."

"What a relief! Thank you."

She reached out to Doug. He grasped her hand and squeezed.

"Where did you find it?" he asked.

I told them, adding, "You can imagine my surprise!"

Celia pressed the hand Doug wasn't holding against her chest. "It's just wonderful. I can't tell you how grateful we are." She gave the building a quick once-over. "Do you have a loading dock?"

"In the back. Why?"

"If we can drive up, it'll be easier to load the trunk into our car."

"Oh, wow. I'm sorry, but I can't release it to you."

"What?" Her brows drew together. "Why not?"

"I can only release an object to its owner."

Celia smiled as if she were about to clear up a silly little misunderstanding. "We'll bring it to Aunt Maudie. That's not a problem."

"I'm sorry."

Celia stiffened all over. She looked at Doug helplessly for a moment, then turned back to face me. "But I told you—Stacy and I only want to help Aunt Maudie."

"Surely you can understand that it wouldn't be appropriate for me to hand over one person's possessions to another person without permission."

Celia's mouth opened, then closed as she wrestled with how to get me to change my mind. When she spoke, her tone was calm and patient, as if she were explaining an unpleasant, complex concept to a four-year-old. "I think I haven't been clear. Aunt Maudie is losing what they call executive function—the ability to make smart decisions. She cherishes her independence, and we certainly respect that. But how can you doubt . . . I mean . . . she left the trunk in a dumbwaiter, for God's sake, which is bad enough, but then she forgot where she put it." Her eyes searched mine for signs of acquiescence. After a few seconds, she added, "We're simply trying to protect her."

"I understand, but unless you have power of attorney, there's nothing I can do."

"Oh, God . . . Doug?"

He patted her shoulder, his eyes on my face. "Maudie refuses to discuss it. We thought it would be mandatory when she entered assisted living, but it isn't, not in the independent wing." He paused, and when I didn't speak, he asked, "What happens now?"

"When I speak to Mrs. Wilson, I'll ask her when and where she'd like me to deliver the trunk. At no charge, needless to say."

"It's not fair," Celia mumbled. "It's just not fair. You need to listen. You need to give us the trunk."

"This is between you and her," I said, growing increasingly uncomfortable by the second. "It has nothing to do with me."

"Come on, hon," Doug said, reaching for Celia's arm. "Let's go."

"Don't patronize me!"

She shoved him, the heel of her hand catching him midchest. He tottered, his eyes flying open.

Celia pressed her fingertips against her cheeks. "Oh, God, what have I done? I'm sorry." Tears welled in her eyes. "Forgive me . . . I'm not myself."

She turned and stood for a moment, then took a dozen steps toward the bench before angling off into a row of cars. Her pace slowed, and she shuffled toward their vehicle.

Doug and I watched her lumbering progress.

"Are you all right?" I asked.

"I'm fine. It was nothing."

"It didn't look like nothing."

Doug kept his eyes on Celia as he rubbed his chest. "She's completely stressed out. I got laid off almost two months ago."

"I had a feeling something was bothering her that went deeper than a missing trunk."

"She's scared, and who can blame her? I was a truck dispatcher for a small dairy, and they replaced me with an app." He snuffled, an unhappy self-deprecating sound. "Can you believe it? An app."

"You don't need to explain, Doug."

He met my eyes. "I have an interview this Friday at Jestran's. Do you know them? They're the largest home heating oil company in New Hampshire, and they need an experienced dispatcher." He lifted his chin. "We're going to be fine."

We both turned at the sound of a car door shutting. Celia sat in the front passenger seat. After a moment, she closed her eyes and leaned back against the headrest.

"With Aunt Maudie moving into a retirement community and selling the house and all," Doug continued, "well, it's the end of an era, and Celia feels it. Anyway, thanks for understanding."

As Doug walked to join Celia, I replayed our conversation. He'd thanked me for understanding, but I didn't understand, on lots of levels.

Prescott's newest cat was black as night with a sheen like coal and an adorable white triangle on her breastbone. That's why I'd named her Angela—angels wear white. She didn't like to curl up in my lap like Hank. She preferred being cuddled like a baby, and just now she was dozing, cradled in my left arm. I sat at my desk, staring out my window past the old maple tree, over the church steeple, wondering if I could trust Tom.

I picked up the shed key earmarked for him, grasping it by the ring. I'd chosen silver metal discs with cardboard centers. I'd written "J&T" on it: Josie and Ty. Not that I had any reason to worry, but I was a cautious woman, and I didn't want to put our last names on a key that might be available to random strangers, making it easy for them to locate our property.

I wanted to trust Tom. I had to if he was going to work for us, and after all, I hadn't asked him to keep quiet about my locating Maudie Wilson's trunk, so it wasn't like he'd done something wrong. The fact remained, however, that he'd been pretty darn quick to pass along the news.

When in doubt, my dad had taught me, tell the truth. It disarms people in a way nothing else can.

I dialed Tom's number and got him. After a little small talk—innocuous chat about the weather, not gossip—I eased into the reason for my call.

"Celia was here at my office when I got back," I said. "She said you told her I found Mrs. Wilson's trunk."

"Yes—she was super jazzed about it."

"Why did you tell her?"

"Huh?" I could hear him breathing. "Oh, jeez. I didn't think . . . I mean, it didn't occur to me that it was a secret."

"I don't mean to make a big deal about it, Tom, it's just that it was my news to share, you know?"

"I can see that. Do you want me to call Celia and apologize, tell her it wasn't my place?"

I was touched by his offer. "No, that's all right. Just in the future, I'd appreciate it if you don't pass along any information you garner while working for me."

"You got it."

"Thanks. One more thing . . . I had the locks changed today, so I need to get you the new shed key."

"I can stop by tomorrow afternoon after I drop Julie at her nanny job."

"I thought she worked at the diner."

"She does that, too. She works a couple of shifts at the diner and two evenings a week as a nanny to make her half of the rent."

"And she's full-time at school. That's tough."

"We feel pretty lucky, all things considered."

"That's a good attitude."

He laughed. "When you hit bottom, there's no place to go but up. I'm joking. We're a long way from bottom. We're doing fine."

Tom was a good guy. I felt it every time I talked to him. I hoped he was sincere about keeping quiet in the future, but I was skeptical. To some people, sharing the skinny was like breathing, as essential as air. I was taking it on faith that Tom wasn't one of those people. I made a mental note to talk to Ty about whether we should get him to sign a nondisclosure agreement, routine for Prescott's employees, but nothing we'd ever done in our personal lives. Even thinking about it felt pretentious, as if we were celebrities at risk of a staff member writing an embarrassing tell-all exposé, or the über-rich, vulnerable to blackmail. Still, if it had to be done, we'd do it.

Ten minutes later, while I was reading my accountant's latest report, confirming that we were on track to earn higher profits than projected, Stacy called.

I heard her say, "Hello, this is Stacy," but the rest of the sentence was lost amid a jangle of laughter and clinking. It sounded like she was at a party.

"I'm sorry, but I didn't hear that last bit." More laughter. More clinking. More lost words. "Should you call back when you're in a quieter place?"

Stacy must have cupped the phone, because her chuckle came through loud and clear.

"I'm in the Blue Dolphin lounge," she said, "so it will never be quiet! Come on down and I'll buy you a drink."

"Thanks, but I'll have to pass."

"Hold on for a sec, then. I need to talk to you. I'll step outside."

While I waited, I drummed a staccato beat on my desk.

"Are you still there?" Stacy asked a minute later. "I'm outside—can you hear me better?"

"Yes."

"Good. I understand you found the trunk. Fantasmic! Is it in good shape?"

"It seems to be, although I never saw it before, so I have nothing to compare it to."

"Celia told me she was going to pick it up. Has she been there yet?"

I repeated what I'd told Celia, that I only released objects to their owners.

"Oh, pooh! Don't be a stickler. Aunt Maudie is in rough shape."

I was struck by the irony. At the Gingerbread House, Stacy had implied I might be so ethically lax as to steal her aunt's trunk. Now she was asking me to cross a clear ethical line.

"I'm sorry to hear that," I said.

There was a lengthy pause, ripe with tension. "Neither Celia nor I will allow Aunt Maudie to be victimized."

I was growing a little weary of Stacy's confrontational communication style, especially since I knew it was optional. I guessed she reserved her buttery-sweet voice for business.

"As I told Celia, unless someone shows me a power of attorney, my hands are tied."

"Have you spoken to Aunt Maudie?" she asked, her tone clipped.

"Not yet."

"Thanks for nothing," she said, and hung up.

Ick, I thought. *It must be miserable being Stacy.*

Ty got home around seven, annoyed and exhausted. He hadn't been able to resolve the training issues, so he would be flying to Washington in the morning.

"What went wrong?" I asked.

"Everything."

"That's comprehensive."

He leaned over and kissed my forehead. "I don't want to recount the multitude of errors. I want a beer and something to eat. Then I want to sit in the hot tub with the most beautiful woman on earth while you tell me about your day."

I went up on tiptoe to kiss him. "Done."

I decided on the fly to skip the chicken. I could tell, don't ask me how, that Ty was in a burger-and-dog mood. He took a Smuttynose from the fridge and leaned against the counter as I placed everything I'd need on a tray. He held the door for me, then sat on an Adirondack rocker with his long legs stretched out in front of him. I fired up the grill.

"I changed the locks today." I described Stacy's unauthorized entry. "I left the new keys on your bedside table."

While I cooked, Ty retied the tomato plants, which seemed to grow a foot a day, to the bamboo stakes that supported them, and I started to fill him in about Celia and Stacy. As twilight descended, we moved to the picnic table. The orange lanterns I'd strung around the patio area cast a warm glow, and I decided to tell Ty the rest of the Celia-Stacy saga later, opting instead to chat about our new home's herb garden and the sound and scent of the ocean. I could see the tension ease from Ty's neck and shoulders. When we'd finished washing up, we changed into swimsuits and slid into the bubbling hot water.

I resumed my summary by telling Ty about Mrs. Wilson's missing trunk, and how I'd found it. "I'll deliver it in the morning." I turned to face him. "I'm a little worried about Tom." I explained about Tom's call to Celia and asked if he thought we needed him to sign the nondisclosure form.

He shrugged it off, saying that he thought it was a nonissue. "What will he be privy to? That we like peonies?"

I laughed and finished recounting my experiences with the Wilson family's confusing and complex dynamics. "I don't know what's really firing up Celia and Stacy," I said, "but whatever is going on feels creepy, as if they're competing for supremacy over their aunt—and each other. I see this kind of bickering in families a lot, and it's always sad."

"And there's never anything you can do."

"Except stay out of it."

"Words to live by."

CHAPTER FIVE

I pulled into the Belle Vista parking lot at nine thirty the next morning, as scheduled. Eric, Prescott's facilities manager, followed in a Prescott's van. He rolled to a stop at the curb and set his flashers blinking. I walked up to tell him to hang tight while I went inside to ask whether we'd need to use the service entrance, as I suspected.

Belle Vista occupied a ten-acre plot on Francis Street, a lovely section of Rocky Point, two blocks from the village green and ten minutes from the ocean. The lawn was manicured, the hedges trimmed, the gardens weeded. The white picket fence toward the rear, separating the open grounds from the private gardens, was freshly whitewashed. I was impressed.

A young woman sat at a cherrywood reception station talking on the phone. She was probably only a year or two out of high school, and striking, with big brown eyes and long, sleek chestnut hair. Her complexion was flawless, the color of Devonshire cream. Her eyes were somewhere between topaz and caramel. She stood to retrieve a notebook from the credenza in back of her, revealing a spectacular figure. A brass tent sign read ELAINE BAGLIO, and I realized she must be the receptionist I'd spoken to the day before, Lainy. She smiled as she took her seat again and raised an index finger, signaling that she'd only be a minute. I nodded. She flipped open the notebook, and I turned away, walking toward the back of the expansive reception area.

The facility was well named—Belle Vista did, in fact, offer a beautiful view. A double-wide plate glass window overlooked a meadow enclosed by poplars, birch, and maples. Wildflowers were in full bloom, purple asters and bluebells, buttercups and snowy-white Queen Anne's lace, a kaleidoscope of summer. In fall, the autumn leaves would add a ring of fire.

"Sorry about that," Lainy called as she hung up. "How can I help?"

I crossed the reception area to her desk, introduced myself, and explained why I was there. She had me sign an old-style guest book, then directed me to the loading dock.

"Mrs. Wilson just got back from shopping," she said. "I'll let her know you're here."

I clanked a polished brass colonial-style knocker, and the door opened wide. A woman my mother would have described as handsome stood with one hand on the door.

She smiled. "Ms. Prescott, this is so kind of you! Please, come in. I'm Maudie Wilson. You can call me Maudie."

Maudie towered over me. She was probably five-ten or taller with a solid frame, big bones, and strong features. Her silvery-white hair was stylishly close cropped. She wore a loose-fitting baby-blue tunic over white slacks with sensible tie-up navy-blue shoes. A shiny silver key dangled from a lime-green plastic-covered wrist coil.

Bright sunlight streamed in through two floor-to-ceiling windows, both open about two feet. Warm air wafted in on a rose-scented breeze.

"And I'm Josie."

I'd expected a small, institutional cell. Instead, the apartment was spacious and homey. On the left was a Pullman kitchen, with modern white cabinets above and below a tan-and-beige-mottled granite countertop. To my right was a sleeping area, separated from the rest of the space by a five-foot-high wall that ran parallel to the kitchen. After a three-foot gap, which provided an entry into the bedroom area, another five-foot wall, this one running side to side, completed the separation and delineated the living room. Through the gap I could see into the bathroom. I took it all in with one sweeping glance, then brought my gaze back to the small kitchen.

What people leave out on their counter tells a lot about them, and Maudie was no exception. A small utilitarian toaster oven and a high-end European coffeemaker took up most of the left side of the counter. A pair of marigold glass candlesticks, maybe carnival glass, stood between the appliances, adding a punch of color. A plain white coffee mug, an old-fashioned wooden rolling pin, and a small white plate were perched on a mini drying rack, which sat on a plastic mat to the right of the sink. All in all, I gathered Maudie's style was half-elegant and half-practical. I walked farther into the apartment.

"Oh!" I said, pausing midstep. Julie was dragging a jumbo clear plastic tub past a folded-up wheeled grocery cart, which was leaning against a Chippendale-style bistro table near the front windows. "Julie! Hello."

Julie looked up. "Hey."

"You know one another?" Maudie asked. "Of course you do. I forgot. Tom told me he's helping you maintain the grounds."

Julie stopped by the front window, positioning the tub against the wall. She straightened up, arching her back as if she were stiff or achy. "What do you think, Maudie? Is this room enough?"

"It should be. Thank you, dear." Maudie turned toward me. "I asked Julie to move the tub to make room for the trunk."

"You're certain you want the trunk in here?" I asked her. "I know we discussed it on the phone, but . . . well . . ." I lifted my arm toward the tall windows. "This place is so open."

"You're nice to think about it. After I go through things, I'll move it to my storage locker in the basement. It will be fine."

I nodded at Eric, who wheeled the trunk in and deposited it at the end of the kitchen counter. He removed the protective blanket. Maudie thanked him, and he left.

Maudie walked over and patted the lid. "I'm glad to have it back." She smiled at me. "Will you join me for coffee? The on-site café isn't bad at all. I'd love to hear how you found it."

I accepted with pleasure, white-hot curious to hear about the presentation box and cat and glad for the opportunity to ask about the chandelier.

Julie grabbed her tote bag. "I'll wait for Tom outside."

"You come, too," Maudie said.

"Are you sure? I'm fine waiting outside."

"Don't be silly. You're more than welcome."

"Thanks," she said with a quick smile. "I'll text Tom. Let me just get the trash."

"Thanks, Julie," Maudie said. "There's a new box of bags under the sink."

Julie used her thumbnail to penetrate the perforated opening and extracted a green industrial-strength trash bag. I held it open while she tossed in smaller bags and other debris—rags and ripped-up packing materials.

"I'm still unpacking and sorting things, if you can believe it," Maudie said. "Having Julie's help makes the process much less painful."

When we reached the small in-house café, Maudie selected a table for four near the front window and ordered a pot of coffee and a basket of breakfast pastries from the server.

"I still can't believe I left the trunk behind," Maudie said. "I'm no more forgetful than I've ever been, I'm just preoccupied." She laughed and raised her left arm to show off her key. "Or at least I'm not much more forgetful. Losing keys is so common around here, they keep a supply of wrist coils at the reception desk. I didn't actually lose my key, by the way—I merely misplaced it. I found it in my refrigerator the next day, next to the mustard."

I smiled but felt a twinge of concern. Finding misplaced objects in unexpected places might indicate nothing more ominous than the preoccupation Maudie referred to, but I'd heard on the news that it was also a symptom of dementia.

After Maudie poured us cups of coffee, she added, "I used to store things in that old dumbwaiter all the time, Christmas and birthday presents, that sort of thing, so you'd think I would have remembered to check."

"How did you get the trunk inside the dumbwaiter? It's not exactly a small Christmas present."

"The day the junk dealer was scheduled to come, I got worried they might scoop it up in the fray. Everything I wanted to keep had already been moved except for the trunk, which I didn't want the movers touching. I planned on asking Tom to help me with it after the junk dealer left. That morning, before they arrived, my real estate agent came over to have me sign something, and he helped me lift it up. As it turns out, I was right to get it out of sight—that junk dealer went through the place like a vacuum cleaner." Maudie smiled. "In case you're wondering how I could manage, well, you might not think it to look at me, but I can bench-press fifty pounds."

I laughed. "Well done! How did you discover the dumbwaiter in the first place?"

"I found it by accident while I was cleaning the pantry a year or so after Eli and I got married. I never told anyone except him. The dumbwaiter had been used when he was a boy, but then it broke and was never fixed. Eli said he hadn't thought about it since he was a kid. He used to leave me love notes inside." She closed her eyes for a moment. "Never mind. Tell me . . . how did you find it?"

"The same way you did, it sounds like. Not that I was cleaning, but I noticed the patched holes and investigated further. I bet I know how you opened it." I paused to extract the crochet hook I'd found in the butler's pantry from my tote bag. "You used a crochet hook." I handed it over.

Maudie's eyes widened with surprise, and she laughed as she took it, rubbing the shaft tenderly. "A little twist, a little lift, the deed was done."

"Very clever."

"Do you think so? Industrious, perhaps. Obviously I planned on retrieving the trunk—that's why I left the crochet hook there. I was so busy those last days . . . forget it . . . it's over . . . and I have my trunk back, thanks to you. So you bought the Gingerbread House. What are your plans for it?"

"We're going to update it, keeping as many of the original components as possible, like the moldings and that gorgeous chandelier. I was so glad you were open to including it in the sale."

"It was purchased for that room. It should stay there."

"I'm guessing it's French."

Maudie's eyes widened. "You're right—but why would you think so?"

"After Napoleon's 1798 Egyptian campaign, the French brought home boatloads of looted artifacts, including palmettes . . . you know, those crystal elements in the center of the chandelier that look like palm fronds. Since Egyptians didn't make crystal chandeliers"—I opened my palms—"and the French did . . . voilà!" I smiled. "It was possible it was Flemish or Italian, but my gut told me it was French."

"You're a wonder, Josie. Eli told me his father found it in an antiques shop outside of Paris during the war—the First World War, I mean—and had it shipped home."

"I don't suppose you remember the name of the shop? Or the place where he bought it?"

Her brow creased. "I don't know whether I ever heard the name of the shop . . . but the town . . . yes, I've got it! He bought it in Saint-Quentin, a small city in the north. I remember because it reminded me of that prison in California." She shook her head. "The shop name, though . . . if I ever heard it . . . it's gone. I must be getting old, which is terrible until you consider the alternative."

I laughed. I hoped I was as cheerful and accepting as Maudie if, when I got to be her age, which I pegged at sixty-seven or sixty-eight, I found myself losing capabilities I now took for granted.

Julie smiled mechanically.

"Are you all right, dear?" Maudie asked.

Julie colored and looked down for a moment, then looked up. "I'm fine . . . just a little tired."

"No surprise with your workload."

"It's not forever. If I don't work hard now, I'll never get anywhere. What is it you told me? The only thing under my total control is self-discipline."

Maudie laughed, embarrassed. "I'm not used to being quoted to myself. At least I gave good advice." She took a mini-Danish and turned to me. "I'm afraid I don't remember anything else about the chandelier, and the receipt, if there ever was one, is long gone."

"Knowing it was purchased in Saint-Quentin is a big help."

"Good. So Tom is going to take care of your garden for you."

"During the renovation, yes. Like moving those gorgeous irises. You must have cultivated them for years."

"They were Eli's pride and joy. He called them his problem children— temperamental and demanding. What are you going to do with them?"

"Tom's going to transplant them into raised beds so they'll be safe during construction."

"You're very fortunate. Tom's a treasure." She glanced at Julie, who lowered her eyes. "Julie is a treasure, too, always pitching in around the house, even though I scolded her for it." She patted Julie's hand but spoke to me. "Now she helps me with this and that, and I'm very grateful."

"I like helping you, Maudie. Nana always said the people that help the most get the best lives."

"I think there's truth in that. I once read—"

Maudie broke off as Lainy hurried across the café to our table. "I'm sorry to interrupt," she told Maudie. "It's your niece Celia." She lowered her voice, communicating seriousness. "She's on the phone. She says it's really important."

"Thank you, Lainy. I'll be right there."

I pushed back my chair. "I need to get going anyway."

"No, please, don't go," Maudie said. "Celia always says things are important, and trust me, they never are. I'll only be a minute."

I hoped for Maudie's sake that she was right, but I was unconvinced. Maybe I was just spooked from witnessing Celia's meltdown in my parking lot, but from where I sat, Celia seemed to be an emotional wreck. I knew from my years as an antiques appraiser working with angry heirs and disenfranchised family members that people can only stomach dismay and disappointment for so long before they react like a volcano and erupt.

CHAPTER SIX

Half my brain continued to speculate about Celia's emotional stability. I focused the other half on Julie.

"You're studying nursing," I said. "I admire that. Do you have a special interest?"

She smiled, but not like she thought something was funny. "Getting a job. Just joking. My dream is to become a school nurse."

"Time off in the summer."

"And holiday breaks during the year. I've always wanted to travel." Her shoulders shot up an inch, then sank. "The way the bills keep piling up, it's just a dream."

"Short-term misery for long-term gain."

"At least I like the coursework."

"What are you studying now?"

"Injections." She smiled, a real one, and her face was transformed; for a few seconds, she didn't look the least bit tired. "We practice with oranges and hot dogs."

"Hot dogs?" I laughed. "That's funny."

"And injection pads. Today we'll practice some more, then tomorrow we go to a clinic to give children vaccinations."

"The children are fortunate to have you."

"Thanks. I work hard, that's for sure, and I never give up."

"There's an old saying: 'The harder I work, the luckier I get.' Hard work and persistence—put those two together and you have a recipe for success."

"I wish Tom could hear you. Maybe that would convince him to go back to school. He could get licensed as a plumber or an electrician or whatever and the GI Bill would cover the costs."

"But he doesn't want to."

"So he says." Julie smiled. "I'm working on him."

Maudie rejoined us. "Sorry about that. All Celia wanted was to confirm that you delivered the trunk as scheduled. She's a worrywart."

"She cares about you," Julie said.

Maudie sighed and shook her head. "You're right, and I should remember it more often. Celia has a good heart."

I smiled. "One woman's worrywart is another woman's devoted niece."

"Perception is all." Maudie turned to Julie. "Julie, you know these old knees of mine . . . Would you do me a favor and get my sweater? The air conditioning . . . I'm chilly."

Julie popped up. "Of course."

Maudie watched her hurry across the lobby. After a moment, she said, "I feel bad for her. She's estranged from her family because, if you can believe it, she's going to college."

"Oh, how sad!"

"I agree. At least she made the right decision—not to sacrifice herself to suit their prejudices." She drank some coffee. "It has to be hard, doesn't it, to step into a close-knit community like Rocky Point and find where you fit. You know what I'm talking about . . . you moved to Rocky Point as a stranger, didn't you?"

"Yes, and it was tough, just like you said. Finding your place is always hard, even in the town you grew up in."

"Only if you're an independent thinker."

"True. And I am. Once I connected with like-minded people, I was home free."

"I think I'm especially sensitive to the issue because of my mother. She didn't have any of Julie's moxie. Just the opposite, in fact. She had a terrible time finding her way. She was an immigrant, from Ireland. The kindest woman in the world, but so timid someone once asked my father if she was mute."

"The poor thing."

"I always wondered what had happened to her to make her so fearful, but she never would say. She insisted she was simply born that way."

"But you don't think so."

Maudie folded her napkin. "No, I don't. She wouldn't ever speak of her father, so it made me wonder if he'd been a yeller, or maybe even a hitter."

"You can't ever really know what's going on with other people, can you?"

"No." Maudie smiled. "I'm not even sure about myself a lot of the time."

Julie returned, sweater in hand. She draped it over Maudie's shoulders.

I pushed my coffee cup aside. "May I ask another question, Maudie, about how you came to own the trunk?"

"It was a flea market find. My sister, Vivian, and I used to love going to flea markets. Your tag sale was always on our list of stops. You do a wonderful job."

"That's great to hear. Thank you."

"Vivian came for a visit every summer. She died last year." She stared into her coffee cup for a moment. "No one teaches you how to gracefully outlive the people you love, just as no one tells you that the hardest part of their dying is that they're gone." She raised a fluttering hand. "They're simply gone. The point is, I bought the trunk at a small outdoor flea market somewhere near Portland, Maine. Vivian was with me."

"I'm so sorry to hear about your sister."

"Thank you. The human spirit is resilient . . . most of the time, anyway. What else would you like to know about the trunk?"

"It looks like it originally included shelves. Do you know where they might be?"

"No. I never had any shelves." She laughed a little. "At least that I remember. What do you think it's worth?"

I smiled. "I can't put a price on an object I haven't appraised, but I can give you what I call a guesstimate. A guesstimate is part estimate based on experience and part guess based on instinct. I'd peg it at around a thousand dollars."

A gleam came into Mrs. Wilson's eyes. "I don't mean to boast, but I only paid thirty-five dollars for it—I don't want to tell you how many years ago."

"And you enjoyed it all this time."

"And I used it to store my most precious items."

"I must say, the presentation box and cat seem very special."

"Oh, they are. Not so much the objects themselves. I never displayed them because, well, frankly, they're not to my taste. But they hold great sentimental value for me. Vivian gave them to me."

"Even though they aren't to your taste?"

"It was the only thing of value she had to give. Vivian's husband died when her daughters were in elementary school. It was so tragic. A heart attack. He was only forty-two . . . can you imagine? From that moment on, Vivian struggled to make ends meet. Luckily she was in a rent-controlled apartment. We helped with the girls' education, paying for music and dance lessons, even their college tuition. After the girls finished school, Vivian gave me the objects as a thank-you."

Tom appeared at the doorway. Julie spotted him, smiled, bounced up, and ran to join him. He touched her cheek, then came to the table. Maudie invited him to have a cup of coffee.

Tom looked at the big schoolroom clock mounted on the wall. "Thanks, sure. We have a few minutes."

Maudie poured him a cup.

I said hello, adding, "If I'd known I was going to see you, I'd have brought your new key."

"That's okay. I can come to you."

"I left it with Cara, in the front office."

"You have class today, don't you, Julie?" Maudie asked.

"Yes." She touched Tom's wrist. "Seeing me enjoy my classes has Tom thinking about going back to school, too."

"No way." Tom laughed. "*Julie* is thinking of my going back to school, not me. I never much liked school when I had to go, so there's no way I'm going back voluntarily. I like what I do now."

"It's like leaving money on the table."

Tom shot her a look charged with annoyance and shook his head, silently asking her to leave it alone.

Julie ignored his unspoken entreaty. "It's not so easy after you've been out for a few years. I know. It takes a lot of discipline."

"Enough," Tom said.

"It's a good idea," she said, sounding peevish.

"Thanks for the coffee," Tom said to Maudie, standing. He nodded in my direction, then frowned at Julie. "Let's go."

Julie stood, thanked Maudie, smiled at me, and hustled after Tom, who was already halfway to the door.

I stared at the doorway long after they'd left the room, turning back in time to see Maudie shake her head.

She pushed her coffee cup aside. "It's not good for one person in a relationship to be so much more ambitious than the other."

"Sometimes people lack confidence. They need to be bolstered."

"I don't think Tom lacks confidence. If people are content with the status quo, it's logical they resent anyone who tries to change it."

"I can see that."

"I suppose it could be that Tom is scared of failing," Maudie mused, thinking aloud. "If you don't try, you can't fail. Especially if you were reared to be a rule follower, not a risk taker. I was always a good girl, which in my case meant letting other people tell me what to do, first my father, then Eli."

"It was a different time."

"Do you think so? I don't know about that. I mean, of course it was, but I still see people doing things they don't want to do all the time. Lainy, for example, the receptionist here . . . she told me that she wanted to move to New York, to see if she could make it as an actress. Her father told her that was stupid, to get a job like everyone else."

"And she did."

"And she did."

"Do you think Tom and Julie's relationship will survive?" I asked.

"It depends on what's more important to Julie—her aspirations or Tom."

"It's awful to have to choose."

"Very much so. I picked Eli, but I've always wished I hadn't had to choose."

"What was your dream?"

Maudie lifted her eyes to a spot somewhere above my head. She smiled slightly. Whatever she was seeing in the past, it was pleasant, a good memory.

After a few seconds, she lowered her eyes. "Travel writing. When I was fifteen, I went with a school group to visit New Orleans. I wrote an essay about the experience. It won a national award."

"Wow! What an accomplishment! Why didn't you continue?"

"I didn't have the money to travel. Later, after I got married, I thought I might take a writing course. Eli asked who'd take care of the house if I went back to school." She pressed her lips together for a moment. "I think about that now and my blood boils. One course. I didn't even argue with him. I just did as I was told, which is all on me."

"And now?"

She tilted her head, her eyes on my face. "Believe it or not, it never entered my mind that I might try writing again, and that's the God's honest truth. I'm still doing what Eli told me, three years after his death, shame on me." She slapped the table. "I moved to Belle Vista because Celia and Stacy pecked at me and pecked at me until I gave in. They were right that the Gingerbread House was too much for me to handle on my own, but I could have hired help or moved into a condo on the ocean." She smiled. "Don't misunderstand—I'm fine here. Except for all these old people sticking their noses in other people's business, I'm perfectly content. All I'm saying is that if Tom doesn't want to go back to school, he shouldn't let Julie make him."

"Relationships are complicated."

"You started your own business. You didn't let anyone keep you down."

I smiled. "It didn't come up—but I can't imagine anyone in my orbit trying to stop me. If they were the kind of person who tried to keep me down, they wouldn't be in my orbit."

"Didn't your parents worry about the risk?"

Now it was my turn to endure hard memories. "My mother died when I was young. I wasn't that old when my dad died, either. His death—or rather, my reaction to not having him anymore—was one of the reasons I moved to New Hampshire. He used to say that when you feel as though you're at the end of your rope, tie a knot and hang on, and if you can't hang on, move on. I lasted in New York City for a little more than a year after his death . . . then I moved on. I'm only sorry my dad can't see me now, can't see how well I've done." My voice cracked. "Sorry. It's been nearly twenty years, but I still get emotional."

"Your father is looking down on you right now." She patted my hand. "He's very proud."

I blinked away an unexpected tear. "Thank you. That's kind of you to say."

We stayed talking for another half hour, mostly about the differences between a travelogue and travel writing. At first Maudie claimed that she wasn't an expert, but I managed to put that contention to rest.

"Who's your favorite travel writer?" I asked.

"Oh, I could never say just one."

"Say more than one."

She rattled off some names. "Nancy Wigston. Sara Wheeler. Mary Jo Manzanares."

"All women."

"Nick Haslam. Joe Cawley. Paul Theroux."

"Want to tell me again that you don't know the difference between a travelogue and travel writing?"

Maudie leaned back and smiled. "You're sneaky."

"Deft, not sneaky."

"A travelogue is to travel writing what an autobiography is to a memoir. A travelogue is a chronological recounting of a trip. Travel writing is a themed slice of the overall experience."

I smiled. "I knew you knew."

"I didn't ever play dumb. It was more complicated than that." She paused, searching for the words. "I've spent a lot of my life pretending I was happy. No, that isn't fair. I was happy. Or at least, I was happy enough. I spent a lot of my life pretending I was satisfied. I sublimated my needs to keep the peace."

"All to meet someone else's expectations. It takes time and energy to throw off that mantle. And courage."

"I don't feel courageous. I feel a certain desperation—I've been pretending everything was hunky-dory for years, forever, and now, for whatever reason, I just can't fake it anymore, but I don't know what to do instead. Maybe moving out of the house, out of Eli's shadow, did it for me. I don't know. My frustration with Stacy and Celia continuing to try to dictate to me, my anger at myself for not telling them to go jump in a lake—excuse my French—well, I've felt increasingly disheartened ever since I moved. Everything is coming to a head because I'm no longer willing to simply go along with things. I want to be in control."

"I'm sorry you're struggling, but"—I raised my cup for a toast—"here's to your emancipation. Here's to self-direction."

Maudie lifted her cup, and we clinked. "Here's to you."

We sipped our coffee to seal the toast.

"I hope you get back to writing, Maudie. With the kind of clarity you displayed about the genres and the authors you admire, well, I bet you'll win another essay contest." I tapped my phone to check the time. It was almost eleven. "I can't believe how the time has zipped by. Thanks again for the coffee, and for the conversation." I stood. "And for telling me what you knew about the chandelier and trunk."

"I'm glad I remembered."

We left the café together. Outside, I took a few steps down the walkway, then looked back. Maudie was leaning against the lobby wall staring at nothing. Just as I was about to turn away, she turned toward me. Our eyes met, and we smiled. She waved, and I waved back.

My smile remained intact all the way to my car. I had a new friend, a woman of depth and intelligence, and I felt exhilarated.

CHAPTER SEVEN

I met Lenny DeVito in the front office at one, as scheduled. Lenny was fortyish, only a couple of inches taller than me, totally bald. He was a marketing whiz and branding expert, a one-man band with clients around the world.

"Josie!" he said, smiling and extending both hands for a clasp.

"Lenny!"

He kissed my cheek, then greeted my staff one by one. He asked Cara how her grandson, Patrick, was doing with crew. Patrick had been elected captain of his team, go Hitchens! He asked Fred, one of Prescott's most experienced antiques appraisers, how his wife, Suzanne, the general manager of my favorite local restaurant, the Blue Dolphin, was handling their expansion into breakfast service. Suzanne, it seemed, was in the final stages of hiring a new assistant manager. I admired everything about Lenny, from his genuine interest in people to his devotion to his wife, Aileen. As I listened in, I realized I'd been so absorbed with buying the house and getting the renovation started, my outside focus had narrowed to a pinprick. Lenny also asked Sasha, my chief antiques appraiser, about the lecture on Victorian seal rings she'd mentioned she planned to attend at a Boston antiques auction house. Sasha reported that she'd fallen in love with an 18-karat-gold and agate ring.

She laughed and extracted it from her desk drawer. "It had an *S* on it, so needless to say, I had to bid on it." She tucked her baby-fine brown hair behind her ears. "And I won."

She placed the ring in the center of her hand to show it to us. The stone was pale blue and oval. The carved letter *S* was backward so when it was dipped in molten wax and stamped on paper, it would read properly. A minuscule latch revealed a tiny gold frame for a photo and a miniature cubbyhole for a keepsake, like a lock of hair. The picture frame hidden in the lid was ornate. The secret compartment was lined in the same blue agate.

"It's gorgeous," Cara marveled.

"Thanks. I'm looking for the perfect photograph; then I'll decide if I want to display it under Plexiglas or wear it like a pendant around my neck."

"Either will work," I said.

"And how about you, Josie? Did you close on the house?"

As I told him about the architectural details Ty and I were determined to retain, I couldn't stop grinning. "But enough of this," I said after a one-minute recounting of the high points. "Tell me what we can do for you."

"Buy back everything we've bought from you over the years." He must have read the bewilderment on my face because he added, "We're moving to London." He held up a hand. "I know, I know, I've always said I'd never leave Rocky Point, but this client I've been working with is relentless. They're moving into entertainment, building or buying everything from video gaming to online gambling to movies, and they want me to commit to a multiyear contract to help them create a cohesive brand. They made me an offer I simply can't refuse. The work sounds terrific, the pay is to-the-moon, and Aileen loves England, so off we go."

I'd known the couple for years, ever since Aileen had discovered we carried a wide range of art deco objects at our weekly tag sale, including fashion plates. Over the years, Aileen had amassed a world-class collection of pochoir prints—a stencil-based printmaking process popular with architects and fashion designers in Paris from the late 1800s to the 1930s. The fashion plates featured meticulously executed details and vibrant colors. In today's market, they'd retail for as much as eighty dollars each.

"Why wouldn't you simply put everything into storage? I can recommend an excellent temperature- and humidity-controlled facility in town."

"We talked about it, but it turns out that Aileen likes the hunt more than the boodle." Lenny smiled. "Since most of those fancy prints she likes come from Paris, she's like a dog with two tails, on the scent, with money to burn. How does it work? Do you buy things outright or do we give them to you on consignment?"

"Both options are fine with us. You'll make more money if we take everything on consignment, but you'll get your money quicker if you sell it outright."

"Let's sell it, done and done." He laughed. "I moved the whole kit and caboodle into the living room. Aileen doesn't want to know from no-how. She's meeting with the relocation team as we speak, so if you can come now with a van . . . hell, what am I thinking." He laughed again. "If you can come with a truck—we can take care of it without anything troubling her."

I exhaled loudly. "You are a man of action, Lenny."

He winked at me. "That's my brand."

I was sad that Lenny and Aileen were leaving, but I was jumping-out-of-my-sandals excited at the prospect of acquiring, in one fell swoop, a truck-load of high-quality antiques, a coup because it's far harder to buy antiques than it is to sell them. Nonetheless, I managed to keep my tone even and calm. "We'd be happy to zip over immediately. I'm going to ask Sasha to take charge of it. She'll be able to make you a firm offer on the spot."

"Let's do it to it!"

Sasha stood. "With pleasure!"

She asked Cara to call the facility guys to bring a truck with appropriate packing materials, and told Lenny she'd follow him in her own car.

As Lenny prepared to leave, I hugged him and kissed his cheek. "I'm going to miss you."

He told me he'd miss me, too, said warm good-byes to everyone, and left.

Sasha got back to the office at five, her eyes wide with awe. "I don't think any of us knew the extent of their collection. There's the print collection, which now numbers a hundred and eighteen separate pochoir prints, but there's also some wonderful art deco odds and ends."

"I'm salivating," I said.

"Wait until you see everything. The guys are unloading now."

I pushed open the heavy door and entered the warehouse. Eric was over-seeing the team as they off-loaded the objects into a cordoned-off area. I spot-ted a stack of light-switch plates in a small clear plastic tub and opened the lid. The pewter-colored plates were typical of the art deco style, fabricated of cast iron and nickel, with a geometric pattern clearly evoking the period.

"Wow."

Sasha stood beside me. "Lenny kept all the receipts, so we have a paper trail."

"Any hesitations?"

When we buy antiques and collectibles outright, we aim to pay no more than a third of the retail value, which allows for the costs associated with storing, appraising, cleaning, marketing, and selling the goods. For rare objects, the only way we could assess fair market value was by conducting an actual appraisal. We always offered to delay our bid, but nine out of ten sellers simply wanted the objects gone. My question to Sasha was code for whether she'd identified any objects that might be especially valuable.

"A couple, if we can identify the maker."

"Lenny wasn't interested in a delay," I said.

"Right. He was determined to settle it all today. I explained my reasoning, but he wasn't interested. I always feel bad when I think a client might be leaving money on the table."

"Well, I suppose we need to remember that selling things is stressful," I said, "and that for some people getting rid of the stress is worth more than money."

Sasha thanked me and smiled. "You have a way of helping me put things in perspective."

I left her to begin the process of videotaping the DeVito collection and went to join Fred at a worktable near the kitty domain. Hank chomped some crunchies. Angela was curled up in a velour-lined kitty bed, enjoying a little nap. Fred had hung our chandelier from a silk-padded brace of my invention.

The chandelier was stunning, featuring four cascading rows of crystal drops, with accompanying bobeches, removable crystal cups devised to catch dripping wax. Each cluster was surrounded by a central candleholder, long since converted to accept electric bulbs. Under the bright work lights, the crystal drops sparked overlapping rainbows on the worktable.

"My initial examination suggests that every palmette, crystal drop, and bobeche is undamaged," Fred said. "You know how rare that is. I'm looking for maker's marks now. So far, I haven't found anything."

I recounted Maudie's memory about the shop in Saint-Quentin, and his eyes lit up. There's nothing an antiques appraiser likes better than a viable lead. Never mind that he would need to trace a purchase made more than a hundred years earlier, in the midst of the chaos that was certain to have raged through the small town during the war—at least he had a starting place.

I said good night to everyone, Hank and Angela included, and went home.

I stood at the open refrigerator considering dinner options, thinking that I could give second life to some leftover roast chicken if I warmed it in a Mornay sauce. Before I could reach for the ingredients, my back door was flung open and Zoë was stomping across the kitchen, glaring at me.

Zoë, tall and thin, had an olive complexion and near-black shoulder-length hair. She was willowy and lithe, and unless she was in one of her tempestuous moods, when she marched with militant passion, she seemed to glide rather than walk. In addition to being my best friend, she was my neighbor and landlady, and I could read her mood by observing her gait. Stomping meant trouble.

Zoë slapped the counter, then spun to face me. "Don't tell me it's okay. It's not."

Before I could reply, she collapsed. She sat on the floor, her back to the cabinet door. She raised her knees and hugged her calves as tears ran down her cheeks. She swiped away the wetness with the side of her hand.

"Oh, God, Josie, what am I going to do? Emma signed the papers today. The marines, for God's sake. She only graduated high school three weeks ago."

I sat beside her, my legs stretched out in front of me. "Oh, Zoë . . . I know you've been dreading this day."

Zoë cried harder. Her shoulders shook as she wept.

"Emma is an athlete," I said. "A star. She's smart and disciplined, a team player." I patted her back as she cried. "I know this isn't what you want for her, Zoë, but it's what she wants for herself. She's wanted it for three years. Maybe longer."

I kept rubbing her back, telling her it was all right, it would be fine, Emma was strong, Emma was smart, over and over again until Zoë ran out of tears.

"How can I stop her?" Zoë asked, her gaze on the floor.

"You can't."

"No, no, no!" she hissed, covering her face with her hands, rocking from side to side.

"Once you're over the shock, you're going to be proud of her."

"No, I won't," she snapped.

I smiled at her rebellious tone. "Ha!"

She sniffed loudly, dragged a wadded-up tissue from her jeans pocket, and wiped her nose. She hiccupped. After a few seconds, she said, "We're sitting on the floor."

"As good a place as any. Want a watermelon martini? I made a pitcher."

"I guess."

I stood and offered a hand, and she took it, getting herself upright.

"Thanks. Sorry . . . I had a moment." She raised her chin, pride triumphing over despair.

"No need to apologize."

She turned on the faucet, letting the water run over her fingers until it was cold enough for her taste, then cupped her hands to drink.

I took a glass from the cabinet and handed it over. "New invention."

She accepted it, filled it to the brim and gulped it down, refilled it, and drank some more.

I got the martini pitcher from the fridge and glasses from the freezer. I kept peeking at her as I poured the martinis.

"How are you doing?" I asked.

"A little better." After another minute and a few more sips, Zoë asked, "Where's Ty?"

"In DC explaining to his boss why his training flopped."

I added a wedge of juicy watermelon as a garnish and slid her martini glass across the counter.

She raised her glass and quoted my dad's favorite toast. "To silver light in the dark of night."

We clinked.

"Tell me about your day," Zoë said. "Take my mind off Emma."

"Let's sit for a minute." I slid onto the long bench behind the farmer's table, arranging the toss pillows as a backrest. "I had a funny experience today."

She sat across from me, in a comfy armchair. "Funny ha-ha?" she asked, calmer now, but still on edge. "Or funny odd?"

"Funny remarkable." I told her about returning the trunk to Maudie Wilson and our lingering, intimate conversation. "Has that ever happened to you? Where you feel a real connection with someone you just met?"

"Once, on a train. The guy sitting next to me and I ended up talking the whole way from Portland to Seattle, more than three hours."

"What did you talk about?"

"Whether he should propose to his girlfriend. He couldn't decide whether his hesitation was cold feet or some instinct alerting him that he should hit the road. I asked questions to help him think it through. And I told him about my marriage, the problems, the way I was trying to extricate myself."

"That's amazing."

"We helped each other, we really did, two strangers. He's the only person who didn't try to convince me to stay, who told me that if I wanted to leave, I should. It was a revelation. By the time we arrived, he'd decided to break up with his girlfriend. He figured that if he was that uncertain, he should listen to his gut, and since he wanted to get married and have kids, if he wasn't going to propose to her, he should end it and find the girl he wanted to marry."

"Did you ever hear from him afterward?"

"No, and I've always wondered what happened."

"Half a story—you know how much I hate that."

She smiled, a weak one, for sure, but it was progress. "What did you and Maudie talk about?"

I recounted the details of our conversation, then said, "It's very unlike me to be so open so quickly. I like her a lot."

"It's great to make new friends."

"Especially so unexpectedly. A real treat!" I sipped my drink. "Can I ask a question about Emma?"

"Ask away!"

"When does she leave for basic?"

"September fourteenth."

A knock sounded at the back door, and Ellis Hunter, Zoë's live-in boyfriend and Rocky Point's police chief, came inside.

Ellis and Zoë had been dating for a decade, taking it slow, trying to protect themselves from future pain. Ellis's wife had died from lung cancer when she was only thirty-three, leaving him heartbroken and rudderless. Zoë had survived a bruising divorce that left her emotionally battered and wary.

"I just spoke to Emma," Ellis told Zoë.

"And?"

"And she's totally psyched."

"Even though she knows she's breaking my heart?"

Ellis sat next to Zoë and took her hand. He kissed her knuckles. "I get the impression she thinks this decision is hers to make."

"And you agree with her."

He kissed her hand again. "I do."

"So does Josie." Zoë teared up again. She withdrew her hand and pushed her chair back a few inches. "Excuse me for a minute. I need to throw some water on my face."

She plodded down the hall toward the bathroom.

"Watermelon martini or beer?"

"Beer. Thanks."

I took a bottle from the fridge and handed it to him. "What do you think?"

"I was a marine."

"I didn't know that."

"Eight years. I was in for the long haul until I fell in love with a Rockette."

"And moved to New York City to be with her. That's very romantic."

"Aw, shucks."

"Thank you for your service."

He smiled. "Thank you for your support."

I smiled back and slid onto the bench. "Any regrets about leaving a career you loved?"

"Not a bit. We all make the best decisions we can with the information we have available at the time. I don't believe in regrets any more than I believe in one and onlys. I loved being a marine, and I love being a cop. I loved Shelby until the day she died, and now I love Zoë." He drank some beer. "Zoë needs to find a way through this. Emma's going. It will be better for them both if she goes with Zoë's blessing."

"I know."

"I know, too," Zoë said.

She stood at the entry to the kitchen. Her cheeks were splotchy, her eyes rimmed in red. Ellis placed his beer bottle on the table, crossed the room, and enveloped her in a hug. She stood with her arms by her sides, her eyes closed, her shoulders shaking, silent tears streaking her cheeks.

CHAPTER EIGHT

T he next morning, Thursday, I sat at the guest table in the front office greeting my staff as they arrived. Fred was last in, no surprise, since he was a night owl, often arriving close to noon and working late into the evening, a schedule that matched Suzanne's at the Blue Dolphin. Today he came in holding a supersized thermos of coffee just after ten. Hank was in my lap, napping. Angela had sashayed away on her own business. I suspected she'd be back soon, carrying a felt mouse by the tail.

While Sasha finished telling me what she'd learned about the art deco light-switch plates, Fred grunted hello, got himself behind his desk, and turned on his computer.

Sasha handed me one of the plates and placed another on her desk. "They were manufactured between 1910 and 1930."

"In other words, they're on the cusp."

Prescott's policy was firm: an object had to be at least a hundred years old for us to call it an antique. These switch plates could be antiques—or they could be mere collectibles. The demarcation mattered on several levels: pricing, promotion, and customer appeal.

"Exactly. From what I can tell, these were produced en masse. They're not rare, but neither are they common, perhaps because they're still popular." She stroked the cold metal. "They're beautiful, aren't they?"

"Very. Can we identify their origin?"

"No. There aren't any marks or stamps."

"How would you price them?"

"I don't know . . . there are minor inconsistencies that indicate the use of a crudely constructed mold and rushed production. Nothing a customer would be likely to notice or mind, since all the imperfections are on the back." Sasha's shoulders lifted, then dropped. "Ten dollars, maybe."

Fred grunted again. "Call it a buck per and get 'em out of here."

Fred was an antiques snob, seeing little merit in an object that wasn't rare, valuable, or important.

"You're harsh," I told him, laughing. "And a snob."

"And proud of it."

I picked up the sample and gently tossed it in my hand, assessing its weight and feel. "It's got real heft to it. Maybe we should price it higher."

"You can buy new ones with an art deco theme," she said, "in brushed nickel for as little as seven or eight dollars."

"Are we competing with the new product market?" I asked.

"If something comparable is available, then yes, I think we are."

"You're right. Ten dollars each is fair and reasonable. Good job, Sasha!"

Sasha twisted a lock of her lank hair into a tight screw. "Thanks."

Sasha's hair twisting was a tell, an unconscious action that revealed her true emotional state. She was gratified that I'd accepted her recommendation, but she was also anxious, worried, I knew from experience, that she'd gone too far, pushed too hard. She hadn't, of course, but don't tell her that.

"You know who'd love these?" I asked. "Lieutenant Commander Silberblatt."

Sasha nodded. "She would. I'll have Cara call to let her know." She turned to Fred. "I got your email. You want me to call that shop in France?"

"Yeah, if you can. At eleven."

"Is this about the chandelier?" I asked.

"Yes. There's only one antiques shop in the town that was operating in 1910 and is still in business today. If this isn't it, I can try tracking down the ones that have gone out of business through the historical society. When I called yesterday, I spoke to a Monsieur Joubert, who is, I think, the current owner, but his English is only marginally better than my French, so we didn't make much progress. I told him I'd call back with a translator at eleven this morning. If Sasha isn't available, I'll call and reschedule."

"I'm available."

"Great. Thanks."

Cara joined in our conversation. "I didn't know you were fluent in French, Sasha."

"I'm not."

Fred drank some coffee. "She may not be fluent, but her French is way better than mine."

Sasha leaned back with a sassy smile. *"C'est peu dire."*

I laughed. "My high school French is limping along behind you, but I think that means 'that's an understatement.' Am I right?"

"Mais oui."

"Ha," Fred said, grinning. "I'm not that bad."

"Just bad enough," Sasha said, laughing.

"Will you call for me? Or do you plan on spending the day embarrassing me in front of the boss?"

Sasha's eyes clouded over; her tone shifted from jocular to appalled. "I'm sorry, Fred. I'm glad to call, and I didn't mean to embarrass you."

Fred pointed his index finger at her chest. "Gotcha."

Sasha exhaled loudly. "What is it you said before? *Ha?* I'll meet your *ha* and raise you a *gee whiz*."

"So you'll call?"

"Of course."

"Merci."

The phone rang, and a few seconds later, Cara told me, "Josie . . . it's Timothy on one."

I reached for the guest phone. Timothy was my TV show's producer and director, and my heart always pounded an extra few beats when I heard his name—I was still a little starstruck. Between having my own show, *Josie's Antiques*, and being around TV industry professionals, well, I found the process intimidating and exhilarating in equal measures.

"Timothy!"

"Hey, Josie. I don't need to ask if I'm calling too early, do I?"

I laughed. "It's nearly ten thirty and I'm wide awake. Why? Are you still in bed?"

"Heavens, no. I'm even dressed and having coffee on my balcony."

"Overlooking the East River."

"It's a beautiful day."

"Here, too."

"I can only imagine. All those trees and grass and things."

I laughed. "You sound like my friend Shelley. She talks about New Hampshire as if it's the Outer Hebrides, not a place you fly or drive to—you trek."

"Speaking of which, I'd like to trek up tomorrow if you're around. I want to scout some location shots. Do you have time? I'll buy you lunch."

"Absolutely!"

We agreed to meet at the Blue Dolphin at twelve thirty, then spend the afternoon checking out specific options so the team would have ample time to organize permits and permissions.

"I'm hoping we can get all the actual camerawork done in a couple of days toward the end of the month," he said. "What does your schedule look like?"

I brought up my calendar on my iPhone. "I'm around all month."

We decided on July 21 through 23 for the actual taping.

Timothy said they wouldn't need me for every shot, but he wanted me on call. They planned to get some ocean footage, various shots around Rocky Point, and lots of me at my desk in my office, working the tag sale venue, organizing the auction room, and walking the floor at Prescott's Antiques Barn, my newest location, recently rebranded to honor its former life as a barn.

"Sounds perfect!"

"Any antiques to set my hair on fire?" Timothy asked.

I described the chandelier and the collection of art deco objects, including the prosaic light-switch plates.

"I definitely feel singed! Keep 'em coming!"

I chuckled, delighted. Timothy was warm, witty, and charming, and he had an innate sense of which antiques and collectibles would work on our show. If Timothy was happy, I was happy.

I was telling Cara which days to block out on my calendar when the phone rang again. It was Maudie Wilson, and she wanted to know if she could come by my office now.

"It's urgent," she said.

I told her to come on ahead. Knowing that she wouldn't use the word heedlessly, I wondered what could possibly be urgent.

CHAPTER NINE

hew," Maudie said, laughing as she sidled out of the backseat of a black Camry. "My hips sure don't swivel the way they used to. Thank you for seeing me on such short notice."

I walked across the parking lot to greet her. "Anytime." I suggested we go up to my private office, but she asked if we could stay on the ground level.

"It's not only my hips that give me trouble. In addition to bench-pressing fifty pounds, I can swim ten laps faster than women half my age, and walk a ten-minute mile with no problem, faster than that if I have to, but climbing stairs is too hard for these rickety old knees of mine."

I offered Maudie two private options: chairs in the currently unoccupied tag sale venue or a bench outside. She eagerly chose the bench.

"I like this kind of weather. Cool and breezy."

"Me, too."

The temperature was in the sixties, and with milky yellow clouds blowing in from the north, I doubted it would be going up anytime soon. I led the way to the same bench Celia and Doug had sat on the other day. The willow tree's long green tendrils swayed in the gentle breeze.

Maudie leaned back against the wooden slats and placed her handbag, summer straw, on her lap. Her gaze drifted from the beds of tiger lilies that lined the walkway to the woods that separated my property from the Congregational church.

After a few seconds, she readjusted her position so she was facing me. "I enjoyed our talk yesterday."

"So did I. Very much. I'm not usually so open."

"Me, either." She twisted her purse's woven handle into a tight screw, then let it unfurl. "You've met my nieces."

"Celia and Stacy . . . yes."

"Did they tell you I'm incompetent?"

I picked my words carefully. "They expressed some concern."

"You're being diplomatic."

I laughed. "A little."

"I would appreciate your keeping my visit here private."

"Certainly."

"I'm thinking of selling the trunk, the presentation box, and the cat. I don't want anyone to know I'm looking into it."

My pulse quickened, but I maintained a calm tone as I assured her that confidentiality was the norm in my business, not the exception.

She nodded but didn't speak.

I was tempted to ask her how I could help, but I didn't. When people are thinking about selling their possessions, it's not unusual for conversations to become charged with anxiety, fear, regret, or resentment, and over the years, I'd learned that patience was essential. It was hard for me, since by nature I wasn't the least bit patient, but allowing potential clients to set the pace made the process easier for them, so I did it.

"You told me your guesstimate of the trunk," Maudie said a minute later. "What about the presentation box and cat?"

"That's trickier than the trunk. I can't give you even a rough idea of value without considering the objects' pedigree and provenance. It's not that those factors don't matter with the trunk. They do. If we knew the trunk's origin and history, it might add value, but not knowing them won't lower the value. The cat and box are a whole different story. If they're genuine ancient Egyptian artifacts with a verifiable backstory, well, they could be worth many, many hundreds of thousands of dollars—or even more. If they're reproductions with no history available, they'd be purchased for their grandeur and craftsmanship, maybe for a few hundred to a few thousand dollars."

"That's quite a range."

"I know. The thing about antiques appraisals is that you need to investigate along two separate, yet equally important, tracks: authenticity and valuation. First you need to discover if an object is real. Then you need to look at the variety of factors that contribute to valuation."

"What are those factors? If it's not too much to ask."

"Not at all. We look at rarity, scarcity, condition, association, popularity, and provenance. Rarity—how many were made or created in the first place? Scarcity—how many are extant? Condition—are we talking normal wear and tear, or what? Association—did anyone interesting or important own it? Did it figure into a notable event? Popularity—there are trends in antique collecting as in everything else, so we want to know whether this object is on trend. One of the ways you measure that is by examining the recent past sales of similar objects. Are the prices going up? Down? Holding steady? Are museums in the mix? Is there a known private collector on the hunt? And lastly, provenance—does the current owner have a clear title? Do we know who made it? Who bought it? We aim to verify how it got from wherever it was made or created to wherever it is now."

"Like a stamp or mark you find on the bottom of some sterling flatware or fine furniture . . . that's how you know who designed or built it."

"Exactly."

"I had no idea the process was so complicated," Maudie said.

"The good news is there's an actual process."

"That is all very interesting." Maudie nodded slowly. I could almost see the wheels turning behind her sharp, intelligent eyes. "Very. I like to see the whole picture before I make a decision, and I like to look people in the eye while I'm doing it, so I thank you for clarifying it for me. How much does an appraisal cost?"

"It depends on the approach, the time it takes, and the expenses incurred. In this case, I'd start with the materials. If the gold is gold and the silver silver, that would be an encouraging sign. If the jewels are real, that would be another positive sign. At some point, we might need to consult an Egyptologist, hire document specialists, translators, and so on. The more time we spend, the more experts we consult, and the more materials testing we undertake, well, no surprise, the more costly the appraisal. At a guess—here's another guesstimate—I would say you're looking at a few hundred dollars to determine whether it's worth pursuing a full appraisal. From there, it might require as much as ten to twenty thousand dollars to finish the job. If you decide to proceed, I'll be glad to give you the names of some reputable appraisers."

"Thank you. Do you do appraisals like this?"

I kept my professional face on. This was the kind of project that had the potential to win the appraiser international acclaim. Equally exciting was the possibility that I could feature the objects on *Josie's Antiques*. My instinct was to leap onto the bench and shout to the heavens, "Oh, yes, baby, we do this sort of work!" But I didn't. I sat quietly for a few seconds to give my raging pulse time to quiet, then said, "Absolutely."

Mrs. Wilson asked about my training and background.

I told her how I'd fallen in love with objects of great beauty as a child by viewing the glass flowers at Harvard University's Museum of Natural History and the James McNeill Whistlers at Boston's Isabella Stewart Gardner Museum; that I'd earned a college degree in art history; and that I'd spent years at Frisco's, a famous New York City antiques auction house. I didn't tell her how I'd been the whistle-blower revealing my boss's price-fixing scheme, or how I'd been shunned by my so-called friends, fired for not being a team player, and hounded by the press. Instead, I expanded on what I'd told her yesterday, how I'd moved to New Hampshire to open my own business, and how it was thriving, and how much I loved the work.

"Thank you," she said. "You've been very helpful. I'd appreciate that list of appraisers."

"Of course," I said, deflating a bit. I was happy to give her some recommendations, but my fingers remained crossed that ultimately she'd choose Prescott's. "Let me consider some options. I can email you the list tomorrow."

Maudie gave me her email address. "I don't really use email, but if I know a message is coming, I'll make a point to look for it on my phone." She chuckled. "Mostly, I use my phone to take photos. Alicia, Celia's oldest, taught me how. Alicia is ten. And I use it to call for an Uber . . . like now." She tapped the app, and after a few more taps said, "Five minutes."

"Would you like a lemonade or an iced tea? I can run inside and get you something."

"Thank you, dear. I'm fine." She smiled devilishly. "There's something else I want to tell you, but I really want to keep it private. Will you keep another secret?"

I used my index finger to draw an *X* on my chest. "Cross my heart. I'm actually very good at keeping secrets. I hate gossip, so I'm never tempted to share someone else's secret."

"I called Rocky Point Computers this morning. In addition to selling computers, they offer private lessons. I have an appointment later today. They're going to get me set up with a lightweight laptop and the right software, and they're going to teach me how to use it." She smiled. "I explained that I'm a travel writer."

"Oh, Maudie."

"I'm quite excited."

"It's thrilling!"

"I don't want to deal with naysayers. Not now. Not at this point in my life."

"No one should have to deal with naysayers—ever. Have you decided on your first story idea?"

"Snorkeling on my own schedule. I love to snorkel, but I hate being part of a crowd. I went to the Caribbean, St. Croix, last winter by myself, and I hired a man with a boat. We sailed to Green Cay, and I went snorkeling there. He showed me things I never would have noticed on my own. It was wonderful. I thought that writing about an older woman with hips that don't swivel and rickety knees traveling alone might make for an interesting niche."

"It sounds fantastic."

"I could try an *Endless Summer* sort of approach—a hunt for the perfect snorkeling site. I always wanted to go to Yap in Micronesia. And the Cook Islands. But there are excellent options closer to home, too."

"You're a woman on a mission."

"A newfound mission, thanks to you."

I was so touched, so moved, for a moment I couldn't speak.

"If there's one thing I've learned over the course of my life," she added, "it's to listen for opportunity knocking. Sometimes the knocking is so soft, it's easy to miss. Now is my time."

"Carpe diem."

"You better believe it. I'm seizing today, all right."

The car arrived on schedule, and I opened the back door.

"I'll call you in the morning when I send the email with those names, so you'll know to look for it. If I don't reach you for whatever reason, I'll leave a message with Lainy."

She thanked me and waved good-bye.

As soon as I stepped back inside the office, I asked Fred, "How did the call to Monsieur Joubert go?"

"Great! We learned he has the previous owners' records, and he thinks they go back to the mid-eighteenth century, if you can believe it. I'm going to send him photos of the chandelier, and he's going to research it."

"That's fantastic!"

"It really is," Sasha said, "and it gets better. Monsieur Joubert's daughter, Yvette, is fluent in English, so he said he'll email me with her availability after they've had a chance to review the photos and their records, and we can schedule a call."

I smiled at them, one at a time, nodding, letting my appreciation register. "You two are awesome. Really, truly awesome."

I decided to stop at the ocean on my way home. I pulled onto the shoulder on Ocean and climbed to the top of a dune. The wind was blowing harder now, and whitecaps dotted the water's surface.

A hundred yards away, a mongrel, part terrier, part something else, tried to wrest a piece of pied driftwood away from a young man wearing blue swim trunks and a long-sleeved Hitchens University T-shirt. The dog's tail wagged so fast it was a blur.

A little farther on, Stacy Collins stood at the bottom of a dune near a jetty where the crashing waves sent spumes of water shooting fifty feet into the air. She wore a mint-green skirt with a white blouse and sandals. Pointing at the jetty, she said something to a man who appeared to be a few years her senior. He wore khakis and a black collared T-shirt.

Stacy turned in my direction. She opened her arms wide, including everything from shore to horizon in whatever point she was making. She broke off when she noticed me, smiled and waved, then spoke to her companion. The two of them picked their way toward me, stepping over driftwood, rocks, and tendrils of slick green and brown seaweed. I sidestepped down the dune and walked to meet them.

"This is Kyle Previns, Josie," Stacy said. "His firm is thinking of investing in my company. I was just sharing your comments about how my designs are unique."

Stacy was using her satiny voice, and she exuded warmth and confidence.

"Totally," I said, smiling and offering a hand to the potential investor. "I deal in antiques, but I recognize good design in all its forms. Stacy's work is spectacular."

He smiled politely.

"I wanted to show Kyle where my inspiration comes from." She faced the ocean. "The power . . . the beauty."

She was positioning herself as an artist, and I wondered if her strategy would work. From his bored expression I inferred he wasn't impressed. I suspected he was inured to needy entrepreneurs' tactics and dismissed anecdotal opinions like mine and touchy-feely concepts like inspiration out of hand. Show him the potential to make money, or go home.

I told him it was nice to meet him, smiled at her, and left. I wished her well, but I got the impression her climb to success was all uphill, and the hill was steep.

As I drove home, I found myself wondering how Maudie was doing for real. Signing up for computer lessons indicated curiosity and motivation, not capability. The same was true for her questions about the appraisal process. Certainly, they were insightful and on point, but I'd done most of the talking. In both our interactions, Maudie had been pleasant, clear, and deliberate. Everything seemed fine, but I'd heard that one of dementia's cruelest tricks was letting people think all is well when it isn't.

CHAPTER TEN

M audie called me at nine the next morning, Friday, before I'd had a chance to call her.

"I just opened your email," she said, "and I wanted to thank you. You said you'd send the list in the morning, and you did."

"You're an early bird! I haven't even had time to call you."

"'Tis true . . . I am an early bird, always have been. How about you?"

"*Mezza mezza*. It depends."

"Fair enough. So of the three names on the list, do you have a favorite?"

"They're all good options for different reasons. The Rocky Point dealer is a generalist, like me. Since you like looking people in the eye, I thought I ought to include another local option. The company in Boston concentrates on ancient artifacts, and the consultant in San Francisco is a world-renowned Egyptologist, in case you'd feel more comfortable with a bona fide expert."

"Wouldn't everyone, you included, consult an Egyptologist?"

"Assuming the preliminary tests are encouraging, yes."

"Why did you pick someone so far away?"

"He's the best."

"Eli always said, you want the best, buy the best." I could hear the smile in Maudie's voice. "Could he do every aspect of the appraisal?"

"No. He'd need to work with a jeweler, and he'd probably recommend that the sale be orchestrated by an antiques auction house, someone who excels at the marketing aspects of the process."

Maudie thanked me again and said she'd let me know what she decided.

• • •

I got to the Gingerbread House to meet Monte, our general contractor, at ten, and found Julie on her knees in the side garden, weeding. It was still cool and windy, with the sun struggling to fight through the clouds.

On the off chance I'd find Julie there, I'd written a thank-you note before I'd left my office, tucking in a fifty-dollar bill. I handed it over. "Here you go, Julie. Thanks again for your help with the measuring."

She leaned back on her haunches and pulled off one of her gardening gloves to accept it. She tore it open it and exclaimed, "Oh!" She looked up at me. "Thank you. Thank you so much. You have no idea . . ." Her voice trailed off.

"You earned it."

"Thank you," she repeated, her cheeks pink with pleasure.

"But you shouldn't be working here today."

"I like to garden."

"You're not being paid."

"It's okay."

"No, Julie, it's not."

"I just want to help."

"I'm sorry," I said, "but you can't."

Tom appeared from the back, grinning. "Hey, Josie! I thought I heard your voice. Monte tells me the engineer has finished his inspection and they're working on the demolition plan. Progress!"

Julie stood up, brushed the dirt from her knees with her gloved hand, and walked toward the front without speaking another word.

Tom's eyes followed her until she rounded the corner, his brow wrinkling. "What's up with her?"

"I told her she couldn't work here anymore."

"And she said she just wants to help."

"Which I know is true, and it's not personal in any way, but between the ethics of letting someone work without paying them and the potential liability if she were to get hurt . . . I just can't allow it. I really am sorry. I didn't realize she'd be so upset."

Tom continued to stare at the place he'd last seen Julie. "I'll take care of it."

He strode off toward the front, and I headed to the backyard. Tom had prepped some handsome raised beds near the stone wall separating our property from the beach, so the irises would be out of harm's way.

Monte came around the corner a few minutes later, and I handed over the set of new keys. I confirmed that his list of the architectural features we wanted to retain was accurate and complete, then got an update on the engineer's findings: He hadn't discovered any additional problems, so they expected the demolition to be fairly straightforward—or as straightforward as this kind of partial demolition could be.

Before I left, I told Monte about Tom's plan to safeguard the bulbs, and he said there was plenty of time, that they wouldn't be in any danger for at least a week. I thanked him and left.

Tom and Julie were standing by the front of his pickup talking. His hand was on her shoulder, and she was nodding at something he was saying.

I kept my eyes on the road, not so much pretending that I didn't see them as signaling that they shouldn't feel obliged to talk to me.

Tom called my name. I looked up, making it a point to smile. Tom nudged Julie.

"I understand about the work thing," she said. "Sorry."

"I hope you know it's not personal."

"Tom explained."

"Good."

I continued to my car, and as I slid behind the steering wheel, I peeked over the dashboard. Tom caught my eye and gave me a thumbs-up. I nodded in his direction and left it at that. I was relieved that he'd smoothed the situation over, but I didn't feel like celebrating. I hated that Julie felt unappreciated. I pulled away from the shoulder and lifted my hand in a friendly good-bye.

I'd never seen Timothy wear anything but black, and today was no exception. He was an inch over six feet and lean, sinewy like a runner. He had a finely manicured three-day growth of reddish-brown beard and brown eyes that seemed to see everything and know everything and judge nothing. I thanked my lucky stars every day that he was my producer and director.

By the time we ordered lunch, we had a solid list of location options. I recommended we check out the tugboats running along the Piscataqua River, the gazebo on the village green where bands played familiar tunes on warm summer nights, the consignment shops that filled Prescott's Antiques

Barn, and the dunes that dotted the eighteen miles of New Hampshire shoreline.

My phone vibrated, alerting me to a text from Cara. Maudie Wilson had called and left a message asking if I would call or visit. She had another question about the appraisal process.

"I need to touch base with a potential client," I told Timothy, "but first I want to show you something." I scrolled through the video I'd taken of the trunk a few days before on my phone, froze the image on the jewel-embedded presentation box, and held it up so he could see it.

His eyes widened. "Oh, my."

I hit PLAY, pausing on the cat.

"I like the box better," he said.

"You like the bling."

"Shouldn't I?"

"Bling is okay in its place, but in this case, it's the cat that caught my eye. It reminds me of the Gayer-Anderson Cat, a famous example of an ancient Egyptian cat statue. It's in the British Museum. It seems that jewels were often placed inside the cats as a tribute to the goddess Bastet. Don't tell anyone, but this cat was heavier than warranted by the materials, ergo . . ."

"Get out of town," Timothy said, ready to share what he assumed was a joke.

"It's true."

"Tell me we can feature it."

"I wish I could, but I don't know yet."

"You're killing me, Josie."

"Maybe I'll let you scout those locations on your own while I go see the owner."

"Go. Go now. You can eat later."

I laughed. "Let me try calling her. I'll be right back."

I walked outside, both to ensure my conversation wasn't overheard and to avoid annoying other diners. Maudie's phone went directly to voicemail, and when I called the facility, the receptionist, Lainy, whispered that Maudie was out to lunch with Julie.

"No luck," I told Timothy as I slid back into my seat. "I'll try again after we eat."

We were halfway through lunch when Cara texted again, this time writing that Celia had called. Maudie had decided to sell everything and to let me handle it all. Celia asked me to call ASAP.

"Hold that thought," I said, awed. "I'll be right back."

Back outside, I dialed Celia's cell phone and got her.

"Thank you for calling back so quickly," she said. "Aunt Maudie has always been decisive, and today is no exception. She was impressed with your professionalism. She hopes you can email whatever documents she needs to sign to me so I can review them, then pick everything up later today."

Having a lawyer or relative review our consignment forms was common, and I was always okay with it. The more transparent the process, the better.

"Needless to say, I'm proud to work with her and touched by her confidence. I won't let her down. I can email the forms now and come by anytime this afternoon. You tell me."

We agreed to meet at two forty-five. I forced myself to walk calmly back to the table, but Timothy wasn't fooled.

"I can feel the heat at the back of my neck—my hair is on fire for real. Take a look." He turned his head.

"You're right, I see the flames. Oh, Timothy, Maudie wants to sell the cat and box. I'll add a paragraph to the contract authorizing us to feature it on the show. I'm sure she'll agree, since the more buzz I can create, the higher the price she'll get." I exhaled loudly, exhilaration and anticipation sending my pulse sky-high.

"When would you plan on selling it?"

"For an object of this quality, nine months to a year is realistic. Marketing well takes time." I smiled. "I can't believe it! Even if the cat and box are replicas, taking people through the process of discovery . . . I'm so excited! This is one for the ages."

Eric and I arrived at Belle Vista at two forty-five, and as before, I left him with the van.

Inside, while I signed the guest book, Lainy called Maudie's room, but there was no answer.

"Maudie got back from lunch nearly an hour ago," Lainy said, "and I haven't seen her go out again. Is she expecting you?"

"Yes. Celia made the arrangements."

Lainy tried calling again, without luck. This time, she left a message saying I was waiting in the lobby.

I thanked her and reconciled myself to the delay. I sat on the bench. A few minutes later, impatient and bored, I turned my back to the window and looked around. A server in the café was clearing a table. Lainy was watching a YouTube video on her tablet. By squinting, I could just make out text running along the bottom of the screen: *The Stanislavski Method*. A middle-aged man in a suit walked alongside an older woman in a turquoise muumuu. When they reached the facility's front door, he kissed her on the cheek. She squeezed his arm affectionately, and he left. Other people came and went.

At three, I called Maudie myself, then Celia. Neither woman answered. I left voicemails saying I was here. A few minutes later, I texted them, thinking that some people pay more attention to texts than calls. I texted Eric, too, to explain the delay. After another ten minutes, I tried Maudie's cell and landline again, then Celia's cell, still without reaching either of them.

I walked back to the desk. Lainy turned her iPad over with faux casualness, and I pretended not to notice.

"I tried calling both Maudie and Celia again." I eyeballed the café. "I wonder where they are . . . We had a two-forty-five appointment."

"Maybe Maudie forgot she was supposed to meet you."

"Celia wouldn't have forgotten."

"True."

"When did Celia sign in?" I asked.

Lainy dragged the big guest book toward her and ran her finger down the entries. "Two twenty."

"About half an hour after Julie and Maudie got back from lunch."

"I don't know exactly, but about that."

"Did Julie come in with Maudie?"

"Yes."

"But she didn't sign in again?"

"No. She'd already signed in when she first got here." Lainy consulted the book. "See? Eleven twenty-seven."

As Lainy pushed the guest book back into position, I asked, "Did Celia wait in the lobby?"

"No, she went straight to Maudie's room. Maudie signed an authorization form allowing both her nieces to enter her apartment anytime. They have their own keys."

I scanned the lobby, looking for inspiration, then brought my gaze back to Lainy's face. "To tell you the truth, I'm a little worried."

Lainy's eyes moved to the brass clock near her phone. It was eight minutes after three. "It hasn't even been half an hour."

"You found me out." I smiled. "I'm known for my impatience. I guess I'll give them another few minutes."

I returned to the bench and caught up on some work emails. Time dragged. At twenty past, I texted Eric again, telling him I planned to wait until three thirty, then consider my options.

At three twenty-nine, just as I decided to leave a message for Maudie and head back to the office, Tom and Julie arrived.

"Tom!" I exclaimed. "Julie!"

"Hey, Josie," Tom said, smiling. "Sorry we're late. Julie got her wires crossed."

"I think I'm going crazy!" Julie said, laughing a bit. "I went to work at the diner . . . God . . . I'm such a ditz! I completely forgot that I was supposed to pick up Tom." She tapped her head and made a funny face, raising her brows and screwing up her mouth. "Today is a nanny day. Tomorrow is a diner day. Duh."

"It's better to show up when you're not scheduled," I said, "than not show up when you are."

"That's true, but I hate being a space cadet."

"You're not a space cadet. Your brain is full."

"You've got that right. Luckily there was no traffic on Travis, so even though school was just getting out, I was able to zip home and get him. Otherwise we'd be way later than we already are." She patted Tom's arm and glanced around. "Did they give up on us? Tom was supposed to be here at three."

I turned toward Tom. "Did Maudie tell you about her plans to sell the presentation box and cat?"

"No. Celia did. She asked me to come by to help load the trunk into your car. I saw your van outside—I guess she didn't know you'd bring your own help." He surveyed the lobby. "Where are they?"

"I haven't seen them. To tell you the truth, I'm a little concerned. When did Celia call you, Tom?"

"One ten, one fifteen, something like that. She said you guys were going to meet here at a quarter to three. She asked me to come at three."

Everything lined up, except it didn't, like when a friend says all the right things and everything seems fine until you figure out she's been dating your boyfriend on the sly.

I walked to Lainy's desk. "I think you ought to call security."

CHAPTER ELEVEN

Lainy called the café, the fitness center, and the wellness center asking if they'd seen Maudie. After receiving a litany of noes, she asked Harry, the security guard, to walk the grounds, explaining to me that they hated to intrude on residents' privacy. Maudie, Lainy said in the lowered tone I'd come to associate with her harmless gossip, loved sitting in the garden.

At ten to four, as Tom, Julie, and I stood around doing nothing, a man in a khaki-colored collared shirt and matching slacks crossed the lobby from a side corridor heading straight for Lainy. He looked old enough to be a resident himself. He was short for a man and slender, with a thick gray mustache and long sideburns. I could see his name embroidered on his shirt pocket: HARRY.

Harry hitched up his pants and said, "She's not outside, and no one I asked has seen her."

"Let me call Mr. Hannigan." To me, she added, "The executive director."

Mr. Hannigan's assistant said he was at a conference and she didn't think he'd be back in the office today. The assistant told Lainy that Carmen Acosta, the director of the wellness center, was the supervisor on duty. Lainy called Ms. Acosta and asked her to come to the front.

Carmen Acosta appeared five minutes later from a side corridor. She was a little older than me, medium height and weight, with short, wavy sandy-brown hair. She wore a white lab coat. A pink blouse with small brown polka dots showed at the top. Her pale pink pumps had little brown leather bows on the sides.

Tom and Julie inched their way toward the window, leaving me at the helm.

Carmen extended a hand for a shake. "I'm Carmen Acosta," she said, her tone all business. "I understand you had an appointment with Mrs. Wilson?"

"And her niece, Celia Akins. It's been more than an hour."

She listened as Lainy and Harry took turns stating what they knew about Maudie's schedule and what they'd already done to try to locate her.

Lainy turned to Julie, who was still standing next to the bench with Tom. "You and Maudie got back from lunch at two."

"About ten of, I think. I don't know exactly."

"Did she mention any plans to go out again?"

"No. She didn't tell me about Celia coming over, or selling the cat and box, or anything. We were eating when Tom's text came in, at . . . I don't know . . . maybe one fifteen or so. I think that's right. He said he got a job and needed the truck. I didn't know the job was here until later, when I picked him up."

Carmen asked Lainy and Harry a few more questions: when they'd seen Maudie last, if she'd seemed normal, if there'd ever been any reports of her wandering away—pro forma, it seemed to me, for when an older person went missing.

"Harry," she said, "will you please open Mrs. Wilson's door for me? I'm going to conduct a wellness check. I'll fill out the paperwork later."

Harry hitched up his pants again and headed down the corridor that led to Maudie's unit. Carmen followed. I joined the procession without asking permission, and Tom and Julie fell in line behind me.

Harry stopped at the third door down, Maudie's unit, and knocked with his knuckles. "Mrs. Wilson? It's Harry, security." He waited a few seconds, then clapped the brass knocker half a dozen times. After ten seconds, he shouted into the sliver of light showing between the door and the jamb: "Mrs. Wilson? We're coming in to check on you." He pressed his ear to the door, waited another few seconds, then selected a key from the oversized ring attached to his belt.

He opened the door a crack.

"Mrs. Wilson?" he called again.

He swung the door wide and took a step in. He inhaled sharply, gulped, and stopped short. Carmen, right on his tail, ran into him.

I went up on tiptoe to peer over their shoulders. Celia lay on the floor, on her back, her eyes fixed on the ceiling, her limbs splayed, her face drenched in blood.

Horrified, I staggered back a step, flailing at the wall for support.

Carmen stepped around Harry and crouched beside Celia, feeling her neck for a pulse, then her wrist.

Tom pushed past me and stepped over the threshold. He gasped. Julie shrieked and lurched backward into the hall, collapsed against the wall, covering her face with her hands, and began to whimper, then cry, wheezing, her chest heaving.

"Call 9-1-1," Carmen instructed.

From the amount of blood pooling by Celia's head and her stony gaze, I was almost certain she was dead. I steadied myself.

Harry extracted his phone from his back pocket and tapped in 9-1-1.

I heard Harry say he was calling from Belle Vista with an emergency, but I didn't listen to the details. I didn't listen to Tom, either, who was murmuring something to Julie, her gusty tears punctuated with high-pitched, soft moans. Instead, I forced myself to breathe deeply, and after a few seconds, I felt steady enough to look around, taking it in, knowing I'd soon be chased away.

Celia's hair was soaked with blood. Red rivulets ran from the puddles surrounding her head and neck to the cabinets. Next to her left thigh was a blood-streaked wooden rolling pin. The coffee mug and plate I'd noticed earlier were still in the drying rack, but not the rolling pin. Evidently, Celia's killer had simply grabbed it and swung. A tan leather handbag sat on the counter in front of the marigold glass candlesticks, next to a ballpoint pen.

I took in a couple more deep breaths and turned to the right, toward the bathroom.

"Could someone be hiding in the bathroom?" I asked Harry in a whisper.

He spun toward the open door and marched in, pausing at the threshold to peek behind the door. He stepped inside, and a moment later marched back. "All clear."

In the living area, an off-white love seat and two butterscotch leather recliners faced a 50-inch flat-screen TV mounted on the wall. The bistro table and two chairs sat in a corner near the front windows, both of them open. A Rocky Point Computers–branded box, sized to hold a laptop, sat on a small desk. All the closet doors were ajar. The trunk was where I saw it last—positioned against the wall at the end of the tiny kitchen. Earlier, the lid had been closed. Now it was up. The Bible and ribbon-wrapped letters were intact, but there was no telltale glint of silver beneath it. I went up on tiptoe again so I could see farther inside. The presentation box wasn't there.

The paramedics arrived within minutes. Carmen spoke to them briefly, then told Harry he could leave and asked him please not to say anything to anyone until Mr. Hannigan got back. As soon as Harry left, Carmen hustled Julie, Tom, and me back to the lobby to wait for the police. We huddled near Lainy's desk. After a minute, Tom led Julie to the bench. She was still crying, her loud moans now hushed mewling. He stroked her hair with a tender, intimate touch. I sat on the other end of the bench, shocked and flustered, trying to harness my tumultuous thoughts into some semblance of rationality.

Carmen came into the lobby, her expression grim. She said something to Lainy, and Lainy stood so quickly that her desk chair skittled backward. Her leaping to action was an empathetic but misguided visceral reaction, and she must have realized it, because a moment later she sat back down. Carmen turned her back to Lainy's desk, facing the three of us on the bench. She punched in a number on her cell phone. When she finished her call, she spoke briefly to Lainy, then left, walking to the same left-side corridor she'd come from earlier.

I approached Lainy's desk. "Is Celia dead?" I asked.

Lainy nodded as tears trickled down her cheeks.

"Do you have any idea where Maudie might be?"

Her bottom lip quivered, and she turned away. "No."

I didn't know what to think. Celia was dead—and Maudie had vanished.

A tall ice-blond police officer named F. Meade was first on the scene, followed shortly by Officer Griffin. Officer Meade was the youngest officer on the force, in her early twenties. She was reserved, observant, and all business.

Griff, the oldest, was close to retirement, a good cop, earnest, always ready to help.

"Where?" Officer Meade called.

Lainy told them, and they tramped down the corridor.

The phone rang. After pausing for a moment with her hand trembling over the unit, Lainy took the call. Her end of the brief conversation was comprised mostly of yeses and noes.

She pushed some buttons, transferring the call, then replaced her receiver and looked at me. "That was Mr. Hannigan. He should be here in about an hour and a half. He's coming from North Conway. The conference center."

I leaned against Lainy's desk, trying to communicate calm despite the upset raging inside me. "I have a question. What time did Maudie sign out?"

"She didn't. No one does, just in."

"That's right," I said, recalling how I'd simply breezed out of the place the last time I was there. "And residents never sign in, only guests."

"Right."

"Wouldn't you have seen Maudie when she left?"

"Only if she went out this way and I wasn't busy with something else. I try to notice, but I can't always. Anyway, Maudie probably went out the side door. It's way closer to the parking lot. If you're meeting someone who's driving, it's much more convenient to go out that way."

"Is that exit limited to people who live on this side of the building?"

"Nope. Most of the staff use it, especially in winter. It's the quickest way to the employee lot."

"What employee lot?"

"You enter from Victory. It's next to the main lot, but you wouldn't have noticed it because tall hedges separate them."

"What about security cameras?"

"There's only one, at the front, facing out. There aren't any cameras anywhere else."

"Really? That's a surprise, isn't it?"

"The residents like their privacy."

"Still, from a security perspective, I would have thought there'd be more."

"We have an intercom system. You can't enter through any door, except the front one, without being buzzed in. There are cameras, but the system doesn't take photos; it just lets me see who's ringing. If I don't recognize the person, I ask them to come to reception. We have a rule—we never buzz in strangers."

I knew about rules. I'd followed a thousand of them in my day, and broken a bunch of others. "What's to stop a staff member who's passing by from opening the door and letting a person in?"

"It's not allowed."

"Even if you know the guy?"

"I suppose then it would be all right."

"What if a resident is leaving as someone from outside walks up? I could see someone thinking that holding the door for a stranger is polite."

Two older men, one leaning heavily on a wooden cane, walked by.

When they were out of earshot, Lainy said, "We call it piggybacking. We teach everyone never to do it at the new resident orientation."

"I bet it still happens a lot. People are nice."

"You're right. We do everything to discourage it, but..." She flipped open her palms.

Before I could ask another question, Ellis walked in, followed by a uniformed police officer I didn't recognize, a man about my age. Ellis took in the reception area with one sweeping look, then headed directly for me.

"Josie," he said, "are you all right?"

My throat closed, and for a moment I couldn't speak. I nodded. When I recovered my equilibrium, I introduced Ellis to Lainy, then wiggled my fingers at Tom and Julie, still nestled together on the bench, asking them to join us.

Ellis acknowledged the introductions and asked us all to wait for a few minutes. Then, following Lainy's directions, he and the officer strode across the lobby toward Maudie's unit. He reappeared ten minutes later, alone, thanked us for waiting, and asked us how we knew the victim, why we were at Belle Vista, when we'd arrived, and what we'd done and seen on-site. He had Tom and me check our phones to get the exact time we'd each spoken to Celia. She'd called me at 1:14 P.M. and Tom two minutes later. Tom had texted Julie at 1:20.

"Did any of you see Celia today?" Ellis asked.

Tom and I said no. Julie just shook her head. Lainy told him about Celia's arrival and explained why Celia hadn't signed in.

"How about Mrs. Wilson?"

Tom and I repeated our noes. Julie stated that she'd helped her sort through some things, and then they'd gone to Ellie's for lunch.

"And she didn't tell you anything about her plans?"

"Not a word."

"Or that she expected Celia to arrive?"

"No."

Julie patted her red and swollen eyes with a wadded-up tissue. Her shoulders were bowed. She looked like she'd just lost her best friend.

Tom rubbed her shoulder.

Griff turned into the lobby from the corridor.

"Officer Griffin will take you and Tom to the station so you can give official statements," Ellis said.

Julie fussed a little about how long it would take since she had to get to her nanny job by six. Ellis promised that she'd get there on time, or if they needed additional time, they'd work it out with her boss, and the threesome left.

"I spoke to Mr. Hannigan," Ellis told Lainy. "As soon as he gets here, he'll get someone to cover for you. We'll ask that you come to the station to give a statement, too."

"Okay," she said, her brows drawing together.

I couldn't tell if she was feeling only the mild apprehension natural to someone told they had to give an official statement to the police, or if her expression indicated a deeper fear.

Ellis explained that crime scene technicians would be arriving soon, that Officer Meade would be staying for a while with another officer posted outside, and that Lainy wasn't to talk to anyone about anything related to Celia's death until she'd given her statement.

She agreed; then Ellis jerked his head toward the window by the meadow, indicating he wanted to talk to me privately. We crossed the lobby and stood by the bench, side by side, our backs to the room.

"What can you tell me?" he asked.

I kept my voice low. "I saw Maudie this morning. I didn't mention it before because she asked me to keep it confidential." I recounted our conversation.

"I assumed it would be weeks before I heard anything else, so when Celia called, I was, as you might imagine, overjoyed. Overjoyed, but surprised." I added that the box and cat were missing—or seemed to be missing. "Maudie told me she planned on moving the objects into storage. Maybe she already did."

"I thought she was having them appraised."

"She was talking about it. I certainly encouraged her to get them under lock and key in the meantime." I paused, wanting to choose my words carefully, to reveal my concern without sounding melodramatic. I'd only just met Maudie, yet her disappearance had hit me hard and left me weak and shaky. I had to clench my hands together to keep myself from trembling. "I know Lainy called around looking for Maudie at the wellness center and so on. I don't know if she called whoever oversees the storage area."

Ellis rubbed the side of his nose, a familiar gesture. He was thinking, and thinking hard. "You're saying the box and cat are worth stealing."

"I'm saying they might be. Maudie's pretty independent. It's possible she didn't call for help to get things into storage. Maybe she wheeled the objects to her locker herself. If I was determined to get my hands on them, and if I knew she'd had a change of heart and was going to get them under lock and key without delay, I could come up with a scenario that ends in violence. I'm worried about her, Ellis. As far as I could tell, she's completely mobile, but she did mention problems with her hips and knees, joking about it, you know. I don't want to make a mountain out of a molehill, but she could be lying in her own storage unit, wounded . . . or worse." At the word, my throat closed again, and I coughed.

"You're right. Let's check."

CHAPTER TWELVE

Harry refused to open Maudie's storage unit without an order from Mr. Hannigan or a warrant.

When Mr. Hannigan arrived, he wouldn't even discuss it. "Our residents' privacy is one of our most cherished commitments."

"This isn't about privacy," Ellis said. "This is about safety."

"You have no reason to think Maudie Wilson is in any danger."

"I know her niece was murdered in her residence and she's nowhere to be found. That sounds like reason to be concerned to me."

"Bring a warrant and I'll be glad to open her storage unit. Without it, I won't even consider it."

"All I'm asking is to see if she's in any kind of trouble."

"The storage units have solid metal doors. You can't see in."

"Do you have a key?"

"No. Residents provide their own padlocks."

"Do you know if her unit is padlocked?"

Hannigan turned to Harry, an interested observer. Harry shook his head.

"Let's look," Ellis said.

Mr. Hannigan didn't want to do it, but he was running out of objections. He was tall and beefy, with scraggly strands of gray hair draped over his mostly bald pate. He wore a navy-blue blazer, a pale blue shirt, and pale gray slacks. From his pursed lips and general air of disapproval, I got the sense that he was a quintessential bureaucrat—he excelled at following rules but floundered when asked to step out of his lane.

"I can't see any harm in checking whether her unit is locked," Hannigan said, as if he were making a concession. "Harry, you come, too. I want a witness."

"Thank you," Ellis said. "I'm going to ask Ms. Prescott to join us. In case the antiques that seem to have gone missing are visible, she can identify them."

Hannigan's lips thinned still further, making his dissatisfaction evident, but he didn't voice his opposition.

He led the way to a utilitarian staff elevator located at the garden end of Maudie's wing. The lights came on automatically when we stepped out of the elevator, and again when we entered the room housing the storage units, which we accessed via a keycard. The keycard dangled from a retractable reel on the key chain attached to Harry's belt.

"No keycards for residents' rooms?" Ellis asked Hannigan.

"We surveyed them a few months ago. There was a fair amount of concern about privacy since keycard systems come with the ability to track usage. We decided to table the issue for the time being."

"Do all residents have a keycard to this room?"

"Yes."

"So you can tell if Mrs. Wilson entered earlier."

"No. As we explained to the residents, we don't track usage. Just because it *can* be done doesn't mean we do it. We don't."

The space was as big as a school gym, with pale gray vinyl flooring and floor-to-ceiling iron-gray metal units arranged in rows. Corridors ran the length of the room between the banks of units. Maudie's unit, labeled with her name and apartment number, was about halfway back. Most of the units were padlocked, securing the doors to the frames, but Maudie's wasn't.

"Since the unit isn't locked, I'm going to ask to open it," Ellis said.

Hannigan nodded. "Yes, that seems all right."

Ellis snapped on a plastic glove and swung the door wide. The room—five feet wide and eight deep, with a ten-foot ceiling—was empty.

I exhaled, and only then did I realize I'd been holding my breath.

Ellis took a small LED flashlight from his pocket and swept it across the floor in a steady back-and-forth motion, then moved to the walls, then the ceiling.

"All right, then," Ellis said, clicking off the flashlight. "There's no indication anyone or anything has been here."

We trooped back to the lobby. Half a dozen people sat at a table in the café facing the reception desk, watching us and murmuring to one another.

Ellis asked me to wait for a few minutes, and I agreed. He asked Mr. Hannigan if there was someplace private they could talk, and the two men walked down the corridor opposite Maudie's wing to Hannigan's office.

Lainy seemed to have calmed down. Her smile wavered a bit but was more or less intact.

"Was the storage unit empty?" she asked in a near-whisper.

I couldn't think of a reason to keep the information secret. "Yes." I nodded toward the café. "I gather word has spread."

"Like the measles. The crime scene team arrived ten minutes ago."

I glanced at her clock. It was twenty-five past five.

"I'm surprised you're still here. How late do you normally work?"

"Five. Mr. Hannigan wanted to talk to the night girl, Karin, before she's inundated with questions, so he asked me to work until six. He wants to tell her what to say."

"Did he tell you, too?"

"Did he ever!" She giggled, then seemed to recall the seriousness of the situation and stopped. "He told me I could only say one of these three things: I don't know. You'll have to ask the police about that. You'll have to ask Mr. Hannigan about that." She raised a hand. "I'm a quick study. Karin not so much. She's very emotional. I guess I'm cold-blooded."

"You're not cold-blooded. You're an actress. You're approaching this like it's a part you have to play."

"Don't tell anyone, but you're exactly right."

The phone rang, and while Lainy fielded the call, I walked over to the window, glad for the time to regroup. Jagged emotions I didn't understand raged inside me. I felt raw, unable to focus, weighed down, almost feverish. My phone vibrated. It was Eric.

"Oh, God, Eric, I'm sorry—I completely forgot you were still waiting. Have you heard what happened?"

"Just now on the radio. The reason I'm calling . . . that reporter, you know, Wes . . . he just knocked on the van window and asked why I was here."

Wes Smith, a reporter for our local paper, the *Seacoast Star*, was notorious.

He had a nose for discord, connections up the wazoo, and no sense of restraint when it came to his job.

"What did you say?"

"Nothing, just like you told us—I never talk to reporters. He was awfully persistent, though. To get away from him, I had to leave. I'm parked around the corner on Victory."

"Good thinking. You can call it a day, Eric. We won't be picking anything up today. Take the van home if you want."

"Are you okay?"

"More or less. I mean . . . I'm fine . . . just a little upset."

I sent an email to my staff telling them what was going on and reminding them not to talk to the press. After I hit SEND, I swung around so I was facing the meadow. I felt as if I needed some time to think, to try to make sense of what had happened. From what I could tell, there were three separate but related issues: Celia's murder, Maudie's whereabouts, and the objects' disappearance.

Celia must have interrupted someone who'd broken into Maudie's apartment to steal the box and cat statue. Except there was no sign of a break-in. The windows were open, but the screens were down, which meant nothing. Screens were designed to keep bugs out, not people. From the outside, I knew, I'd be able to slip a penknife under the flange and force the screen up just enough to wiggle my fingers through and onto the lift tabs. From there, I could lever up the screen the rest of the way. Thirty seconds would be sufficient, maybe a minute. Not that I was an experienced burglar, but I knew my way around everyday products like window frames and screens. To close the screen from the outside, I'd simply repeat the process backward. Once I was outside, I'd lower the screen as far as I could, lacing my fingers under the frame, using the lift tabs. I'd pull my fingers clear, then force the screen down the rest of the way.

Maybe the intruder didn't need to do such fancy handwork. Perhaps he used keys. Harry had keys; probably every security guard did. So did Celia and Stacy. Certainly Mr. Hannigan did, and who knew who else.

Possibly, Celia had been in Maudie's apartment and opened the door to a knock. Whoever she let in killed her, took the objects, and left by the window. Or maybe the killer simply slipped the presentation box into a rolling trolley or suitcase, strolled down the corridor, exited via the side door, and left.

"Sorry to keep you waiting," Ellis said.

I flinched as if he'd struck me, then smiled. "Sorry."

He straddled the bench sideways. "Are you okay?"

"Sure. You know me . . . I fall apart *after* the crisis has passed."

"Are you sure? You seem kind of keyed up."

"I know. For some reason, this has hit me hard."

"It's a terrible situation."

At a scraping sound, Ellis looked toward the front. I skewed around in time to see an older woman slide into the receptionist's chair and Lainy slip her iPad into a canvas tote bag. She said something to her replacement that I couldn't hear.

"I'm bringing Lainy to the station," Ellis said, turning back to face me. "She says she's too upset to drive. How about you—want a lift?"

"No, thanks. I'm fine." I caught my breath, choking on air. "Oh, wow! I must be shakier than I realized. Has someone contacted Celia's husband, Doug? Or Stacy, her sister?" I gripped the smooth beveled edge of the bench to steady myself. "Oh, God . . . what about her kids?"

"We reached Stacy in Boston. She's on her way back to New Hampshire and should get to the station no later than six. The kids are with the school principal. Detective Brownley is trying to locate Doug now."

"He said he had a job interview today at Jestran's. I don't know when."

Ellis took his phone from his pocket and texted someone.

"I just had another thought. Did anyone find a grocery cart? It might be folded up in a closet or under the bed. Maudie used it when she went shopping. If it's missing, maybe she's just at the store."

He texted again.

"Ellis, I really must be rockier than I thought. I just realized . . . I mean, I can't imagine why it didn't occur to me before . . . Maudie might be meeting with an antiques appraiser right now—and she might have the objects with her." I told him about the list of appraisers I'd emailed Maudie earlier in the day.

"Can you call them and ask?"

"Let me get outside for some privacy."

We crossed the lobby, pausing at the reception desk so he could speak to Lainy.

"Josie and I are going to step outside to make a couple of phone calls. Join us when you're ready."

She said she'd be there in a few minutes, once she clocked out, and we left.

Ellis started for the front, and I touched his elbow to stop him. "Lainy tells me the side door is quicker."

We walked past Maudie's apartment. Her door was open. I spotted two technicians, one squatting near a bloodstain on the floor, the other one photographing the open trunk. Twenty paces farther on, we came to an exit on the left. Ellis pushed open the heavy fire door and held it for me. Once we were through, the door closed with a loud snap. I turned to look back. A sign on the door read THIS DOOR IS KEPT LOCKED AT ALL TIMES. PLEASE ENTER THROUGH THE FRONT. We were in a small vestibule. A stairway on the right led to the upper floors. The outside door bore the same sign, stating it was locked at all times.

Outside, I stood for a moment, orienting myself. The gardens were to the right. The street was to the left. We followed a winding path edged with tall laurel, designed, I was certain, to provide privacy. A black wrought iron bench was tucked into a setback. Lanterns mounted on tall black poles illuminated the walkway after dark. The path ended at a gate that accessed the parking lot.

When we reached the lot, I said, "I'll make the calls from that bench we passed."

"Good. I'll wait by my vehicle."

I retraced my steps to the bench.

I checked messages before starting my calls. Wes Smith, the reporter, had texted twice and left a voicemail demanding an immediate callback. Everything with Wes was urgent. Emma, Zoë's daughter, had texted, too, asking if I had time to get together. I texted back saying I'd love to see her, and after some back-and-forth, we settled on ten the next morning, Saturday, tag sale day, at my office. *Don't tell Mom, okay?* I stared at the words. I hated secrets, although I was good at keeping them. *I'm not comfortable with that, Emma. Best friends . . . you know.* Her reply came quickly. *Please. Just this once.* I said okay, and immediately regretted it. Emma wrote *THANK YOU!!* in all caps. I leaned back against the hard iron for a moment, considering what

Emma was going to ask me to do that she didn't want her mom to know about, and all the ideas I came up with placed me in a difficult position. Emma might want me to try to persuade Zoë to support her enlisting in the marines; fat chance. She might ask that I convince Zoë to shut up about her objections; another fat chance. It was possible, I supposed, that she wanted to know my opinion, which I'd be leery to give. Any opinion I voiced would please Emma and alienate Zoë. More to the point, I was a believer in independent decision-making. And from all reports, Emma had already made her decision.

I tapped in the phone number for the Rocky Point–based antiques appraiser, Melvin Farrow, the owner of Farrow Antiques, the first name on the list I gave Maudie.

I knew Melvin fairly well. He was an old-school gentleman who dealt mostly in fine British antiques but was, as any dealer who operated in a small city had to be, a generalist. He knew a little bit about a lot of things and had access to experts for the rest.

His assistant said he'd left for the day, and she was just closing up herself. When I explained who I was and that I was helping the police try to locate Maudie Wilson, she gave me his cell phone. He answered on the second ring.

"I'm sorry to bother you after hours, but it's really important. I referred Maudie Wilson to you. Have you seen or spoken to her?"

"Thanks for the referral, Josie. That's very kind of you. Mrs. Wilson and I chatted for a few minutes this morning."

"Did you make an appointment to get together?"

"I tried, but she said her schedule was in flux and she'd call back when she was ready. I wish I could have nailed something down, but that's the way that cookie crumbled."

I called Lisa Rollins next. Lisa was a rising star at the venerable Brandt-Larkin Antiques auction house in Boston. She was still in her twenties, but between her antiques know-how, media savvy, and gracious style she'd already made a name for herself.

Lisa was effusive in her thanks. She'd spoken to Maudie for fifteen minutes around ten this morning. Lisa tried to get Maudie to make an appointment, even offering to drive up to Rocky Point, but Maudie said she had plans and would be in touch, probably next week.

"Mrs. Wilson sounds like a super client," Lisa said. "Why are you giving her away?"

"I'm not. She asked for options, and I gave her some. I hope she chooses Prescott's."

Lisa laughed, an appealing tinkling sound. "I'll do my best to see that never happens!"

The San Francisco–based Egyptologist, Edward L. Moss, whom I'd known for years, since my days at Frisco's, looked like an absent-minded professor and spoke with gentle authority until he got his teeth into an antiquity that interested him, at which point he morphed into a pit bull. Dr. Moss said he hadn't heard from Maudie, so he didn't know I'd referred her. He thanked me, and I asked him to call me if he heard from her, and he said he would.

I spotted Lainy by an old silver Ford Focus and Ellis by his big black police-issued SUV. Lainy placed her tote bag in the trunk. She had earbuds in, and her shoulders rotated to the beat. She took a step, then paused to read something on her phone. Ellis was staring into space.

"So," I said to Ellis as I drew close enough for him to hear, "nothing." I summarized the three conversations.

"Mrs. Wilson told Rollins she had plans."

"It might have been a fib—that's a common white lie to get out of doing something you don't want to do without going into your reasons."

Ellis rubbed his nose. "Knowing who she called this morning doesn't help us figure out where she is now."

"I noticed a laptop box on her desk. Did it contain a laptop, or is it empty?"

"Why?"

"If it's empty, she took the computer with her. She wants to get back to travel writing. I bet she went on a snorkel trip and took her laptop so she could write about it."

Ellis texted someone, then asked, "Where would she go?"

"She mentioned Yap and the Cook Islands, but she's not doing that as a weekend jaunt. It would take a couple of days at least just to get to either place—they're in the middle of the Pacific. She said there were plenty of good options in the Caribbean. Can't you check if she's used her passport?"

"No, of course not. The privacy laws are clear."

"This is an exception."

"Not in the eyes of the law. Adults are allowed to travel freely. You know that."

"I'm worried about her."

"I know." He patted my shoulder. "I'm going to ask you to post stolen-antiques notices. Until we know that the objects are safe and sound, I'd rather err on the side of caution. The worst that happens is that she turns up with them and we withdraw the notices."

"Okay. Luckily, I video-recorded everything, so we can capture some still shots for the posting."

"You took video? Why?"

"Innate prudence and habit. I think we should send the flyer to jewelers, too, with a note that the thief might have pried the stones loose."

He agreed, and I told him I'd take care of it. His phone vibrated, and he read a message.

"There was no computer in the apartment. The box was empty. There's no grocery cart, either. I'll get a canvass going of stores. Good idea."

I loved it when someone I respected, like Ellis, told me an idea of mine was good. There is no tonic more powerful than affirmation.

"Thanks."

He caught Lainy's eye, and she pulled out one of her earbuds.

"Ready?" he asked.

She said she was.

I watched them leave, then called Fred, and sure enough, he was there even though it was after six. I asked him to arrange for an international stolen antiques posting. In addition, I asked that he prepare flyers featuring still shots of the presentation box and cat, and close-ups of the jewels, and send it to all local dealers and jewelers.

Disconnecting, I saw that Wes had left a new message. Before listening to it, I called Ty. My call went straight to voicemail. I gave him the one-minute version of events and said I hoped to be home in an hour or so, which was probably wishful thinking.

Wes's message was predictably dramatic. "Call me," he said. He lowered his voice conspiratorially. "It's about you—we need to talk."

I called him back.

CHAPTER THIRTEEN

D id you take photos?" Wes asked, skipping hello, like always.

"I'm fine, Wes. How are you?"

"Good, good. So have you got some pictures of the corpse? Video? What?"

"Don't be crass, Wes. No, I didn't take photos or video. It was horrible . . . terrifying . . . there was so much blood."

"Good. What else?"

Here I was trying to bring him to a sense of real-world misery, and there he was hearing it as useful color for his next article. When on the trail of a hot lead, Wes was like a particularly malevolent yellow jacket, ready to attack. For years I'd put up with him, because the rest of the time he seemed like the kid brother I'd never had, affectionate, protective, and loyal, and while I disliked his in-your-face style of journalism, I admired it, too. Lately, though, Wes's reporting had edged perilously close to yellow journalism. Still, Wes had a remarkable network of contacts he could tap at will, and I knew the drill. If I wanted information, I had to share information.

"I'll tell you what I saw, but only off the record. You can't quote me."

"That's not how it works, Josie. You know that."

We'd had this tussle before. I always won. "I'm hanging up now, Wes."

"Wait!" he yelled. "Don't hang up. I need to be able to name my sources, and you've proven fairly reliable in the past."

Fairly reliable. I didn't roll my eyes, but I could have. "I'm not negotiating, Wes. I really am going to hang up."

Wes sighed deeply, Wesian for his profound disappointment in me. "All right." He sighed again, just as loudly. "Off the record."

"I'll tell you, but first, your message said you wanted to talk about me. What about me?"

"Just this—what you saw."

"It was a ploy to get me to call you back?" I asked, aghast.

He chuckled. "It worked."

"That's outrageous, Wes!"

"Thanks."

"That wasn't a compliment."

"Sure it was. So talk to me. What did you see?"

I gave up trying to reason with him. Wes had his own worldview. "It looks like Celia was struck on the head. There was a bloody wooden rolling pin on the floor near her body. I'd seen it in the drying rack earlier in the week."

"You're saying the murder was an act of passion. Spur of the moment. Unplanned."

"Not necessarily. The killer could have come with a weapon, seen the rolling pin, and used it instead."

"Why would anyone kill her?"

I thought of Doug, out of work, tormented by guilt, bearing the brunt of Celia's anger. He seemed worn and weary, but still understanding, even after he'd been shoved by his wife. I kept my reflection to myself. "I don't know."

"Come on, Josie. You paused. You only pause when you know something and don't want to tell."

"I only pause when I think I know something. You know me, Wes. If I don't have evidence, I don't say a word."

"Tell me what you're thinking. I've already promised not to quote you."

"Forget it."

Wes sighed again. When I didn't acquiesce, he shifted gears.

"Why was Eric at Belle Vista today?"

I recounted finding the trunk in the Gingerbread House, described the contents, and explained the confusion surrounding Maudie's intentions— whether she planned to have the box and cat appraised, or sell them outright. I could hear Wes scratching notes. He used to write on a ratty old piece of paper. Now he used nice notebooks, a professional upgrade instituted by his wife, Maggie, along with his classy business casual attire, instead of his old scruffy jeans, and a new car, instead of his ancient rattletrap.

"How about Maudie Wilson. Why did she disappear?"

"I don't know that, either, but I'm afraid for her. I'm really scared, Wes."

"Tell me."

"You know I never gossip."

"This isn't gossip—it's off the record. You're giving me leads so I can do my job. I might be able to help."

"I have the impression that Maudie is wealthy."

He soft-whistled. "And early reports show that Doug and Celia were in a real financial jam. They're behind on their mortgage. Their credit cards are maxed out. From what I can tell, they're close to bankruptcy."

Wes's analysis matched my initial impression—Doug and Celia had seemed desperate for money, flat broke, or close to it. "I'm so sorry to hear that."

"It's always the husband, natch."

"I don't know, Wes. Things might have been on the upswing for them. Doug told me he had a job interview today at Jestran's."

"I'll check. You've met him. What's he like?"

"Salt of the earth . . . sincere, you know? I simply can't imagine him killing Celia."

"You're too nice, Joz. You can never picture someone killing someone else."

I smiled. "If I have to have a flaw, I guess I'll take 'too nice.'"

"I didn't say that was your only flaw."

"Ha ha."

He chuckled again. "If Maudie sold those objects, how much would she get?"

"Lots, if they're genuine, which is not at all certain. Replicas can be astonishingly convincing and beautiful."

"Let's say they were the real deal. You're saying there'd be plenty of cash for everyone."

"Only if Maudie offered it."

"You're saying Maudie is selfish."

"Not at all. Maybe she's a believer in self-reliance."

"So Doug hears that Maudie is going to sell the stuff out from under them, and he kidnaps her, saying he'll release her only when he gets the booty

Celia deserves. Maudie objects. He tries to whack her, misses, and kills his wife instead."

"That sounds like something out of a really bad movie. I suppose it's possible that Celia and Doug tried to convince Maudie to sell the objects, and if Maudie said no, they decided to steal them instead. Murder? No way."

"Don't be so quick to dismiss it."

"Even if you're right, Wes, you still need to consider the logistics. Sneaking out of Maudie's apartment isn't easy. Sure, you could get yourself out through the window or even simply walk out the side door, but Celia was killed in the middle of the afternoon, with plenty of people around, and you're suggesting Doug managed to escape with the presentation box *and* Maudie?"

"How about this? Maudie catches Celia red-handed trying to steal the box and reaches for the phone to call the cops. Celia tries to stop her. They struggle. Maudie grabs the rolling pin—boom, she strikes. Or Celia grabs it and Maudie wrestles it away from her. Same ending. Maudie panics and runs. There aren't any logistical issues in this scenario. She just walks out."

"Absurd!"

"Why? What's wrong with it?"

"Maudie wouldn't kill her niece."

"Even in self-defense? Sure she would. Anyone would."

"Even if Maudie killed her, which I don't for a minute believe, she wouldn't run."

"You're on Team Maudie all right. What about security cameras?"

I reported what I'd learned from Lainy.

"All right, then," he said, "if not Doug or Maudie, who?"

"Ninety-plus percent of art heists are inside jobs—a security guard who games the system, a curator who creates a fraudulent paper trail so she can abscond with a treasure for her personal collection, a trusted docent with sticky fingers. Why not a member of the Belle Vista staff?"

"Good one, Joz! I'll see if the facility does background checks."

I didn't want to know how Wes planned on flushing out that information.

"What else?" he asked.

"Nothing. Remember, Wes—I'm just thinking aloud. You can't quote me."

"I know, I know. What about pics of the box and cat?"

"That I can do." I explained how I came to have them in my possession, adding that we were posting stolen-antiques and -jewels notices, worldwide.

"Cool beans! Catch ya later."

I texted Fred to send me a link to the still shots, and when he did, I forwarded it to Wes.

I pulled into the Rocky Point police station parking lot and parked facing Ocean Avenue and the dunes across the street. The station resembled a sprawling cottage, with shingles weathered to a soft dove gray and trim painted colonial blue.

Cathy, the civilian admin who'd worked the front desk for as long as I'd lived in Rocky Point, smiled. "Ellis asked me to tell you he won't be long. He hopes you're okay with waiting."

I assured her I was and sat on the hard wooden bench. I leaned back, resting my head against the unforgiving backrest. I hadn't heard from Ty all day, and here it was, six thirty-five. After a moment, I texted him, asking how it was going, then stared at my phone for a few minutes, hoping for a quick reply. Nothing.

To distract myself, I walked across the lobby to the community bulletin board. The eleventh annual beach volleyball competition was slated for next Sunday afternoon. Rocky Point Community Theater was casting for the much-loved musical *Chicago*. The flyer invited members of the community to come to the open casting calls, which started next week. My favorite brass quartet, Academy Brass, was playing on the village green Saturday evening. Rocky Point Community Center was offering free swimming lessons. As I read about the genial, normal activities that defined us, I felt the tension that had twisted the muscles in my neck and shoulders into steel ease. I loved Rocky Point. I'd come to New Hampshire hoping for a second chance at happiness, and I would always be grateful to the town that had welcomed me.

"This way," a woman said.

I turned toward the front. It was Detective Brownley, and she was holding the door open for Doug, Celia's husband.

Doug pushed his way in, tripping on his own feet. He wore a navy-blue suit that seemed too big for his slender frame. His blue-and-red-striped tie was loosened. His eyes were harrowed. He didn't see me, or maybe he saw me but it didn't register that he knew me. Detective Brownley, tall and slim, with short black hair and alabaster skin, kept her hand cupped under his elbow as if she were concerned he might collapse. She escorted him across the lobby and directed him down the left-hand corridor toward a series of interview rooms.

I paced. I was too impatient to sit and too antsy to stand. I texted Ellis that I was going to wait outside, that I'd be in the parking lot or across the street on a dune, and left.

CHAPTER FOURTEEN

T he temperature had dropped into the low sixties, and the wind was biting, so I slipped on the windbreaker I kept in my car for just-in-case moments like this. I crossed the street to the beach. Pink wild roses grew amid the tall grasses and scrub oak that separated the asphalt from the sand. I pushed through the low growth and climbed the tallest dune, and when I reached the top, I zipped my jacket to my neck. The sky was more gray than blue. Whitecaps charged across the near-black water, racing to shore. No one was in sight. It was a lonely scene, isolated and harsh.

As I watched the roiling ocean, I thought about Doug and desperate men, hoping against hope that Maudie was still alive. After ten minutes, I started shivering and decided to head back inside. While I stood on the shoulder waiting for traffic to pass so I could cross the street, Stacy walked out of the police station. She took a few steps, then paused and closed her eyes.

I dashed across the street.

Stacy was as stylishly dressed as the last two times I saw her. Today's outfit included a cobalt-blue pleated skirt with a matching asymmetrical jacket over a cream collared blouse, and open-toed pumps, off-white with blue trim. She opened her eyes, spotted a wooden bench near the front door, and sat down. A sand-filled canister sat nearby, a concession to smokers. She extracted a water bottle from her Prada tote and took a healthy swig, then clutched the water bottle to her chest like a flotation device. She leaned forward, rocking a little as if she had a stomachache. Her eyes were fixed on the asphalt.

When I was close enough to be heard, I said, "I'm terribly sorry for your loss."

"Thank you." She studied my features for several seconds. "You were there."

"When the security guard went inside . . . yes."

Her eyes filled with tears. "I can't believe it. My big sister. I just can't believe it."

Not wanting to encroach on her space, I stayed standing. "I know."

She covered her face with her hands, dropping the bottle, sending it rolling under the bench.

I picked it up and held it while she cried.

After a minute, she sniffed loudly, lowered her hands, and wiped away the wetness from her cheeks using the side of her pinky. She dug around in her bag and found a tissue and patted her cheeks dry.

"I'm sorry," she said.

"You have nothing to apologize for."

She made a fist, scrunching the tissue. "I don't understand any of it. The police said that Celia called you . . . that Aunt Maudie wanted to sell the presentation box and cat. Why wouldn't Aunt Maudie have told me? I spoke to her this morning."

I handed over her water bottle, and she grasped it, murmuring, "Thanks."

"When was that?"

"Early . . . around seven. Just before I left for Boston. Do you have any idea where Aunt Maudie is?"

"I wish I did, but I don't."

"I don't know how much more I can take. I'm full up. Just full up."

"Losing someone you love is devastating."

"Add in the load of bad news I'm facing on the business front, and you'll understand how I'm feeling—overwhelmed, completely overwhelmed." Her eyes filled again. She reached into her bag and patted around until she found an old-fashioned silver cigarette case, a relic from another era. She lit up. After a couple of puffs, she added, "It's not a secret—I wish it were. My chief investor pulled out of the deal last week, leaving me high and dry. I found out about it from a *WWD* tweet, if you can believe it."

"*WWD—Women's Wear Daily?*"

"Right." She lowered her eyes to the black pavement again. "It was awful . . . humiliating. Kyle, the investor you met on the beach, bowed out.

So did the company in Boston." She looked into the distance, over the dunes, toward the horizon. "So here I sit, starting a new line of trend-setting tables, with orders in hand, and no way to fill them."

"That's awful. I'm so sorry. What will you do?"

"Find another investor—fast. My first investor, a venture capitalist who's been funding my company for more than a year, didn't like my designs, which is outrageous, since he knows nothing about design. All he knows about is leveraged buyouts. Kyle couldn't see the way to profitability, his words, the loser. The investor in Boston, who owns an interior design company, said my designs were derivative." She slapped the bench, and her water bottle skittered away again. "Why am I sitting on orders if my designs are bad or derivative? Tell me that."

I retrieved the bottle again and handed it back.

She smiled wanly. "Want to invest in an up-and-coming niche furniture brand with verifiable purchase orders?"

"I'm strictly an antiques girl, but I'm sure you'll have lots of takers."

"You bet. Then I get the call about Celia and Aunt Maudie." She rubbed her temples for a moment. "This is maybe the worst week of my life—it started bad and has been getting steadily worse."

I felt bad for her, but I was also shocked. She seemed more upset by her business setbacks than her sister's murder and her aunt's disappearance.

She took a long drink. "I'm not usually such a wuss. Forget it—chalk it up to momentary weakness, soon to be forgotten." She drank some more, then pulled back her shoulders, ready to cope. "Are you coming or going?"

"I'm on hold, waiting for my turn to give my statement."

"They'll ask you about Doug and Celia," she said.

"It's an obvious question."

"Not once you meet Doug. One look and you can tell he couldn't hurt a fly. He's constitutionally a milquetoast."

"You don't like him."

"How many people do you like?"

Names popped into my head, a lot of names. Zoë and Ellis, and Zoë's children, Emma and Jake. Gretchen, Sasha, Fred, Eric, and Cara, my key staff. Timothy. Helene, the director of New Hampshire Children First!, where I volunteered; Shelley, my best pal from New York; and others. I liked a lot of people, but I couldn't say so. Not only was her question rhetorical, it seemed to reflect her own hurt and dismay at being abandoned, dismissed, and left behind more than anything else. Stacy might have an edge sharp enough to slice a loaf of bread, but that didn't mean she didn't have feelings that got hurt like everyone else. She seemed to be waiting for my reply, and I realized her question hadn't been rhetorical after all. She was hoping that I shared her derisive view of people. I understood that she felt lonely or isolated, or both, and that the burden of those emotions was no doubt weightier now; still, her abrasiveness made it nearly impossible to empathize. I knew misery loved company, but I could never understand why miserable people expected me to be miserable, too, as if my despair would help them feel less alone, when to me it only served to accentuate the dearth. All I could do was avoid making a bad situation worse. My dad taught me that if you don't want to talk about content, talk about process instead.

"Everyone is different," I said.

Stacy waved it away. "Whatever." She took another drink, then tossed the bottle into her bag. "Celia got what she wanted in Doug, which is something, I guess."

"From what I could tell, Celia loved Doug very much."

"Celia wanted a puppy dog," Stacy said, "someone to fawn over her and love her unconditionally." She stood and smoothed her skirt over her thighs. "Don't mind me. You nailed it when you said people are different. Celia and I were different in every way, but we loved each other. You're right that she and Doug loved one another, too, and I was truly happy for her. I don't mean to pooh-pooh it. With everything going on, I'm a mess, but my heart is in the right place, and I'm a survivor. Always was . . . always will be." She looked at the sky, pale yellow dimples on slate-gray clouds. "Is it supposed to rain?"

"So they say. Not for a while, though. Tomorrow, maybe."

Stacy stood and stretched, arching her back, rolling her head, reaching for the clouds. "I have to get back into the melee."

Before I could respond, Stacy turned and sauntered back toward the entrance. She walked like a model on a runway, a woman who was used to being watched, who liked being watched.

My phone vibrated, startling me. I'd forgotten I was holding it. It was Ty, calling.

"How's my beautiful wife?"

"Missing her gorgeous husband. Are you okay?"

"Yes. Sorry I missed your text. I convinced the powers that be to let me try it my way—that monitoring remote border crossings with cameras and drones makes much more sense than trying to organize human surveillance. I just landed at Logan. How are you doing?"

"About as you'd expect. I'm at the police station now, waiting for Ellis or somebody to take my statement."

"I should be home by eight or eight thirty, and I'll be ravenous. If I get home first, I'll get started with dinner."

"I have chicken marinating, ready for the grill, but I don't know if I can deal with cooking—or cleaning up, for that matter."

"Plan B: I'll pick up a pizza."

I felt myself relax a few notches. I loved our life together. "Great idea."

We chatted for a few more minutes, then Ty said, "I go back to the border Monday morning to meet with the team about our strategy. It'll take a couple of days, not longer, I hope."

Ellis stuck his head out of the door and asked if I was ready.

"More than ready. I'm beat."

"This won't take long. Sorry to keep you waiting."

He was right. It only took half an hour. Ellis asked about the antiques and the people involved. He confirmed the timeline, then told me I could go. It was twenty to eight when I said good-bye to Cathy and left.

I listened to the local radio station on my way home. Stephanie Bolton, the Hitchens University student who hosted the evening classical music series, introduced Wes, announcing he had an update on the Celia Akins murder.

Wes reported that Doug was still being questioned by the police. Celia, Wes said, with an air of revealing a seminal fact, had arranged for me to take possession of some of her aunt's rare objects. The police were investigating whether I had actually received the pieces. I spun the steering wheel sharply and stopped on the side of the road. The way Wes worded it, and from what he didn't say, it would be easy to infer that something wicked was in the works, and that I was in on the scheme.

I called him, but his phone went directly to voicemail, which made sense, since he was on air.

"Wes, you need to correct your story immediately," I said through clenched teeth. "If Celia didn't have her aunt's permission to sell those objects, this is the first I'm hearing of it. I didn't meet Celia, I don't have Maudie's possessions, and you need to stop implying that I was a participant to fraud. Yes, you may quote me."

On the off chance he had his phone with him in the studio, I zipped off a text saying the same thing.

"This just in," Wes announced portentously a few seconds later. "Josie Prescott is holding firm on her denial, insisting she had no prior knowledge of Celia Akins's intention to sell her aunt's objects without permission and that she, Josie, doesn't have them."

Leave it to Wes to make my righteous anger come across as a weak and self-serving denial. Wes had crossed a line, and if I had anything to say about it, he'd be sorry.

"Are we talking big dollar values here, Wes?" Stephanie asked.

"Yes. For sure."

Sophistry—using facts to tell a lie. Wes didn't say the objects were worth big bucks. He simply said he was talking about big bucks. Wes was getting out of hand, more than out of hand. Aggressive reporting was one thing. This was something else altogether. He had ventured beyond hyperbole, beyond embellishment—by leaving out salient details, essentially, Wes had told a whopper, and I wasn't going to be a party to it, not as his victim or his patsy.

"Thanks, Wes," the host said. "And now here's Serena Matthews with the weather."

CHAPTER FIFTEEN

y was tearing lettuce for a salad when I got home around eight.

"You beat me!" I said.

"No delays, snags, or snafus."

"Yay!"

I leaned in for a kiss, and Ty placed his hands on my waist, his kiss searing.

When we separated, I snatched a piece of carrot and popped it in my mouth. "What a day."

"Tough all around."

"It was horrible enough without Wes implying I'm a crook."

"I heard his report. He's on a tear, all right, filled with conspiracy theories and ominous what-ifs. We know he's wrong about you, but do you think he might be right about Celia? That she set out to rob Maudie?"

"I wish I could say 'no, absolutely not,' but the truth is . . . yes, I think there's a chance." I told him about Celia's calls to Tom and me. "As to Wes . . . I'm getting angrier by the minute. His wording was incendiary—he said I was continuing to deny it, not that I didn't do it."

"Your word against a dead woman. Don't worry about it . . . everybody knows what Wes is. It'll blow over."

"Not everyone knows what Wes is, and I don't care if it will blow over. He has no business doing it."

"You're right. So what are you going to do?"

"I don't know."

"You'll figure it out." Ty sprinkled sea salt over the salad.

"And meanwhile, Maudie is missing."

"You hit it off with her."

"Big-time. So . . . did your boss agree with your insights? Or did you wear him down?"

"He was impressed with the evidence. And, yes, he agreed with my analysis—although I wouldn't call my conclusions insights."

"You're too modest."

"You're biased."

"True. So what's the bottom line?"

"He approved my funding request. All's well that ends well."

He poured apple cider vinegar and olive oil into a cruet, added stone-ground mustard, salt, and pepper, and shook. He poured a little on the salad and tossed it using the olive-wood salad spoon and fork set I'd given him last Christmas.

"I want some sliced tomatoes, too."

"If you get them, I'll slice them."

I plucked two red beauties from the vine.

He took the meatball pizza from the oven and transferred it to a platter.

"That looks incredible," I said. "Luscious."

"I open a mean box of takeout pizza."

"You keep it warm perfectly."

"Thanks. Setting the oven to two-fifty is a real skill."

"You mock me."

"Also true." He smiled, and my heart skipped a beat. "Let's eat outside, while you tell me something good."

I carried out a bottle of white Bordeaux in a cooler and two glasses. We sat across from one another at the picnic table, and I poured for us both. The air was thick and moist with the promise of rain. The orange lanterns encircled us with warmth.

I shared some good-news updates: that Fred thought every element on the chandelier was original, that he was hot on the trail of its provenance, that Timothy had zipped up to take me to lunch, and that he and the crew were coming at the end of the month to film some location shots.

"Can I ask your opinion about something that's in the not-such-good-news category?" I asked.

"You don't even need to ask."

"It's Zoë." I described Zoë's reaction to Emma's decision to join the marines. "Did you know that Ellis had been a marine before he joined the police?"

"No."

"So what should I do?"

"Be there for Zoë. Congratulate Emma. Thank Ellis for his service."

"That's it?"

"That's it."

"I was thinking we could host a going-away party for Emma. A big one."

"Okay, that, too. Now let me ask you something. What do you think of a sectional couch for the living room?"

I laughed. We traded ideas on furniture styles and arrangements. Just before eleven, we gathered up the dishes and headed inside. We reached no decisions about furniture, but none needed to be made. It was enough, more than enough, to escape from the frightening chaos of the unknown into the safe harbor of Ty's love.

After a mostly sleepless night worrying about Maudie, a woman I'd only met twice in my life, I rolled out of bed. It was eight minutes after six. Ty was still asleep. I made a pot of coffee and sat down with my iPad to check the morning edition of the *Seacoast Star*.

I braced myself for more of Wes's venom and was pleasantly surprised to see that he didn't repeat his unfounded speculation in print. In fact, he'd done yeoman's work overnight, talking to a dozen people and reviewing a score of records, reports, and other documents. He reported that the police hadn't found anyone who'd seen Maudie after she and Julie got back from lunch.

One of the photos accompanying Wes's article showed Celia as she arrived at Belle Vista. I wondered if he'd sweet-talked it from someone at the facility or bartered for it with a police official. Wes had tentacles everywhere, and nothing he managed to learn or acquire surprised me. I stared at the image, the last known photograph of a woman on the brink. Her eyes were mere slits. The corners of her mouth turned down. One of the muscles running along her neck was bulging. A recent professional headshot of Maudie was positioned beside it and offered a telling contrast. In that photo, Maudie was half-smiling, polished and confident. The photo credit read "Rocky Point Women's Club." In his mini-bio, Wes stated that Maudie was on the organization's board. Wes had selected two photos from the array I sent him, one of the jewel-decked chest, another of the cat statue. They were in a sidebar. The text asked anyone who had any information about these potentially priceless objects to contact me.

Another sidebar, bearing the byline of an intern named Cary Finley, stated that the murder weapon was definitely the rolling pin. The killer hadn't tried to hide the weapon, just their identity. It had been scrubbed with a Clorox wipe, probably taken from a container Maudie kept under the sink, so it was unlikely any forensic evidence remained that might indicate who had wielded it. The Clorox wipe container had been wiped, too, removing fingerprints and touch DNA. The murderer had evidently washed up in the kitchen sink, then splashed some bleach around. Blood residue was found in the drain, but it was so degraded by the bleach as to be useless in the investigation. No bleach was found in the apartment.

I walked to the window, thinking. Wisps of fog veiled the meadow, muting the colors of the wildflowers and softening the shapes of the trees that grew along the perimeter of the property. It was as if I were viewing an impressionist painting from afar.

I refilled my coffee cup, then sat back down to finish the article. It ended with Wes's hallmark provocative flair: Doug, Celia's recently laid-off husband, was still, as of 5 A.M. when Wes posted the article, at the police station. According to the sign-in sheet at Belle Vista, though, Doug hadn't been there. Unless someone let him in by a side door or he entered Maudie's unit through the window. Wes added that staff, residents, and visitors were all being questioned.

Someone knocked on the door, and when I turned to see who was there, Zoë smiled.

She stepped inside. "You're up early."

"You, too. Have some coffee."

"Sorry for losing it before," she said as she poured herself a cup. "There's no excuse for stupid."

"I didn't think you were stupid. I thought you were terrified."

"I was. I am. But it's not my life."

"You don't get a vote, but surely it's okay to venture an opinion. You're the mom."

She slid into a chair opposite me. "And having so ventured, I now get to shut up."

"Among the hardest things in the world for either of us to do."

"You got that right. Are you okay? I read in the paper that you were at Belle Vista."

"I'm fine. Or I will be."

"I wonder if I will be." Her eyes filled. "I think I'm coping better, then I fall apart again."

"It will get easier." I reached across the table and squeezed her hand, wondering again what Emma had wanted to tell me, and why it had to be a secret. "I promise."

She began to cry, tears running down her cheeks. "Oh, Josie, what am I going to do?"

"Tell her you love her and you'll always be there for her, no matter what."

"And then what?"

"Tell her again."

After a few more seconds, Zoë stopped crying. She sat quietly for a while, drinking coffee. When she left, she hugged me, a big wraparound hug, the kind you see in the movies, fueled by devotion and a deep, unspoken need.

On Saturdays, tag sale day, everyone worked, me included. First, though, I wanted to look at Maudie's windows from the outside.

I reached Belle Vista at seven thirty and parked in the back, by the employee lot Lainy had told me was on Victory Boulevard. Dedicated to Rocky Point's military heroes, the street featured a wide median, which was maintained by the Rocky Point Military Family Association. This summer, they'd planted pink and white petunias arranged in star shapes, with a three-foot-high American flag in the center of each star.

I crossed the parking lot toward the facility and walked through the gate onto the path that led to the side door near Maudie's unit. I passed the bench where I'd sat to call the antiques appraisers, then followed the walkway, hoping to find inspiration about whether Celia's killer had escaped through the window—or entered that way. I left the path and trod on packed dirt toward the building, keeping myself hidden behind the laurel hedge. When I was even with Maudie's windows, I separated twigs so I could peek.

A uniformed police officer I didn't recognize was stationed near her unit.

I peered into the flower beds below her windows, both now closed, seeking out stomped-down areas. The dirt near the window looked slightly lower than the rest of the garden, but that might be due to a gardener traipsing around, a drainage gully, or simply my imagination.

I was able to confirm my initial speculation, though. It would have been astonishingly easy to slip in or out via the window, even while carrying the presentation box and cat, especially if you'd secreted them in a bag or larger box. The grassy areas, manicured thickets, and gently curving walkways were all screened from view by artfully arranged bushes and hedges. Anyone fleeing via Maudie's window could make their way to the road or parking lot without hindrance and with a good chance of escaping notice even from the residents Maudie had described as busybodies. I surveyed her neighbors' windows. Even though lights were on in both units, I didn't see a soul. That the killer could manage to maneuver an unwilling or unconscious woman out the window and drag or carry her through the garden to the parking lot seemed less plausible.

I walked back to my car. I hadn't found inspiration, but neither had I seen anything that contradicted my theory that sneaking in and out of Maudie's apartment was doable, and that was something.

CHAPTER SIXTEEN

mma arrived at ten, as expected, and greeted everyone with friendly hellos. She'd been in and out of Prescott's since I first moved to New Hampshire, when she was three.

Emma inherited her height and lissome frame from Zoë and her ivory skin, blond hair, and cornflower-blue eyes from her dad. She wore tan cargo shorts with a sleeveless white collared blouse and Skechers. Muscles rippled along the insides of her thighs and arms. She was a beautiful young woman, inside and out.

We crossed the warehouse and mounted the steps to my private office. She sat on the love seat. I sat across from her on one of the wing chairs.

She leveled her eyes at me. "Mom's upset."

"Understandable."

"Not to me. I expected her to be happy for me. All my life she told me I was smart and capable, that I could do anything I set my mind to." She lowered her eyes for a moment. "It was all a big fat lie. She meant that I could do anything I set my mind to, but only if she approved."

"In other words, you don't merely want to enlist—you want her approval."

"Is that too much to ask?"

"Evidently, yes. Don't tell me you're surprised your mom is scared."

"This is way more than scared. She's falling apart! I thought she'd express concern, I'd reassure her, and that would be that."

"Surprise!" I called, smiling, raising my arms, and wiggling my fingers, as if Emma were the birthday girl at a surprise party.

"Very funny," she said. "What should I do?"

"Tell her you love her."

"That's it?"

"Hug her."

"What's that going to do?"

"Are you going to change your mind?"

"No."

"Then don't argue the point. Empathize. Tell her you love her. Hug her."

She nodded slowly, thinking it through. "That's good advice. Thank you."

"You're welcome."

She lowered her eyes again and rubbed her thighs. Something was churning inside her, something she didn't want to address. "There's more."

"Okay."

"I don't know how to tell you."

"You're pregnant."

"What? No!"

"You've committed some kind of crime and need me to help you get it quashed before you leave for basic."

"Don't be silly. It's not about me. It's about Mom." She clamped her teeth onto her bottom lip for a moment. "I was looking for my birth certificate. There was an envelope labeled 'important docs' in her desk drawer. I didn't mean to pry."

"You opened it."

"It was already open. I went through the papers, yes. Did you know?"

"Know what?"

"If she told anyone, she would have told you. Did she?"

I no longer felt like joking around. "What are we talking about, Emma?"

"She doesn't know I know."

"Maybe she doesn't want anyone to know."

"That's what I think."

My innate curiosity bubbled to the surface, but I managed to call on my better self and tamped it down. "If it's about something she did a long time ago, or a family secret, or a secret she's keeping for someone else, you should pretend you didn't see it. It's not your information to share."

"It's none of those things."

"You're saying there's a problem."

"I don't know."

I sensed an unseen chasm opening in front of me. If Zoë was in trouble and hadn't said a word to me, I would feel both dismayed and hurt, but I couldn't share either of those emotions with her daughter. Instead, I said, "So respect that—she doesn't want you to know."

"I thought maybe she told Ellis."

"Maybe she did."

"No. I asked him like I'm asking you, just now. At first he tried to guilt me into telling him, then, when I refused, he peppered me with questions. I didn't know what to do. Finally, he asked if Zoë was sick or dying, and when I said no, he brushed me off. He told me to come back when I had something to say, that he was too busy to watch me dance around a topic."

I didn't comment. I didn't know what to say. I worked on maintaining a neutral expression and hoped Emma couldn't tell how hard and fast my heart was beating.

"It was a printout of an email from—"

"Stop!" I interrupted, deciding in a flash I had to stop Emma from revealing Zoë's secret. All of me wanted to know, but I couldn't let her tell me. "If Zoë doesn't want me to know, I don't want you spilling the beans."

"You're right. Of course you're right." She stood and smiled. "Sorry."

I walked her out. We didn't speak again until we reached her car.

"I love you, Josie."

"I love you, too, Emma."

Apparently, Zoë was struggling, but until she approached me for help, there was nothing I could do.

I spent the rest of the morning working Prescott's Instant Appraisal booth at the tag sale, which helped take my mind off my worries.

As a little perk to my staff for working Saturdays, I always provide pizza. I chose a slice of mushroom, a nice change from last night's meatball, and went to my office.

Timothy's assistant producer, Starr, the recently promoted pink-haired queen of makeup, called to finalize our plans for later in the month. They'd selected two beach locations, one by the jetty and the other a series of high dunes. Sasha and Fred came up together to share their ideas for the themed high-end antiques auction we'd slated for next spring, tentatively titled

"Pining for Pineapples," highlighting antiques that featured a pineapple motif, long a symbol of affluence. I approved the title and their plans. I answered a few emails, then tried to read an accounting report, but my mind kept wandering from our impressive numbers to Emma and Zoë, each wanting something from the other person she didn't want to give, and from Celia, burdened by debt she couldn't manage, to Maudie, a woman whose whereabouts were still unknown.

I knew investigations took time, but I felt fidgety and unsettled.

I gave up on the accounting report and returned to the tag sale venue. I took a turn working the floor, guiding customers to objects they might find interesting, answering questions, ringing up sales.

Retired Lieutenant Commander Cynthia Silberblatt, a tall blonde with a big smile, came in and headed right for me.

"I got Cara's call," she said. "The light-switch plates sound like just my cup of tea."

I waved Eric over. "You know Lieutenant Commander Silberblatt, don't you, Eric?"

"I've seen you here, but we've never met." He shuffled back a step, as self-effacing as ever. "Hi."

"Hi," Cynthia said, smiling broadly. "I've seen you here, too. Nice to meet you!"

I touched his elbow. "Eric, Cara asked you to set aside some art deco wall-switch plates. Would you get them?"

Eric hurried away.

I turned to Cynthia. "May I ask a favor?"

"Name it."

"I have a friend whose eighteen-year-old daughter just enlisted in the marines. My friend is terrified, and I don't know what to say to comfort her."

"Does the daughter know what she's in for in terms of the physical requirements and training standards?"

"Yes, and she's up for it. I suspect she'll sail through at the top of her class."

"Then you can tell your friend that whatever situations her daughter might face, she'll be able to handle them, and handle them well. The marines train for all eventualities, including lots of things that will never come to pass. She'll be ready."

I repeated Cynthia's words to myself, memorizing them. "Thank you. That's just the information I needed."

Eric returned with the tissue-paper-wrapped plates. He unwrapped one piece, and Cynthia exclaimed, "Oh, they're even more beautiful than I expected! I'll take it! I'll take them all."

She thanked us again and again for the call, and Eric, unable to withstand her enthusiasm, smiled warmly. As I waved good-bye, I repeated her words to myself: *Emma will be ready.*

By midafternoon, just as I was about to leave, to walk through the woods or along the beach to try to clear my mind, Wes called.

"Whatcha got?" he asked.

"I'm not talking to you. You're a provocateur."

"Oh, puhleeze . . . all I did was repeat what you said."

"I understand there's an intern at the paper, Cary Finley. I bet she's going to be a terrific reporter once she gets some experience . . . I think I'll give her a chance to prove her reporting chops with an exclusive."

"What?" Wes exploded. He sputtered and stammered, whining that I should know better than to trust my important perspective with a newbie, that maybe he'd taken too strong a position before, and that he'd fix it immediately.

I smiled, pleased with his reaction. "Good. When you've published your correction, call me, and we'll talk."

"Don't contact Cary."

"You have an hour." I hung up.

I opened the *Seacoast Star* website and scanned the listing of top stories. Ten minutes later, after my third refresh, a new link appeared. The headline read JOSIE PRESCOTT HELPS POLICE. The short article touted my expertise and integrity. He even included a quote from Ellis thanking me for working with the police to locate Maudie's missing objects. I had just finished reading when Wes called.

"Did you see it?" he asked.

"Yes. How did you get the quote so quickly?"

"I've had it for a while. I was saving it."

"For what?" I demanded.

"For when the objects were found. I'm sorry, Joz . . . my enthusiasm got the best of me."

"That's no excuse."

"You're right," he said, sounding young and vulnerable. "I won't do it again."

My anger melted, at least a bit. "Apology accepted."

"Thanks. So whatcha got?"

"You called me, remember?"

"I need information—talk to me."

"I have nothing but questions."

"Questions are good. They can point me in the right direction. Do you have time to meet? Our dune in ten?"

I still felt bruised and raw from Wes's perfidy and was about to tell him to forget it when I remembered something my dad once told me: If you expect people to be perfect, you'll spend a lot of time alone. I believed Wes's remorse was genuine, and I trusted his commitment to never betray me again.

"Okay," I said. "I'll leave now."

I grabbed my tote bag, told Cara I'd be back in a while, and ran for my car.

CHAPTER SEVENTEEN

W es was in his midtwenties, seven or eight years younger than me. He had slimmed down since his marriage, and he'd cleaned up his act, at least superficially, but he hadn't lost a bit of his enthusiasm for the hunt. Now that he'd promised to corral his errant bad boy instincts, I could support his efforts to find the truth.

I got to the dune first, our dune, the place where Wes and I met to talk without fear of being overheard. I climbed the sandy hill and stood at the top surveying the scene. The sky was solidly pewter. The ocean churned, waves pounding against the beach, landing with a thunderous roar.

A car engine revved, and I knew it must be Wes. Only Wes revved the engine as he jerked to a stop. I turned to watch. He parked on the shoulder and leapt out of the car.

"Hey, Wes," I called.

"Hey." He wore crisply creased tan slacks and a white collared shirt with the sleeves rolled up three turns.

He clambered up the shifting sand. "So I guess you're up the creek this time, huh?"

"Me? What are you talking about?"

He scanned my face, trying to see if I was pulling his leg. "You mean you don't know?"

"Know what?"

"It's what I said on air, except more so. An idea's being floated that you and Celia worked out a deal on the QT—you were to sell the box and cat without Maudie being any the wiser. You stashed the goods in your car, and as you walked back to Maudie's unit, you realized that you could eliminate a witness, to say nothing of keeping all the proceeds for yourself, if you ix-nayed Celia, so you did."

My brain slowed. I opened my mouth to protest, then closed it.

My first instinct was to shove him off the dune. He'd paw the air in a futile effort to save himself, then catapult toward the beach, rolling through the sand like a pig in mud. He wouldn't be hurt much, possibly a few bruises and a wrenched muscle or two, nothing long-lasting. Then maturity kicked in and I laughed.

"God, Wes, you're unbelievable. Did you come up with this theory all by yourself? Or did you hire a novelist?"

"Why?" he demanded. "What's wrong with it?"

"Everything. Why don't you close your eyes for a minute, take a few deep breaths, and when you're ready to join me back here in the real world, let me know."

He grinned, and his entire demeanor was transformed into the boyish imp I knew and adored. "Okay, okay, so I was just trying it on for size. After apologizing to you earlier, I figured I'd better show you I wasn't turning soft."

I thought again about shoving him off the dune, then got pragmatic. "Have you told anyone else?"

"Nah."

"You're some piece of work, Wes. Have you heard anything about Maudie?"

"Nothing. She's vanished."

"With no sign of foul play."

"Right. No one saw her leave Belle Vista, and no one has seen her since."

"How can that be? There are security cameras everywhere, in bank park-ing lots, on streetlights, in residential driveways, yet no image has surfaced that would help explain Maudie's disappearance? Don't you find that hard to believe?"

"Totally. The police are still canvassing. They surveyed stores, too. My po-lice source says that was your idea, and it was a good one. A good one, but no dice. As far as they can tell, Maudie wasn't in any Rocky Point shop or store yesterday afternoon."

"Is Maudie's purse in her apartment?" I asked. "Her toothbrush?"

"No to both."

"Have they checked her credit cards?"

"No can do without a court order, and no judge will issue it."

"Even though her apartment is a crime scene?"

"Unless the person has a proven physical or mental disability that places them or someone else in danger, or they were kidnapped, or—and here's the only section of the law that might apply—the adult is missing after what they call a 'catastrophe,' the police can't do squat."

"A catastrophe probably refers to an earthquake or something of that nature."

"Right. I'm with you, though, in being skeptical. I mean, if she went away on some kind of trip, don't you think she must have heard what happened? Surely she would have gotten in touch."

"Not if she went out of state, where the murder wouldn't make the news, or to an off-the-grid place, like one of those health spas that collect your cell phones when you check in."

"Does that sound like her?"

"Out of state? Yes. A spa? Not really. How about Doug? Was he at Belle Vista yesterday?"

"There's no evidence he was, but there's no evidence he wasn't, either. I followed up on your tip about his job interview at Jestran's. The cops have Doug on video arriving at nine fifty-five for his ten o'clock meeting and leaving an hour later, just before eleven."

"So he had plenty of time to get to Belle Vista."

"Bingo on that. No one admits seeing him or letting him in or anything, but that doesn't prove anything—that place is a security sieve. They're still sifting through everyone's stories. It's a lot of who was where when and who saw you there."

"No blips on anybody's radar at all?" I asked.

"Nope. Belle Vista routinely does background checks, which I guess makes sense given that the staff is in and out of residents' units all day every day. No one has ever been convicted of a felony. Most of them have never even gotten nabbed for speeding."

"You sound surprised."

"Aren't you? There's almost two hundred people who work there. And not one is even a little bit dicey?"

"That shows Belle Vista does a good job screening people. They're diligent. Back to Doug for a sec—how did his job interview go?"

"No news." Wes sounded annoyed, as if his contact had let him down by not sharing the details of Doug's interview.

"Where did Doug go when he left Jestran's?"

Wes chortled. "Who knows? He said he drove around. Talk about lame."

"Lots of people find driving relaxing."

"He was on the phone with Celia for fifteen minutes while he was driving, from eleven ten to eleven twenty-five."

"How can you possibly know that?"

He grinned. "I've got game. Doug won't say what they talked about because it was, quote, 'personal,' end quote."

"What's surprising about that? Don't you and Maggie talk about private things?"

"Not so private I wouldn't tell the cops if I was suspected of murder."

"Is he really a suspect?"

"From what I hear, he's the one and only." He chuckled. "Except you."

I smiled politely. "Cute."

"I bet they were talking about making the rent," Wes continued once he realized he wouldn't get a rise out of me. "When you don't have enough money, you can't think about anything else, and as we know, Doug and Celia were riding on fumes." He waggled his fingers at me. "Your turn . . . talk to me. You gotta know something."

"I wish I did."

"When you do," he said, waggling his index finger again at my face, "I'm your first call."

Before I could reply, Wes crab-walked down the dune and was gone.

When I got back to Prescott's, I locked my bag in my car and set out for the Congregational church. The quarter-mile walk through the woods that separated our properties was one of my favorite ways to declutter my brain.

I followed the packed dirt path under a thick lattice of maple leaves until I reached the church parking lot. I'd hoped I'd find Ted, the pastor, puttering in his garden, and I did.

Ted maintained a large vegetable garden at the back of the property.

Anyone, congregant or stranger, was welcome to help themselves anytime. I often took some arugula in spring, a few cucumbers in summer, and a Halloween pumpkin or two in fall.

"Josie!" he called, leaning back on his haunches. "Are you here for some tomatoes?"

"No, just stretching my legs."

"The cherry tomatoes are especially good," he whispered.

"Why are you whispering?"

"I don't want to hurt the Big Boys' feelings."

"You make me smile, Ted."

"You look like you could use one." He stood, pulled a small jute bag from his pocket, filled it with plump red cherry tomatoes, and handed it to me. "Come have a cup of coffee with me."

"Thank you. I'd love a coffee."

Ted's office was airy and bright. He'd cranked open every one of the half dozen Gothic-style windows, and the moist, cool air was as invigorating as the steamy hot coffee he poured from a Mr. Coffee machine.

"Talk to me," he said.

"I don't want to impose."

"Is it the murder of that poor woman?"

"Yes, sort of. Mostly, it's the missing woman. Maudie Wilson. I only met her a few days ago, so I can't understand why I'm so upset."

"You have a big heart, Josie. You feel things deeply."

"That's nice of you to—" I broke off as a dragonfly sailed in, its iridescent blue-green wings whirring. "Look! How gorgeous!"

The dragonfly lit on the top molding of a mahogany bookcase by the door. Ted and I swiveled to watch it.

"It's so beautiful," I said.

"Luminous."

"What do we do?"

"Call Winnie," Ted said, reaching for the phone.

"Who's Winnie?"

"Winnie Thornton. A congregant. She works here part-time now, mostly in the office. This isn't the first dragonfly to get inside, but I'm not worried.

Winnie has a sixth sense when it comes to God's creatures. She's gotten them all out safely."

"That's wonderful, but you need screens."

"They're custom windows, which means we'd need custom screens, and I'm afraid the budget doesn't allow for that. Excuse me for a moment while I call Winnie. She lives nearby."

I didn't hear a word of Ted's conversation with Winnie. I was watching the dragonfly, a universal symbol of self-awareness, of the ability to embrace change and adapt. Like Maudie was trying to do for herself. Maudie went to Rocky Point Computers for training. She told them she was a travel writer. I wondered what else she might have mentioned in the course of their conversation.

"Winnie will be right here," Ted said as he replaced the receiver.

"Something's come up. Sorry. Thanks for the coffee, but I've got to go."

Ignoring his startled expression, I jogged back to Prescott's, retrieved my tote bag from the trunk, and jumped behind the wheel. I turned inland out of the lot, toward the village, where answers lay.

CHAPTER EIGHTEEN

Rocky Point Computers occupied a one-story stand-alone building a block from the village green. It shared a parking lot with a strip mall containing a pizzeria, a nail salon, a Chinese takeout restaurant, a children's clothing store, and an outpatient physical therapy facility.

It was packed, not a surprise on a gloomy Saturday afternoon. Inside, computers and peripherals were displayed on shelves that ran along the left side of the store. They sold and serviced cameras, cell phones, and tablets, too. Carrels lined the right side. Every unit was in use, some with two people working together at one machine. A big schoolroom clock was mounted high on the wall. It was eighteen minutes past four.

A woman in her early twenties walked up, smiling. She had four gold studs running up the outer edge of her left ear and a nose ring. Her shoulder-length toffee-brown hair was full and curly. When it bounced a certain way, I could see a blue-and-yellow anchor tattoo on the side of her neck. A name tag pinned to her blouse read GILLIAN.

After we exchanged greetings, I smiled warmly, hoping to disarm her. "Maudie Wilson told me how excited she was about the training on her new computer. I'm hoping you can tell me who she worked with."

"Maudie Wilson. That's the woman who—" Gillian's brows lifted. "Why are you asking?"

I smiled even more broadly. "It's a surprise. Maudie's going to be over the moon!"

"Uh-huh," she said, unimpressed.

"I want to buy Maudie a present," I said, maintaining the pretense, "whether it's more training, a professional camera, some software, you know, whatever would be special for her. I'm hoping that whoever Maudie worked with would know what she'd want."

Her brow cleared. "Fun! But I don't know who did her training."

"Can you look it up?"

"No, sorry. We're really busy."

"I can wait."

"It'll be a while."

"Maybe I can talk to the manager."

From Gillian's expression, I could tell she'd decided it would be easier and quicker to get rid of me by answering my question than it would be to wait me out or deal with her manager.

"Okay," she said. "I'll just be a minute. You can wait here."

Gillian went to the customer information booth and tapped something into a computer. After a minute, she walked back to join me.

"She was here on Thursday afternoon, and she worked with Lara." Gillian scanned the room and spotted Lara, a curvy blonde in her late twenties, sitting at one of the workstations with an older man, and pointed. "Lara's doing training now."

"Would you mind asking her if she can give me two minutes when she's done? I don't want to interrupt her." I smiled again. "As I said, I don't mind waiting."

Gillian crossed the room and spoke to Lara, who nodded at me. I nodded back and mouthed, "Thank you."

Gillian walked back to me. "Lara will be done with this session at four thirty and will be glad to talk to you."

"You're the best!"

"No prob!" Gillian said. She returned to cruising the sales floor.

I stood by the carrel closest to the front door, out of the way, but able to keep my eye on Lara. She finished with her client right on the dot and came to join me.

"How can I help?" she asked.

"First, thank you for seeing me without an appointment. Do you have a few minutes to talk?"

She checked the time. "My next appointment isn't until five. Do you mind if we go outside so I can have a smoke?"

I said that would be fine. She said she'd grab her cigarettes from the back and meet me at the bench in front of the pizza place.

I stood by the bench. A few minutes later, Lara rounded the corner. She paused to light up, then sauntered my way. She sat down, slouching and stretching her legs straight out, crossing her ankles. I sat next to her.

She tapped her cigarette on the bench arm. "Gillian said you had questions about Maudie Wilson. I heard the news—is she all right?"

"As far as I know, she's fine. She told me how excited she was to begin training. How did it go?"

Lara exhaled slowly, watching me through a haze of smoke. "Why are you asking?"

"It's a surprise!" I said, smiling, giving a small gurgle of laughter, and replicating the bubbly answer I'd just given Gillian.

My silliness drew a reluctant smile from Lara. She cocked her head, her expression more curious than suspicious as she debated whether to probe deeper.

"So how did she do?" I repeated, betting she'd decide to skip asking any follow-up questions. It's always easier to do nothing than make waves.

"Good. I mean she was rusty and all. She said she hadn't used a computer since her husband died, but she was familiar with all the basic settings and some of the software, so she felt comfortable with the laptop. She'd never worked with a touch screen before, though, and she didn't like it. That's okay. Not everyone is ready to make the switch. I adjusted the settings so the one she bought has dual capability. The touch screen works if you want it to, but you don't have to use it. She's a fast typist, so that boosted her confidence."

"Did she want to learn a photo program?"

"Yeah. I stayed simple because she wasn't going to be doing heavy retouching or anything fancy. She just wanted to be able to crop photos and do some minor adjustments, you know, exposure, color saturation, the basics. She picked it up real quick. I showed her how to email photos from her phone to herself so she could download them easily, but the quality wasn't good enough for the kind of photos she needed, you know, for publication. She has an iPhone 5, for God's sake."

"What was your solution? A camera or a new phone?"

She laughed. "I tried hard to sell her on a new phone, but she wasn't having any of it. She loves that old dog. She bought a Fujifilm camera. It's perfect for her: high quality, intuitive, small, and lightweight." Lara tossed her cigarette butt onto the ground and rubbed it out. "She practiced using it and downloading the photos. By the time she left, she felt pretty comfortable."

"It sounds like she was here for a long time."

"Three hours. That's what she signed up for when she called for the appointment, and we used every minute of the time."

"Something tells me you're patient."

She laughed again. "I didn't need to be, not with Maudie. She was fearless."

"Did she tell you her plans?"

"About the travel writing? Not much. She wanted to go somewhere she could snorkel from the shore. She was going to talk to someone, a girlfriend, she said. I asked whether she wanted a waterproof camera since she was going snorkeling, but she said no, that she was going underwater, not the camera."

"Did she mention her girlfriend's name?"

"Nessie. I remember because it's the same as the nickname for the Loch Ness monster, which you definitely don't want to see when you're snorkeling. She said her friend Nessie was as adventurous as she was."

"Did she mention Nessie's last name?"

"No. Sorry."

"Did she say where she and Nessie were planning to go?"

Lara tucked her hair behind her ear as she thought about it, reviewing their conversation, trying to dredge up more specifics. "If she told me, it didn't stick."

"That's okay." I stood up. "You've been really helpful, Lara. Thank you."

"Did you get what you needed?"

"Maybe. I wish I knew where to find Nessie."

"Try the Rocky Point Women's Club."

"Why do you say that?"

Lara shook another cigarette from her pack and lit it. "We're not supposed to discuss anything strategic or tactical with clients. We're here to train them on computers and whatever software they want to learn to use. We don't make suggestions. Can you hear my boss? *We're not proactive. We're reactive. Proactive gets you in hot water. Reactive gets you repeat business.*

What a crock." Her shoulders lifted an inch, then fell. "I helped Maudie set up a website. Just a rudimentary placeholder, but if she's going to get travel writing assignments like she said she wanted, she has to have a place to showcase her portfolio."

"That's terrific of you, Lara. Really."

"I don't know. If she gets pissed off about something, and reports me, I'm toast."

"Maudie's not like that. What does the Rocky Point Women's Club have to do with anything?"

"I wanted to post a headshot, and I offered to take one with her new camera."

"And she told you she had a nice headshot on the Rocky Point Women's Club's site."

"Exactly. She felt uncomfortable just having her photo snapped. I get that, so I scooped that one up. Maudie was in a bunch of photos, groups and duos and so on, but this one was a pro shot, you know?"

"Some of the photos on their site included Nessie."

"You didn't hear this from me."

"Hear what?" I asked, smiling and extending my hand for a shake.

I was glad to sit in my air-conditioned car for a while to get out of the humidity and still, thick air.

I brought up the Rocky Point Women's Club website on my phone and navigated to what they called the "Photo Gallery." In addition to the formal headshots, Maudie was in a half dozen photos, and in every one she looked like she was having a blast. I read the captions. There was a Nancy, a Naomi, and a Natalie, but nary a Nessie.

I called Cara and told her I wouldn't be back, called Ty and said I'd be home in about an hour, and then drove to the Rocky Point Women's Club.

I turned onto Lynden Street, not far from Old Mill Pond, and spotted the gilt-and-black ROCKY POINT WOMEN'S CLUB sign. The club was housed in a well-maintained Edwardian mansion surrounded by mature trees and lush gardens. The front door was open. Through the screen door, I could see a short young man wearing a white collared shirt standing behind a mahogany bar polishing wineglasses with a dishcloth.

I knocked on the doorframe, and he looked up and smiled. "Come on in. It's open."

I walked into an entry hall with alcoves on both sides, passed under a high archway, and stepped into a large square room. Dark wood paneling covered the bottom half of the walls. The top half was painted a creamy white. Mini tent cards were laid out in a chevron pattern on a round cherrywood table. A podium stood at the end of the room near a window. A dozen paintings dotted the walls, all portraits from a bygone era in gilt frames. Ten tables set for eight were covered with crisp white linen tablecloths. Silver flatware glistened.

I walked to the bar and introduced myself. "I'm hoping you can help me . . . I have a quick question about one of the members: Nessie."

"Sorry. I'm only here for special occasions. I don't know anyone's name except Leesa." He grinned. "And I only know her name because she's the one who hires me."

I smiled. "Fair enough. Where's Leesa now?"

He jerked his head toward a set of swinging doors to his right. "In the kitchen."

"I'm guessing she's meeting with the staff about tonight's gala."

"Which begins at six thirty. Early birds will arrive around six."

"Which means I'm in the way."

"Not to me. I'm a man of many talents. I can shine up these glasses and talk at the same time."

A nicely dressed middle-aged woman came through the swinging door, pausing for a second to look back through the small window at the top. She started walking toward the bar, stopped short when she saw me, then continued on, smiling with professional warmth.

"Hi," I said.

I introduced myself, and so did she. She was the program manager, Leesa Tobin.

I smiled, glancing around the room. "This place looks gorgeous. I know you're busy, so I'll only take a minute of your time. It's about Maudie Wilson."

Leesa's smile faded. "Have you heard anything?"

"No. I'm hoping you can tell me if you're expecting her tonight."

"I'm sorry . . . what did you say your name was?"

"Josie Prescott. I own Prescott's Antiques and Auctions, here in Rocky Point. Maudie is a friend."

"Sorry . . . I'm upset about the situation. Yes, we expect Maudie tonight. I called her, but I didn't reach her."

"Does she have a friend named Nessie?"

"Yes—Agnes, but everyone calls her Nessie."

"I'd like to talk to her. How can I reach her?"

"I'm sorry, we never release member information."

"I understand, but this is an emergency."

She shook her head. "I can't."

"What's her last name?"

"Please . . . I'm sorry."

"Would you call her for me and ask if she'll talk to me?"

"That wouldn't be appropriate. I'm going to have to ask you to leave. We're getting close to the event start time, and I have a lot to do."

"I understand," I said. "Thank you for talking to me."

I headed out, but when I reached the entryway, I tucked myself into the alcove on the left side of the arch. I might understand Leesa's refusal, but I didn't have to accept it as the final word on the subject.

Leesa spoke to the bartender for a minute, then walked out of my line of vision. A few seconds later I heard a loud, resonating tap-tap. Leesa was confirming the sound system was working. A moment later, she spoke into the mic. "Testing one, two, three. How does it sound?"

I peeked out in time to see the bartender give a thumbs-up.

Leesa walked to the swinging doors. "I'll be in the kitchen if you need me."

"Got it," he said.

As soon as I heard the soft whoosh of the door swinging closed behind her, I stepped into the large room and beelined my way to the table holding the tent cards.

The bartender continued his work. He didn't speak to me, and I didn't speak to him.

The attendees' names were organized in alphabetical order. Maudie

Wilson was near the end of the arrangement. I started at the beginning seeking out an Agnes.

It was taking too long. Leesa was going to reappear any minute. I kept an eye on the swinging doors. The bartender, now cutting limes, continued to ignore me. When I reached the *T*'s, he left. Probably he figured that discretion was the better part of valor—it wasn't his job to chase me away, but he didn't want any guff from Leesa in case I got caught.

Footsteps sounded from inside the kitchen, close to the door. I looked up in time to see the back of Leesa's head through the window in the door. She was speaking to someone, her voice audible, the words unclear.

I turned back to the tent cards. *Maudie Wilson. George Willis. Marie Willis.*

A whoosh sounded as the kitchen door swung open.

Trevor Winslow. Charlie Wynn. And there it was: *Agnes Wynn.*

I darted out the door.

CHAPTER NINETEEN

I drove around the corner, zipped left, then right, and rolled to a stop at Old Mill Pond. It was twenty to six, and I wanted to get to Nessie before she left for the club, but I needed to alert Ellis about the possibility that Maudie would also be at the gala before I did anything else. I called his cell phone, and it went directly to voicemail.

"Ellis, it's Josie. I just learned that Maudie Wilson is scheduled to attend a gala tonight at Rocky Point Women's Club. My hope is that she spent a night at a fancy resort somewhere and she'll sweep into the club wearing a new gown she bought at some chichi boutique. I know, I know, it's not likely. No one goes to a fancy resort for one night. Anyway, I wanted to let you know she's on the guest list, and as far as I can tell, she hasn't canceled. Bye."

I hung up, then brought up a search engine and typed in "Charles Wynn," hoping I could find their address easily. I did. Unlike the more than forty percent of people who'd jettisoned their landlines, Charles Wynn still had one registered in his name, and the number and corresponding address were publicly available. The Wynns lived on Chestnut Lane, around the corner from the Rocky Point Women's Club.

I dropped my phone into my bag and drove to their house. I parked in front, ran up the paved walkway, and rang the bell.

An older man opened the door with a warm and welcoming smile. He was tall and lean, with a glisten of perspiration on his brow. He wore old-school tennis whites and carried a racquet.

He smiled. "Howdy."

"You're Mr. Wynn."

"Charlie, that's me."

"I've interrupted your game."

"Nothing interrupts my game. We just finished. I won. Big."

"Congratulations. I'm Josie Prescott, a friend of Maudie Wilson's. I was wondering if Nessie is here?"

"Any news about Maudie? If it's bad news, tell me first."

"No news."

He turned toward an open door at the rear of the hall and shouted Nessie's name, then invited me in.

The two-story hall was as big as my bedroom. The floor was tiled in black and white marble squares to form a checkerboard pattern. A stairway to the right curled around a fluted column. The chandelier featured a series of brass rods with asymmetrically positioned circular openings that sent dots of light crisscrossing through the room. The artwork was all abstract, slashes and dollops of purple and gold.

Moments later, a woman appeared in the doorway. She was a little younger than her husband, midsixties or so. She had curly white hair that highlighted her blue eyes. She was of medium height, thin and wiry, like an athlete. She wore a short pleated gold skirt with a white cowl-neck short-sleeved blouse, a more contemporary tennis outfit than Charlie's. I wondered if their apparel reflected their personalities. If so, I'd bet big money that Nessie had decorated the hall.

I introduced myself. Charlie called out a friendly "Nice to meet you!" and disappeared through a door on the left.

"Did Charlie tell you he won our match?"

"He did."

"Braggart. He can't resist."

"You have a tennis court out back?"

"And a pool." She gently knocked her skull twice. "You better believe I know how fortunate we are, and I never take it for granted. I know your name. Maudie loves your tag sale. She told me she was going to ask you to help her decide how to sell that old box and cat."

"You've spoken to her recently, then."

"Thursday, the day before Celia died. Have you heard anything?"

"No, I'm afraid not."

Her shoulders drooped, and her eyes moistened. "I'm shattered about Celia, just crushed. To say nothing of Maudie. I'm so worried. We've been friends for more than thirty years, ever since Charlie and I moved to Rocky Point."

"You don't know where she is?"

"I don't, but I can make a good guess. I told the police the same thing. She wanted to go snorkeling. She asked me to join her, to blow off everything we had planned this week and just go, but I couldn't. Charlie and I are walking the Appalachian Trail, one leg at a time. We leave tomorrow for Virginia to tackle another chunk."

"Snorkeling . . . where?"

"She didn't say, but she's gotten so much more adventurous as she's gotten older, I'm betting it's somewhere exotic."

"Do you think she'd go alone?"

"Absolutely. She's one of the lucky ones—she enjoys her own company. Now that I think of it, Gerard would know where she is. Gerard Martin, our travel agent."

"Where is the agency located?"

"On Route One, next to the Betty's Flooring."

"I know just where that is." I rooted around in my tote bag for my business card case, a sterling silver beauty Ty had given me years ago. I handed her a card. "Thank you. If you think of anything that might help me find Maudie, please let me know."

"I've left Maudie three messages. I keep telling myself not to worry that she hasn't called back . . . Maudie's not very good at remembering to check messages." She rubbed her fingertip over the surface of my card. "Why are you looking for her?"

"I've only known her for a few days, but I'd like to think I'm her friend, too."

She nodded. "She's about as special as they come."

I didn't comment further because I didn't think I could keep the prickly fear that was driving me to act from showing in my voice. Instead, I thanked her and left.

I drove by Martin's Travel Agency. It was closed, and the sign on the door indicated it wouldn't be open until nine on Monday. I headed home.

The rain started just as I pulled into the driveway. I retrieved the spare umbrella I keep on the front passenger-side floor and dashed for the porch.

I shook off the wetness and wiped my shoes on the coir mat before I went inside.

"Hey, beautiful," Ty called from the kitchen.

"It's wet out."

"That's called rain."

"Ha ha." I slid the umbrella into the blue-and-white Chinese-patterned stand and kicked off my shoes. "What's the point of having a mudroom in the back if you park in the front?"

"That's one of those pesky conundrums that bear careful consideration."

I walked into the kitchen and slipped my arms around his torso, leaning my head against his chest. "I love you. What's for dinner?"

He leaned back a bit, cupped my chin, and kissed me. "The chicken you've had marinating."

Rain slashed the windows, sending waves of water sweeping across the glass.

"We can grill inside."

"Being known for my prescient thinking, I moved the grill under the overhang."

"No wonder I married you. On top of everything else, you're brilliant."

He kissed me again.

We sat at our picnic table, dry and safe, protected from the driving rain. I made a tarragon Dijon sauce for the chicken, a familiar recipe I'd mastered years ago by following my mother's careful directions. In the weeks before she'd died, when I was only thirteen and utterly unprepared for the loss, even though I knew it was coming, she'd written a cookbook by hand, complete with side notes and little drawings. It was one of my most cherished possessions.

After we finished eating, Ty went upstairs to his closet-sized home office to respond to an urgent email from his Canadian counterpart, and I cleaned up. I was placing the last of the flatware in the dishwasher when someone knocked on the back door.

It was Zoë, wearing a bright yellow hooded slicker. She took it off in the mudroom and hung it from a peg, stepped out of her dripping sandals, and fluffed her hair.

"Nice weather for ducks," I said as she entered the kitchen.

"Quack, quack. Do you have a minute? Or ten?"

"Always. Here or private?"

"Private."

Zoë looked thin, thinner even than yesterday, reed thin. Anxiety rippled up my spine. She didn't want a martini, or coffee or tea, so I poured us glasses of water and led the way to my study.

Zoë sat on the love seat, her arms resting on her thighs, her eyes on the red-and-blue-patterned Oriental rug. I turned the desk chair to face the couch and sat across from her.

She raised her eyes. "Emma told me she spoke to you about going through the envelope she found in my desk."

"She didn't reveal anything."

Zoë nodded. "I know. She told me that, too. I didn't plan on telling anyone, but since Emma snooped around, that ship has sailed."

"I'm good at forgetting things. Whatever it is, you don't have to tell me. I'll forget Emma spoke to me and everything will be copacetic."

"Sweet Josie. You're not just good at forgetting things. You're good at everything."

"Hardly."

"I applied for a job on a cruise ship."

"What?" Once Emma told me the secret wasn't from the past, and despite her reassurance to Ellis, I'd been prepared to hear that Zoë was ill, maybe from a dread disease with a dismal prognosis, but a job on a cruise ship? "Why?"

"Emma." She looked away, out the window, where the rain pelted the glass. "I've been reading everything I can get my hands on about empty nest syndrome. The consensus seems to be to change it up, find new interests, break the patterns of your schedule. All in all, I figure why the heck not? Jake is happily living in Boston, with no plans to move back after graduation. Emma's heading off to the marines. When you think about it, there's nothing keeping me here."

The same sickening sensation I felt on roller coasters roiled me, tossing my stomach into my throat, only to have it slam against my ribs as it lurched to my knees. *What about me?* I wanted to ask. I'd understood Zoë's reaction to Emma's enlisting on an intellectual level. Now I understood it emotionally. *How could Zoë even think of leaving me?*

She sipped some water. "I got an offer a minute and a half after I applied. It was smart that I decided to get my nursing license. The contract calls for four months on, two months off. Once I'm assigned a ship, you and Ty can book a cruise, and we can hang out during my time off."

I felt as if I'd stepped unknowingly through the looking glass. Zoë was no longer acting like Zoë. I had to make sense of the nonsensical. I grasped the chair arms to steady myself.

"What about Ellis?"

"I haven't told him yet. When you and Ty come on a cruise, he can come, too."

"Zoë, you know I adore you. I want whatever is best for you. What about your job? You love being a sexual assault medical advocate."

"I'll take a leave of absence."

"What other options have you considered?"

"None. Like what? What other options should I consider?"

"Taking a cruise with Ellis for a shorter time."

"What makes you think he'd want to go with me?"

"Because he loves you." I leaned forward. "Where is this coming from, Zoë?"

Zoë turned her head aside. Two tears ran down her cheek in a zigzag pattern. "I always knew Ellis was too good to be true. I've talked to you about that."

"Not for years now."

"I became complacent. Silly me."

"You're not making any sense. Did you and Ellis have a fight?"

"No, of course not. But we're in a holding pattern, and I need to shake things up, not continue in a rut."

I felt the earth right itself, the chasm inching its way to closure. Zoë was caught in a vortex of unwanted change—Emma's enlisting, Jake not coming home after college, realizing that her nest really was going to be empty. She felt unmoored, purposeless. She'd spent decades being needed, and now she wasn't. I could see her dilemma as clear as day, but that and a dime wouldn't get me a cup of coffee or Zoë happiness. Luckily, I saw a way out.

"I bet some of the empty nest success stories featured smaller changes than escaping on a cruise ship," I said.

"Is that what this seems like to you? Like I'm running away?"

"A little bit. I understand the instinct . . . I think everyone has felt that way at some point."

Zoë looked down at the carpet for a few seconds. "What do you think I want?"

"A new set of commitments to replace the ones you're losing."

"I'd marry Ellis in a heartbeat, but he hasn't asked me."

"Name other things you love—not people . . . things."

"Why?"

I smiled. "I have an idea."

"What?"

"Name them."

"I don't know . . . lots of things. Making soup. Journaling. Dogs. Botanical gardens."

"How long before you have to accept the cruise ship position?" I asked.

"It's kind of open-ended. They always need nurses on one ship or another."

"I want you to trust me."

"I do. You know that."

"I need to talk to a couple of people, and I don't want to tell you anything about it."

"Emma?"

"Yes."

She looked out the window again, the rain still pounding the glass. "And Ellis."

"And Ty. And Jake."

She turned to face me, her eyes moist. "It sounds like you're planning an intervention."

"Do you think you need one?"

She rubbed her forehead. "Yes, I guess maybe I do. I was already in bad shape. When Emma enlisted, well, that finished the job. Do you really think my idea is a bad one?"

"No, not at all. I think escaping for a few months sounds heavenly. I just don't think it's going to give you what you really want."

"What do you think I really want?"

"That's the surprise. Give me a week."

She stood and walked to the French doors. "I will. I won't talk to anyone or do anything for a week. I know I'm adrift. I just don't know how to find my way back."

"I can help, and I will."

I walked her into the kitchen and leaned on the doorjamb while she put on her slicker. "One of my tag sale customers is a retired lieutenant commander, Cynthia Silberblatt. I asked if she had any advice for me to pass along to you about Emma enlisting."

Zoë wiggled her feet into her sandals. "She said I shouldn't worry, right?"

"No, she said Emma will have all the training she needs. There's nothing she'll face that she won't be prepared to handle."

She met my eyes for several seconds, the words resonating. "I'd hug you, but I'm still wet."

I lifted my arms and mimed hugging her. "Virtual hug!"

She mimicked my position. "Virtual hug!" She opened the back door, and the sound of the rain pummeling the roof grew louder. She looked over her shoulder. "Please thank Lieutenant Commander Silberblatt for me. It's comforting to hear from someone who knows, even if I don't think I'll ever stop worrying. I know she's grown up, but she's still my baby." She blew me a kiss. "Thank you, Josie."

Having a family, whether biological or created, doesn't guarantee stability any more than someone leaving the nest means you aren't loved. Zoë might sign on for that cruise ship someday. Ty and I might move to Washington, DC, for his job. In a matter of months, once the Gingerbread House's renovation was complete, Zoë and I would no longer be next-door neighbors. Things change. People move on. It's love that endures, if you're lucky.

After Zoë left, I went upstairs. Ty was reading something online.

"Am I interrupting?"

"Not a bit. I went downstairs a few minutes ago and saw you and Zoë holed up in the study. Is everything okay?"

"Well, it's complicated. I want to explain, but I need to think about it first."

"Okay."

"Are you done? Let's go sit outside and listen to the rain."

"I'm totally done. I had some back-and-forth with the team, and we're back on schedule, ready to start Monday. Disaster averted."

I took his hand. "No surprise to me."

Outside, we sat on Adirondack rockers under the overhang.

"You'd never know it now," Ty said, "but tomorrow's supposed to be beautiful."

"Let's do something fun."

"Like what?"

"Let's go for a hike." I told him about Nessie and Charlie's trek along the Appalachian Trail. "Let's walk the Ridge Trail at Fox Forest, then have lunch at the Hancock Inn."

"Lunch is good, but I like the Mud Pond Trail better."

"We did Mud Pond last time."

We decided to defer the decision until morning, opting instead to sit and hold hands and watch the rain batter the flagstones. It was as relaxing as a massage. I tried to put my amorphous worry about Maudie aside, but I couldn't, not completely, and before I went to bed I texted Wes asking if Maudie Wilson had attended the Rocky Point Women's Club gala.

I awakened Sunday around eight to the irresistible aroma of bacon and a text from Wes. Maudie had been MIA from the gala. A surge of panic jolted me upright. It was getting harder and harder to believe Maudie was okay, just out snorkeling somewhere, having fun.

It was still overcast when we left, but pale shards of light were cutting through the cloud cover, and by the time we arrived at Fox Forest, the clouds were feathery and blowing away.

We decided on Barred Owl Trail, a new walk for both of us. I spent most of the time thinking about Zoë, planning my strategy, rehearsing what I'd say to Ellis.

We climbed along a muddy path replete with sodden moss. After twenty minutes we rounded a bend on the trail and came to a flat hunk of granite, a natural seat, big enough for two. We got ourselves positioned to watch the waterfall a hundred feet away, sitting so our shoulders touched.

Water trickled through striated rocks on the facing cliff, landing with a steady, staccato beat in the water basin below. The sun angling through the water sparked flecks of gold on the cliff wall. Ten feet below the top ledge, a ragged oval opening provided a clear view into a valley I hadn't known existed. By tilting my head to the right, I saw a shimmering pool of water, a secret world mostly hidden from sight by the cliff. I was staring at this natural wonder, but I wasn't seeing it at all. I was remembering Maudie's windows, low to the ground and open to the world.

CHAPTER TWENTY

A t seven o'clock Monday morning, an hour after Ty left for Canada, I Googled Gerard Martin. His name sounded familiar, but I couldn't place him until I saw his photograph. I'd met him at a few Chamber of Commerce breakfasts. He was middle-aged and middle-sized, and, if I recalled right, rather quiet.

Martin's Travel Agency occupied a double-wide storefront in a strip mall next to Betty's Flooring, one of the largest retailers on the seacoast. I'd passed by Martin's dozens of times, maybe more, without noticing it, proving once again that you only notice those things that interest you, or that you need or want.

Everything in the agency was modern, from the recessed lighting to the open layout. The staff worked at convertible desks, the kind that raise or lower as the worker prefers. Of the dozen or so people visible from the front entrance, about half were standing at their desks. All wore headphones. A private office enclosed in glass had been partitioned at the rear. Semitransparent blinds provided a modicum of privacy. A shadowy shape, silhouetted through the blinds, was seated at a big desk. I pushed open the heavy entry door.

A young man in a summer-weight slim-fit suit came out from behind his standing desk to greet me.

"Hi. I'm Ivan. Welcome to Martin's."

"Hi, Ivan." I handed him a business card. "Would you tell Mr. Martin I'm here? I'd love to talk to him if he has a minute."

Ivan walked to the back, and a moment later, he stepped out, followed by Gerard Martin, who was smiling warmly. Ivan returned to his workstation, and Gerard waved me into his office.

When I reached him, he extended his hand for a shake. "Josie! What a nice surprise! Come in, come in!"

Inside, Gerard opened a palm toward an upholstered armchair next to the near corner of his desk and waited for me to sit before sitting himself.

"Thank you for seeing me without an appointment."

"I've been an admirer of yours for years. Congratulations on your TV show and your expansion."

"Thank you. I've seen you at some Chamber breakfasts, I think."

"That's right." He readjusted himself, settling into his chair, signaling he had all the time in the world. Gerard was an experienced salesman, glad to let me set the pace.

"You know Maudie Wilson."

He nodded, his expression shifting from eager-to-please to sad. "I've been following the news. Her niece—tragic."

"Nessie Wynn suggested I talk to you." He didn't speak, and I let the silence linger for a few seconds before continuing. "She thought you might know where Maudie is."

After another period of silence, Gerard said, "What's your interest?"

"My husband and I bought her house." Unexpected tears welled in my eyes, and I looked aside for a moment, blinking. "I've only met her recently, but I feel an unusual connection. We became friends in an instant."

"Yes, Maudie has that gift. She's a fine woman. I've known her for many years. As you may know, since most consumers prefer to book their own travel, a large part of my business is homestays and interest-based tours. I was sorry to see Maudie move into an assisted living facility. She hosted seven international students over three years, ever since Eli died."

"I had no idea." I smiled. "That's wonderful."

"I, too, consider her a friend, as much a friend as a client, so I'm sure you understand my hesitation to reveal anything she wouldn't want discussed."

"It might help find her."

"Maybe she doesn't want to be found."

"Have you spoken to the police?"

"My conversations with my clients aren't privileged like a lawyer's would be, but I consider them confidential and do my best to protect their privacy. If I spoke to the police, which I'm not acknowledging, I'd tell them the same thing I'm telling you."

"You're not going to let the cat out of the bag."

"I'm not even acknowledging there's a cat or a bag."

I nodded, understanding his reticence but racking my brain as to how I could overcome it. I leaned forward, pinning his eyes with my own. "I'm worried about her, Gerard."

He paused for an extra second before replying, but neither his eyes nor his words gave anything away. "With all respect, Josie, if she'd wanted you to know where she is, she would have told you."

"Would you check in with her? To make sure she's okay, to let her know about Celia?"

"I'll tell you what I told the police—if I know where Maudie is, which I'm not saying I do, it's not my place to check on her or deliver bad news."

I couldn't think of anything else to ask, so I thanked him and let him walk me out. He chatted about the beautiful weather after Saturday's torrential rain and the next Chamber meeting, saying he hoped he'd see me there.

The glorious weather didn't last long. The sunny warmth gave way to overcast skies and cooler temperatures. I was snuggling with Hank in my private office as I researched chartering yachts when I spotted a dragonfly hovering outside my window. No wonder Clara Driscoll chose dragonflies as a theme for Tiffany's lamps. No wonder they were so enduringly popular. It was more than their astonishing shimmering incandescence; it was their resilience, their capability, and their adaptability. They were magnificent creatures. Watching it, I had an idea for the church. Before I could develop it, Cara called.

Gretchen was downstairs, wondering if I had a minute. I said I did, and within seconds, I heard the click-clack of her stilettos as she crossed the warehouse floor.

My eyes widened as Gretchen sat on a guest chair across from me. "You've cut your hair," I said.

She patted the sides of her pixie-short hair. "What do you think?"

"Give me a minute." The super-short cut accentuated her cheekbones and eyes. "I think I love it. You look more sophisticated somehow. The truth is that you're so beautiful, you could wear a paper bag and it wouldn't matter. How much did you cut?"

"Twenty-three inches. I donated it to a nonprofit that makes wigs for kids."

"Oh, Gretchen, that's fantastic of you."

"I hope it helps. In any event, I'm sorry to barge in, but I have a request and I wanted to make it in person. I've been thinking about my workload. I don't think I'm as productive as I might be. I think I defer to small tasks as a palate cleanser, as it were. I have so many big things to do that it's nice to get down in the dirt sometimes. To help me become more productive, I need an assistant."

"You have too much on your plate."

"Not exactly. It's not that there's too much . . . it's that I'm feeling overly fragmented. An assistant will help me keep track of all the details."

"Do you have a proposed job description?"

She extracted a turquoise plastic sleeve from her tote bag, removed a sheet of paper, and slid it across the desk.

I read the bulleted list of duties carefully. "Budgeting. Project management. Scheduling. Supervising. Merchandising. This is high level."

"Yes."

"I'm not sure that it's reasonable to expect one person to have such disparate skills."

"I do."

I laughed. "True. But you're extraordinary." I placed the single sheet under a paperweight, a snow globe featuring a winter forest scene, then tapped the paper with my index finger. "I say go for it."

She smiled. "Thank you. I'll keep you posted."

She reached for her tote bag, preparing to leave.

The dragonfly flew away. I turned back to face her. "You know the Congregational church next door."

"Sure! I love Pastor Ted's garden! Jack and I bring Johnny each season. Johnny's only four, but Pastor Ted talks to him as if he's an adult. It's wonderful to see. Johnny just asked Jack why we haven't planted more varieties of lettuce."

I laughed again. "What was Jack's answer?"

"'Good idea—we'll do it next year.'"

"I didn't know you gardened."

"I don't. Jack does—because Pastor Ted created a gardening monster in Johnny. The little guy just loves it."

"That's really spectacular."

"It is, isn't it? Pastor Ted is exceptional."

"Speaking of which . . . there's a congregant named Winnie Thornton who works at the church part-time. I need to talk to her without Ted being any the wiser. Please find her for me so the three of us can have a private conversation."

Gretchen stood, her emerald eyes alight. "I'm on it."

Around eleven, I went downstairs to catch up with my staff.

Gretchen had left for Prescott's Antiques Barn.

Sasha was at her desk writing catalogue copy.

Eric was outside inspecting the asphalt in the parking lot for potholes or cracks.

Cara was adding the names we'd gathered at the tag sale into our database.

Fred was at the Hitchens University library, which housed an excellent art and artifact history collection, researching a brass umbrella stand adorned with pineapple fittings.

Another busy day at Prescott's.

Lainy had said that piggybacking wasn't allowed at Belle Vista. At the time, I'd assumed it was one of those rules that organizations implement at their lawyer's insistence to offer cover if something goes wrong, not an actual prohibition they enforced. Most people would agree that there's really no harm in letting someone follow you in if they live or work there or if they're a relative you've seen around. That kind of complacency can lead to disaster. You may not know that the resident's daughter you've seen for years is now persona non grata or that the employee got fired earlier in the day. Now, as I stood at the window staring into the dense forest across the road, I found myself wondering just how easy it would be to sneak into Belle Vista without anyone being the wiser.

CHAPTER TWENTY-ONE

I parked near the employee lot, in a corner spot where my car was hidden from casual observation by the laurel hedge, and took the path that led to the garden. Before passing through the gate in the white picket fence, I looked back toward Maudie's unit. The uniformed police officer was gone. The gate opened with a simple self-closing latch, and just like that, I was in the private garden. Anyone could walk in, day or night. I passed under a matching lattice, thickly twined with purple clematis.

Twenty feet down, I came to a fork. I followed the branch to the right, the tine closest to the facility. The path ended at a stately fountain, water dripping from a cement finial into a circular bowl. Wicker chairs and chaise longues ranged around the fountain.

Two older women sat to my left. One started laughing at something the other one said. I chose a chair on the right, near the back door, which bore the same sign I'd seen posted on other outside doors: THIS DOOR IS KEPT LOCKED AT ALL TIMES. PLEASE ENTER THROUGH THE FRONT.

A few minutes later, the door opened and an elderly man stepped onto the pavers, followed by a young woman.

They took a few steps toward the fountain.

"It's kind of cold, Gramps," she said. "Are you sure you want to sit outside?"

He glared at the gray sky. "You're right. I thought it would have warmed up already. Let's go to the café."

He used his key to open the door, and his granddaughter held it for him. After he passed through, she let it go, and I scooted out of my seat and caught it just before it closed. I held it ajar for a few seconds, letting them get ahead of me, then slipped inside and eased the door closed. I looked out the window built into the top of the door. The two women, partially hidden from view by the fountain, were still chatting and laughing. From what I could tell, they hadn't noticed me at all. I turned the corner in time to see the grandfather's leg slip into the elevator.

Another question answered: It was easy to piggyback into Belle Vista if you knew the lay of the land.

I climbed the nearest flight of stairs and exited through the side door by Maudie's unit, making my way to my car without seeing anyone. I drove into the guest lot and parked close to Francis Street, then followed the walkway that led to the main entrance. As I advanced closer to the door, I glanced up at the security camera.

Inside, Lainy was at her desk watching something on her iPad. The Rocky Point Community Theater's *Chicago* audition flyer lay next to her, partially covered by a pad of paper.

I pointed at it. "I love that show. Are you going to try out?"

"Oh!" she said, embarrassed. She turned her iPad over. "I don't know. Probably not."

"My lawyer, Max Bixby, was in their production of *Oklahoma!* a couple of years ago. They do such a professional job, you'd never guess it was a local theater company."

"There's a lot of talent in Rocky Point."

"Including you, I suspect."

She smiled. "Thanks. But I mean people who've been in a lot of shows over a lot of years." She lowered her eyes. "I've never even auditioned, except once in school."

"Did you get the part?"

Her eyes fired up. "Yes." The light dimmed. "I couldn't accept it, though. I had to work."

"Would you like me to contact Max for you? I bet he could give you some pointers."

"Oh, I wouldn't want to impose. Thanks anyway."

"I don't think it would be an imposition."

"I don't know. I guess I'll pass. I'm not ready."

"If you change your mind, give me a call." I took a business card from my case and handed it over. "Really."

She placed the card carefully into a zippered pocket in her handbag. She looked at me straight on, and when she spoke, her tone was solemn. "Thank you."

I smiled. "You're very welcome. Other than audition jitters, how are you holding up?"

"Okay, I guess. I'm sad. How about you?"

"The same." An older woman and an even older man sat in matching club chairs near the café talking in earnest whispers, neither paying any attention to us. I leaned in a little closer. "Has anyone come forward saying they saw Maudie leave the day Celia was killed?"

"No," she whispered. "And the police have spoken to everyone—residents, their relatives, staff, even outside vendors."

"Maudie mentioned that some of her neighbors sit at their windows to watch the world go by. If one of them saw something suspicious, surely they would have reported it."

Lainy laughed. "If Maudie was complaining about busybodies, she was referring to Selma, who lives in one of the units next to Maudie's. Maudie and Selma are like oil and water. Selma is on every committee and likes to keep track of everyone's comings and goings. Maudie keeps to herself and resents Selma trying to get her involved. It made Maudie feel like a little kid who needs to be coaxed out of her shyness. Maudie called her 'bossy boots.' Selma's not here, though. She's been on a long visit to her daughter in Lewiston, about an hour and a half from here, in Maine. She won't be back until tomorrow afternoon."

"What happens if a resident locks herself out of her unit?"

"It depends. In the independent living section, I call security to open the resident's door. Other wings have different protocols."

"Security . . . that's Harry."

"Or whoever's on duty. There's always someone here."

"Who else has a master key?"

"Mr. Hannigan, of course. And the nurse on duty."

"And you?"

"Well, sure, in case of an emergency."

"Where's it kept?"

Her eyes flew to the center drawer of her desk, then came back to mine. "I'm not allowed to say."

"Out of curiosity, have you checked to be certain the key is where it's supposed to be?"

"This morning. Detective Brownley asked the same thing. It's there."

"Could someone have used it and put it back?"

"I guess, but only if they know where it is."

"So you talked to Detective Brownley. She's good. Really solid."

"She kind of scared me, truth be told. She acted like I was keeping something back."

I smiled and leaned in close to whisper, "Were you?"

Lainy giggled. "Just about Katrina Marlow's grandson, Mitch. He's super cute. I finally fessed up."

The phone interrupted us. When she finished the call, I set my eyes twinkling and asked in a low voice what she told Detective Brownley about Mitch.

"Nothing juicy." She giggled again. "I wish. It's just that once when Mitch was visiting, a cleaner from Macon's—that's our service provider for the common areas. The housekeepers who take care of the individual rooms, they're employees. Anyway, the cleaner from Macon's suddenly popped out from the independent living wing. Naturally, I asked her how she got in, and she told me that one of the residents' relatives happened to be walking by the side door and let her in. From the description, I knew it was Mitch. I told Mitch that very day that he shouldn't do that, not ever. He promised he wouldn't, and that was that."

"When was this?"

"A few months ago. Around last Easter." Lainy lowered her voice another notch. "Detective Brownley asked me how Maudie got along with people. She asked about grudges and personalities and so on. I said there was nothing to tell. Maudie got along with everyone."

"Except Selma."

"That wasn't bad blood. That was just Selma being Selma and Maudie refusing to play along. No biggie."

"Did you mention it to Detective Brownley?"

"Yes. She asked for Selma's daughter's contact information, which I gave her." Lainy lowered her voice another notch. "She called then and there and spoke to both Selma and the daughter. The day Celia died, they were at the Ossipee Valley Fair in South Hiram, Maine. Selma didn't know anything that would help."

"No surprise, I guess. I noticed the police officer isn't stationed outside anymore. When did he leave?"

"A couple of hours ago. Stacy—you know, Maudie's niece—just called. She wanted to know if her aunt's apartment was still under police seal."

"Is it?"

"Yes, but I think they're winding up. I mean, it isn't just that cop who left. None of them have been here for a while now. Mr. Hannigan is raising Cain about the police seal still being on the door. The residents are terribly upset about the murder, and seeing the police tape upsets them even more."

"I understand. Does Stacy's question mean she plans on coming over?"

"I think so. She said she didn't want her aunt coming home to such a mess. She's going to ask Tom to clean everything once she gets the all clear."

Before I could share my surprise that Stacy would take it upon herself to organize the cleaning, the phone rang again. I wondered if I'd misjudged Stacy—maybe she wasn't as self-centered as I'd thought.

Lainy seemed to be settling in for a long call, and since I was out of questions, I mouthed "Thank you" and left.

CHAPTER TWENTY-TWO

I leaned against my car and scanned the neighboring houses and buildings.

Looking left, I spotted a red-light camera at the intersection of Francis and Bradmor Streets, then another at Delany's, an upscale pub half a block away. There was an additional one to the right, at Francis Street and Victory Boulevard. If the cameras had turned up anything, Wes would have known, and he would have reported it.

I tucked my phone and car key into my back pockets, tossed my tote bag into my trunk, and crossed the parking lot toward Victory. I turned right, away from Francis, and walked to the next intersection, Zelligan Street. I paused at the corner and did a slow survey. As far as I could tell, none of the old Victorian houses that lined the street were outfitted with security cameras.

Farther down the block, at another sprawling home, a girl of thirteen or fourteen was directing a younger boy to attach patriotic red, white, and blue bunting to the porch. She stood with her hands on her hips, assessing his work. A swinging chair hung from big hooks screwed into the porch ceiling. An American flag fluttered from an outrigger-style pole attached to one of the porch columns.

I extracted my phone from my pocket, brought up Wes's *Seacoast Star* article where he'd featured Maudie's Rocky Point Women's Club headshot, scrolled down until I came to it, and enlarged it so it filled the screen.

I crossed at the light and walked toward the house, reaching it in time to see the girl nod, setting her ash-blond ponytail swinging.

"That's good," she said to the boy.

"It looks great!" I said. They both turned, and I smiled. "I'm Josie Prescott, and I'm a complete sucker for bunting. Since it's after July fourth, I'm guessing there's a special reason you're putting it up."

The boy bounced from one foot to the other and back again as if he couldn't contain his excitement. "Our dad's coming home from Afghanistan! He's in the army."

"Oh, that's wonderful! When do you expect him?"

"About one," the girl said. "It was all last minute. Mom went to the airport to pick him up."

"I wanted to go, too, but Mom said we had to stay here and decorate."

"You're doing a terrific job." I held up my phone and showed the girl Maudie's photo. "I'm sorry to interrupt, but I have a question. Have you seen this woman?"

She barely glanced at the photo. "I don't know."

I smiled. "It's important." I held the phone closer. "Take another look. Please."

She looked at the display, then raised her eyes to my face. "Sorry."

"It might have been last week."

"Last week?" She glanced at the phone again. "I'm sorry . . . but really, who can remember this morning, let alone last week?"

"Try to think . . . It really is important."

She turned to the boy. "Did we do anything last Friday?"

"I dunno."

"You hung out with Bobby."

"You went to the beach with Nina."

"Right. In the morning. Then I came home and helped Mom put up strawberry jam." She nodded, smiling. "Then I sat on the porch, reading." She squinted at the image. "I remember! She waved, and I waved back."

I kept my voice calm. "What time was that?"

"After lunch. I don't know . . . maybe around two."

"That sounds right. Which way was she heading?"

"Up Victory." She pointed in the opposite direction from Belle Vista. "I don't know where."

The boy continued to bounce around, his impatience apparent. "We better get going, Tammy. We're only half done."

"Cory's right. I need to bake a pie. Dad loves my cherry pie."

I smiled. "Yum! Just one more thing—was she alone?"

"Uh-huh."

"Just walking along?"

"Yeah . . . wait! She was pulling a suitcase. Not a suitcase . . . I don't know what you'd call it . . . some kind of bag on wheels."

"Like one of those metal carts for groceries?"

"No, more like a briefcase. My mom is an insurance agent, and she has a wheeling briefcase. That woman's was larger than Mom's, though."

"A duffel bag?"

"No, Dad has one of those."

"A tote bag."

"Sort of, I guess. I don't know."

"Tammy!" Cory called.

"Sorry," Tammy said. "I've got to go."

I thanked her, said goodbye to them both, and walked back to my car. Once inside, I called Ellis. Cathy picked up.

"He's in a meeting, Josie. Can I take a message?"

I considered trying to explain what I'd learned to Cathy, and rejected the idea. "Tell him I need a minute of his time—it's urgent. I'll be there in ten minutes."

Ellis met me in the lobby and led me into his private office. We sat at the round guest table by the window. I told him about Tammy and how she'd seen a woman she thought might be Maudie walking by her house last Friday, the day Celia died and Maudie went missing, around two.

"What's Tammy's last name?"

"I didn't think to ask. The house is at 452 Victory."

He reached behind himself for his cell phone and tapped in a message.

"I understand that adults are allowed to leave their homes without permission," I said, "so you can't just demand Maudie's credit or debit card records or her phone log, willy-nilly. But at this point, days out, isn't this a special situation?"

"If she doesn't turn up soon, we'll try to make that case to a judge." He touched his phone. "In the meantime, I want to get going on this new lead. Thank you for the tip." He stood. "There's something else I want to talk to you about. Can you sit tight for a minute?"

I said I would.

I'd been in Ellis's office a bunch of times, and nothing ever changed. The furniture was standard issue, brown veneer meant to look like walnut. The desk was bare except for a phone, an old-fashioned calendar blotter, notebooks and pads of paper, and a Rocky Point Police Department mug filled with pens and pencils. From past visits, I knew his laptop was kept in a drawer under lock and key. In addition to the desk, there was the table I was sitting at, a bookshelf, mostly empty, and a large, locked storage unit. Two Norman Rockwell illustrations hung on the wall.

"Sorry for keeping you waiting," Ellis said as he opened the door. He sat across from me and leaned back, lacing his fingers behind his head. "I don't know what you've heard, but Doug Akins, Celia's husband, is here, helping us out."

"Again? Or still?"

"Again. I wanted to give him some time with his kids."

"He must be out of his mind."

"Pretty much. What's your impression of him?"

"I only saw him a couple of times, and under difficult circumstances."

"And your impression?"

"I thought Doug was devoted to Celia, and earnest. I thought he was worried about her."

"Worried about what?"

"Celia was totally stressed out, a taut wire about to snap."

"Have you had any responses to the stolen-object postings?"

"Not yet."

He adjusted position, resting his elbows on the table. "No matter where I look or who I talk to, the unifying element in Celia's death and Maudie's disappearance seems to be the presentation box and cat sculpture. I need your help."

"What do you want to know?"

"What were Maudie's plans for the objects? Were her nieces in line with her ideas?" He paused for a moment. "I'll tell you what I really want to know if you'll agree to keep it between us."

"Of course."

"I think there's a chance that Celia planned on steamrolling Maudie into selling the box and cat whether Maudie wanted to or not. Celia's been telling people, relative strangers included, that her aunt is getting forgetful.

Labeling a relative as senile might serve to cover a multitude of sins. It's also possible that Celia planned to steal the objects outright. The thing is, I can only ask Doug whether his wife was a crook so many ways. I ask. He says no. What do I ask next? It's not reasonable to expect a man to say anything bad about his wife, even if telling the truth might help catch her killer." Ellis flipped a palm. "If I'm off base, I'm wasting a lot of time barking up the wrong tree."

"If you expect Doug to help, you must think he's not the killer."

"Not necessarily."

"If Celia planned to steal the objects one way or the other, she'd need a partner," I said, "someone wise in the ways of antiques."

"Also not necessarily."

"I'm confused."

"She might have been prepared to sell the box for the jewels and be done with it. So will you help us out?"

"What do you want me to do?"

"Get Doug talking about Maudie and Stacy and the antiques."

"I'll try." I stood. "May I ask you something?"

He stared at me for a few seconds. "What?"

"Did you find my company's consignment forms in Maudie's apartment?"

"No. Why?"

"Were they in Celia's purse?"

"No."

"How about her key to Maudie's unit?"

"What's going on, Josie?"

"I'm not sure. I'm just trying to piece things together."

"The key was on her ring, and the ring was in the purse."

"Did you find Maudie's checkbook?"

"No."

"Maudie might have taken her checkbook with her," I said.

"That's what I think. She's old-school about payments. She writes checks for all her regular bills. From the receipts, which are neatly filed, she never pays anything online or uses her debit card."

"She has a credit card, though. She has to—she uses the Uber app."

"More than one. Why are you asking?"

"If Celia was up to no good, she would have had to forge Maudie's signature on the consignment forms. If they're missing, it's likely that whoever killed her stole them."

"Why?"

"To protect Celia's reputation."

"Do you really think a killer would care about her reputation?" he asked.

"Doug would. Or Stacy."

He smiled. "You think Stacy would care about Celia's reputation?"

I smiled back. "I think it's possible. I got the impression Stacy loved Celia . . . really, I did. More to the point, though, Stacy cares about her company's financing. If her sister were charged with grand larceny, bye-bye investors."

"That sounds right. Do you want to wait here or in the lobby?"

"The lobby, I guess." I stood. "Can I ask you something else, something unrelated to Celia or Maudie?"

He paused with his hand on the doorknob. "That's one of those questions."

"You know me."

"Exactly my point."

"You're not going to like it."

"I already don't like it. Go ahead."

"I have a question that is in the none-of-my-business category except that Zoë has kind of made it my business."

He dropped his hand. "Zoë?"

"I've tried to think of how to ease into this, but I can't, so I just have to ask you directly."

"Cut to the chase, Josie."

"You have to promise you'll tell me the truth."

"Not knowing what we're talking about, I can't."

"Promise me you'll tell me the truth or you will refuse to answer."

He walked back to the guest table and sat down, pointed to the chair I had just vacated, and said, "Sit."

I sat.

"Are you in trouble?" he asked.

"No."

"Is Zoë in trouble?"

"Yes, but not the way you mean, so no."

"Are we discussing a crime?"

"No."

"Enough of twenty questions," he said. "I promise to answer truthfully or decline to answer at all."

"Do you want to marry Zoë?"

"What?" Ellis jerked back so quickly his chair rattled against the desk, then righted itself.

"You heard me."

"Why are you asking?"

"Answer me and I'll tell you."

"Yes. I'd love to marry Zoë. I adore her. The timing hasn't been right."

"That's what I suspected. You're wrong, though. The timing is perfect." I smiled. "I have a plan."

Back in the lobby, sitting on the hard wooden bench, I called Cara and got the word that nothing required my immediate attention. I sat there enjoying a moment of private pleasure, recalling Ellis's reaction to the one-minute version of my plan. After a minute, I got up and walked to the front window, saw nothing that interested me, and sat down again. I drummed my fingers on the wood, trying to channel my impatience into productive thinking, without luck, when the front door opened and Julie stepped in.

She looked tired, not a surprise, given her schedule, two jobs and school. She half-smiled at me as she walked to the counter. She gave her name to Cathy. I overheard Cathy tell her to have a seat, that she'd let Chief Hunter know she was there.

Julie perched on the edge of the bench across from me. I said hello, and she nodded but didn't smile.

"You, too?" she asked, her tone somewhere between serious and sarcastic.

"What are you here for?" I asked, adapting a technique I'd learned from Wes. If you don't want to answer a question, ask one instead.

"They want to go over my last conversation with Maudie, you know, when we went to lunch. I don't know what they think I'll remember." Her shoulders lifted an inch, then dropped. "Or maybe they just want to know more about orange marmalade."

"Orange marmalade?"

"It's just an example of the nothing things we talked about. I was with Maudie a few weeks ago when she took my recommendation and bought a new orange marmalade, the store brand, and during lunch, she told me that she liked it. She laughed at herself for paying extra for a fancy brand all these years."

"There's a lesson there."

"Be poor?"

I laughed. "No. Don't be a snob."

"Only rich people worry about things like that."

"Do you think so? I think everybody, or almost everybody, has a little bit of keep-up-with-the-Joneses in them. Regardless, it doesn't matter, that's for sure. What else did you talk about?"

Julie bit her lip for a moment, thinking, replaying the event. "She said you got her thinking about those shelves, for the trunk, that it showed how knowledgeable you are—you hadn't studied the trunk, you simply knew it came with shelves. She mentioned that she was going to reread all of Eli's love letters but couldn't bring herself to do it yet." She sighed. "We talked the whole time, but not about anything special." She shrugged again. "We ate lunch, then I walked her back. I picked up my tote bag, which I'd left in her unit, and left."

"It sounds like a fun lunch."

"Always. Maudie's wonderful to me."

"How did the children's injections go?"

She smiled, an unexpected easing of tension. She looked younger and less careworn. "I got an A, so Tom and I are going to celebrate. We're going out for Chinese. I know that doesn't sound like much, but it's a real treat for us."

"That's great, Julie."

Ellis walked into the lobby from the hallway on the left.

He nodded at me but spoke to Julie. "Thanks for coming in, Ms. Simond. We'll be with you shortly." He turned to face me. "Ready?"

I stood, realizing that I wasn't ready at all. I hoped I'd find my way and told Julie I'd see her later.

I agreed with Ellis that Doug knew something. He had to because Celia had, and if she did, he did. If I could ask the right questions, worded in the right way, and in the right sequence, maybe I could ferret it out.

CHAPTER TWENTY-THREE

s Ellis and I approached the interview room where Doug was waiting, I checked my phone. It was nearly one, later than I thought.

"I'm hungry," I said. "Can you bring in some food? For me and Doug."

"We asked Doug already, and he said he didn't want anything."

"Let me ask him again."

We stopped in front of Interview Room Two. Doug sat at the far end of the long rectangular table with his back to a pair of windows and a human-sized cage, reserved for what the police called "unruly guests." The windows, which faced the rear parking lot, were covered by off-white curtains. Detective Brownley sat at the head of the table, close to the entry door. One of the uniformed officers who'd come to Belle Vista, Officer Meade, sat with her back to the wall, a pad of lined paper on her lap. A blue plastic tray holding a box of tissues, a pitcher of water, and a stack of paper cups sat next to the detective's right hand. Red pricks of light on the three video cameras mounted high on the walls indicated they were recording. As I entered, the only sound I heard was the soft, steady hum of the central air-conditioning.

Doug slumped in his chair, his eyes fixed on a deep scratch in the wooden table. He didn't look up when I came in, not even when I sat next to him.

Ellis stood by the door. "Doug?" Doug raised his eyes to Ellis's face. "You know Josie Prescott."

He swiveled to look at me, but there wasn't even a flicker of recognition. His skin was blue-white, as if he'd lost blood or was half-frozen.

I nodded at him. "I'm so sorry, Doug."

He kept his eyes on my face, but he didn't reply.

"As you know," Ellis said, "Josie is an antiques expert. I asked her to talk to you a bit about that box and cat."

Doug turned back to face him. "I've already told you everything I know."

"And I appreciate it. Josie's asked for lunch. What do you want, Josie?"

"I don't know . . . a grilled chicken Caesar, I guess. What about you, Doug? Do you like salads?"

"I'm not hungry."

"Do you prefer sandwiches?"

"I don't care."

"Let's get a large chicken Caesar salad and a large turkey sub. Doug and I can share. You like turkey, don't you, Doug?"

"I told you . . . I'm not hungry."

"How about something to drink?" I asked.

"I guess a cup of coffee would be all right. Regular."

I turned to Ellis. "I'll take an iced tea, please. Sweet, if they have it."

"It shouldn't take too long," Ellis said. "Detective Brownley and I are going to step out and organize the food. Officer Meade will stay here in case you need anything. Doug, I want to thank you again for your cooperation."

As soon as the door closed behind them, Doug asked, "Have you been deputized?"

"Not at all. It's just what he said—I'm here as an antiques expert."

"But this isn't a casual chat. There's a police officer in the room and video cameras whirring away."

"True. We're all just so concerned, Doug."

He covered his face with his hands for a moment, then took in a deep breath. "I don't know what I'm going to do without Celia. She was the best mother. The best wife."

"You don't need to decide anything just yet."

"Sure I do," he snapped, anger flaring. "I have three kids and no job. That sounds pretty darn urgent to me." The anger seeped from his eyes and voice, replaced by sadness. "I have no family. My folks died when I was a kid. I was raised in foster care."

"I'm so sorry."

"I'm keeping the kids home from school for a few days."

"Where are they now?"

"Our next-door neighbor is taking care of them. Celia would never let Stacy watch them. Stacy gets distracted, and they're too young."

"How did your interview at Jestran's go?"

He leaned back. "I guess good, but who knows."

"There's plenty of help available, Doug, until you get back on your feet."

I reached for the water pitcher and a cup. I poured one for him, then one for myself. He drank some. I took a sip, then pushed it aside. It was lukewarm.

"I'm worried about Maudie," I said.

"The police are, too, but I'm sure she's fine. She likes to be up and doing."

"Would she go away without telling anyone?"

"She's done it before. Lots of times."

I nodded. "And she might not be checking her messages."

"Almost guaranteed."

"She pays attention to the news, though."

"Has Celia's murder made the news anywhere but here?"

"You make a fair point," I said. "Who are Maudie's best friends?"

"I don't know. When we see her, it's all family stuff."

"She's never mentioned a name?"

His shoulders lifted, then sank. "Not to me."

"How often did Celia see her?"

"It varied. If Maudie needed something, like when she was packing to move, fairly often. Otherwise, a couple of times a month, maybe less frequently."

At a soft knock, Officer Meade opened the door and spoke to someone outside. A few seconds later, she slid a white paper bag onto the table. "We got extra," she said. "Just in case." She extracted two deli-packed salads and two white-paper-wrapped subs, laying them near me, along with a large coffee cup encased in a cardboard heat-protector, a bottle of lemon iced tea, and a cup of ice.

"So quick," I said. I divvied up the food and started in on one of the salads. "I know Maudie wasn't particularly fond of the presentation box and cat. Did you like them?"

"I appreciated the history and the sentiment, but I thought the box was ostentatious, flashy. And the cat was just ugly."

"Did Celia and Stacy agree?"

Doug forked some salad and ate it, then did it again. I wasn't sure he knew he was eating.

"Not really," he said between bites. "Neither one of them appreciated the history or the sentiment."

"You know that nothing Celia did can be held against her now."

Doug tilted his head to the side, his eyes boring into mine as if he were trying to see inside me.

"You were very open with me, Doug, about your financial challenges, being out of work and all. Anyone determined to protect her family would think nothing of selling the box—all those jewels! No one would blame her."

"You're assuming the jewels were real."

"Not at all. I'm assuming anyone trying to save their family would think it worth finding out if they were real."

"You're saying Celia stole it."

"I'm wondering about that, yes. If I were in her position, I'd sure as shootin' have been tempted. It wasn't like she was taking food out of someone else's mouth."

He took the last forkful of salad and pushed his plate aside. I unwrapped one of the sandwiches and moved it closer to him.

"No more for me, but thanks." He glanced at the empty salad container. "I guess I was hungry after all." He drained his cup, too.

I turned to Officer Meade and asked, "Any chance Doug could get a refill on the coffee?"

She said, "Of course," and texted someone.

I moved the leftover food aside. "No one seemed to like either the box or the cat. You're the first person I've talked to who even appreciated its history."

Doug lowered his gaze to his long, bony fingers resting on the table. "Celia thought it was petty and mean for Maudie to insist on keeping it."

"That Maudie was selfish."

He nodded. "I didn't. Maudie's helped us a lot over the years."

"What was Celia's plan?"

He didn't reply.

"To sign Maudie's name on the consignment documents?" I prompted.

His shoulders rounded, and he seemed to sink farther into his chair. He nodded.

I drank some iced tea, trying to place myself in Celia's shoes. "Celia thought that when Maudie found out, she'd keep quiet. After all, Maudie didn't care about those objects, but she did care about her nieces. This would show Maudie how desperate things really were."

"Celia was certain that Maudie would see that it was best for everyone."

"So she printed our consignment forms at home," I prompted.

"She couldn't use the e-sign option because an email would go to Maudie automatically," he said. "Maudie doesn't use email often, but she checks periodically."

"What bank account did Celia plan to specify for the direct deposit once the sale was completed?"

"None. She planned to ask for a check." Doug raised his eyes to my face. His lower lip quivered, and he clamped his upper teeth onto it, holding the position for several seconds until he regained control. "I didn't try to stop her because, well, I couldn't see any harm in it, and we . . . you know . . . fortune favors the bold."

"What did Stacy think?"

"She didn't know anything about it. If she had, the only thing she would have cared about was that she got her cut. The only thing Stacy cares about is Stacy."

"So Celia printed out the consignment documents, signed Maudie's name, and drove to Belle Vista. She knew Maudie's signature well, and I didn't know it at all, so that was low risk, but what made Celia think Maudie wouldn't be there?"

"Celia called Maudie at twenty after one," he said, "just after she spoke to you and Tom, asking if she could come talk to her." He shut his eyes. "She called from a burner phone she bought last week in Rye." He opened his eyes. "Maudie told her no, that she wouldn't be around. I saw Celia smile. Celia had all sorts of plans up her sleeve to get Maudie out of the way, from sending her to get a manicure or a massage, to pretending one of the kids was sick and Celia had to take him to the doctor so she needed Maudie to babysit for the others. With Maudie off somewhere, she wouldn't need to finagle any of it."

"Where did Maudie say she was going?"

"Celia was so relieved, it didn't even occur to her to ask. All Maudie said was 'Let's catch up in a few days.'"

"What do you think happened to the consignment forms?" I asked.

"I hadn't thought . . . Someone must have . . . ? I don't understand. Why would someone take them?"

"I don't know."

He leaned back, raised his chin to the ceiling, and scrunched his eyes closed. "I can't believe this is happening. I just can't."

His confusion and despondency were hard to witness.

"I'd feel the same, Doug. I'm so sorry."

He opened his eyes and resumed his study of the table. "We had to do it. We were out of options."

I aimed for a rational tone, as if planning to steal your aunt's treasures were a normal, reasonable activity. "But doesn't Maudie have plenty of money already? Why didn't you just ask her for help, or a loan, or whatever?"

"We did. Celia asked a year ago, and Maudie said no, she'd given us money when Eli died and again when Stacy started her business, to keep things even, and that was it, she was done. It's true she gave us money . . . she's always been generous . . . but that didn't help us now. I went to her alone when I got laid off. Maudie said her decision was final. She encouraged me to look at the situation we were in now as an opportunity, not a problem, said that someday we'd look back on this struggle and laugh. She told me that the only way to build self-esteem is through accomplishment, that only by standing on my own two feet would I regain my pride."

"You must have been devastated."

"Mostly I was ashamed. Ashamed I had to ask and ashamed I muffed it. She acted like she was doing us a favor by saying no, like she thought I was lazy, and this would spur me to action. I'm not lazy. I've worked like a dog for everything I've ever had."

I recalled Doug's humility, his apology for Celia's grumpiness, and I wondered if it had been all part of an act—no one would think that a man who blames himself for his family's dire straits would kill his wife.

While I was ruminating, Ellis walked in carrying a fresh cup of coffee. He placed it in front of Doug.

"Thanks, Josie," Ellis said. "I'll ask you to step out. I need to talk to Doug for a while."

I pushed my chair back. "Doug . . ." I waited for him to meet my eyes. "I'm so very sorry for your loss."

As I walked to my car, I rubbed my upper arms, trying to warm myself up. I was chilled to my core, as much from the difficult conversation I'd just had with Doug as from the cool air blowing in from the west.

Halfway back to my office, my phone vibrated, and I pulled onto the shoulder to take the call. It was Wes. He said he had an info-bomb and we needed to meet immediately.

"Tell me on the phone."

"No can do. This is big, Josie, to-the-moon big. It's going to be my lead on the late edition, but I'm willing to let you in on it early in return for the inside scoop on your conversation with Doug."

"What makes you think I talked to Doug?"

"I have ears and eyes everywhere. I thought you knew that. Meet me at our dune in fifteen, okay?"

"Even if I spoke to Doug, I couldn't tell you anything about our conversation."

"Sure you could."

"No, I really couldn't, Wes. I look forward to reading your late edition. I'm hanging up now."

"Wait! I have news about Doug's interview at Jestran's, too. Let me ask you some questions. If nothing else, you can confirm what I already know. I won't quote you."

I agreed, as Wes had known I would, and drove straight to the beach.

I struggled up the still-wet sand. The sun was trying to break through the clouds, a losing battle. The wind riffled the water, but the ocean itself was calm.

I had a niggling feeling that I had overlooked something significant, that a comment I'd taken at face value had deeper implications than its surface meaning, and I'd missed it. I stared at the waves rolling to shore, replaying my conversations of the last few days, but nothing leapt out at me. The more I tried to recall the memory, the fuzzier it grew.

Wes arrived a minute later, and the memory slipped away, its tendrils evaporating like ether.

CHAPTER TWENTY-FOUR

T alk to me," Wes said as he scrambled up the dune. "What did Doug say about the murder?"

"I haven't acknowledged that I spoke to Doug."

"I know you were with him at the police station. Don't try to snooker me."

"I'm not trying to snooker you. I told you I couldn't tell you anything, and I meant it."

"I won't quote you."

I turned to face the ocean. Far out to sea, a big tanker was steaming north. "What's your info-bomb?"

Wes sighed, his disappointment evident.

I knew he was waiting for me to turn, to meet his eyes. I also knew I could outwait him. He wanted to share his news, whatever it was, more than I wanted to hear it. He'd insisted we meet in person not so he could try to wheedle something out of me, although he certainly hoped he could; rather, he was expecting a megareaction and wanted to enjoy it.

"All right . . . I'll tell you, but you're gonna owe me, Joz. You're gonna owe me big-time. When Celia was killed, Stacy wasn't in Boston like she said." He leaned in close, his voice vibrating with energy. "She was in New Hampshire."

Stunned, I spun to face Wes. "What?"

"Yup." He grinned, pleased at my astonishment. "The police confirmed that Stacy's investor meeting ended at ten thirty."

"So? Maybe she went shopping or something."

"They have evidence she hotfooted it to New Hampshire. Here's how the police are figuring it: Consider motive . . . as far as the cops know, there's no one who benefits from Celia's death. She didn't even have life insurance. Killing her was either an accident, during a struggle to claim the presentation box and cat, for instance, or necessary to remove the threat of exposure, like if she walked in on the thief. So that takes care of motive, and means is evident—the rolling pin was in plain sight. Which leaves opportunity, so the police are checking everyone's alibis. And Stacy was definitely here in New Hampshire. Want to guess how they proved it?"

"She had a rental car equipped with E-ZPass and they traced it. They have a photo showing her passing through the toll booth, entering New Hampshire."

Wes's eyes shone with excitement. "Her E-ZPass wasn't used."

"She paid at the cash lane."

"Nope. She wasn't photographed at the toll booth."

I thought through the options. "She drove up Route One. It's the only other option."

"Bingo! There are two security cameras close to the border, one a red-light camera, the other attached to a bank's roof facing the entrance to their parking lot, which takes in a chunk of Route One. The police used facial recognition software, and boom! They got her! She passed by both cameras just before noon."

I looked out over the ocean again, puzzled by Wes's revelation. "This doesn't make sense."

"Why not?"

"If she had nefarious intentions, she would have disguised herself and taken the bus. In today's world, surely she would have assumed she'd be caught by a camera at some point along the way and acted accordingly. Therefore, she had another reason for lying. Maybe she had an appointment she wanted to keep private."

"You're skipping the obvious: She's a New Yorker—she doesn't drive much. She doesn't even own a car. I bet things like red-light cameras didn't even occur to her."

Wes made a valid point. When I lived in New York City, I didn't own a car either, and I didn't pay any attention to motor vehicle laws or policies. "What does she say about it?"

Wes grinned again. "She says it's none of anyone's business how she spends her time."

"Have they tried to place her in Rocky Point after noon?"

"Yeah, but no luck so far. The police are still checking security cameras all around town."

"So she didn't enter through the front door at Belle Vista—that's the only place they have a camera."

"Right. But she still could have gotten in."

"I know. Just for the heck of it, I tested it myself. It was easy."

Wes asked for details, which I provided once he accepted my terms—that he attribute the story to a source who insisted on anonymity, which would, I suspected, lead most people to assume that Wes got the information from someone on the Belle Vista staff.

"Hot bananas!" he said when I finished.

"Did Doug get the job at Jestran's?"

"You first. You've gotta give me something."

"I just did."

"I need more. Did Doug confess?"

"No."

"Is he going to? They're leaning on him hard."

Doug had described his lonely childhood, contrasting it to the stability, love, and contentment he'd found with Celia. What would it feel like to see the dream life you've constructed for yourself through sweat and devotion slowly, inexorably slipping away through merciless, seemingly insurmountable financial difficulties? Some men would dig deep and rise to the occasion. Others might go feral.

Wes was waiting for my assessment. "So . . . will he confess?"

Since lots of people knew I'd talked with Doug, I decided to acknowledge the meeting and share my impressions. "I doubt it. His focus was on his kids, his responsibilities. His grief."

He pinned me with his eyes. "Josie, you were with him for a long time. What did the chief ask you to do?"

"Talk to him about antiques."

"And?"

"Doug respects the history behind the objects."

"You mean about that missing box and cat."

"That's right. He said he has no idea where they are, and I believed him."

"You're not being very helpful here, Josie."

"I warned you. What about Jestran's?"

"Why do you care?"

"What kind of question is that, Wes?"

"Whatever. Do you think Doug was the mastermind? Is that it?"

"I think that until we have answers, we need to track everyone and everything, seeking out inconsistencies or anomalies. Did Doug get the job?"

"Yup. They're a little nervous, though, because the position comes in at ten percent less than he was making before, and that's a surefire recipe for see-you-later-alligator. You know how it goes . . . Some people see that as an insult and begin their next job hunt before they even start."

"Not Doug. I bet he said that was fine, that he just wanted to work."

"That's nearly word for word. How'd you know?"

"Because I have a fair sense of Doug's character. He needed the job, so he didn't allow his pride to get in the way."

"That's all well and good, but how does he expect to make ends meet? He couldn't do it before, and now he'll be bringing in even less and have childcare expenses to boot."

"He'll take a second job. He'll ask Maudie for help, and this time he'll approach her with a plan, not merely a request. He'll ask community or church groups for help. He might qualify for certain government aid. He'll find his way."

"You make it sound doable. What else you got?"

"Nothing."

"Can't you give even a little color? How did Doug look?"

"Exhausted."

"Good, good. What else?"

"That's it. You know I tell you what I can when I can."

"See you do," he said sternly. "Catch ya later!"

Wes slid-walked down the dune, and within seconds, he'd fired up his car and driven away. I stood a while longer, watching the sun trying to pierce the clouds, thinking.

My initial shock on hearing about Stacy's lie had passed, leaving me more stunned than surprised. I suspected Stacy embraced situational ethics as her philosophy of choice, maybe even veering into what might be called flexible ethics, where she'd consider it wrong to lie, unless it was necessary. Which begged the question: Why would Stacy lie about when she got back to New Hampshire? Sometimes the obvious answer is the truth—it was certainly possible that Stacy had killed her sister unintentionally, in a panic-heightened rage, or on purpose, to hide another crime, like the theft of her aunt's treasures. While sororicide was rare, it wasn't unheard of.

I couldn't stop watching the ebb and flow of the water. The waves were mesmerizing.

If Stacy had flipped out after her Boston-based investor abandoned the deal, she might lie to hide what she would certainly consider a weakness, thinking that her emotional fragility was no one's business but her own. She might also be concerned that if the word got out, other investors would think twice about partnering with a woman on the verge of ruin.

I wasn't a mind reader, and there was no question I could think to ask that would force Stacy to reveal her true reactions to the loss of three investors, two of them in the past week. When I'd seen her at the police station, she'd been visibly upset, and she'd made no secret of her frustration.

My phone vibrated, startling me. I didn't recognize the number, although it was from a local area code.

It was Lainy. "If you still think your lawyer friend wouldn't mind talking to me about auditioning, I'd love to take you up on the offer."

"I suspect Max will be more than happy to chat with someone who shares his love of theater. I'll contact him today and let you know what he says."

"I appreciate it." She lowered her voice. "Did you hear Wes Smith's announcement just now? About Stacy lying to the police?"

"I did. I wasn't expecting that at all."

"What do you think it means?"

"I don't know. It could mean something, or it could be nothing."

"But she lied to the police! How could that be nothing?"

"Not all lies are equal. You fibbed about Mitch, remember? Maybe what Wes calls a lie is something like that—an innocent fib."

"Because she was embarrassed, like me?"

"It's possible. Or to protect someone else."

"You're right. I shouldn't judge, and I shouldn't jump to conclusions. I deal with that all the time at home, and I hate it."

"No one likes to be judged."

"If no one likes it, why does everyone do it? In any event, she just called to confirm the police seal had been removed. She wants to get the unit cleaned so Maudie won't come home and see all the bloodstains and police guck and grime. Ick. I mean, that's really nice, but yuck. It's so awful to think about." A ring chimed in the background. "Oh! There's the phone. I've got to go . . . sorry. Thanks again for introducing me to Max."

And she was gone.

I still found it hard to imagine Stacy undertaking cleaning her aunt's apartment without one heck of an ulterior motive. The Stacy I knew was far more narcissistic than altruistic. Her warmth was professional, not personal, and could be turned on or off, as needed. I wished I could see Stacy simply as a loving niece, but I couldn't. The truth was that I wouldn't be the least bit surprised to learn that she didn't think the presentation box had been stolen after all, and that she planned to search for it. Sure, since Maudie had signed an authorization form, Stacy could enter her apartment anytime, but that would call attention to herself. If she wanted a cover story, overseeing the cleaning was a beaut, and if I was right, she'd arrive before Tom.

Oh, Maudie, I thought as a fresh wave of fear washed over me. *Where are you?*

While I was on the phone with Lainy, Gretchen had texted me to ask if I had time to meet Winnie, the dragonfly savior, at four, in half an hour. I replied that I did, and she suggested the Rocky Point Diner. I said that was fine, knowing Julie wasn't scheduled there today. I was excited to meet Winnie and go over my plan. I knew Gretchen could make it happen. If anyone could handle a cloak-and-dagger operation of goodwill, she could.

I shivered. Standing on the top of the dune, buffeted by the sharp wind, I'd gotten chilled. I was glad to get back inside my car. Since I had the time, I decided to take the scenic route to the diner. Circling Old Mill Pond, I was able to catch glimpses of slate-blue still water.

My phone vibrated again. This time, it was Tom. I pulled onto the shoulder next to a grassy slope that ran into the pond.

"Sorry to bother you, Josie, but I wanted to clear a schedule change with you. I hope it's okay. I'm at your place setting up the rest of the raised beds and planned on moving the irises tomorrow. Here's the thing: Stacy called. The police say she can access Maudie's apartment, and she wants me to clean it tomorrow at eleven. So I thought I'd call and ask you if it's all right if I reschedule the move."

"We'll need to check with Monte to see if it fits his schedule. If there's no problem on his end, it's fine with me."

"He's here now, so if it's all right with you, I'll ask him."

"That's fine. Text me what he says."

"Will do. Thanks, Josie."

I got out of my car, tucking my phone in my back pocket, and stood on the grass watching a sord of mallards paddle around a clump of yellow pond lilies.

As I watched the ducks splash around, Tom's text arrived. Monte said it was okay by him, that he had nothing planned for the next few days that would put the irises at risk. I kind of loved it that we were working this hard to protect some flowers. Would that the rest of life were that simple.

I was ten minutes late because Travis Drive was closed for construction, and the only way to access the diner was via the interstate.

I slid into the booth next to Gretchen and apologized to them both.

"No worries," Winnie said. She smiled, exuding graciousness and kindness. "You got caught in the construction."

"I had no idea."

"There was a water main break last Thursday."

"Isn't that supposed to be an easy fix?" I asked. "A few hours, and boom, you have a new pipe."

"I think you're right for a typical break, but from what I hear, this time the old pipes were rusty, and the rust got in the water that feeds Travis Elementary, so they had to close the whole street down. The last estimate I saw was a week." She smiled. "But then we'll have new pipes and the kids will be safe."

"You walk on the sunny side of the street."

She laughed. "I guess I do."

Winnie must have been a knockout when she was young, because she was a knockout now, and I pegged her at over seventy. Her silvery-gray hair was parted in the center and hung to her shoulders in elegant waves. Her eyes were hazel. She wore a short-sleeved cherry-patterned sundress, circa 1960. We placed our order, coffee for me, peppermint tea for Gretchen, and a chocolate milkshake for Winnie.

"I wouldn't have pegged you as a milkshake girl," I said.

"When you reach a certain age, you realize it's time to eat and drink what you want. I love chocolate milkshakes."

We compared favorite foods and drinks until the waitress delivered our order. Then I told them my idea to protect the dragonflies that seemed to love the church next door to Prescott's.

Winnie was enthusiastic, and I left them to discuss the ways and means.

Outside, I texted Max to ask him to help Lainy with her audition. While I waited for a reply, I tried to recapture the elusive memory that had teased me, intimating that I'd missed a detail or misunderstood the meaning of a known fact.

I had been at lunch with Timothy when Celia called to tell me that Maudie had decided to sell the objects. That was Friday, at fourteen minutes after one. Cara emailed her the consignment forms. Celia wanted the forms sent to her own email address so she could review them in advance. She'd told me she'd print them out, that Maudie didn't trust electronic signing systems, that she wanted to touch the paper to confirm it was real. That rang true to me. Since Maudie wanted to look people in the eyes before she agreed to do business with them, it made sense that she'd want to hold papers in her hands before she signed them. A pen had lain on Maudie's counter next to Celia's purse, yet the forms were missing.

I'd assumed that the killer—whoever it was—had taken the box and cat with them when they escaped, and maybe they had. Surely they would be smart enough to lie low, to wait before selling either piece. If the thief had merely pried a jewel or two loose and tried to sell them on their own, a jeweler might be alarmed when large unset superior-quality gems appeared at his door, or he might not. The jeweler might have seen our flyer alerting him to the possibility, or he might not. He might care, or he might not. It wasn't a coincidence that lots of people involved in illegal transactions used loose jewels as their currency of choice.

The box and cat were missing, maybe stolen, maybe hidden somewhere we hadn't thought to look. Maudie was missing, too. The pieces of the puzzle didn't align, which meant some were missing as well.

My phone vibrated. It was Max. *Super*, he wrote. *Have Lainy text me.*

The feeling that I was misinterpreting something important was with me still. In fact, the sensation had grown from a minor irritation to a full-blown annoyance. It was hobbling me, like a pebble in my shoe.

CHAPTER TWENTY-FIVE

I t was just after six when I pulled into the driveway of my rental house and parked. Zoë was on the porch, sitting on a bench staring at nothing. The clouds had finally blown out to sea, and the sky was bright and streaked with red, sailor's delight. Tomorrow would be a stunner.

"Hey," I said as I climbed the steps.

She turned her head. "Hey."

"Aren't you cold?"

"A little, but I like the fresh air."

"Let me drop stuff inside and grab a sweater."

I brought out an afghan for Zoë, then went back inside to retrieve a tray containing a bowl of pistachio nuts, some napkins, two plastic martini glasses, and a plastic pitcher filled halfway with watermelon martinis.

I raised my glass for a clink. "To us."

"To us." Zoë sipped. "I spoke to Mark."

"Your ex-husband? In Oregon?"

"I thought I'd be delivering the news about Emma, but she called him herself last week. She called her no-good loser of a father, and she didn't even tell me."

"She probably thought you wouldn't approve."

"She would have been right."

I could have pointed out that Emma was an adult and didn't need permission to talk to her father, but that wasn't the issue. Instead, I read between the lines. "You hoped he'd talk her into reconsidering enlisting."

"He said he was proud of her. Proud."

I felt myself skittering across a superthin, slippery sheet of ice. I was proud of Emma, too, but I couldn't say so, not now.

"If anything happens to her, I'll kill myself, Josie. I will."

"Zoë."

"I'd wade into the ocean, just about this time of day, and swim out."

"Are you suggesting that Emma shouldn't enlist because you're not strong enough to handle it?"

She turned and stared at me.

I touched her hand. "You promised to give me a week."

She lowered her eyes to her hands.

"Adapting to change is a process, Zoë, you know that. You're reconciled to Emma's choice one day. The next, you panic. Up and down. Eventually, the needle on what's normal will shift, and Emma being a marine will have become the new normal. You'll adjust."

"I don't know why you think so."

"Because you're you. You feel things passionately, and you express yourself freely. Ultimately, though, you're ruled by your head, not your heart."

Zoë took my hand and squeezed. "Thank you, Josie."

"You're welcome."

"You're saying I don't have any choice but to get a grip."

"There's an alternative. You could stay in a state of perpetual melt-down."

She laughed. "It may come to that." She sipped some martini. "Has anyone heard from Maudie?"

"No. Her best friend thinks she's snorkeling."

"But you don't."

"No, I don't. Between you and me and the porch railing, I'm scared to my bones."

"And there's nothing you can do."

"You know me, so you know how much I hate that."

"Me, too." Zoë leaned back against the siding and shut her eyes. "When Emma is deployed, I won't know where she is. There's nothing worse than not knowing. I'm still thinking about taking that job."

"You gave me a week."

"Have you made any progress?"

"Yes."

She sat up and opened her eyes. "You have?"

I patted her forearm. "Trust me."

Ty and I went to dinner at the Lobster Pot, our favorite summer seafood joint. The clams steamed in white wine and garlic were briny and rich. The lobster stuffed with crabmeat was sweet and tender. Ty was more cheerful than he'd been in days. His meetings were going well, he said, with everyone now seeming to be on the same page. They had a plan. He was going to drive up in the morning for a couple more days to ensure the plan would be implemented the way he envisioned.

Ty crashed as soon as we got home. He planned on hitting the road by five.

I stayed downstairs, continuing my research on behalf of Zoë and typing up notes for Ellis. My plan for her had two prongs. I'd signed up Ellis for one of them, providing source names and timing suggestions. I made my recommendation: *Perfect Knot*, a 50-foot fiberglass sloop, that the owner, Captain Ken, told me was a truly exceptional sailing yacht. Captain Ken was a justice of the peace, and as such, he was authorized to perform marriage ceremonies by the state of New Hampshire. I'd booked it for the week of August fifteenth. My idea had us sailing far enough out so all we saw was open water; then, after the ceremony and the party, the guests would disembark, and off Ellis and Zoë would go to Bimini and points south. That gave them three weeks back home before Emma's deployment.

I had more research to do regarding my other plan—helping Zoë cope with empty nest syndrome by channeling her endless fount of love and her innate ability to nurture into an ongoing good deed. I figured she should start on September fifteenth, the day after Emma left.

I sent Gretchen an email, too, explaining my ideas for Emma's party, which I wanted to schedule for September twelfth, the Saturday before Emma left for Parris Island.

After I was done, I still wasn't sleepy. The temperature had dropped into the fifties, and I curled up on the sofa under an afghan. I rarely took time to reflect on life and myself and my dreams, yet every time I did, I was glad I'd done so. I leaned back and closed my eyes. I had so many balls in the air, I worried that one might drop. Emma's party. Zoë's wedding. Zoë's next endeavor. To say nothing of my regular work—the TV show, our auctions, the weekly tag sale, the column I was writing for *Antiques Insights* magazine, managing Prescott's growth, planning our next steps—plus the renovation of the Gingerbread House, and everything swirling around Maudie, Celia, and the presentation box and cat sculpture. I had more questions than answers about that mysterious triad . . . If only I could remember the memory that was flitting in and out of my consciousness, like a dream.

I woke up at seven, jelly-rolled in the afghan, feeling unrested and fidgety. I unfurled myself and stood, stretching, trying to chase away the cricks and lingering goblins. I tottered into the kitchen, where the first buttery ribbons of sunlight were striping the kitchen counter and floor.

Ty had made a pot of coffee and I poured myself a cup. He'd left a handwritten note on the counter. *You look so relaxed, I didn't have the heart to wake you. Talk to you soon. XOXO.* I pressed the paper to my chest.

I made myself some scrambled eggs and read Wes's article about Stacy while I ate. There was nothing that was new to me. I tidied up and got ready for work, pausing before I left to enjoy the view from the kitchen window. The meadow was in shadow, the colors muted. Closer in, the pale morning sun touched the dew-specked tomatoes, and they shone like beacons. Since Ty had tied up the vines, I could see the tomatoes clearly—I loved that. Before, all I saw was vines and leaves. The tomatoes had been there, but hidden. A minor adjustment that led to a major shift in perception.

Perception.

I stared out over the meadow, but what I saw was Maudie's apartment. It was as if the memory I'd been chasing had been enveloped by thick fog, and now the fog had lifted, so I could see what had been there all along: Celia's lifeless corpse and the trunk, the lid open, revealing the Bible and stack of letters. The implications pinballed through my brain, setting my heart hammering against my ribs, and I grasped the counter to steady myself.

Slow down. Look again.

I closed my eyes and let the picture come, viewing again, in more detail, what I'd seen from the entryway of Maudie's apartment: Celia's body, the puddles of blood, and the rolling pin; a brown handbag on the counter near a pen; the open windows; and the trunk with the Bible and letters visible. I opened my eyes. It wasn't an illusion or a mirage. My observation was accurate, and the meaning was clear.

The clock mounted high on the wall told me it was three minutes after eight. I called Ellis on his cell, but it went straight to voicemail. I didn't leave a message. Instead, I called the station.

"I'm sorry, Josie," Cathy said, "but he just got in, and he's already in a meeting."

"Please. Tell him it's urgent."

She told me to hold on, sounding doubtful.

Three minutes later, Ellis came on the line. "Josie? Are you all right?"

"Yes, thanks. Question: Is the trunk still in Maudie's unit?"

"Why? What's going on?"

"I need to show you something. Is it there?"

"Yes, it's there, but the techs have been all over it, and they didn't find anything of note."

"They didn't know what to look for."

"And you do?"

"Yes."

I could hear him breathing for the few seconds it took him to decide. "I can get there by noon."

"Stacy has arranged for Tom to clean Maudie's unit at eleven, and I think she'll arrive early. We need to get there first."

"What's going on, Josie?"

"I need to show you. Can you come now?"

"No. Give me a sec."

I tapped my foot impatiently.

A minute later, he came back on the line. "I can do nine thirty."

"Good."

I stopped in at my office to greet my staff, say hello to Hank and Angela, and ask Sasha for any updates they might have about antiques.

"I spoke briefly to Yvette Joubert," Sasha said. "She confirmed that she and her father are going through the old business records. She'll email when she finds something about the chandelier, or if she doesn't. She expects to get back to us by the end of the month."

"Waiting makes me crazy." I smiled. "But you already knew that."

Sasha laughed.

I thanked her, told Cara I'd be back in a while, and left for Belle Vista.

The sun was shining brightly when I pulled into a space close to the front. A man wearing safety earmuffs steered a riding lawn mower toward the back gardens. It was nine fifteen when I passed Belle Vista's front security camera.

The woman who'd covered for Lainy the day Celia was killed sat at the reception station. The brass tent sign read LOIS BAXTER.

"Hi," I said as I walked up. "I'm Josie Prescott, here to meet Chief Hunter. I'm a little early. I might as well sign in, if that's all right."

She slid the guest book toward me.

"Is Lainy here?" I asked.

"Yes—she just stepped away from her desk for a few minutes." The phone rang. "Excuse me."

I thanked her, signed in, and walked to the window. I sat on the bench and watched Lois's back.

Lois was busy. She took a string of phone calls, transferring them all, and answered several in-person questions from residents. The café was busy, too, nearly all the tables occupied. I stood, keeping my eyes on her back, and took three steps toward the corridor that led to Maudie's apartment. I thought I'd take a peek to confirm that the police tape had been removed. I waited a few seconds for Lois to answer another call, then sidled my way across the lobby. As soon as I rounded the corner, I stopped to reconnoiter.

The hall was empty, but that could change at any moment. I continued down it until I reached Maudie's door. The door was only partially latched, as if the last police tech to leave hadn't pulled it all the way closed. I pressed my ear to the cold wood and listened. I didn't hear anything, but I wasn't certain I could with the lawn mower still at work.

I turned to face the lobby and listened. Faint murmurs emanating from the lobby told me Lois was busy with her work. Probably she wouldn't even miss me, or if she did, she'd assume I'd gotten tired of waiting and left, and she simply hadn't noticed.

I reached for the doorknob and turned it slowly as I pushed. The door swung open easily, silently. I stepped inside and shut it behind me, leaving it as I found it, partially latched.

Signs that a forensic team had been on-site were everywhere. Black powder littered the kitchen counter. The drying rack was in the sink. The pools and streaks of blood had dried into cordovan globs and splotches, and blood-smeared footprints led from the spot where Celia's body had lain to about a foot from the front door. I could imagine a technician slipping on plastic booties as he navigated his way to the exit so he wouldn't traipse blood down the corridor.

Only one window was open, the screen raised an inch. The rolling pin had been removed. So had the purse and pen. Everything seemed to have been moved, at least a little. The bistro table was pressed against the closet door. The marigold candlesticks sat on the top of the room divider. The toaster oven rested on its side. The trunk, its lid open, had been moved closer to the windows. The pile of ribbon-tied letters sat next to the Bible, just as I recalled.

I walked toward the trunk, freezing midstep at a rustling coming from somewhere nearby. I spun around, but didn't see anything. I stayed still, listening, but didn't hear anything else. The lawn mower had moved away, its drone a distant hum. I rubbed my suddenly moist palms against my skirt. I hadn't imagined the rustling. A strong burst of wind caught one of the sheer panels and sent it swirling, bringing with it the delicious summer aroma of freshly cut grass. I turned toward the window. A crow cawed, and a chipmunk darted across the lawn, disappearing into the bushes. The rustling must have come from outside, its pitch different enough from the mower to be perceived. I was jumpy for no reason. I turned back to the trunk and forced myself to laugh a little, pure bravado. My dad always said to fake it until you make it.

I took another step toward the trunk, heard a whoosh on my right side, and whirled. Something struck me, a jarring blow to my left upper arm.

"Uh," I exclaimed, a grunt, surprise tempering pain.

Off balance, I teetered a few steps, trying to right myself, confused and frightened.

A second blow landed on my upper back between my shoulder blades, and I tumbled forward, crashing headfirst into the trunk. I collapsed, facedown, the wind knocked out of me, heaving, trying for air, covered by glass confetti.

Pounding footsteps added to my terror, and I raised my arms to protect my head. I wanted to roll over, but I was scared that the glass covering my arms and back would cut me or fall into my eyes. The pounding footsteps stopped abruptly, followed by a scraping sound, metal on metal, then silence, punctuated by birds chirping and calling. I closed my eyes and willed my racing pulse to slow.

CHAPTER TWENTY-SIX

D on't move."

I recognized Ellis's voice, but I didn't understand why I was hearing a police command. Was I being arrested? It didn't make sense. I was one of the good guys. I decided I must have heard wrong. "What?"

"Don't move."

"Why not?"

"You're covered with glass, and you might have a back or neck injury. An ambulance is on the way."

"I don't need an ambulance."

"It's not optional. Did you lose consciousness?"

"No. I haven't moved because I was scared of getting cut."

"Good thinking. Do you know who attacked you?"

"No."

"Are you in pain?"

"I'm kind of crampy from being in this weird position, but other than that, no."

"I'm going to take some photos and video while we're talking so we can study the glass distribution pattern later. Does your head hurt?"

"No."

"Your neck?"

"No."

"Your back?"

"No. I told you . . . I'm not hurt."

"What were you doing here?"

"Looking at the trunk."

"Looking? Or approaching?"

"Approaching. The attack came from behind me. I was struck twice, once on my arm, the other time between my shoulders. You need to get some officers here to make sure no one messes with the trunk."

"I will. This apartment is a crime scene again. It will be sealed."

"Station officers in the hall and on the lawn. Remember, Stacy and Tom are coming at eleven. I think Stacy will be here sooner. Maybe she already was."

"You think she attacked you?"

I recalled the footsteps, which I'd described to myself as pounding. They weren't the higher-pitched patter of high heels. They were the thumps of boots.

"I don't know." I recounted my recollection. "The only times I've seen her, she's been in heels. Maybe she wears boots when burgling."

"Could it have been regular shoes?"

"Maybe."

"Sneakers?"

"Probably not. They're too soft."

"Bare feet?"

"No."

Voices sounded from somewhere close by, followed by footsteps. The paramedics had arrived.

One of the EMTs told me to keep my eyes closed and used a small brush to sweep the glass bits off me. They slipped on a neck brace and strapped me to a spinal board. At the hospital, I was x-rayed, examined, monitored, and assessed for signs of confusion, and I passed every test with flying colors. I was bruised, and I had a small bump on the top of my head, but nothing was broken, and I hadn't been cut by flying glass. I wasn't dizzy or nauseated, and I had no memory loss. All signs indicated that I was fine.

The doctor gave me a list of symptoms to watch for and told me he didn't expect me to have any problems. I thanked him and prepared to leave.

I didn't want Ty or my staff to hear about my misadventure on the news, so as soon as the doctor finished with me, just before noon, I texted Ty that

I had been attacked but was fine and didn't want him to worry. I also texted Gretchen so she could alert everyone at Prescott's to the situation. I called Zoë to ask her to spend the night, just in case any problematic symptoms appeared, and she agreed, announcing that she'd start cooking tomato basil soup. I laughed. Zoë was the soup queen, creating delicious concoctions for every occasion, and sometimes for no occasion. Ellis said he'd arrange for a police officer to drive me home in my car, still in the Belle Vista lot.

"I'm fine, just a little bruised up. I still want to show you something in Maudie's unit."

"While you were here, I had detectives go over the trunk again. There's nothing there, Josie."

"Yes, there is." I stood, preparing to leave. Sitting still, I'd begun to stiffen up, and my upper back ached. "Five minutes. That's all it will take."

I winced as I struggled to get into Ellis's huge SUV.

"Are you sure you're up to this?" he asked, helping me step up.

"Absolutely." I was feeling more battered than I wanted to let on. My hot tub was calling. "It's important."

"If you're feeling good enough to do this, you're up to hearing that I still haven't decided whether to charge you."

"Me? What are you talking about?"

"You didn't actually break and enter since the door was unlocked and un-latched, but I could definitely charge you with trespassing and maybe with tampering with evidence."

"What evidence?"

"The trunk."

"I didn't touch it."

"You know you did the wrong thing, Josie. We arranged to meet. I was on time. You had no excuse for going in without me."

I turned to gaze out the side window. "Sorry."

"Don't do it again."

"I won't."

"You could have been seriously injured."

"I know." My phone vibrated. "I need to take this—it's Ty." I tapped the ACCEPT button. "Hey." He asked how I was, his worry pulsating through the phone line. "I'm fine. Ellis called an ambulance as a precaution. You'll be glad to know that other than a couple of bruises, I'm perfect."

"I knew you were perfect a long time ago. What happened?"

I gave him the one-minute version and told him we were going back to Belle Vista and then I was going home. I reassured him that there was nothing to worry about since Zoë had agreed to stay with me overnight.

"There's no need. I'll be there in a few hours."

"Don't be silly. There's already been too much fussing over a minor incident."

"Maybe your injuries are minor, but the incident isn't."

"You sound like Ellis. He's just been yelling at me."

"Good man."

He told me he loved me, and I told him I loved him back.

I had a dozen voicemail messages and just as many texts. I appreciated my staff's many expressions of concern and good wishes, and I wasn't surprised by Wes's nonstop demands for information, but I wasn't going to respond to anyone now, and I didn't want to be bothered. I turned my phone to silent.

The same uniformed police officer I'd seen on the lawn before was back in position. Ellis asked him if he'd had any problems. He said Wes Smith had been sniffing around, taking photos and asking questions of anyone passing by until Mr. Hannigan, the director, tossed him off the property.

When we went inside, I saw Lainy was back at her station, her expressive eyes radiating concern. I asked Ellis to give me a minute and went to say hello.

"We were so worried," she said.

She looked more stunning than ever in a lilac sundress with beige lace-up chunky-heeled boots.

"You're very kind. I'm okay. Listen, before I forget, Max said to text him—he's glad to talk to you about auditioning. Let me give you his number." She tapped it into her phone as I called it out. "He's a good guy and very knowledgeable. Ask him anything."

"Thank you, Josie. I really appreciate this."

"You look excited."

"It's funny how sometimes the stars align. First you put me in touch with

Max to help me learn how to audition well, then I found this open showcase in New York next fall—agents looking for new talent. New York City! That's always been my dream." She giggled and lowered her voice. "'Excited' doesn't even begin to describe how I'm feeling. I'm going to text Max now and try to connect with him in the next few days. I've been preparing an audition piece from *Chicago*, too. Between you and Maudie . . . all the encouragement . . . I'm going to give it the old college try. Thank you, thank you."

"You're more than welcome. I think it's great, Lainy!"

She scanned my face. "Are you sure you're okay?"

Fighting fatigue and an inclination to hunch over to favor my bruised shoulder, I smiled and gave her a thumbs-up. I rejoined Ellis, and we walked to Maudie's apartment. Officer Meade leaned against the wall.

"Anything I need to know?" Ellis asked her.

"No, sir. Everything's been quiet. The crime scene techs finished at eleven thirty."

"Call over for me, will you? Ask about fingerprints or anything else they can give us. Call Detective Brownley, too. I want to know the whereabouts of Doug and Stacy during Josie's attack."

She took her phone from her pocket as Ellis opened the door.

The room looked the same as I recalled. The floor was littered with bits of iridescent yellow and orange glass, which I recognized as coming from one of the marigold glass candlesticks. The other one was intact and lay on the floor. I had no idea why it hadn't broken, too. The window screen had been punched or kicked out.

"Did Stacy or Tom show up?" I asked.

"Both, separately. Stacy arrived around ten, Tom at eleven. Needless to say, they were shocked and upset to hear about your attack."

"What was Stacy wearing?"

One corner of Ellis's mouth shot up. "Jeans and black leather half-boots."

"Her housekeeping outfit. Any alibis?"

"It's too early to reach any conclusions."

"The attacker must have been hiding in the bathroom." I pointed to the dividing wall that ran parallel to the kitchen. "The candlesticks were on this ledge. Whoever attacked me must have grabbed one of the candlesticks and swung it at me. I dodged just enough to escape the brunt of the blow, and it didn't break but skittered onto the floor. The attacker swung the second candlestick and got me on the back. Lucky for me, he—or she—gave up, probably because I catapulted into the trunk and hit the deck, so there was time to escape."

"You didn't see anyone, is that correct?"

"Right. Not even a shadow."

"How about a smell? Any perfume or cologne? Aftershave?"

"No."

"Cigarette smoke?"

"Stacy smokes."

"And?"

"No, nothing like that."

"Coconut oil?"

His question seemed such a non sequitur, I found myself momentarily confused. "Coconut oil?"

"It's popular now. It's an ingredient in certain shampoos and skin creams. It has quite a distinctive aroma, and it lingers."

"You've asked people what shampoo and skin cream they use?"

"I'm very thorough. Did you smell any coconut oil?"

"No."

"As it was happening, did you think it had to be so-and-so?"

"Stacy, but only because I'd gotten it into my head that she'd be arriving early."

"If you were me, trying to identify your attacker, what would you do?"

"Look for fingerprints on the unbroken candlestick and footprints outside the window."

Ellis walked to the window and peered into the dirt. "Nothing distinct, just a mush of footprints." He crossed the room and opened the door. "Anything?" he asked Officer Meade.

"Yes, sir," Officer Meade replied. "No forensics. Doug was meeting with the principal at his kids' school. Stacy was on the phone to a London-based investment committee."

"The whole time?"

"Yes, sir. Both."

"Did you hear?" Ellis asked.

"Yes." I walked to the door and stood on the threshold. "Come stand beside me."

Standing shoulder to shoulder, we filled the doorway.

"I was standing right here," I said. "The trunk was in the same place it is now, maybe a little closer toward me. Squat so you're my height. Look at the trunk . . . What do you see?"

Ellis crouched next to me, dropping his height by almost a foot.

"A large black book with the word 'Bible' written in gold on the cover. A pale blue ribbon that appears to be wrapped around a bunch of envelopes."

"You can stand now." He did so, and I continued. "When I opened the trunk in the Gingerbread House pantry, I was standing six inches away and had to lean in to see both the Bible and the letters. Now I can see them plainly. If I couldn't see the Bible and the envelopes in the pantry, why can I see them here?"

"What are you saying? That they've been raised up somehow?"

"I asked Maudie about shelves. She said there weren't any. Nineteenth-century dome-topped trunks like this one came with two shelves. Julie told me that Maudie said she was going to look for them. She must have realized that what she thought was the bottom of the trunk wasn't. Instead, it was the missing shelves stacked on the bottom."

"So she installed one. So what?"

"Why? What's underneath?"

Understanding lit up Ellis's eyes. He tramped across the room to the trunk. "I'm going to take some video."

I watched for a moment, then took my phone and duplicated Ellis's efforts. I couldn't send Wes anything now, but if and when I was able to deliver it to him, my debt would be wiped clear, and then some.

He extracted some plastic gloves from his jacket pocket. "Anything I should know before I lift the Bible and envelopes out?" Ellis asked.

"We need to find a safe place, a clean place, to set them down. How about on the bed, under the duvet?"

He tossed back the duvet and laid the objects on the clean bottom sheet; then, together, we peered inside the trunk. The shelf fit snugly on the ridge below it.

I pointed to a slight half-moon-shaped opening on the left side of the shelf. "Do you see that half-circle indentation? Whatever tool came with the trunk to lift the shelves is probably long gone. I'd use a hooked probe or something similar. Slide the implement in and tug. Maudie had a metal crochet hook in the pantry to work the dumbwaiter, which would, I think, work well on this, too. I gave it back to her. Anything like that, even a metal knitting needle, for instance. You don't need the hook, now that I think of it. All you need is something strong to act as a lever."

We both scanned the living areas. I wouldn't have been surprised to find a basket filled with yarn on the floor by a chair or the sofa, but there wasn't one.

I pointed toward the kitchen. "The crochet hook might be in one of those drawers. Or she might have a lobster pick."

"What about a knife?"

"Too wide."

"So we need a knitting needle. You're saying you don't have one on you?"

"Funny. Do you?"

"I left mine in the car."

I laughed. "My toolbox is in my car for real, but I don't think we need to get fancy." I slipped my penknife out of its sheath, used my fingernail to access the narrowest blade, and held it up. "How about this?"

"I have one of those."

"Beat ya."

I eased the blade into the aperture and pried up the shelf. When I'd raised it about an inch, Ellis asked if I could hold it there for a minute so he could continue his video recording, and I assured him I could.

I was wondering how I could sneak in a few shots myself when he said, "If you promise not to give any of the footage to Wes until I give the go-ahead, I'll take some with your camera, too."

"I wasn't going to hand it over to Wes."

"Not now, anyway. Did you think I wouldn't notice you shooting video earlier?"

"I think you notice everything."

"You're right. Promise not to share it with anyone until and unless I give the okay?"

"I promise."

When he'd finished recording using both our phones, he worked his fingers under the shelf and lifted it clear of the trunk. He carried the shelf to the bed and placed it on the clean sheet next to the Bible and stack of letters.

"Did you peek?" he asked as he returned to the trunk.

"No. It felt like it should be a shared experience."

He smiled. "That's what I thought, too."

We looked inside the trunk together.

It was empty.

My stomach plummeted, and I couldn't drag my eyes away from the empty trunk. "We're too late."

CHAPTER TWENTY-SEVEN

E llis and I stood in front of the trunk. "The trunk may be empty, but it was a good idea, Josie."

"Someone had the idea before me, and they stole Maudie's presentation box and cat."

"You're thinking Maudie repositioned the shelf so no casual observer could see what was in the lower section . . . that was clever of her." He pointed at the bottom. "Is that another shelf?"

I eyeballed the space. "It looks that way. See the beveled edge? It's a match to the one we lifted out."

"Let's see if anything is under it."

I held his camera while he turned the trunk on its side. The shelf flipped over.

"Maudie might have just moved the one shelf," he said as he pulled it out and placed it on top of its twin. "You planted the seed when you told her trunks like hers came with shelves. She wanted to find out if she had some. She found them and slipped one in place to confirm it fit."

"Theoretically, I guess, you're right—there's no evidence that she moved the presentation box and cat, but neither is there evidence that she didn't. All we know for certain is that they're still missing."

He nodded, thinking.

"Maybe she took them with her," I said.

He shook his head. "They'd be too heavy for her to manage."

"Not really. Maudie told me she could bench-press fifty pounds, and I'm certain the box and cat weigh more than that. The problem I see is that it's twenty-four inches long, which makes it too big for carry-on if she went by plane, and no way would she check it."

"Do you have a theory about what happened?"

"I have several. It's possible Maudie managed to hide the presentation box as the bad guys were breaking into her unit, then escaped. She's hiding out somewhere."

He scanned the small apartment. "Where could she hide it?"

"I don't know."

"Who are the bad guys?"

I stared at the bloodstained spot where Celia had died. "Someone who was enraged and took it out on Celia."

"Was Doug that angry at her?"

"I don't know. Maybe Celia's drama wore him down and he snapped." I raised my eyes to meet Ellis's piercing gaze. "Where does Stacy fit into all this?"

"We're following all sorts of leads, some more promising than others. You said you had several theories. Tell me another one."

"Maudie hid the box after she got back from lunch. She'd made plans to go away. After she was gone, someone came in or broke in and stole it."

"Where did she go?"

"Mountain climbing?"

Ellis smiled. "What's your second guess?"

"She said she wanted to go snorkeling."

A firm clap-clap sounded from the brass knocker.

"One second," Ellis called.

It took him ten seconds to slip a shelf into position. I was there with the Bible and letters and lowered them into place as he tossed the duvet over the second shelf. I stayed by the trunk while he opened the door. It was Officer Meade.

"Sorry to bother you, sir. Mr. Hannigan, the manager, is here. He says it's urgent."

Ellis swung the door wide.

Mr. Hannigan was just as buttoned up as the last time I saw him, maybe more so. He wore a suit and tie, and his expression was solemn, bordering on grim.

"I've consulted with our board," he said, "and pursuant to our Residency Agreement, paragraph twelve, subsection (e), we are withdrawing Mrs. Wilson's acceptance, effective immediately. Due to her continued absence, we'll be packing up the contents of her apartment as specified in paragraph fourteen as soon as you allow it. We'll secure everything in a locked unit downstairs and deliver it to any Rocky Point address she specifies."

"You're kicking her out?" Ellis asked.

"We've determined her needs can't be properly met here at Belle Vista. We will be returning her entry fee."

"What's really going on?"

"We can't allow this ongoing situation to continue to upset the other residents. It's not good for them, it's not good for us, and it's not helping her. I understand you need to complete your investigation, but I want to make certain you aren't unnecessarily delaying it."

"We hope to be finished within a day or so. I'll keep you posted."

"Not today?"

"No. But you can go ahead and fix the screen."

Mr. Hannigan tightened his lips, his dissatisfaction patent. "Very well."

He marched off, and Ellis closed the door.

"Nice guy," I said.

"He's between a rock and a hard place."

"Can you always see both sides of an issue?"

Ellis smiled. "I always try."

"I think Maudie getting the boot is a blessing in disguise. She'd been thinking about a condo on the beach before Celia and Stacy strong-armed her into moving here."

There was another knock on the door. This time, Officer Meade said it was Lainy with a question.

Ellis said that was fine, to let her in, and Lainy stepped over the threshold. Her big eyes were alive with curiosity, and she looked everywhere at once, peering, registering, filing.

"Sorry to break in," she said. "Mr. Hannigan just told me about Mrs. Wilson. I'm so upset . . . If he's withdrawing her residency approval, it made me think you must have news about her."

"We're following multiple leads," Ellis said. "Have you thought of anything else that might help us find her?"

"No. I wish I had." She shook her head, her sadness evident—unless she was acting. "And you still haven't found the presentation box and cat?" She sent her eyes around the room again. "The way Tom described it . . . those jewels! I'd love to see it."

"Any ideas for us on that front?"

"Sorry, no. The real reason I'm here . . . I thought maybe you'd like some coffee or a Coke or something."

Ellis turned to me. "Josie?"

"That's very thoughtful of you, Lainy. Thank you. I'm fine, though."

"I'm good, too," Ellis said. "Thanks."

As he closed the door after she backed out of the room, I said, "That we haven't found the missing objects will be all over town before you can say *I have a secret*."

"What's her agenda?"

"Chronic nosiness. She's a nice girl but an incorrigible gossip."

"It will be interesting to see how people react to the news."

"It will indeed." I paused for a moment. "I have an idea. Let me slip Wes a few nuggets. I could tell him that I dragged you here because I was convinced that there was a hidden compartment in the trunk, but I couldn't find it. The objects are still missing. I'll assure him that I'm okay, that whoever attacked me apparently didn't want to hurt me badly—he or she simply wanted to get away. If you remove the officers and hide cameras around the apartment, nanny cams, for instance, the scene is set."

"I can't do it without Mrs. Wilson's permission."

"We don't know where she is. Can't you do it as part of your criminal investigation?"

"You have an elastic view of privacy laws."

"This is a good idea, that's all I'm saying."

He rubbed the side of his nose. "I can certainly set the plan in motion pending her permission."

"Shall I text Wes?"

"That can't do any harm. Why don't you have a seat? I need to make a bunch of arrangements."

I sat on a bistro chair to text Wes, then stood at the window, half-listening as Ellis spoke to Cathy, asking if there was anything he needed to do right away.

Maudie and I had talked about the risk of leaving valuable objects in her apartment, that too many people knew about the box and cat. Given her physical capability, I knew she could have moved the presentation box on her own. The tough part would be lifting it out of the trunk, but after that, rejiggering the shelf and lowering the presentation box into the lower section would be a piece of cake.

It was certainly possible she repositioned the shelf simply to confirm it fit, but I thought it was more likely that she had hidden the box and cat sculpture so they were safe during her trip. If I was correct, she'd planned her getaway; she hadn't run away on the fly. Maybe her plan had come together last minute, but it was a plan, not a flight. Evidently, she'd left within minutes of her return from lunch, and there was no doubt in my mind that Maudie hadn't been planning on traveling when we talked Friday morning, which meant she'd arranged the trip after we spoke. Something had changed her mind or spurred her on.

I caught Ellis's eye and raised my index finger, indicating I wanted to talk to him, and he asked Cathy to hold on.

"Did you talk to Gerard Martin? Maudie's travel agent? Maudie's friend Nessie Wynn told me she gave his name to the police."

"We talked to him. Why?"

"When I spoke to him, he wouldn't answer any questions. Did he tell you anything?"

"No. Did you think of something I could use to change his mind?"

"No."

I turned back to the window. A small brown bird flitted from a nearby branch to another one a few feet away, then, a moment later, flew off toward the meadow.

Ellis told Cathy to connect him to Katie, the police tech expert. When he had her on the line, he detailed what he wanted in terms of hidden camera placement, external feeds, and absolute discretion. When they were finished, Katie transferred Ellis to Detective Brownley, who was charged with overseeing the sting.

"Since Hannigan plans on moving Mrs. Wilson out of here ASAP," Ellis told the detective, "we can use that as a cover story. We'll tell him that we'll be in and out all day today, completing our investigation. Other than repairing the screen, he has no reason to be in here, which means you can control access. Once I receive the go-ahead from Mrs. Wilson, we can activate the hidden cameras. If it's a go, I'll want eyes on the camera feed nearby, maybe in a car parked around the corner. Under different circumstances, I'd try to coordinate with management to use a room on-site, but the facility is now hostile to our presence, so I don't want to involve them. Wherever the placement will be, it needs to be unobtrusive, but close enough to make an arrest, if needed."

I continued listening with one ear, but most of my brain was thinking about Maudie, to try to differentiate truth from lore. Not all lies are equal. I'd learned that lesson young. My dad told me that sometimes lying was the right thing to do, the only thing to do.

I'd been in the eighth grade, and none of my friends knew what to do or say when my mom died, even my best friends. One girl was especially insensitive, asking prying questions about Mom's cancer, her last days, her pain. I tried to stay strong and tough, but after a few days of what felt like a thousand pricks, my dad caught me crying and dragged the story out of me. He told me to avoid the issue, and if that didn't work, to lie. He said I should thank her for her concern and smile and walk away. If she pursued it, I should say that Mom had no pain at the end, that her passing was peaceful. No one but us, he said, needed to know about her agony or frailty. He explained that it was completely okay to lie when answering a question no one had a right to ask. It worked like a charm. Soon she lost interest, and I was allowed to grieve in peace.

Two of the three antiques appraisers I'd recommended, Melvin Farrow and Lisa Rollins, had spoken to Maudie on Friday morning, the day I'd given her their names. Dr. Edward Moss, the third on the list, told me he hadn't. Perhaps Maudie had decided that he was out of contention based on his distant location, but there was another possibility worth considering. People who work in the high-end art and antiques field have to develop finely honed skills of deception. A husband who discovers that his wife charged a pair of antique cuff links wants to know if she told you who they were for. You know it was some hottie named Sam, but you don't reveal that tidbit because her relationship with Sam is none of your business. The husband has to be put off, hopefully without alienating him, because after he recovers from the shock of her betrayal, he may want to buy a set of antique cuff links for himself. A daughter whose father has recently died insists that you tell her the details of the consignment deal you just struck with her brother. You have to explain you never reveal who is or isn't a client, nor any arrangements, because while you're plenty excited he decided to consign his share of his dad's antiques to your firm, you want her share, too.

Ellis continued his instructions to Detective Brownley. "The bottom line is that everyone has to believe that we haven't found the missing objects—which, by the way, we haven't. I'll get Officer Meade to park herself inside the unit until you arrive." Ellis listened for a while, responded to some questions, then ended the call.

As soon as he was off the phone, I said, "Do you have a colleague you can trust in San Francisco?"

He pocketed his phone, his eyes on my face. "As it happens, I do. Why?"

"Who?"

"You first. Why?"

"Because I think Dr. Moss, that Egyptologist I told you about, is a really good liar."

CHAPTER TWENTY-EIGHT

llis was a good listener. As I detailed why I thought Maudie might be in San Francisco, he kept his eyes on my face, his attention absolute.

I concluded by saying, "I think it's worth talking to Dr. Moss in person. It's easier to fib on the phone than it is face-to-face."

"I can ask the SFPD to help out, but I'd rather keep my interest in one of their city's upstanding citizens unofficial if I can. Let me call a buddy of mine who moved out there, Vincent Stein. We were in Homicide together in New York. When he retired, he took a job as head of security for one of those high-tech start-ups. He's been out there as long as I've been here in Rocky Point, a dozen years or so. From what he tells me and what he doesn't say, I suspect he'd like to get back out in the field and do some detecting." He gave me a once-over. "While I'm trying to locate him and finalizing the arrangements here, you are to sit and chill. Then we're going to get something to eat."

"I'm not tired and I'm definitely not hungry."

"If you're not tired, you're not human, and if you're not hungry, you're more injured than I realized."

I was about to argue the point but stopped. There was no reason for me to try to tough it out. "You're right—I'll be glad to sit down, and I should have something to eat."

I sat on Maudie's sofa, and after a minute, I fluffed a red velour toss pillow and stretched out, nestling my head in the soft cushion. I dozed while Ellis spelled each of the officers on sentry duty, giving them short breaks, left messages for Vincent on his cell and at his job, and touched base again with Detective Brownley, reviewing the tech plan and discussing contingencies.

"Are you asleep?" Ellis whispered a while later.

"No," I said, opening my eyes and smiling. "Just resting my eyes. Is it time to go?"

"Yes."

I sat up and took stock. My shoulders ached, my neck was stiff, and the top of my head was tender to the touch, and truth be told, I was weary to my bones, not so much sleepy as worn out, the exhaustion that follows a fright-fueled adrenaline rush.

Ellis told Officer Meade to come in, directing her not to leave the apartment until Detective Brownley arrived. Once the detective was on-site, Officer Meade was to resume her post outside the unit until she was relieved or dismissed. He told the officer standing outside that he, too, was to stay in place until Detective Brownley told him he could go.

Ellis's phone vibrated. It was Vincent. After an exchange of greetings and one-minute personal updates, Ellis described what he needed, and as he had expected, Vincent was eager to help. Ellis gave him the details, asking him to confirm, if he could, whether Dr. Moss had heard from Maudie, and if so, when. Any information he could garner about her present whereabouts would be a bonus.

"Okay, then," Ellis told me after he'd ended the call. "He'll call back as soon as he's spoken to Dr. Moss."

I struggled to my feet and shuffled alongside Ellis to the parking lot. I didn't want to flame out before I knew Maudie was all right and helped her, if I could. She was in for a terrible ordeal—the shock of her niece's murder, the stress of the investigation prying into the corners of her life, the distress that her presentation box and cat sculpture were missing, and the tumult of losing her apartment.

I insisted I was fine to drive. I followed Ellis to a small coffee shop in an industrial park, anonymous and utilitarian. It was brightly lit and decorated in yellow and turquoise, too cheerful for my mood. When we arrived, just after one, more than half the tables were occupied. Ellis chose a table by the window. I opted for the house special: half a sandwich and a cup of soup. I went with grilled cheese and, since Zoë was making me tomato soup, chicken orzo. I also ordered sweet iced tea, black currant, heaven in a glass.

"Thank you," I said after I'd taken two bites of the sandwich. "I didn't know I needed this, but you might have just saved my life."

"Good. And after this, you go home."

"I'm not going to argue, so long as by 'this' you mean tracking down Maudie."

"I don't. I mean after lunch."

"Stop coddling me."

"I'm not coddling you. I'm reacting to your limited mobility and frequent grunts of pain."

"I haven't grunted once. I don't grunt."

"Don't be stubborn."

"I'm tenacious, not stubborn."

I'd just requested a refill on the iced tea when Vincent called back.

Ellis listened for more than a minute, then said, "Good deal. When?" He glanced at his watch. "A full hour, that's a lot of conversation . . . Okay . . . Got it . . . When did she make the appointment?" He listened for another minute. "All right, then. Let me tell you what I think we should do. We're about to dump a whole lot of bad news on her, out of the blue." I listened while Ellis described his plan. "Whatever Mrs. Wilson needs, I want to be certain she gets. I don't want to get ahead of myself. I just want to be prepared . . . Good . . . Great . . . Skype, I think." The two men finalized the logistics, and Ellis tapped the END CALL button. He smiled at me. "Maudie is fine. She's been in San Francisco since Friday, staying at the Fairmont."

"What a relief! I infer she hasn't heard about Celia."

"Not as of a little bit ago."

"Did Vincent ask Dr. Moss why he said he hadn't spoken to her?"

"It was just what you suspected. Maudie called him last Friday morning around eleven, eight Pacific time, just after he got into work. They made the appointment for today, and she asked him to keep it confidential. He agreed, and nothing you told him gave him a reason to break his commitment. As soon as Vincent filled him in, he changed his tune and was glad to cooperate. Vincent is heading to the Fairmont now." Ellis flagged the waitress. "Time to get you home."

"I don't need to go. I feel a thousand times better now that I've eaten."

"If Maudie's not in her room, it may be hours before we connect. I want to use my laptop for Skype, and it's at the station, so I'm going to escort you home." He held up his hands as if to fend off an attack. "Not that I think you need an escort. I want to say hey to Zoë and see how she's doing. I'll be certain to convey your condolences and concern to Maudie."

"All right. I give up."

Ellis pulled into my driveway in back of me and had just stepped out of his vehicle when his phone vibrated. I walked to join him. From his side of the conversation, I gathered that Vincent was with the hotel's manager on duty, a woman named Amy Chen. Vincent handed her his phone so she and Ellis could talk directly. Ellis reviewed the situation, and Ms. Chen said she was glad to facilitate whatever support the hotel had to offer, from scheduling a doctor's visit to pouring a shot of brandy. At Vincent's request, she had just called Mrs. Wilson's room, pretending to check on whether she had everything she needed, and was therefore able to confirm that Maudie was there.

"I'll need fifteen minutes to get back to the station and set up," Ellis told Vincent.

I waved my hand to catch his attention.

"Use my laptop," I whispered. "It's ready to go. Please? I won't interfere—I just want to be available to help Maudie if I can. She's going to want to see a friendly face."

He kept his eyes on mine for a few seconds, then nodded.

"Change of plans," he told Vincent. "I can Skype you within five minutes. Call me when you're in Mrs. Wilson's room. Just tell her the Rocky Point police chief needs to talk to her. She'll freak out, but that can't be helped."

I led the way to the kitchen. My laptop was where I'd left it, on the table. I slid onto the long side of the L-shaped bench, swallowing a loud "ouch" as aches and stiffness reminded me where I'd been struck. I brought up Skype and pushed the computer toward the short side of the bench, where Ellis was getting organized, then scooched out. I decided to sit on a chair, much easier to get into and out of than a bench packed with pillows. I positioned one so it was perpendicular to where Ellis sat. The pain radiating from my shoulders was becoming more present, a wearing, steady, dull ache, merging with new twinges and sharper stabs in my thighs, probably from my fall. I was a mess, but game. I poured two glasses of water, delivered one to Ellis, and surreptitiously took two ibuprofen.

Vincent called. Maudie was ready to talk. Ellis gave him my Skype username and was connected within a minute.

I had a side-angled view of Maudie. She was frowning at the camera. Closed curtains hung in back of her. A sliver of TV showed on the right. Because Vincent's phone was perched against a pile of books, the camera was aimed upward, never a good angle for a woman. Every droop and wrinkle on Maudie's neck and face was accentuated. To make matters worse, she looked terrified. Her eyes were as round as silver dollars, and her lips were slightly parted as if she expected to scream.

Ellis nodded at the monitor. "Mrs. Wilson? I'm Chief Hunter of the Rocky Point police. I have some bad news, and I didn't want you to be alone when you heard it. I'm here with Josie Prescott, who is available to talk to you after I'm done. I know Mr. Stein introduced himself. He's a former colleague of mine from when I was a police detective in New York City, and a friend. I understand Ms. Chen is with you, too. Both are ready to help."

"Whatever it is, please . . . just tell me."

"It's your niece, Celia Akins. I'm sorry to report that she's dead."

Maudie stared blankly into the camera for a few seconds, then her lips quivered and her eyes filled. She covered her face with her hands, shielding herself. She murmured, "No, no, no." After a few seconds, the murmuring was replaced by whimpering, heartrending exclamations of despair.

Ellis waited close to a minute before speaking again. "I'm terribly sorry for your loss."

Maudie lowered her hands, her cheeks wet, tears clinging to her lashes. "Did she . . . Was it suicide?"

"Why would you think that?"

A woman's fingers appeared, offering a tissue. Maudie took it and patted her cheeks dry.

"Celia's always been high-strung. Nervous. If I missed clues that she was in worse condition than I thought, I'll never forgive myself."

"It wasn't suicide. She was attacked Friday afternoon, around two."

"Attacked?" Maudie's voice cracked, and she coughed and looked aside. The same woman's hand passed her a glass of water, and Maudie took a sip. "I'm sorry. I don't understand. You said Celia was attacked?"

"I don't want to sugarcoat the situation. What I have to tell you is going to be hard to hear. If you need a minute, just tell me. Your niece was murdered in your apartment last Friday afternoon, within minutes, apparently, of your departure."

Maudie's brows scrunched together, and her chin jutted forward. "Killed?" Maudie asked as if the word was unfamiliar. "In my apartment?"

"Yes. She was beaten to death with a wooden rolling pin."

Maudie's hand flew up to her mouth as the horror she was hearing sank in. "Who would do such a thing? Why?"

"We're working on who and why. We think whatever is going on might be related to an attempt to steal your presentation box and cat."

"Steal? Or sell?"

"You tell me."

"Celia begged me to sell the presentation box and cat sculpture." Her voice quavered as she added, "I told her she was selfish and encroaching." Maudie looked aside for a moment. "If she was planning to sell the objects out from under me, counting on my reluctance to create a scandal in the family, I can't say I'm surprised. She was wrong, but that's what she believed. That's why I hid the objects as soon as I got back from lunch."

"Where did you hide them?"

"In the trunk, under a shelf."

"I have more bad news, then. I'm afraid the objects are missing."

She pressed her fingers against her mouth. "Oh, no. Celia stole them after all."

"I don't think so. I think it was her killer."

"And you don't know who that is?"

"Not yet. Do you have any ideas?"

"Heavens, no." She covered her face again, her shoulders shaking. When she lowered her hands, she added, "I'm reeling. Just reeling."

"I understand. We'll talk more when you get back. Just a few more questions now, if you're able."

She used the tissue to wipe away more tears. "All right," she managed.

"Why didn't you move the box and cat to the storage facility?"

"I didn't have a padlock, and I didn't have time to get one. It sounds so silly now, but that's the truth. I'd never noticed there was extra room in the trunk, so I didn't think anyone else would, either."

"You made your travel arrangements Friday morning?"

"Yes. As soon as I talked to Dr. Moss, I called Gerard."

"Gerard Martin?"

"Yes, Martin's Travel Agency."

"What luggage did you take?"

"My wheeling tote bag. Why?"

"That's not much."

"I needed a new suitcase anyway, and I thought it would be fun to buy some new outfits and bathing suits and so on. I haven't bought any clothes since Eli died." She looked aside. "Fun."

"I'm sorry, Mrs. Wilson, but I do have some more difficult news." Maudie turned back to the camera. "I won't go into all the details now, but I want you to hear it from me, not on the news. Josie Prescott was also attacked in your unit this morning. She's all right, just a few bumps and bruises, but the apartment is once again a crime scene."

"Oh, my God. Josie, are you there?"

Ellis moved the laptop so we were both visible.

"Yes, Maudie, I'm here. What the chief said is correct. I'm fine."

"Thank God for that."

"I'm so sorry about Celia, Maudie."

"Thank you. I can't believe it. I just can't believe it. Poor Doug . . . he was so devoted to Celia, to the children. And Stacy must be beside herself. I know how awful it is to lose your sister."

Stacy had clearly been rattled by Celia's death, but only she knew how upset she really was. I'd seen many shades of Stacy's personality, from sweet to bitter, poised to frazzled, confident to despairing. Through it all, she'd shown a chameleon-like ability to turn off her acid tongue and turn on the charm, which made her an unreliable witness, even, perhaps, to herself.

"It's a rough situation," Ellis said, his tone matter-of-fact.

Maudie patted her eyes with the tissue again. "And you have no idea who's responsible?"

"We're working on several leads. If it's all right with you, I'd like to install hidden cameras in your apartment to see if someone comes after the box and cat once we clear out. We'll be monitoring them continuously, in real time. If someone enters the unit, we'll know it. If not, no harm done."

"All right."

"Thank you. I'm going to ask that you stay away from Belle Vista until we know it's safe for you to come back."

"I don't think I'll ever want to live there again. Not after this. Poor Celia. My poor niece."

"I certainly understand. I hate to have to tell you this now, and I'm very sorry to be the bearer of more bad news, but it seems there's a cancellation clause in your residence agreement. Mr. Hannigan, the manager, has informed me that the Belle Vista board has decided to exercise that option. They're withdrawing your acceptance and refunding your fee. He plans on packing up your possessions as soon as I unseal the unit."

"I'm being tossed out of my home?"

"I'm afraid so."

Maudie stared at the camera, her lips pressed tightly together, her eyes slits. "I don't want him, or anyone I don't know, touching my things. I'll get on the first plane home tomorrow morning. I should be able to organize the move in a day or two."

"I'll let him know. As far as I'm concerned, the apartment remains a crime scene, and it's sealed. What with our plan to monitor access via remote video feed, I won't allow him to reclaim the unit for a couple of days, minimum."

"If he insists on getting me out before I can take charge, would you be able to ask Tom Hill to pack me up?"

I touched Ellis's elbow and pointed at my chest.

He nodded and moved the computer so she had me full face.

"I'll call Tom, Maudie, and let him know he may be needed."

"Thank you, Josie."

"Maudie, do you have your new laptop with you?"

"Yes."

"Good. Then we can confirm it wasn't stolen. How about your checkbook?"

"No." Her eyes rounded. "I'll have to call my bank." She rubbed her forehead. "Is anything else missing?"

Ellis shifted the computer back and said, "I don't think so, although until you go through everything, there's no way for us to know for sure."

Maudie pressed the sides of her index fingers under her eyes for a moment, quelling tears. "I don't even know what to ask. I'm in shock." She turned her head aside and took a few deep breaths. After a few seconds, she turned back to the camera. "Why did you think to lift the shelf, looking for the box and cat?"

"Josie realized that the Bible and letters were higher than they were when she discovered the trunk in the dumbwaiter, and she knew what that must mean—you'd discovered the shelves and used one."

"All those years, I simply took the trunk at face value. It makes me wonder what else in my life I missed." She shook her head. "I'm sorry. I've been sitting here asking myself why no one contacted me about Celia until now, and then I realized I never checked my phone or email for messages. I forgot my charger, or maybe I lost it, I don't know."

"I'm sure you have a bunch of messages," Ellis said. "A lot of people have been worried about you."

"I don't know what to do first, who to call, how to get things organized."

I leaned into the camera's view. "You mentioned changing your flight home. Can I help you with that?"

"Thank you, Josie, but I'll call Gerard. He'll take care of everything. I was going on to Hawaii. He'll cancel that leg of my trip and get me straight home."

Ellis turned the monitor a bit so he had Maudie in direct view. "Mrs. Wilson, I have another request. I know you're going to want to talk to your family and maybe some close friends. I need to ask you not to talk about the murder or my plan with the hidden cameras. Talk about how upset you are and how much you loved your niece. Help plan the funeral. Ask if there's anything you can do, but don't speculate about who might be responsible, or why, or how they gained access to your apartment. I hate to burden you like this, but it's crucial. When you and I talk in person, which is a preference I know we share, I want you to express your uncensored views to me, frankly and openly, not the views that might have been colored by listening to other people's opinions and conjectures."

Maudie nodded slowly, letting the implications penetrate. "That makes perfect sense to me, and it's an apt warning. I've spent a lot of my time here in San Francisco thinking about how and why I let myself be swayed by other people's estimations, some well-meaning, others not. I can assure you it won't happen this time. It won't ever happen again."

Ellis had her write down his cell phone number and extracted a promise that she'd call him as soon as she knew her new flight information.

"If there's any pressure put on you to speculate," he said, "or you just don't want to engage with someone, blame me."

"You're kind, but I won't need to make excuses anymore. I'll call you with my flight information, and I'll call you when I'm in the car en route home." She gave a little snort, a soft, ironic nonlaugh. "En route to a hotel, I should say, since I no longer have a home. I'll have Gerard take care of that, too."

Maudie thanked Ellis for his courtesy in making sure she wasn't alone during the conversation. "I'm all right now. I'll call Gerard, then Doug and Stacy, just to let them know we connected. You asked me to keep certain things confidential. I'd like to ask you to do the same thing for me. I'm going to tell Doug and Stacy I was in San Francisco for a little vacation in a city I love before going on to Hawaii. Until I decide what to do with the presentation box and cat"—she paused and gulped—"assuming they're found . . . I don't want to engage with them on the topic."

"I can do that."

She thanked him again, and they ended the call.

"What do you think of her?" I asked as he lowered the laptop's lid.

"She's a sensible woman. Direct. Intelligent. I look forward to meeting her."

"She's changed since I first met her. It's amazing what a week can do."

"How so?"

"Her nieces worked to make her feel weak, diminished. Whether they hinted or even more than hinted that she had early-stage dementia on purpose to further their own agendas or simply allowed the fear to take hold and become the commonly accepted view, like an urban myth, she ended up believing that she was incapable and failing. Now she's back to trusting herself. There's a strength in her now that was simmering just below the surface when I first met her."

"Interesting," he said, giving nothing away. "You can go ahead and call Tom. Be excited that she's safe and en route home. Tell him it will be at least two days before the police unseal the unit, and Maudie may not need his services by then, but she asked you to give him a heads-up."

"Planting another seed in case someone wants to take one last crack at finding the presentation box and cat."

He stood. "Thanks for the use of your computer. I'm going to go next door to see how Zoë is doing. I'll let her know you're home."

"Can I ask you something first?"

"You know how much I hate that question."

I smiled. "What did you decide about my idea for your wedding?"

He leaned back against the wall, relaxing, smiling. "I love it. Captain Ken and I are in sync about the wedding ceremony, brief and romantic; the reception, long and filled with joy and fun; and the trip—Bimini was a good call, and he recommends Andros Island, too. In terms of the proposal itself, that's where you come in. I was going to ask you today, but then you got yourself all banged up. I need a ring, and I'd love your advice. What do you think Zoë would like?"

"Zoë's going to be thrilled with whatever you choose, of course, but I think she'd like a ruby, or a ruby-and-diamond combo. I know rubies are her favorite stones, and with her coloring, it would be perfect. Are you thinking new or antique?"

"You tell me."

"I suspect she'd prefer an antique ring. Let me see what we have in stock. We don't carry a huge selection of jewelry. It's too specialized for us. That said, everything we carry is at least a hundred years old, set in eighteen-karat gold or platinum, and fully appraised by an expert."

"Great. Do it."

I called Sasha and asked her to search our inventory. Moments later she reported that we had five beauties in stock.

I covered the mouthpiece to ask Ellis, "Can you wait ten minutes? I'll have Sasha drive them over."

"You're a ball of fire. Sure—I can wait for ten minutes."

I asked Sasha to come on the fly, then offered Ellis a cup of coffee, which he declined.

I refilled my glass and said, "I've had another thought."

"You've done enough. Paying for the yacht is above and beyond—a stellar wedding gift."

"I'm not talking about another gift. My idea is for Zoë, but it involves you, too. It's the empty nest thing. Zoë is worried that once Emma leaves, she'll be lonely and bored. I don't know whether that's realistic or not, but I do know that Zoë is scared that life as she knows it is over. I also know she has plenty of love to give." I smiled. "And she's nuts about dogs."

"You think we should get a dog?"

"I think you should volunteer to help train service dogs. They place puppies with volunteer families for a year or so. You teach them the basics, manners and so on. You bring them to what they call 'puppy club' meetings, which is such an adorable name, I can't stand it. Etcetera. Doesn't it sound perfect for her? For you?"

A grin slowly crossed his face. "It does. It really does."

"I'll email you the link to the volunteer application. It's quite a process to get approved. I calculated that if you start now, you'll be able to accept your first puppy just after Emma leaves. Your first endeavor as a married couple."

He raised his fist for a bump, and I tapped it with my own.

We chatted about dogs and the Bahamas until Sasha arrived. She set a black velvet tray containing five ruby-and-diamond rings on the table.

Ellis's eye was immediately drawn to the largest one. "I like this one."

"That's my favorite, too. The center stone is a ruby. The shape is called a step-cut oblong, and it's surrounded by narrow rectangular diamonds, set in platinum."

He looked at each ring, turning them this way and that to catch the light, then smiled and handed me the one he'd first selected. "This is the one."

Ellis asked the price—$2,100—and he said he'd take it. Sasha commended his choice as she returned it to the tray, then headed back to Prescott's. I told him that we'd package it in a special box.

"Thanks, Josie. I'll stop by tomorrow, pay for it, and pick it up." He smiled. "The timing is perfect. I was going to propose and let Zoë pick her own ring, but this is better."

"And needless to say, if she doesn't love it, you can return it. When's the big moment?"

"Thursday night. Emma's going to stay with Jake in Boston for a couple of days."

I applauded softly. "I'm thrilled, Ellis, totally ecstatic! For both of you."

"You're a good friend, Josie. I wish I hadn't needed the nudge, but since I did, I'm glad you were comfortable nudging. Now I'm going to go see how Zoë's doing."

"If she wants to come over, tell her to bring her bathing suit—my next stop is the hot tub."

CHAPTER TWENTY-NINE

Before I changed into my bathing suit, I called Tom. I explained Maudie's situation and passed along her request that he stand by to help her move out of Belle Vista, if needed.

"Maudie's safe! That's great news, Josie! Julie and I have been so worried about her."

"I know. I agree. She's going to need a lot of support when she gets back. She's had a lot of bad news rain down on her."

We chatted a minute longer; then Tom ended the call. I could tell from his clipped good-bye that he couldn't wait to get off the phone with me and pass along the news. I would have been willing to bet that Stacy would be his first call.

I decided to take a peek at Wes's latest post on the *Seacoast Star* website.

I was pleased. He could have shared the news about my failed effort to find a hidden compartment in Maudie's trunk as if he were revealing a crack in a hegemony, implying my previously infallible powers had waned. Instead, he positioned the information as an example of complexity, adding that I remained convinced the presentation box and cat were hidden somewhere in the apartment.

I texted him. *Nice post.*

He texted back almost immediately. *Thx. What else ya got?*

Give Wes an inch and he'll take a foot and try for a yard.

I was about to climb into the tub when Zoë appeared at the back door, carrying a big pot of soup. I held open the door and she placed it on the stove to simmer. It smelled scrumptious, rich tomatoes mixed with pungent basil.

The ibuprofen had done its job, and I was feeling far less rickety and beat-up.

I took a spoonful of soup. "Oh, wow. You should bottle this, Zoë—no joke. You'd make a million dollars."

"I'll tell you my secret." She lowered her voice confidentially. "Select the best tomatoes, the most aromatic basil, the crispest celery, the sweetest onions . . . are you noticing a theme?" She resumed her normal tone. "I'm glad to take credit, but the truth is that if you use only the best ingredients, everything tastes good."

Zoë was doing her best to be the happy, peppy girl, yet from the haunted look in her eyes, I knew she was still fearful, still depressed. While I could admire her effort and intention, it was painful to watch. I hoped that Ellis's Thursday surprise would lighten her emotional burden.

"You're too modest," I said. "I've tried lots of recipes over the years using only the finest ingredients, and I've had as many failures as successes. You, my friend, have a gift." I started for the back door. "I'm getting into the hot tub. Coming?"

"Try to stop me!" Zoë whipped her terry cloth cover-up over her head and tossed it on a chair.

Outside, I eased myself into the steamy water, leaned back against the built-in bolster, and semifloated, the heat and pulsing soothing more than my sore muscles. I drifted into relaxation mode, and soon my thoughts turned to Maudie, to the missing presentation box and cat sculpture, and to my attack.

I knew from experience the dramatic shift in perception that occurs when you leave a tunnel and look back, but it hadn't happened to me yet, not this time. I could see only the pinprick of light far ahead of me, not the bigger picture that would be revealed once I was out in the open. I kept thinking, assessing, conjecturing, waiting to emerge, to escape, to see the tunnel as merely a slender tube in the wider landscape, but so far, the same scenarios kept playing in my head, over and over again, like a broken video. All I could do was invite the images in and hope they rearranged themselves into a different picture.

When I had arrived at Maudie's unit, the door wasn't completely closed, and the window was wide open. The screen had been raised an inch. Whoever struck me had been hiding behind the wall divider or in the bathroom.

Who?

Someone who needed money.

Someone who wore boots.

Someone with a key or the ability to raise the screen from outside, not impossible, but not the easiest of tasks. Whoever it was probably unlatched the door to facilitate a quick departure and lifted the screen in case an alternate exit was needed.

Stacy needed money, she wore boots, and she had a key and plenty of chutzpah.

I sat forward, my mouth falling open.

My initial dislike of Stacy had limited my vision like blinders on a horse, but the truth was that she wasn't the only person with a key to Maudie's unit. Doug could have copied Celia's key.

Doug lacked Stacy's chutzpah, but he was, if anything, more determined than Stacy to get his hands on some money. Stacy wanted to save her business; Doug wanted to save his children.

Doug had worn boots the first time I saw him.

So had Tom. Tom didn't have a key, but he was more than handy enough to jury-rig access through the window.

"What is it?" Zoë asked, reacting to my expression.

"I just realized . . ." I stopped, my voice trailing off, my brain firing on all cylinders.

Zoë leaned toward me, the water bubbling under her chin. "Josie? Are you all right?"

I blinked myself back to reality and slapped the water. "I'm missing something."

"What?"

"Someone stole the presentation box and cat sculpture, probably the killer. Whoever attacked me must have been in Maudie's apartment to steal them—why else would anybody be there? That means the person who attacked me didn't know the box and cat had been stolen. There were two separate crimes and two separate criminals."

"That's logical."

"Take them one at a time. If Stacy intended to kill Celia, surely she would have prepared an alibi."

Zoë leaned back. "Maybe the murder wasn't planned."

"If she and Celia were there to steal the presentation box and cat sculpture, she'd still have needed an alibi."

"So she's not the killer. Why do you think she won't say where she was?"

"It could be anything," I said, thinking aloud. "People lie all the time, for all sorts of reasons. To protect themselves, or someone else, or something else. Or for fun, to see if they can pull it off. Or to cover something up."

"Like what?"

"A crime or a sin. Or something that might be embarrassing or that you fear might hurt your business. You and I might think it's fine for someone to consult a psychotherapist, but maybe Stacy was worried her investors would be put off by it. Or maybe she's having an affair with a married man."

"Why don't you ask her?"

"I have no leverage."

"If you had to guess where she was, where would it be?"

"I don't know . . . but if I had to guess what she was feeling after her latest investor pitch failed, I'd say despondent." I met Zoë's eyes. "And if she was feeling despondent, I can, in fact, guess where she went."

I scrabbled out of the hot tub, thanked Zoë, ran for the house, grabbing a towel as I darted through the mudroom, and dashed upstairs to change.

At four fifteen, the lounge at the Blue Dolphin was just beginning to get busy with the after-work crowd. I chose a barstool near the far end. The bartender, Jimmy, was a longtime acquaintance, one of the first people I'd met when I moved to Rocky Point. He was routinely cheerful and always competent.

"Hey, Josie!" He spun a cocktail napkin toward me with a flick of his wrist, as if he were skipping a stone on the ocean's surface. "What's your pleasure today?"

"Ginger ale, please."

"You got it." He opened an old-fashioned small bottle, poured the effervescent amber liquid over ice, and placed the glass on the napkin. "I heard about what happened to you on the news. How are you feeling?"

"Good, thanks." I smiled. "Can I ask you something?"

"Fire away!"

"Do you know Stacy Collins?"

A subtle change in his expression told me that he did. He wasn't exactly wary, but neither was he his usual happy-go-lucky self.

"I've known Stacy for years. She stops in every time she visits her aunt."

"Was she here last Friday? Around lunchtime?"

"Her sister was killed that day."

"I know . . . it's so horrible . . . but I'm asking because it might help me find a missing antique."

"You know me, Josie. I'm the soul of discretion."

He was, and usually I admired his ability to look the other way. "Under normal circumstances, a wonderful quality."

"But not now?"

I lowered my voice, hoping my tone would communicate both significance and urgency and preclude follow-up questions. "It's crucial."

"Will you keep it on the down low?"

"If I can—but I can't promise."

"I guess I should have said something."

"Why didn't you?"

He wrung out a dishrag and wiped down a section of bar, avoiding my eyes. "I assumed someone else had already told the cops. She was here for hours, seen by lots of people. And, you know, customers don't want to think you're keeping track of their movements." He tossed the rag onto the counter below the bar.

"That makes sense," I said. I had a different view of civic duty, but that was me. "Stacy was here all afternoon?"

"In and out."

"From when to when?"

"From around noon to sometime after five."

"What do you mean by 'in and out'?"

"When she first got here, she ordered a lobster roll and her regular drink, an old-fashioned. She skipped most of the sandwich, but finished a second drink, and left just after one, returning close to three, when she ordered another drink. She received a phone call shortly after she got back, maybe three fifteen, that upset her enough that she moved from the bar to a table, where she downed two more cocktails before leaving at five something."

"Do you know where she went from one to three?"

"No. She just held up crossed fingers and said to wish her luck."

Jimmy walked to the other end of the bar to serve a customer. I sipped some ginger ale. I was certain the phone call Stacy had received was from the police informing her of Celia's murder. She'd refused to reveal her whereabouts because she didn't want anyone to know she'd spent so many daytime hours at a bar drinking whisky, two of them after she'd learned of her sister's death.

I walked around to the back alley, a lovely enclave overlooking the Piscataqua River, bordered by an old fieldstone wall. The river was nearly black and running fast.

I called Ellis to tell him what I'd learned. I got his voicemail and left a message.

I watched the savage current for a few more minutes as I planned my next move.

CHAPTER THIRTY

I called Stacy and invited her for a drink. "How's the Blue Dolphin?" I asked.

"Perfect. Give me ten minutes."

I went back inside and sat at my favorite table in a corner by the window. "I'm back," I told Jimmy. "Stacy will be joining me. I won't repeat what you told me."

"I appreciate that. Another ginger ale?"

"Club soda, please. With lemon."

Ten minutes later, Stacy threaded her way through the tables to join me.

"Hi, Jimmy! Bring me an old-fashioned, hon!" She sat with her back to the window and scanned the room. "I'm glad you called. Talking to the police is thirsty work."

"You've been with them again today?"

"And every day. I've never answered so many questions in my life. Did Celia have any enemies? No. How would I describe Celia's relationship with Doug? Tense. Tell us about her financial situation. Bad."

"Did they ask you where you were this morning?"

"Yes, but they wouldn't say why."

Jimmy brought her drink, and she took two big gulps.

"What was your answer?" I asked.

"I was on a call to London with a team of hedge fund analysts."

"How'd it go?"

She smiled and raised crossed fingers. "What happened this morning?"

"I was in your aunt's apartment and someone attacked me."

She leaned back, studying my face, her eyes communicating her surprise, then her concern. "Are you all right?"

"Yes, thanks. The police think the attacker was after the presentation box and cat, and I was simply in the wrong place at the wrong time."

"So the killer didn't find it."

Stacy downed her drink and raised her glass, catching Jimmy's attention, silently asking for a refill.

"I guess not." I drank some club soda. "You heard your aunt has been located."

"Yes! What a relief! I spoke to her a couple of hours ago, just for a minute."

"And she'll be home tomorrow. There is something I'm a bit confused about. I know from the *Seacoast Star*'s news reports that you've refused to tell the police where you were when Celia was killed. But you didn't hesitate to share your whereabouts during the time I was attacked today. What's the difference?"

She thanked Jimmy when he placed her drink in front of her and took a sip before she spoke. "I didn't kill my sister. It's an insult that they're treating me like a suspect. When you asked, when they asked, I didn't know I was providing an alibi. I thought I was chatting. If I'd known, I might have answered differently."

"I suspect I'd feel the same."

"I think a lot of people would." She shook her glass gently, sending the ice spinning. "Let me take a turn with the questions . . . Why did you ask me to join you today?"

"I feel for you. Your life is in New York. Here you are without a support system, with your business in flux. I wanted to help, if I could."

"That's very nice of you, but pointless." She took another sip. "The truth is that I'm beyond help."

"You're having a little setback, that's all. I don't know if you were aware, but I lived in New York City for years. The point is that I get what the city can mean to a person. Everything you need or want is right there. When you're not there, you feel, well, all at sea."

"You do get it . . . Why did you leave?"

"A business opportunity. We're both entrepreneurs, so you know what I mean. It was a good decision for me. I'm very happy in New Hampshire, and"—I opened my arm to the lounge—"the Blue Dolphin is my favorite hangout."

"Oh, me, too. Jimmy's a doll. A complete peach!"

I continued leading the conversation onto neutral, pleasant topics. Soon Stacy was telling me about her dreams for her business—to celebrate her clients' individuality as an antidote to oppressive conventionality—and I found myself warming to her. Her communication style might often be brusque to the point of rudeness, but as she'd said, her heart was in the right place, and there was no denying that her ideas were inventive and her observations thought-provoking.

When she was almost done with her third drink, I asked, "You said you wouldn't tell the police where you were on Friday because you don't appreciate being suspected of killing your sister, but isn't it understandable that the police want to know where you were? It isn't personal to you. They've asked everyone."

Stacy shook her head, refusing to discuss the issue, then took a long drink.

I lowered my voice. "Someone told me they saw you here having a few drinks starting at noon and that you left around one for a couple of hours."

Stacy kept her eyes on her glass, seeming to watch the ice melt.

"It sounds to me like you were drinking to screw up your courage," I whispered, "that you must have had to do something you found distasteful or uncomfortable."

"Whoever told you that is a liar."

"Really?"

"Really."

"Now that the word is out, the police will be able to find lots of other people to confirm the story."

"Let them try."

"It's over, Stacy."

She met my gaze for a moment, then lowered her eyes again. She placed her elbows on the table and rested her forehead on the tips of her fingers.

"You had to push," she said, signaling Jimmy for a refill. "You just couldn't leave it alone."

"What?"

"Push, push, push." Jimmy delivered her old-fashioned, and she took a long drink. "I just couldn't do it."

"What couldn't you do?"

"Ask Aunt Maudie for money. That's what I was doing. Are you happy now? I drove to New Hampshire directly after that disgusting investor meeting in Boston, knowing that I was going to have to do the one thing I most dreaded—beg Aunt Maudie for money—again. It was my only hope of keeping my business alive. I came straight here, had a couple of quick ones, liquid courage, then set out for Belle Vista."

I knew Stacy hadn't signed Belle Vista's guest book, and she didn't appear on the security camera footage. "You never went."

"I couldn't. I just couldn't face Maudie's contempt. I drove around for an hour or so, then returned to the home of Jimmy's foolproof cure for whatever ails you."

"Asking for money is tough."

"I have no problem asking investors for money. That's business. But Aunt Maudie . . . She isn't going to judge my business plan. She's going to judge me. I was ashamed and embarrassed."

"You're sounding stronger now."

"I'm drunk."

"Tipsy, maybe."

"You do have a way with words, don't you? I'm not stronger. I just know how to put on a good show."

When Stacy went to the ladies' room, I settled with Jimmy. On her way back, she asked him for another drink.

Once she was seated, I said, "You need to tell the police where you were on Friday. They'll understand."

"They'll think I'm a loser just like everyone else."

"I don't think you're a loser. I think you're trying to cope as best you can."

She tilted her head. "I can't decide if you're naïve or dumb."

I stood. "Neither. I'm open-minded and fair. I give everyone the benefit of the doubt. I've got to go . . . Can I drive you somewhere?"

"Thanks, but no thanks. I'm here for the duration."

"You shouldn't drive."

"I never drive when I've been drinking. That's why God made cabs."

"Good." I started to leave, then turned back. "I'll need to tell the police we spoke."

Stacy sipped her drink, then took a larger swig. "Everyone does what she has to do."

Ty arrived at seven, after I'd texted Ellis about Stacy's alibi, just as I was surveying the refrigerator, weighing options for dinner. Zoë told me she'd be back around ten, ready to spend the night. I walked into his embrace and rested my forehead on his chest, then leaned back to ask, "What are you doing here? I said I was fine."

"If I told you I'd been whacked upside the head but I was fine, would you stay away?"

I laughed. "Well . . . when you put it that way . . . I wasn't hit on the head, though. I got the bump when I crashed into the trunk."

He examined each of my hands, kissing my palms, then brushed his lips against my bruised upper arm. "I'm noticing some colorful bruises."

"True." I smiled and kissed him. "I'm so glad you're home."

CHAPTER THIRTY-ONE

Ty left the next morning, Wednesday, at six. I got up to say goodbye, and when he left, I lay down again, falling into a dreamless sleep. I woke again at eight, late for me.

I called Zoë. "I'm sorry I ran out on you yesterday, then canceled your sleepover. I'm going to soak my weary bones right now, then have breakfast. Come and join me. I'll make you French toast."

"Yum. I can't, though. Emma and I are making a day of it. We're going to take in a museum and have a nice lunch. Emma feels sorry for me. Either that or she's trying to appease her guilt."

"I hope you can put all that self-pity and anger aside and have a good time. Live in the moment and all that."

"You know me too well."

"Not too well—just well. I think it's really nice that she wants to spend time with you."

Zoë sighed, the sound of something artificially inflated deflating. "So do I. Thanks, Josie. Was your errand yesterday a success?"

"Yes. I realized there was a way to get Stacy to come clean about her alibi. I had to try."

"Did it work?"

"Yes."

"And?"

"It's complicated. What museum are you going to?"

"Currier. Emma wants to see some of her favorite pieces, the Wyeth and the O'Keeffe."

"She always had good taste."

"Want to come? You can bridge the communication gaps."

"I wish I could. But I'm confident you can avoid communication gaps by reminding yourself how much you love her."

I got to work by ten. Cara was alone in the office.

After I greeted her and poured myself a cup of coffee, I asked, "Where is everyone?"

"Sasha is meeting with a curator about an impressionist painting she bought from a picker. She thinks it might be a . . ." Cara consulted her notepad for the name. "Jacques Lambert. She says he's not well known, but his work is excellent."

"Early twentieth century."

Cara consulted the note. "That's right. 1902. Fred is meeting with a professor who's getting ready to retire and wants to know his options about selling some antiques. Eric is out back, overseeing the power washing of the gutters." She picked up another note. "Gretchen called. She plans on stopping by at eleven." Cara leaned forward. "And you? How are you feeling?"

I smiled. "I'm fine. Just a couple of bruises."

"When Gretchen told us . . . well . . . you can imagine."

"Thank you, Cara. I think I'm going to—" I broke off when the phone rang.

Cara answered with her usual cheery greeting, then said, "Bonjour, Mademoiselle Joubert. No, I'm sorry, he's not here right now."

I waved my hand to catch her attention.

She nodded. "Josie Prescott is here, though. May I put her on?"

I took the call at the guest table. I introduced myself in French, apologized for my limited command of the language, and asked if she was comfortable speaking in English. She said she was, that she had news, and asked that I call her Yvette.

"My father found the original bill of sale and the ledger containing the purchase record." Yvette laughed with delight. "My great-great-grandfather was a very organized man. The chandelier, item number 17412 in the ledger, was sold to a Major Wilson in 1919. It was shipped to a private residence in Rocky Point, New Hampshire."

She called out the date of sale and the shipping address, my address now, and a burst of joy and enchantment charged through my veins. I always felt exhilarated when we took a step on the path to provenance, but this was personal, and oh, so meaningful.

"This is beyond expectation. Do the records indicate how it came into your shop?"

"Yes. A young war widow of a most well-respected family named Genevieve Vermandois sold it to us. Madame Vermandois told my great-great-grandfather that the chandelier had been made to her mother-in-law's specifications by Jean-Charles Delafosse, the preeminent designer of that era. My father said to tell you that in his estimation, it would sell at auction in Paris today for close to a million euros."

"I'm speechless, Yvette. Honored, dazzled, and speechless."

"I have scanned in these documents, and I will email them to you. My father said to tell you that this was a superb moment for him, to read his great-grandfather's notes, to verify the provenance."

"Please tell your father that if I can ever help him with an appraisal, all he has to do is ask."

She laughed again, a sweet, tinkly sound. "I assure you, he will. When he needs help, he is not shy."

Monte called. He said he wanted to show us something at the Gingerbread House. I told him that Ty was out of town, but I could come.

I got there around eleven thirty and parked in back of a Dumpster wedged against the hedge. The lawn was covered with materials and supplies, a daunting sight. A steady stream of men wheeled loads of rotten wood and broken bricks along the front walk and up the Dumpster ramp. They flipped the debris into the Dumpster, wobbled back down to street level, and did it again.

Tom, outfitted with a yellow hard hat and sturdy work boots, came from the side of the house, wheelbarrow in hand.

Monte was in the backyard, pointing at the eaves, saying something to a tall, thin man who was staring at the roofline and nodding. Both men wore hard hats.

Monte greeted me and introduced me to Roland Thurston, the master carpenter he'd retained to replicate all the decorative wood elements that had to be replaced.

"We're almost done," Monte told me. "Give me a minute, okay?"

"Sure."

I walked to the stone wall at the back of the property.

It was warmer today, maybe eighty-two degrees, with a light breeze blowing from the west. The ocean was calm, waves gently rolling to shore. Suntouched sequins skipped across the water.

The iris beds looked good. The bulbs had been transplanted and the flowers raised their heads to the warm sun, a sheen of water clinging to the leaves. Tom must have watered them earlier. The lawn was cut up where the beds rested, as if the heavy wooden frames had been dragged instead of lifted into place. A spade lay on the grass, half-hidden by the shed. I picked it up and leaned it against the stone wall. The lawn was in worse shape in back of the shed, maybe from heavy tools being tossed onto the grass, a handy place to store things out of sight. I wasn't going to let myself get upset. Monte had warned us that renovation projects were disruptive, intrusive, and annoying. The shed door was slightly ajar, so I guessed Tom planned on doing some other gardening chores before he left for the day.

A scraping sound broke into my reverie, and I turned toward the shed in time to see Julie heading in, weighed down by a coiled garden hose.

"Julie!"

She spun toward me, so startled she nearly dropped the hose.

"Hi!" she said. She licked her lips and took a faltering step backward. "Sorry."

She looked all around, seeking help or an escape, I wasn't sure which.

"How are you?" I asked.

"Fine, thanks." She juggled the hose, trying for a more comfortable position, then lowered it to the ground. "We were so excited to hear about Maudie."

Her expression belied her warm and friendly tone, her eyes reflecting fear more than surprise, and I thought I knew why. I'd warned her not to do any work on the property, yet here she was, caught red-handed.

I smiled and nodded at the hose. "Helping Tom?"

She stared at the hose, calculating how to best reply. "I'm like a sub," she said, raising her eyes to my face. "You didn't like it that I was working without getting paid. Now I'm getting paid. I mean, Tom does the billing, but it's fair. You can think of us like one unit."

I didn't want to say no. If Tom was doing unskilled construction work, obviously they needed the money. I also admired their work ethic.

"I'll tell you what . . . I'll add you to our worker's comp insurance plan, then you're good to go."

Tears sprang to her eyes, and she smiled as if she'd won a Vegas jackpot. "Thank you."

"I'll get it done today, so you can go ahead and work."

She flashed me another quick smile, scooped up the hose and placed it in the shed, used a key she extracted from her front pocket to lock it, then called "'bye" and scuttled away, disappearing around the left side of the house.

I texted Cara to let our insurance agent know he should add her to our personal policy, listing her duties as outside gardening and light maintenance, effective immediately.

I turned to the left, looking north. A half mile farther up, New Hampshire gave way to Maine.

Monte walked up. "Sorry, Josie. Roland is booked solid for months, so if he says he wants to get going on your work, you accommodate him."

"Terrific news." I opened my arms toward the ocean. "I'm glad for any excuse to commune with the ocean."

"I don't blame you."

"From the line of men carrying away refuse, it looks like you're making good progress."

"We're on schedule, which brings me to why I asked you to stop by. We need to talk zones for the HVAC."

He said that in our previous discussion we'd decided to install four zones, but he thought we should consider adding more.

"Let me talk to Ty," I said, "but I think you're right. We might as well double it. A little extra cost now, but we'll save on energy forever."

I called Ty, and he agreed. We almost always did.

I had just gotten back to Prescott's and climbed the stairs to my private office when Ellis called to tell me to stop talking to suspects—in particular, Stacy.

"I don't work for you," I said.

"That's my point exactly. Not only is your going rogue potentially dangerous, but you risk messing up a case. You gave her a chance to practice her replies."

"I don't accept the premise of your objection. I didn't go rogue. I met Stacy in a public place, and I'm not stupid. I didn't try to trick her or anything. Nothing got messed up."

"You might not have been in danger during that particular conversation, but that doesn't mean you're out of danger. Likewise, you might not have realized you were helping a witness prepare for an interrogation, but you were. You need to lay off. I mean it, Josie. Your intentions are good. That isn't the issue."

"I still don't agree with your assessment, but it's moot because I don't plan on talking to anyone else."

"If you change your mind, you call me *before* you talk to anyone."

"You're being absurd, Ellis!"

"Fear festers."

That two-word reply brought me up short. He was right—fear does fester, and everyone in Celia's orbit was afraid of something: losing independence, failure, going broke.

"Point taken," I said. "How's Doug?"

"Figuring out childcare. He starts his new job on Monday. How are you feeling?"

"Fine—more or less. Thanks for asking. Any nibbles on who broke into Maudie's apartment?"

"Not yet."

Not yet, I repeated to myself once we'd ended the call.

Yesterday I'd been hoping to finally escape the tunnel and see the situation through a wider lens, yet I remained stubbornly stuck inside. Sitting in the hot tub, I'd concentrated on specific facts, seeking linkages or contradictions, finding none, but today I had the sense that something, one of those linkages or contradictions, had jostled loose. That I couldn't put my finger on it added to my frustration and gnawed at me like hunger.

I spent the next several hours catching up on work and other pending issues. Gretchen told me she'd posted the listing for her new assistant position and already received applications. She also told me that she and Winnie had conspired to get Pastor Ted out of the way for an hour so the window rep could take the measurements.

Wes called at two trolling for dirt, but I had nothing to share.

"You were firecracker hot with Stacy—you're the only person to get the truth out of her. How'd you do it?"

"I empathized."

"No, I mean carrot and stick, you know ... empathy might be the carrot ... what was the stick?"

"Wes, you never cease to amaze me. There was no stick. Jeesh!"

"Give me some color. Did she cry?"

"No!"

"Talk to me."

"I have nothing to say. I've got to go."

I touched the END CALL button.

Hank sauntered into the office. He leapt into my lap and curled up, and I began to pet him, gentle strokes. His purring machine whirred onto high. I was still petting him with one hand, and replying to emails with the other, when Maudie called at ten after four. She was in the car, on Route 95, north of Boston.

"I'm calling to ask a favor," Maudie said. "I called my friend Nessie, but she's out of town. With everything going on, I forgot she and Charlie were off hiking. I thought about who else I'd like to see, and the only name that came to me was yours. I'm booked into the Austin Arms. Would you be able to meet? I know it's last minute ... I hope I'm not imposing."

"I'd love to see you, Maudie." With Ellis's admonition fresh in my mind, I asked, "What about the police? I know Chief Hunter said he wanted to talk to you as soon as you got back."

"I just got off the phone with him. I'll meet with him in the morning. I'm trying to decide whether to bring a lawyer."

"If it makes you feel more comfortable, why not?"

"I'm afraid it might make me look guilty."

"Guilty of what?"

"Nothing, since I didn't do anything ... but haven't you ever noticed that you don't need to *be* guilty to *feel* guilty?"

I smiled. "All the time. The good girl's curse. I think you should bring a lawyer. Do you have one?"

"Just our family attorney. She handled the house closing, prepared our wills, simple things. Do you have a recommendation?"

"Yes, as a matter of fact, I do."

I told her I'd email her Max's name and contact info and assured her that she couldn't do better. We agreed to meet at six.

I called Max on his cell to give him a heads-up.

"Josie! I was just thinking of you. I'm in my car en route to meeting Lainy. She's so enthusiastic . . . I love it. I'm auditioning for the part of Billy Flynn. Maybe we'll end up working together. How're things in your world?"

"Good, good." I told him I'd passed along his name to Maudie and shared how much I liked her.

"Do you think she's mixed up in this?"

"No. I mean, I don't know, but I don't think so."

"Something's got you all jittery."

"I'll just feel better knowing you're there with her and on her side."

"Fair enough. Come and join Lainy and me for a drink. Listen to us talk about the Great White Way."

I laughed, charmed as I always was by Max's joie de vivre, and accepted. He told me they were meeting at five at Delany's, the pub near Belle Vista.

I got to Delany's early and sat in the parking lot, thinking about keys, and all at once, I realized there was another person who had a key to Maudie's apartment—Lainy.

CHAPTER THIRTY-TWO

called Ellis and got him.

"It's Lainy," I said.

"How did you know?"

"What?"

"We just arrested her. I'm en route to Belle Vista now. How did you know it was her?"

"She broke into Maudie's place?" I asked, aghast.

"Yes . . . your idea about the hidden cameras worked. For the third time—how did you know?"

"I didn't. I mean, I didn't know she'd broken in. I just remembered she had access to a master key, and she wanted money—in her case, to fund her career in New York City. Ellis, she was wearing boots when I was attacked. Do you think she broke in then, too? Did she attack me?"

"She has no alibi. We'll see what she says."

"Oh, Ellis! What was she thinking?"

"I doubt she was doing a lot of thinking. Probably it's an opportunistic crime. She saw a chance to make a big score and decided to go for it."

"You have her on video?"

"Clear as day."

"I'm sick."

"I know."

He thanked me for the call and said he had to go.

I was tempted to stay where I was, to avoid the ugliness, but decided I wanted to see Lainy for myself, to look her in the eye, to see if she turned away, so I drove back to Belle Vista, arriving just as a patrol car pulled up, its siren blaring, its lights spinning.

Officer Meade flipped a switch, and the sirens stopped, the abrupt quiet startling. She stepped out, said something into her collar mic, and jogged up the walkway. Ellis arrived as I was getting out of my car. I didn't wait. I ran into the building.

I heard Lainy before I saw her. "No!" she shrieked. "No, no, no." Her voice was piercing, her panic palpable. "No, no, no . . . stop!"

Lainy, her hands cuffed behind her back, tried to wriggle away from Detective Brownley. Officer Meade clutched Lainy's right arm, with Detective Brownley gripping the left one. Lainy continued to struggle, to screech, her voice growing shriller with each word.

"No! Stop! No, no, no!"

I stopped ten paces into the lobby and pressed my back against the wall, watching in horror.

"No! Stop it! It's a mistake! Stop!"

Ellis raced inside and took charge. He stepped directly in front of Lainy and held up his hands chin high, palms toward her, pumping air, gesturing that she was to stop, to pause, to listen, to breathe. "Ms. Baglio, you need to stop resisting. Do you understand?"

"I didn't do anything! Let me go!"

"We can talk about this at the station, but right now, you need to accompany the detective and officer outside."

"No, no, no!" she screamed, working herself into a hysterical dither.

"Stop!" Ellis boomed.

Lainy froze, petrified, her chest heaving.

"I understand you're upset, but you need to cooperate with us. You're under arrest for burglary. You'll have an opportunity to tell us your side of the story. No one is trying to railroad you. All we want is the truth. The first thing that has to happen, though, is that we transport you to the police station. If you resist again, we'll have to add that charge. Do you understand?"

Lainy nodded and walked forward, slowly, her tears flowing.

When she reached me, she looked straight at me. "I'm sorry."

She took another step, then paused again and looked back at Ellis. "Please," she whispered, "don't tell my father."

Max was at a table by the fireplace. Instead of wood, there was a nice arrangement of white pillar candles, unlit in the still-sunny late afternoon.

"Lainy won't be joining us," I said, plunking down on a chair across from him.

"Trouble in paradise?"

"There was never any paradise, only trouble. I just witnessed her arrest."

Max leaned back, his eyes locked on mine while I described what I'd seen and what I knew.

He shook his head. "Proving once again that you can't judge by appearances or first impressions."

Max waved the waitress over and ordered a Macallan single malt neat. I asked for club soda with lime.

When the drinks arrived, Max said, "Are you flipping out?"

"A little. I can't believe Lainy attacked me. I mean, I know she didn't intend to hurt me, she just wanted to escape, but still . . ." I shook it off. "Did you speak to Maudie?"

"Yes, we're meeting at her hotel in the morning. My first impression was positive. Will I be disappointed?"

"It was Malcolm Gladwell who said, 'We don't know where our first impressions come from or precisely what they mean, so we don't always appreciate their fragility.' I like Maudie a lot. You're not the only one who hopes a first impression sticks."

The Austin Arms was the most luxurious hotel in Rocky Point, old-style in decor and service. There were murals of clouds and cherubs and angels painted in muted colors on the ceiling, and gilt everywhere, from the crown moldings to the picture frames. The building and grounds sprawled over seven acres at one end of Rocky Point's village green, within easy walking distance of shops and restaurants.

Maudie met me in the lobby and led the way to a small alcove. We sat on club chairs near a window facing the back garden. A waiter took our order for tea.

"I just heard about Lainy," she said. "On the news."

"I'm still stunned."

"Did she kill Celia?"

"I don't think so. I think she was after the presentation box. Tom described it to her."

She turned toward the window for a moment, then looked back at me. "I spoke to Stacy and Doug from San Francisco. Neither call went well."

"I'm sorry to hear that."

"I should have been better prepared."

"You had no way of knowing what was going on with them."

"That's true," she said. "And I don't know why I'm surprised. Stacy was as acerbic as always, acting as if Celia's death was one of a dozen tragedies designed specifically to overset her plans. Doug was angry. I asked if he'd like me to stay with him for a few weeks, to help with childcare and the house. He said no."

"Stacy is Stacy, and I don't think Doug knows which way is up. He's overwhelmed."

"I suppose."

"You said you wanted to talk to a friend." I patted her hand. "How can I help, Maudie?"

"You've helped me so much, Josie, more than you know, more than you can imagine." Her expression softened. "I don't need anything in particular. Just a friendly voice, a bit of kindness."

"That I can do."

"People never know what to say in times of tragedy," she said, echoing the thought I'd had on Tuesday, the thought that had led to our locating her in San Francisco, "so they don't say anything, or they only speak in platitudes. I've found that it's better to talk about what's bothering you, no matter how hard it is; that it's *not* talking about things that leads to problems."

A waiter slid a gilt-edged tray onto the table between us. He poured two inches of a dark mahogany brew into bone china cups, topped it off with steaming hot water, and left. I stirred in a teaspoon of sugar and a dollop of milk. Maudie squeezed a piece of lemon into hers.

I left the tea to cool. "How are you doing for real?"

"I don't know how to describe it. Sad, but more than that. Alone. Celia and I had issues, but she had a genuinely good heart. She was a loving wife and mother. Perhaps I should have done more for her. Perhaps the fact that I didn't led to her death." She reached for her cup, then pulled her hand back. "It's hot." She made an effort to smile. "I know I'm not responsible for Celia's death, any more than I'm responsible for Stacy's business failing, but I certainly understand why people who win the lottery give blank checks to the flood of long-lost relatives who come begging. It's easier to bear than the guilt."

"Doug said you helped them out before."

"When Eli died, I gave Celia and Stacy fifty thousand dollars each, telling them it was from him. When Stacy told me her business idea, I felt so proud of her. It takes real courage to start a business. She asked me to invest, and I said I wouldn't, that I wasn't comfortable investing, but I gave her twenty-five thousand dollars as seed money. That's what I called it: seed money. To be fair, I gave the same amount to Celia, encouraging her to invest in herself somehow, just as Stacy was doing. A few months ago, just after I moved in to Belle Vista, Stacy asked for a loan."

"You said no."

"That's right."

"Why?"

"I'm very conservative with my investments. Eli inherited a nice amount of money from his family, and he did very well in his career. I have been blessed. I feel no need to earn big returns. I feel the need to not lose my principal. Except for those gifts, I have never dipped into it."

"How did Stacy handle your refusal?"

Maudie touched the cup with a fingertip, testing the temperature, and decided it was still too hot. "Stacy used it as evidence that my alleged dementia was worsening. Doug and Celia asked for money at about that same time, and when I said no to them, too, Celia jumped on Stacy's bandwagon, implying that I wasn't dealing from a full deck. The two of them hovered over me, looking as if they expected me to start babbling or drooling any minute. Their apparent concern got me wondering if they were right." Maudie turned her face aside. "A month after I moved into Belle Vista, I went to a neurologist. Turns out, I'm fine. He put me through a battery of tests at my request, and I passed them all. I joke about losing my memory and so on because I got tired of arguing about my mental acuity with my nieces. They eased up once I stopped arguing. I never did sign the power of attorney form, though, and that rankled."

"Oh, Maudie, that's awful. I mean, it's wonderful you're healthy, but it's awful you had to go through such a thing."

"I agree. I spent a lot of my time in San Francisco thinking about what I should do about their nagging, what might happen if I sell the presentation box and cat for a bundle, how I'd handle their renewed requests. I decided to stick to my guns. I don't owe anyone anything. I've done my best to help them, but enough is enough. And their efforts to make me doubt myself, well . . . it was cruel."

I blinked away a tear. Poor Maudie.

She tested the tea again. It passed muster, and she drank some. "However, I'm a fan of education. Just as Eli and I paid for Celia and Stacy's education, I called my lawyer, that family lawyer I mentioned, and asked her to establish a trust to cover all of Celia and Doug's children's educational expenses. And Stacy's kids, if she ever has any, and Doug's, if he wants to go back to school himself."

"That's wonderful of you, Maudie."

"I hope it helps. I don't believe in handouts, but I do believe in rewarding initiative, and I certainly believe in second chances."

"I do, too. People learn from their mistakes—if they want to. Not to imply that Doug made a mistake. Lots of people just need a break. And I believe in giving it to them, if I can."

"Those breaks often cost money."

"Almost always," I said. "It's amazing you're including Doug in your offer. His hands aren't completely clean when it comes to stealing the presentation box."

"I've known Doug for years. I think he's essentially a good man who was simply pushed to the limit. Once again, it comes back to second chances. He's all those kids have now. I emailed him that I'd cover his tuition and all expenses, including childcare, household expenses, everything, while he's in school. He's always been good with numbers, so maybe accounting would be a good choice." She placed her cup on the saucer, and it rattled. "If I'd made this offer before Celia died, maybe she'd still be alive."

"Don't do that, Maudie. You can't know what someone might have done. Celia might have been grateful at first, then decided she needed more, and found herself in the same situation—trying to steal from you, and ending up confronting someone else who was trying to steal from you. You can't second-guess decisions, not based on speculation."

"You're right. It's just my guilt talking. I tell myself to focus on the positive and on the future, but it's hard."

"I know." I drank some tea. "Tell me something about Celia. What's your best memory?"

"Banana bread. She made the best, most succulent banana bread, and she kept me supplied with it. She made those little loaves and brought one over, oh, I don't know, once a month or so. I'd cut it up and freeze it."

"So thoughtful!"

"Yes, she was thoughtful. I loved her, which was often challenging. Celia didn't handle life's difficulties easily or well. She was very needy. Her best quality, I think, was her ability as a mother—she cherished her children. They'll have the memories of her love to buoy them forever."

"And Stacy? What's her best quality?"

Maudie smiled. "I care about Stacy, too, but the truth is that she's always been hard to love. She lives in a state of perpetual disappointment. She has a chip on her shoulder the size of Montana, and she doesn't handle setbacks gracefully. I also . . . and this is a terrible thing to say about your own niece . . . I think she's manipulative. Stacy is so self-absorbed, I suspect she thinks I don't notice the superficial nature of her affection."

"You're saying she's just after money."

"Yes, I guess I am. I've given her every opportunity to be friends, but she always circles back to business. Oh, well . . . I've done the best I can, and that's all I can do."

Maudie drank some tea as she surveyed the lobby. It was quiet. Everything was clean, pristine. An older couple sat nearby, their conversation hushed.

She lowered her cup to the saucer. "I like it here. I'm not sorry I had to leave Belle Vista. I shouldn't have agreed to move in."

"Where do you think you'll go permanently?"

"I may try to negotiate a monthly rent here. It's not likely to be higher than Belle Vista."

"What about that condo on the beach?"

"Yes, that's worth considering, too." She turned back toward me. "I spoke to that lawyer you recommended, Max Bixby. He sounded assured and knowledgeable. He's coming here for breakfast at seven thirty."

"Because you want to look him in the eye before retaining him."

She smiled. "Wouldn't you?"

I smiled back. "Yes."

"I have another favor, but I'm hesitating to ask you."

Joyous shrieks sounded outside the window. Two boys, about nine or ten, ran by, carrying badminton racquets, their laughter contagious.

I laughed. "When I was a kid, I was killer at badminton."

"Me, too."

"Oh-ho! I sense a challenge about to be issued."

"I haven't played in decades."

"You're either managing expectations or setting me up as a mark."

She smiled. "You'll just have to find out for yourself, won't you?"

"Name the date. In the meantime, what's the favor? I appreciate your hesitation and promise I'll say no if I can't do it."

"Chief Hunter said that the first thing he wants to do is take me to Belle Vista so I can see if anything besides the presentation box and cat and my checkbook were stolen. I'm certain I'll notice myself if anything is missing, but if that police chief starts asking me questions . . . I'm being silly, I know . . . but . . . I'd appreciate a second set of eyes. You were just there, so your memory is fresh. I know it's a lot to ask, but will you come?"

"Yes. I don't think you're being silly—four eyes are always better than two. I'm glad to help you."

"Thank you. That's such a relief . . . something I don't have to fret about."

"I'm glad. It's funny, isn't it, how little things can mess with your head in a way big things don't. I guess because we expect big things to be problematic. In any event . . . if you're up for it, I'd like to ask you a couple of questions, but I don't want to upset you."

"Fire away. I'm glad to talk. It's good to talk."

"When did you decide to go to San Francisco?"

"Last Friday. I know your next question is why I went. Eli and I visited for our fifteenth wedding anniversary. I liked it very much, and when I decided

I wanted to meet Dr. Moss in person, I asked myself, Why not? My plan had me in San Francisco for a week, followed by Maui for ten days. I asked Gerard if he knew places in Hawaii to snorkel from the shore, and he recommended Maui."

"Black Rock."

"I read about that! And the thirty-mile marker."

"I love Maui."

"I'll go another time."

"So you called Gerard, and off you went."

"He got me a first-class ticket on the six P.M. out of Logan. I was so excited!"

"I can imagine. I found someone who saw you wheeling your tote bag down the street. I'm guessing you had Uber meet you a few blocks away. Why?"

"I didn't want to give any of those busybodies something to talk about."

"Isn't wheeling a tote bag down the street more conspicuous than getting into a car in the parking lot?"

"Not at Belle Vista. Every time I got dropped off by Uber, that busybody Selma peppered me with questions about where I'd gone and what I'd done. Since everyone was used to me walking to stores pulling my grocery cart or tote bag, no one would even notice."

"Why didn't you tell anyone where you were going?"

"I didn't want to listen to all the reasons why my trip was a bad idea. I could hear Celia: *What if something happens to you? You'll be so far from home.* Stacy would ask how much it costs. My mother had a saying—don't give your head for washing. If you volunteer information, you're giving someone permission to judge. Another aspect is that it never occurred to me that anyone would notice I was gone. It's not like I saw them on a daily or even a weekly basis."

"You called me at lunchtime on Friday and left a message asking me to call or meet."

"Oh, my! I never called you back . . . how rude. What did I want?"

I laughed. "How would I know?"

"Good point." Maudie laughed heartily, and I got a glimpse of her future—free-spirited and open to adventure.

Maudie invited me to stay for dinner, and I thanked her but declined, explaining I needed to get home. It wasn't an excuse. It was true. I needed to be alone, to think, to add these new tidbits of information to the puzzle and see if the picture would finally come into focus.

The essential questions hadn't changed: Who had a key to Maudie's Belle Vista apartment or the ability to get in through the window? Who needed money badly enough to take the risk? Who had the wherewithal to spirit away the presentation box and cat sculpture and hide them somewhere they would be safe and accessible, but not accidentally stumbled upon or easily found?

I fell asleep with those questions revolving in my mind like an unending carousel, and when I awakened, I discovered that the fuzzy image was indeed beginning to resolve itself into one cohesive picture.

CHAPTER THIRTY-THREE

When we arrived at Maudie's apartment the next morning at ten, it looked the same: grimy, stained, and disheveled.

She gasped as she entered and steadied herself by grasping the bedroom dividing wall. "How awful," she stammered.

"Your niece, Ms. Collins, planned to have Tom Hill clean it," Ellis said. "She didn't want you to see it this way." He moved toward the kitchen counter. "I know you want this to be as quick as possible. If you would start in your clothes drawers and closets . . . Let me know if anything is missing, large or small, important or insignificant, valuable or worthless."

Maudie opened the front hall closet and flipped through her coats and jackets, crouched to peer behind the row of boots on the floor, and lifted scarves and hats from the top shelf. She did the same with another closet, this one packed with dresses, skirts, tunics, and blouses. A shoe caddy hung on the inside of the door. She pawed through her drawers, filled with intimate wear, tops, socks, slacks. She opened her jewelry box and poked around.

"As far as I can tell, nothing is missing."

Maudie stepped into the kitchen and began a methodical inspection, moving from left to right.

When she reached the cabinet under the sink, she said, "The bleach is missing."

Ellis jotted a note. "Can you describe the container? The brand?"

"It was the store brand, fifty-five ounces, if I remember right. I recall thinking that was an odd size, less than half a gallon. The container was white plastic with a built-in handle."

"Good. What else?"

She pointed to a box of large trash bags. "I'd just opened that box. It contains ten bags, and I know we used one . . . but look . . . I'm guessing three or four are gone."

Maudie continued her examination but didn't notice anything else missing.

"What about your grocery cart?" I asked. "The last time I saw it, it was leaning up against the bistro table."

"You're right."

I took a step toward the kitchen. The picture snapped into focus. "That's the last piece of the puzzle." The grocery cart. The trash bags. The key. A desperate need for money. Easy lies.

Ellis said something.

So did Max.

When Ellis stepped in front of me, I realized he'd been talking to me.

"Josie?" he asked. "Are you all right?"

"What? Sorry. I'm fine. I was thinking." I met Maudie's eyes, then Max's, then came back to Ellis. "I know what happened and how and why—and I know how to prove it. I know where the presentation box and cat sculpture are, and I know they're safe."

Ellis demanded that I explain.

"I think we should get the box first," I said. "Then I can answer all your questions." I turned to Maudie, who was standing with her mouth agape. "The police are going to take possession of the box and cat. They'll be safe in the police lockup."

"That's fine, but I'm going to be a witness. Let's go."

"We're not going anywhere until I have some answers," Ellis said. "Tell me what's going on."

"Let me tell you about it en route," I said, and he agreed. "We're going to the Gingerbread House."

Ellis and I went in his SUV. Max drove Maudie and followed us.

I described what I'd observed and heard, and when I was done, Ellis asked, "How deep is it buried?"

"Three to four feet, at a guess."

He took his car radio in hand and told Cathy where we were going and why. "I want the crime scene team to do the digging, so we can be certain to preserve the evidence properly."

The radio squawks were hard to understand, but I gathered the team would meet us there in ten minutes. Ellis asked for two police officers, too.

When he was done, I said, "Tom Hill was working for our contractor the other day."

"Doing what?"

"Hauling debris."

When we arrived, just ahead of Max's Prius, Ellis grabbed a roll of yellow crime scene tape from the backseat while I found Monte and told him we were going to be in the back and he should ignore us.

"Is Tom here today?" I asked. "Tom Hill?"

"Not now. He worked for me for a couple of hours this morning, then had to go to another job. He said he'd be back to do some watering."

"Did he say when?" Ellis asked.

"After lunch, nothing more specific."

We thanked him, and I led the way to the backyard.

Ellis used the tape to cordon off a wide swath of land surrounding the shed. We stood around, not talking, waiting for the officers and crime scene techs. Occasionally, one of Monte's crew popped around the corner of the house, checking us out.

"The dig is going to be all over the news," I remarked.

"Can't be helped," Ellis replied.

I took a few photos of the shed surrounded by yellow tape.

Two men wearing Rocky Point Crime Scene–branded collared T-shirts marched across the lawn. Each one carried a large rectangular box bearing the same gold-and-blue logo.

The two officers arrived next, Griff and a young man I'd met a couple of times named Daryl. Griff was stationed at Ocean Avenue to keep curiosity-seekers and the press at bay. Daryl was posted on the beach, just in case trouble came calling from that direction.

Max, Maudie, and I stood on the sandy incline that led to the water, out of the crime scene team's way, on the beach side of the stone wall.

Fast-moving clouds scudded across the pale blue sky. The temperature was dropping, the humidity rising.

The techs began their painstaking work, digging with miniature shovels, brushing dirt aside, examining the hole, removing another shovelful of dirt, brushing, viewing, over and over again. Ellis rested his hip against the stone wall.

Wes appeared on the beach, popping onto the sand from a narrow public access path a hundred yards to the south. A Nikon hung across his chest. He jogged toward us, his expression fierce. I looked down again, my gaze fixed on the men digging with archaeological precision.

Wes began taking photos, of the scene, the techs, the witnesses. He called to Ellis from the beach side of the wall. "What are they digging for, Chief?"

"Nice to see you, Wes. No comment."

"Come on, Chief."

Ellis ignored him.

Wes peppered me with questions, too, and when I didn't answer, he tried to provoke Maudie into an indiscretion.

"How does it feel to be betrayed by someone you love?" Wes asked, edging closer to her as he spoke.

Max laid his hand on Maudie's shoulder, indicating she shouldn't react. He stepped between them, blocking Wes's view of Maudie.

"Why do you need a lawyer, Mrs. Wilson? Are you a suspect in your niece's murder?"

Max glared at him. Maudie didn't seem to hear. Her eyes remained on the men methodically working, digging, brushing, assessing.

Wes gave up with a heartfelt sigh and resumed taking photos.

We waited.

After fifteen minutes, one of the techs called, "Chief, we have something."

Ellis peeled off the wall and walked toward them.

Wes placed both hands on the top of the wall, preparing to vault over, onto my lawn, and probably land on one of the iris beds.

"Stop!" I yelled, punching the air with my hand like a traffic cop. "Private property. Stay off."

"Come on, Joz! It's me."

"Look where we're standing—only the police are allowed on the lawn."

He sighed again.

Ellis helped stretch out a clear plastic tarp. The two techs worked together to haul out a heavy-seeming green trash bag.

"That's one of my trash bags," Maudie said.

"It appears similar," Max corrected.

"That looks like one of my trash bags," Maudie said, nodding.

The men laid it on the tarp.

We all leaned in closer as they opened it up and drew out a second, seemingly identical bag.

"Can you believe it?" Maudie whispered. "The killer took time to double-bag it after murdering Celia."

The techs slipped the box clear, and I took in a deep, satisfying breath. The clicks from Wes's camera punctuated the silence.

Max kept his eyes on the presentation box. "Jazzy."

Ellis looked over his shoulder and smiled at me. "Well done, Josie."

I pointed at the box, embarrassed by his praise, glad to change the subject. "It's beautiful, isn't it?"

"Those look like emeralds," Ellis said.

"They do indeed."

"Are the red ones rubies?"

"Probably garnets."

"Why?"

"Garnets were common in ancient Egypt. Rubies weren't."

"What are the blue stones?"

"Maybe nothing. Maybe lapis lazuli and turquoise."

"Is there any reason I shouldn't open it?"

"No."

Ellis snapped on plastic gloves and lifted the lid. He stared at the unimpressive cat sculpture without comment. After a moment, he asked me, "Do you recognize these objects?"

"Yes," I said. "Everything looks the same as when I first saw the box and cat in Maudie's trunk."

"Mrs. Wilson?"

Maudie looked stunned. "Me, too."

Ellis called out instructions to the techs, arranging for a video recording of the objects and the hole where they were found, and for their transport to the police station.

"Stay off this property," Ellis told Wes. He turned to Daryl. "Officer, if he encroaches, arrest him for trespassing."

I heard Wes's gobbled protests until we passed under the lattice. When we reached the street, Ellis stood by his SUV with Max on one side and Maudie on the other, the three of them facing me. I felt as if I were facing a tribunal.

"I need details, Josie," Ellis said.

Before I could say anything else, Tom drove up, his pickup clanking as he rolled to a stop on the rocky shoulder. He smiled and jumped down from the cab.

"Hey, Maudie! Josie!" His smile dimmed. "Chief Hunter."

Ellis introduced Max as Maudie's lawyer.

"Perfect timing," Ellis said. "Monte said you'd be back after lunch, and here you are."

"When it's this hot, I like to give the irises a little extra water."

"You'll have to skip today. We need to talk."

CHAPTER THIRTY-FOUR

Ellis followed Tom's pickup to the police station. Max brought up the tail.

"I thought maybe Julie would be with him," I said as we drove. "She often is."

"We need to talk to them both. I'll have someone pick her up."

While Ellis dispatched an officer to the Rocky Point Diner, where Tom said Julie was working, he set Detective Brownley talking to Maudie. Tom was left alone in an interview room.

Ellis took my statement himself, explaining this was preliminary, that he would no doubt have many more questions, but they could wait. All he wanted now was for me to repeat for the video camera what I'd already told him in the car. I described the torn-up lawn behind the shed, the missing grocery cart, all the disparate details that finally coalesced into one clear picture.

When I was done, he thanked me and chased me away, asking an officer to drive me back to my car.

"What's your next step?" I asked.

"Scoot. Time for you to go."

"I'd like to speak to Maudie first."

"Why?"

"I want to offer to help. I'll ask one innocuous question, that's it."

"Nothing you do or say is innocuous."

"Ha!"

He brought me into the next room, the same one where I'd talked to

Doug. Maudie's mien remained stolid, aghast. Max sat next to her, a legal pad in front of him. They each had a paper cup of water nearby.

I waited for Maudie to look at me. "I suspect you're not in a mood to talk about anything as mundane as packing, but I wanted to offer. If you'd like, I'll go there now and get your clothes and jewelry and anything you want right away, so you won't have to go back. I have boxes and packing materials in my car."

"Thank you, Josie, but don't do anything today. The way I'm feeling at this moment, I don't want to see anything that would remind me of this wretched experience. I may donate everything . . . I don't know. I'm too upset right now to decide."

"I understand." I turned to leave, then paused to add, "If I can do anything to help, please call."

I drove to work. Everyone was busy, and nothing needed my attention.

To distract myself, I called Gretchen for an update on the dragonfly situation and learned that my big surprise would be ready in a week. We talked about ways and means of keeping Ted away for an entire day, the time required to implement my plan, no easy task. She said she'd consult with Winnie.

I picked up a report on a marketing plan Gretchen had asked an outside firm to prepare, but couldn't concentrate. I tried to read my emails, but found my mind wandering. Wes called, and I let it go to voicemail. He texted, too, wanting a quote. After a frustrating half hour doing nothing productive, I drove home.

I ate a bowl of Zoë's soup and some salad, then changed into jeans and hiking boots and set off on one of my favorite walks, a trail through the woods. After a mile or so, the packed dirt path swung left and zigzagged through some wetlands. The trees grew tall and close, the leaves forming a high canopy. On bright days, with the sun dotting the path, it felt cozy. On cloudy days, it felt bleak. Today was in between. Speckles of sun penetrated the leaves, but the light was pale, washed out.

I called Ty and got him between meetings. He said he'd be home by seven and expected to be able to stay home for the next week. Then I filled him in about Maudie and the presentation box—and Celia's killer.

"How sure are you?" Ty asked.

"A hundred percent. Ellis will never get a confession, though. There may be evidence, but only of the theft . . . Maudie's checkbook, for instance."

"You don't think Lainy stole the checkbook? She was in the apartment to steal."

"No—it wasn't her." I paused where the trail curved. "I wish I knew what Ellis was doing right now."

"Half a story . . . you've always hated that."

"True, but also—" I broke off when call waiting clicked in. "There's another call. Hold on." It was Ellis. I asked him to hold and went back to Ty. "It's Ellis. I'll let you know what he wants. Love you . . . See you tonight!" I clicked back over.

"Cara said you went home. I'm outside your place now."

"I'm in the woods. I'll turn back."

Between the wind whipping up fallen leaves and the storm clouds that were rolling in fast, I was glad to reach open terrain.

Ellis stood in the driveway I shared with Zoë, chatting with Emma.

"How was the museum?" I asked.

"Stellar. So was lunch."

"Where's Zoë?"

"Getting a mani-pedi." She smiled at Ellis. "Apparently Mom has a hot date tonight."

"Very cool," I said. "And you're going to spend a few days with Jake."

She grinned. "Who says?"

"I have reliable sources. Say hey for me."

"Will do. I've got to grab my backpack and hit the road. See ya!"

When she was in the house, out of hearing, Ellis said, "Tom isn't talking."

"What about Julie?"

"She's in the wind."

I stared. "Julie? She'd never go anywhere without Tom!"

"And Santa Claus is real. She finished her shift at the diner at three. A coworker named Allison said she agreed to drive Julie to the Gingerbread House, where she was supposed to meet up with Tom. We've talked to Allison. According to her, Julie blew her off. No one else there knows anything except that Julie clocked out on time, changed in a flash, and was gone. Julie's not at the apartment she shares with Tom, her college library, the home of the family she babysits for, her parents' trailer, or anywhere else anyone can think of. Wes has been blasting the news we found the box and cat, so I figure she's gone to ground. I've left messages for her. We've notified the bus companies and airports to be on the lookout. She doesn't have wheels, so that's a help. I'm hoping you can think of something I've missed that will help bring her in."

"Money. Someone should offer her a job—you know, a couple of hours' work, high-paying, away from prying eyes, but on a bus route—or better yet, make it some snooty-sounding snob who offers to send a car for her. Julie won't think it's a stupid stereotype. She'll think it's her lucky day."

"I can get Dawn LeBlanc, the undercover cop from Portsmouth, to help. She's good—you remember her."

"She's terrific, but Julie has already been gone for how long?" I looked at my phone. "More than an hour. It's five after four. By the time you got the paperwork in order and Dawn up to speed, Julie could be in Florida. She's probably already in a rig heading south."

"Hitchhiking?"

"If I were her, I'd have headed straight to the nearest truck stop to ask a driver for a favor. Someone is bound to be eager for company. Long distance driving is lonely work." I smiled. "As to who can play the snooty role, I have an idea."

Max was eager to cooperate and signed the liability waiver Ellis passed him.

"This is fine," he said, handing it back. "I promise to do my best, and you indemnify me from any unfortunate consequences. Give me the details."

We sat in Ellis's office. The rain had started as mizzle, my mother's word for misty drizzle, while Ellis and I were still standing in the driveway, but by the time we reached the police station, it was drenching.

I sketched out Max's role. He took notes, nodding and smiling.

"This is good, Josie."

"You need the voice." I raised my chin and put enough nasal in my tone to float the Mayflower back to England. *"I'm terribly concerned about Mother."*

Max chuckled. "You ought to try out for Roxie, Josie. You're fabulous."

I laughed. "I can't sing. I can't act. I can't dance. I'm a triple threat, all right."

Ellis double-tapped the desk with his knuckles. "A discussion for another time." He turned to Max. "Can you do it?"

"No problem."

"I'm thinking I want to talk to her away from the police station, where her guard won't be up."

"Forget that," I said. "Her guard is always up."

"All the more reason to try for the element of surprise. I'll get us an off-site location."

"Get me the address," Max said. "In case she refuses my offer of a limo, I need to be able to tell her where to go."

"She won't," I said.

"She might," he argued.

"You're right. She might."

We both turned to Ellis and waited expectantly.

He rubbed his nose for a moment, then stood and walked to the door. "I'll be back. In the meantime, rehearse."

Ellis was back in ten minutes. He handed Max a slip of paper.

Max's brows drew together. "Isn't this Josie's address?"

"Next door—a woman named Zoë Winterelli. I've cleared it with her and have officers en route, just in case Julie shows up on her own."

Julie didn't answer her phone; no surprise. Max, in his role as Mortimer Peterson-Fox, an investment banker who'd been living in London for the last five years, left a message.

"Ms. Simond," he said at his haughty best, "my name is Mortimer Peterson-Fox. I understand you are a superb organizer—and that's what I need. It's for my mother, who is getting on in years. I live in London, and I'm here on a brief visit. Needless to say, time is of the essence. Mother has accumulated quite a lot, not hoarding exactly, well, not *exactly* hoarding, I suppose, but close enough for you to get the idea. Things must be culled. I hate to push—I truly do—but I must get things in order. Please tell me you're available now." He listed an hourly wage that made me stare. "Don't think I'm being overly generous. I assure you, you'll earn it. I can send a car for you. Please call me as soon as you get this."

He hung up and grinned.

I smiled. "You've got the part."

"I do like to act. It gives me quite a feel . . . I can't explain it."

Ellis leaned back. "For that kind of money, I'll help your mom myself."

"Was it too much?"

"No," I said. "She'll bite."

Two minutes later, Julie called. She was at the Mall at Fox Run in Newington, three miles northwest of Rocky Point, heading, perhaps, for Canada. They settled on the place where his limo would pick her up, and Ellis chose an officer I didn't know to play the driver, safely ensconced behind a locked divider made of bulletproof glass.

I was in my kitchen peeking out the window when the limo drove up. Ellis and I had both been dropped off by a patrolman, the same one who'd driven me to Belle Vista to pick up my car. Ellis went into Zoë's house, and I went into mine. He'd tried to get me to stay away, but after I promised to keep out of sight, he gave up. He had two additional police officers with him and sent them to hide in the bushes on the sides of the house.

The plan went off without a hitch. The police officer pretending to be the driver held the limo door, and Julie stepped out. Between the murky light and steady rain, her hair took on a coppery sheen. He shielded her with an umbrella. She looked around, then started up the walkway. He escorted her to the porch, then returned to the car.

The officer stood by the passenger side of the car and unbuttoned his jacket. I saw a glint of silver, his weapon, holstered on his left side.

Before Julie could ring the bell, Ellis stepped out.

Without pause, Julie vaulted to the walkway. Her sangfroid was fully as unexpected and startling as Lainy's anguished howls. As I stood and watched, stunned, she streaked across the street and lunged into the woods. A moment later, the driver and the two police officers sprang into action and charged after her.

Within seconds, they'd nabbed her. The two uniformed officers towed her clear of the woods. As soon as she hit the asphalt, she went limp, and they half-dragged her back. While Ellis snapped on the handcuffs and spoke the words I assumed were to inform her that she was under arrest, she raised her eyes to the sky. She seemed to see through the clouds and pelting rain to the heavens, as if she were praying. A patrol car pulled up. Ellis said something else I couldn't hear, and Julie shook her head no, no, no. After another brief exchange with Ellis speaking and Julie shaking her head, presumably his asking if she'd be willing to talk about the situation here and now, and her indicating no way, he led her to the patrol car. He assisted her in getting into the backseat, placing his hand over her head, protecting her. So much for Julie letting down her guard.

Two minutes later, they'd all left. I sat on my sofa and did nothing.

So many people affected by one young woman's ambition, impatience, and greed.

Wes called, interrupting my musings.

"I heard on my police radio that something went down at your house. What?"

"It wasn't my house. It was next door. Julie Simond has been taken into custody."

"Custody? What for? Talk to me!"

"Where are you?"

"Driving up Elliott, about half a mile from the takedown place."

"'Takedown' is a little strong."

I asked him to give me a ride to my car in return for filling him in, and he agreed.

We sat in Wes's car. The steady rain drummed a persistent beat. A wall of water running unchecked across the windshield blurred the outside world, cocooning us. I stared into space, explaining the inexplicable.

"Julie just couldn't take it anymore. She felt like everyone had been taking advantage of her good nature, and she'd had it. She went from being an unpaid helper when she lived in the Gingerbread House with Tom to working two jobs to cover her share of the rent once they moved out. Worse, she felt demoralized doing what she considered menial work. Here she is trying to better herself, to become the first person in her family to graduate college, to become a nurse, and she's stuck running from tedious job to tedious job, trying to make ends meet. From her perspective, Tom just doesn't get it. He's content simply getting by, but Julie has big dreams—a house, nice clothes, a new car. At this point, though, all she wanted was what she thought she earned, what she felt entitled to. If you were to ask her, she'd say that she's always tried to do the right thing, to be kind and helpful. She quoted her grandmother as saying that the people who help the most get the best lives. She was a true believer . . . She was wired to help, and she was reared to help, but she wasn't getting her due."

"I get it. She wanted more. So what happened?"

"Like everyone, Julie knew that Maudie was thinking of selling the presentation box, which meant she had to act before the opportunity slipped away. Julie didn't know if the jewels on the presentation box were real. No one did. I'm speculating here, but I think I'm on firm ground. If they were, great . . . if they weren't, no harm done. I suspect that she wasn't going to try to sell the box or cat. She was after the gemstones, probably just a couple of them. She might have planned to try to replace the ones she stole with fake stones before anyone noticed they were missing. With any luck, when the fakes were discovered, say, during an appraisal, everyone would assume they'd gotten lost at some point over the centuries and someone replaced them with replicas. I could see her justifying the theft by saying that no one would miss them, yet the money they'd bring to her would change her life, would give her options."

"Okay, so that's the justification and the plan. How'd she pull it off?"

"She snuck back into Maudie's apartment after Friday's lunch, after Maudie left for San Francisco. That's when Celia arrived. They must have been floored to see each other. Celia was planning a major scam of her own, so she had to be all twitchy from the get-go. I imagine Celia caught Julie in the act of prying a jewel loose. Celia, already frazzled, said she was going to call security—maybe even the police. Julie would have begged her not to, to forgive her, to let her go. She would have promised never ever to do anything like this again. Whether Celia refused or agreed, Julie probably wouldn't have trusted her to keep quiet, which meant her future hung in the balance. She convinced herself that Celia was an existential threat that had to be stopped. The rolling pin was in the drying rack. Julie grabbed it and struck."

"Why didn't she dig out the jewels then and there?"

"With a dying woman at her feet? She went into crisis mode. She was in and out of Maudie's apartment all the time, so she didn't have to worry about fingerprints, except on the bloody rolling pin, so she doused it with bleach."

"Why didn't she take the rolling pin with her?"

"I suspect it simply didn't occur to her. She was completely focused on the presentation box."

"Not just the box. She took the bleach, too, which doesn't make any sense."

"Sure it does. Probably she planned to sterilize the grocery cart after she was done with it."

"Come on," Wes said, sounding incredulous. "She didn't take the rolling pin, but she took the bleach?"

"She wouldn't want to be seen buying bleach right after the murder. And don't forget that time was of the essence."

"Okay," Wes said. "But wasn't it risky as all get-out for Julie to wheel the box out using Maudie's own grocery cart?"

"Not at all. She double-bagged the presentation box so it would be protected from the elements, which means no one would see anything noteworthy. I actually think using Maudie's grocery cart was smart—she was with Maudie a lot, often wheeling that same cart. Obviously, her plan worked. No one noticed her."

"She didn't pry out the jewels, though."

"My guess is that she decided to wait until after the brouhaha died down."

"You said she let herself back in," Wes said. "How'd she pull that off?"

"She had a key. The first time I met Maudie, the three of us had coffee. Maudie asked Julie to get her sweater. Maudie didn't hand Julie a key, which means she already had one. In terms of getting into the facility unseen, I did it myself with no problem."

"So she wheels the box in the grocery cart to her car. Then what? Where did she go?"

"The Gingerbread House. I was certain that she'd stashed the box and cart in the shed. She had a key to the shed—I saw her use it. All the guys working on the renovation are so used to seeing Julie in the garden, they wouldn't think anything of her wheeling in a bag of what they'd assume were supplies, probably for the iris beds. Later, after the crew had left for the day, while Tom was on some job or other, she buried the presentation box in back of the shed. I noticed the freshly torn-up lawn."

"Good one! Where's the grocery cart now?"

"Well bleached and in some Dumpster, would be my guess."

Wes tapped his pen on his chin. "My police source tells me that after lunch on the day Celia was killed, Julie said she went to the diner, that as soon as she got there, she realized she'd made a mistake about the day of her shift, so she turned around and left. But . . . hello! . . . if she was at the diner she couldn't have been at Maudie's apartment at the same time. Something isn't jibing here."

"She never went to the diner. She told that lie solely for Tom's sake. She needed a reason to explain why she was late. It never occurred to her she'd actually be a suspect, that she'd need a real alibi, so she just made it up."

"No way."

"It's true."

"How do you know it was a lie?"

"Julie said traffic wasn't bad on Travis or she would have been even later. Travis was closed to repair a water main break."

"Gotcha," Wes said, jotting a note. "You sure ate your Wheaties on this one, Joz!"

"There's more. Julie stole the consignment documents and Maudie's checkbook. Celia had already forged Maudie's signature on the forms."

Wes soft-whistled. "So Julie, thinking it was Maudie's real signature, saw an opportunity to steal some money by writing a fake check."

"I bet she rationalized it by saying she would only take what she was due for all that unpaid labor."

"Why didn't she take the pen?"

"Why would she? She didn't need it."

Wes shook his head. "Lots of people were up to no good: Celia, Lainy, Julie. All out for a quick buck."

"Different situations. Lainy simply wanted to finance her dream without saving for it. Celia felt she was out of options—poverty had worn her down. Julie felt she was doing everything right, yet she was just treading water."

"All women who felt Maudie or the world owed them," Wes said.

"What do you make of that?" I asked.

"I don't know. You?"

"Be careful who you trust."

We talked a while longer; then I raced through the buffeting rain to my car and drove home.

CHAPTER THIRTY-FIVE

Wes's late-night post revealed that Julie was refusing to cooperate and was being held on a material witness charge. Her court-appointed lawyer told Wes that he was looking forward to meeting with his client in the morning. Wes included a video clip he'd recorded at 9 P.M. of Tom, sitting on the hard wooden bench in the Rocky Point police station lobby. Tom had been cynical about human nature, but now that the dark side was touching him personally, he looked perplexed. It was heartbreaking to see.

Wes, out of camera view, asked Tom what he was doing there.

"I need to talk to Julie."

"She's been arrested," Wes said, "so I don't think they'll let you talk to her."

"I'll wait."

"Did you know of her plan to steal Maudie Wilson's presentation box?"

"There was no plan. There was no theft. Julie's not a thief."

"The police searched your apartment. They found Mrs. Wilson's checkbook and consignment forms from Prescott's Antiques in Julie's bedside table."

"What?" Tom squinted at the camera, at Wes. "That doesn't make any sense."

Detective Brownley's voice interrupted their conversation, telling Wes to stop recording, and a moment later, the video ended.

The rain stopped overnight, but it was still cloudy, and the temperature remained in the mid sixties. Ty was going to work from home, so he didn't have to get up before dawn. I made us scrambled eggs around eight. After we finished, Ty went upstairs to his office to set himself up for the day, and I washed up. I was drying the frying pan when Zoë came inside.

Her smile told me everything I needed to know. I laid the pan in the sink, dried my hands, and hugged her. I pulled her to the bench and sat on a chair.

"Tell me everything," I said.

She presented her left hand, palm down. The ruby winked under the incandescent lights.

"Oh, Zoë! It's breathtaking."

She giggled like a schoolgirl, jiggling her fingers to better catch the light. "Isn't it remarkable? I can't tell you how surprised I was." She reached across the table and took my hand in hers. "Ellis told me everything you did—goosing him to propose, the cruise, the dog fostering. I'll never, ever be able to thank you enough."

"You just did. Have you told Emma and Jake?"

"Ellis and I are driving down to Boston tonight. We'll take them out to dinner and tell them . . . and make sure they're available on the fifteenth. Also, we want the wedding to just be us six, so we'll pick a date for a bigger reception later, before Emma leaves."

"Don't pick the Saturday before she goes," I said, explaining that Ty and I planned to host a surprise party for her.

"I can help."

I touched her arm. "I'll count on it." I smiled. "You're getting married!"

"I'm so excited! Ellis is such a wonderful man."

"He really is. Shall we toast your future happiness with mimosas?"

She slid out of the booth. "Rain check. It wouldn't be the first time I've had champagne before nine in the morning, but I need to have all my wits about me. I'm going to an information session at the dog place to get the ball rolling."

I left for work around nine thirty.

Outside, the air was still damp, although the rain had stopped, and the sun was winning the battle for supremacy over the clouds. I hopped over puddles to reach my car.

When I got to my office, I pulled into a spot by the front door. Before

I got out of my car, Tom pulled up in his pickup. From his gray pallor and numb expression, I suspected he hadn't slept all night.

"Did you hear?" he asked without even a hello. "About Julie? She's confessed as part of a plea bargain."

"Oh. I hadn't heard that."

"I can't . . . I mean . . . it just doesn't . . . I can't . . ."

"I'm sorry."

"Julie is so sweet." He rubbed his brow as if he had a headache. "A killer? Julie?"

"What was the deal?"

"Negligent homicide—seven to twelve years. They were going to charge her with manslaughter—up to thirty years. Wes quoted you in his article this morning. He said you figured out that Julie was after money. Is it true? She killed Celia for money?"

"You need to talk to the police, Tom."

"It's my fault, isn't it? I should have realized the burden she was under. Here she was, a nursing student, struggling to pay the bills, while I'm diddling around." He rubbed his forehead again. "If I'd gotten a full-time job, taken the pressure off, or if I'd gone back to school like she wanted, none of this would have happened."

"Maybe you weren't as aware of her feelings as you could or should have been, but that still doesn't justify murder. You can't blame yourself."

Tom met my eyes for a moment. "Yes, I can."

He got back in his truck and drove away. As I watched him leave, I thought of Doug, another man who blamed himself.

At noon, the district attorney called to set up a meeting. She wanted to discuss a plea deal they were considering offering Lainy.

When I arrived, Maudie, accompanied by Max, was already there. So was Ellis.

The district attorney was a woman I'd met before named Cheryl Tavery. She was pragmatic and efficient.

She squared up her notes. "Thank you all for coming. Mrs. Wilson . . . Ms. Prescott . . . I want to talk to you about Ms. Baglio's alleged crime. You two are the victims. Mrs. Wilson, she burglarized your apartment. Ms. Prescott, she assaulted you. She seems genuinely remorseful. I'd like to know your thoughts if we drop the burglary charge and proceed only with simple assault, a misdemeanor. She could get up to a year in jail and a fine of two thousand dollars, but we're considering three years' probation. She'd have to give a full allocution."

Max turned to Maudie.

"Ask Josie first," Maudie said. "She's the real victim here."

All eyes turned toward me.

There was no excuse for Lainy's behavior. She wasn't desperate for money with small children to feed. She wasn't under attack, striking out in self-defense. She was greedy, entitled, wanting something for nothing. I got that her behavior was wrong, even dastardly. But I also knew that forgiveness was sometimes transformative.

"What are Lainy's plans?" I asked Cheryl.

"She wants to move to New York City to pursue an acting career."

"How will she support herself?"

"Waiting tables."

"She'll have trouble getting good work with this on her record."

"It's only a misdemeanor."

"Still." I turned to Maudie. "We talked about second chances. We both believe in them."

"Yes."

I turned back to the prosecutor. "I think you should just let her go."

Cheryl looked incredulous. "After breaking into an apartment and attacking you? No way."

I stood. "You asked my opinion. That's it. Give her a second chance." I stood. "Nice seeing you all." I walked out.

Two hours later, Wes posted a breaking-news alert on the *Seacoast Star* website. The district attorney, citing unspecified mitigating circumstances, announced that all charges against Lainy Baglio had been dropped.

Five days later, the day after Celia's funeral, I walked through the woods to the church. It was four in the afternoon, another glorious summer day, in the low eighties, with a balmy breeze.

Winnie and Gretchen had conspired with Pastor Ted's wife to get him out of town. Peg told Ted she needed a fun day with her husband, so they were going to Boston to walk the Freedom Trail, eat some steamers and lobster, and ride the Swan Boats. Ted, after getting over his astonishment at such an unprecedented request, was delighted to comply. Peg promised to have Ted back between four and four thirty.

The screens were perfect, unobtrusive and easy to open. I congratulated Winnie and Gretchen on their speedy and excellent work.

"You do the honors," I told Winnie.

"You should. It's your donation."

"Nope, I want to be an observer."

Ted and Peg drove into the lot, right on schedule. We all listened to Ted's amazement that they hadn't thought about playing hooky before, kissing Peg's cheek and saying that it was now going to be a regular occurrence.

"I sense that you're not here by coincidence," Ted said, looking from Winnie to Gretchen to me. He took in his wife's expression and added, "And Peg's in on it."

"It's a surprise!" Winnie said. "Follow me."

We trooped into Ted's office and stood in a cluster by the entryway.

"Notice anything?" she asked Ted.

He took his time, examining the ceiling, the floor, the walls, his desk. When he spotted the screens, he gasped and pointed. "Screens!" He turned to Winnie. "You got us screens!"

"Josie did."

He hugged me, a big warm bear hug, then walked to a window to touch the wire mesh.

"They're incredible. So thoughtful. So generous."

I smiled. "Now I won't have to worry about those dragonflies."

He extended his hand, and I took it. "Thank you, Josie."

We traipsed down to the commercial kitchen, where Peg found a pitcher of lemonade in the fridge, and we toasted the new screens and summer days spent toodling around Boston.

When I got back to Prescott's, Maudie was waiting for me.

I sat across from her at the guest table and asked, "I know you're not a fan of stairs. Would you like to go outside so we can talk in private?"

"There's no need. Thank you, though. Actually, I'm here on business. I'd like you to appraise the presentation box and cat. After you're done, I'll decide if I want to sell it. Chief Hunter says I can pick them up anytime. I asked him to release the objects to you or your staff."

I grinned, excitement bubbling inside me. "I'm very pleased, Maudie. We'll get the objects today. Now." I turned to Fred. "Take Eric."

Fred smiled broadly and pushed through the heavy door that led to the warehouse. Hank and Angela zipped out into the front.

While Cara prepared the appraisal agreement form, including a paragraph allowing me to feature the presentation box and cat on *Josie's Antiques*, the cats frisked around Maudie.

"Are they bothering you? I can chase them away."

"Not a bit. I love cats!" Angela sprang into her lap. Hank nuzzled her calf.

Maudie read the form carefully, signed it, and tucked her copy into her purse.

"What can you tell me about the objects' history?" I asked.

"Not much. Vivian's husband inherited the box and cat. They had been originally acquired by his great-great-grandfather while he was on his honeymoon in Rome sometime in the early 1900s. Most of the family had assumed the objects were nothing more than attractive collectibles with a nifty story. I'm sorry I can't tell you more."

"It's a start."

Maudie placed Angela on the floor and stood. She smiled. "You know why the cats like me? Because they heard that I own a cat beloved by the gods. Mark my words—the cat sculpture is real. Cats know everything."

CHAPTER THIRTY-SIX

T hursday morning around ten, I stood next to Nate Blackmore, Prescott's go-to jewelry expert, in the cordoned-off work area we'd allocated to the Wilson appraisal.

Nate slipped on white cotton gloves, standard operating procedure to avoid transferring oils from skin to potentially valuable objects. We knew these had been handled without protection for generations, but once the formal appraisal process began, our protocols kicked in. I wasn't particularly worried about it. While the oils from skin can break down certain materials like the papyrus ancient Egyptians used as paper, it was unlikely that anything on the box or cat sculpture was vulnerable.

"The most valuable gems, if they're real, are the emeralds," Nate said. "The others are likely to be semiprecious stones common to the era: garnets, onyx, lapis lazuli, and turquoise."

"Am I right that it's easy to tell if an emerald is genuine?"

"Yes. There are three tests. Assessing value is more complex, as it is in any appraisal, but authentication is fairly straight-ahead."

He bent the gooseneck lamp so the light shone directly on one of the emeralds. He fixed a loupe in his eye and bent over to study the stone.

"Take a look," he said. "Note the inclusions, the crystals throughout and a needle on the right."

The flaws were apparent. "I see them."

"That's a good sign. Essentially all emeralds are flawed. Now I'll breathe on it. If it's real, it will begin to evaporate in a second or two, and it will dissipate fast. Fakes take seconds longer, which doesn't sound like much, until you calculate it on a percentage basis. Fakes take up to five hundred percent longer for a breath to begin evaporating and two to three hundred percent longer for the evaporation process to complete."

He breathed on the stone. The film of air was evident, then gone.

"Another good sign," I said.

"The last step is to apply a coating of oil. If it's real, clarity will be enhanced. If it's fake, the oil has no effect."

Nate used a small brush, the velvety soft bristles certain not to harm the stone. He spread a microscopically thin coating of oil across the surface, then examined it again with the loupe. When he was done, he straightened up and invited me to look.

I leaned over the box. "I see the crystallization in more detail."

"We just proved that this green stone is a genuine emerald."

I took a magnet from the worktable drawer and placed it against the side of the box. "I know many metals available to ancient Egyptians contained nickel."

"And nickel is a magnetic material."

"While silver is not."

The magnet tumbled to the table, and I smiled.

"I'm going to turn the box over to test both the silver and gold."

"Nitric acid?" I asked.

"Yes . . . the acid test."

I helped him access the bottom.

He changed gloves, replacing the white cotton ones with a heavy protective pair, and he put on safety glasses.

"I'm going to make a tiny scratch in each colored metal. If they're genuine, it will be easy to do because both gold and silver are soft."

"Don't we risk hurting the value?"

"The scratches will be so small they'll be impossible to discern. We're watching for a reaction. For the gold-colored metal, green means fake gold; milky white froth, gold-plated sterling silver; and if there's no reaction—it's gold."

"Am I right that for the silver, a green reaction means it's not silver, but if it's creamy white—not milky, just a clear cream color—it's sterling."

"You got it."

"Fingers crossed."

He used an eye dropper to apply the nitric acid. We watched for a reaction.

Nate smiled. "Look at that—nothing on the gold, and cream on the silver."

"The emeralds are real. The silver is real. The gold is real. That suggests everything is real."

"That would be my conclusion, but I'll need to examine every gemstone. A physical examination can verify garnets, lapis lazuli, and turquoise with a high degree of confidence. I can use other tests, like color stability and Mohs hardness, if needed."

I left Nate to his work and carried the cat sculpture to another bench. I wanted to examine the material. My first step was to weigh it. Typically, an eighteen-inch bronze hollow-cast sculpture from ancient Egypt would weigh between nine and fifteen pounds. This one weighed twenty-five pounds. The logical next step was to x-ray it, which would reveal if anything was secreted inside, most likely jewelry or loose stones. I was certain there was. The sculpture was simply too heavy for its size and material—assuming the material was bronze.

I used a wooden pick to scrape along the bottom edge. The patina didn't scratch or flake off, and the minuscule bit of underlying metal I'd exposed gleamed with a dark golden hue, a sign it was bronze, an alloy comprised largely of copper, the material I expected. I stuck it gently with a wooden dowel and heard the telltale clear ring. Another encouraging sign. The statue wasn't magnetic. I smiled. A minute examination with a loupe showed there was no rust. My smile broadened.

The bottom had been sealed eons ago, perhaps upon forging. The seal was also evidently bronze. It was round, six and three-quarters inches in diameter, leaving roughly an inch of the cat's bottom circling it. We might be able to pry it open without harming the statue—that was a question for Dr. Moss, the San Francisco–based Egyptologist.

Years ago, when we needed to see inside a doll, we'd used an x-ray machine at Portsmouth Diagnostic Imaging. After that experience, I bought Prescott's a portable x-ray machine, easy to use and highly reliable. I scanned the cat. To my surprise, nothing was inside. I repeated the test. Nothing.

"How can that be?" I asked myself.

Hank mewed, telling me he didn't know.

"Let's consider provenance. What do you think, Hank? If I can find anything about where the objects were created or who owned them, maybe I can find something to explain the extra weight."

Hank got bored and ambled away.

Per our insurance company's regulations, no one who isn't a bonded Prescott's employee, not even a jeweler of impeccable reputation, is allowed in the warehouse unescorted. I called Cara and asked her to send in Sasha to keep Nate company. As soon as Sasha arrived, I said good-bye to Nate and went up to my private office.

Using one of the proprietary art library sites we subscribed to, I located an old sales catalogue from a 1915 auction. The auction, titled "Divine Cats: Sacred Animals of Egyptian Gods," had been organized by a long-defunct Rome antiques auction house. The cat and presentation box featured in a two-page spread were listed as owned by "anonymous," a not unusual occurrence. Many sellers don't want savvy thieves to know they possess valuable art or antiques. The catalogue copy was written by an art historian, Dr. Anthony Russo. One of his entries described a cat sculpture and presentation box that exactly matched the size, style, coloration, and appearance of Maudie's objects—down to the centimeter.

I called Maudie at the Austin Arms and got her.

"I have good news. We've been testing the materials, and so far, everything indicates that the box and cat are genuine. I'm working on the provenance now, and I was wondering if you'd object to my calling Stacy and talking to her about it. I know you want to keep the appraisal confidential, so if you'd prefer I don't, I understand completely."

"Thank you for asking. I think I'll say yes. I'm really determined not to let myself be intimidated. I have some good news, too—I'm trying to give myself a second chance. I'm back in touch with Doug."

"That is good news."

"Very. I called to ask if he'd like some moral support at tomorrow's sentencing hearing."

"For Julie? I hadn't heard the hearing was tomorrow."

"Yes, at ten. I'd planned to go, of course, but now I'll be able to sit with him, to help, if I can."

"You must be distraught."

"I should be, I suppose, but I'm not. I don't think 'distraught' is in my emotional lexicon. What I feel is sad. Very, very sad. But I'm determined to put my sadness aside and be there for Doug."

"I'm sure it will mean a lot to him to have you there."

We chatted for another minute; then I called Stacy and made my request. "Do you know how the box and cat came into your family?"

"Through my dad's great-great-grandfather. His name was Ethan Holmes. He was a college professor in Rutgers's Classics Department. I know he earned his Ph.D. at Princeton and that he spent two years in Cairo as a visiting professor and traveled extensively throughout Europe. I'm sorry, but I don't remember which university he worked at there or where, specifically, he traveled. I assumed that he acquired the objects during that period."

"I'm guessing he was overseas in the early 1900s . . . does that sound right?"

"Yes. I know he came back before World War I."

"Do you have any cousins or other relatives who might have additional information?"

"No . . . sorry."

"Thanks, Stacy. You've been helpful. How are you doing?"

"Better. I decided that if I wanted to keep my sanity I had to stop pounding my head against the wall. I sold my designs and licensed my machine to a competitor, so at least the orders will be filled. Don't get me wrong. I haven't given up. I'm going to continue to hunt for funding, and I hope I'll be able to launch my own line within a couple of years, but clearly now isn't the time."

"That sounds like such a smart plan, Stacy. Congratulations."

"I don't know that congrats are in order, but at least I can sleep at night."

"Have you gone back to New York?"

"Oh, yeah. I can only take Rocky Point for so long, no insult intended."

"None taken. I wondered if you planned on going to Julie's sentencing hearing tomorrow."

"No. I said everything I had to say to the district attorney. She killed my sister, left her to bleed to death alone. I hope they give her the max."

"I understand. Any news about Doug?"

"He likes his new job, and he's planning on going back to school, accounting, I think. We decided to get together for Thanksgiving, if not before. Aunt Maudie's hosting the dinner at the Austin Arms."

"I'm glad to hear that."

"And I promised him that I'd try to get better around the kids."

I smiled. "You don't like them?"

"It's not them in particular . . . it's all kids. What's to like? They're little narcissists. I'm of the children-should-be-seen-and-not-heard theory of child-rearing. I don't know why that approach ever fell out of favor."

I laughed, thinking that I wasn't surprised that she didn't warm to children. "Maybe you'll like them better as they get older."

When we were done, I swiveled back to face my computer monitor. Given that Stacy had no more specific information about where or when her ancestor purchased the box and cat, I could infer the objects came from this auction house, but I couldn't document it. I clicked on the next link, which led to a sheaf of Dr. Russo's original handwritten notes, a copy of which was archived at the University of Rome. The English translation was available online.

Dr. Russo wrote that jewels were alleged to be hidden inside the cat sculpture. From the x-ray, I knew this wasn't true, and I wondered why he'd speculated that they were. Another article, published in 1987, suggested that the rumor persisted because the cat, which was made of bronze with silver and gold inlays, backed by lead, weighed almost twice as much as the Gayer-Anderson Cat, the exemplar owned by the British Museum.

"Holy moly!"

I called Sasha. Nate had left, and she was at her desk.

"I'll be right down," I told Sasha. "Get the endoscope."

With Sasha holding the insulated cord, keeping it straight, I threaded the tiny camera into the cat through its open mouth. Together we watched on the monitor.

The inside metal was streaked with verdigris, a green patina.

"The outside must have been coated with wax," Sasha said. "Otherwise, it would be green, too."

"Sealing bronze sculptures was common." I inched the scope lower. "Look, do you see those pins?"

"Yes. Is that what held the mold in place?"

"The wax mold, yes," I said. I moved the camera closer to inspect the remnants of the pins. They were coarsely hewn. "After creating a wax mold, the artist covered it with clay and fired it in a kiln. Naturally, the wax melted away."

"Which is why it's called the lost-wax process."

Something gleamed in the camera's concentrated light. "Wow." There was something inside, but not jewels. "I was right, but wrong." The object was just shy of six inches square, all gold, as bright as the sun. I looked at her. "See if you can reach Ed Moss."

We got him at his studio and sent him the live camera feed.

"What do you think it is?" I asked.

"I don't know. It's not a familiar object."

"I'm going to show you the bottom of the inside of the cat, then the outside bottom. It's sealed."

I manipulated the endoscope so he could see a close-up of the inside seal. It was jagged, as if whoever added the metal disk was only concerned about the outside appearance. Sasha used our professional camera to take a detailed image of the outside. It was smoother than what appeared on the inside, but lopsided. Sasha emailed the photo.

"Any thoughts?" I asked Dr. Moss.

"I need to examine it in person. The seal is uneven, which suggests it was added some time after the statue was created."

"How soon can you get here?"

He could come immediately, and I transferred him to Cara, so she could make his travel arrangements.

Sasha packed up the endoscope. "Since the x-ray was negative, what made you think something was inside?"

I smiled. "A 1987 article saying a cat similar to ours was heavy because it contained lead. X-rays don't penetrate lead."

I checked my calendar and saw I had an appointment with Gretchen. She wanted to discuss the finalists for her new assistant position.

"Do you have a favorite?" I asked her.

"Zach. I like his reason for wanting a new job—he's always looking to better himself. He's an assistant manager at a furniture store, and he was knowledgeable about quality construction. He cares. If they'd had an opening for a manager, he would have stayed. If you agree, I'd like to offer him the job, and as part of his onboarding process, I think we should sign him up for Hitchens's weeklong gallery management course. It will be good for him to learn some of the vocabulary and special considerations we deal with."

"Yes, I agree, because it's your decision to make. Remember that part of your job is to continually groom him for his next position at Prescott's."

"Will do. I'm excited."

"Me, too. You did a fabulous job, as always."

Later, as Ty and I sat in the hot tub watching stars twinkle, we discussed our plans for Emma's party.

"I'm thinking I need to rent a hall."

"How big are you thinking?"

"Big." I told him my ideas. "What do you think?"

He said he loved it, and I slid deeper into the hot tub. Everything was coming together.

CHAPTER THIRTY-SEVEN

 got to the courthouse at a quarter to ten the next morning, Friday, located the correct courtroom, and paused by the door. I felt oddly nervous.

Wes stood with his back to me, talking to Tom. Tom shook his head and walked into the courtroom.

I nodded at Tom as he passed by. Wes joined me at the door.

"How's Tom?" I asked.

"Feeling played."

"He prided himself on his ability to read people."

"And messed up big-time."

"If someone is a good liar, there's no way you can tell."

"Don't you think you can read people? Their eyes? Nervous tics?"

"I like to think so, but who knows? If someone cons you, how would you know unless they get caught? Have you heard how Julie is doing? Is she contrite?"

"I guess we'll find out soon enough. No one from her family showed up."

"That's awful."

We walked in together. Wes sat in the front. I sat in the back not far from Tom. I was pleased to see Maudie sitting next to Doug.

Julie was led in. She wore an orange prison jumpsuit. She didn't look at anyone, not her lawyer, not Tom, not the judge.

She stood when told to do so, sounded robotic when she delivered her allocution, which contained no new information, and sat when she finished.

The judge asked if there were any victim impact statements. Maudie patted Doug's arm. He stood and dragged himself to the podium positioned to face Julie, giving the gallery and judge his profile. Julie kept her eyes on the table in front of her.

"You killed the love of my life, the mother of my children, a woman who did you no harm. I will never forgive you. After today, I will never again speak your name."

He carefully refolded the paper, placed it into his pocket, and returned to his seat.

The judge asked if there were any other statements. There weren't.

He sentenced Julie to seven to twelve years, and she was led away.

After everyone else had left, I sat on the bench thinking about love and loss, independent thinking, and second chances.

I returned to Prescott's and ate lunch outside, a tuna salad sandwich, sitting under the willow tree. When I was done, I stayed a while longer, enjoying listening to the birds chat.

An old brown car pulled into the lot. I didn't recognize the driver, a young man in his twenties. The passenger was Lainy.

I stepped out from under the willow so she'd see me.

She said something to the driver and got out.

She walked toward me, stopping ten feet away.

She nervously pleated a fold of her skirt. "I just came from seeing Maudie. She looks good, better now that she's out of Belle Vista. Not that there's anything wrong with Belle Vista—I didn't mean that." She paused. "I went to thank her for asking the district attorney to let me go, and she said it was all you, that she went along with it, but it was your idea, that it wouldn't have happened without you, that you argued for it. Thank you. I'm so sorry for what I did. I'm *so* sorry."

"I've always thought that a couple of mistakes, even a couple of really bad mistakes, shouldn't define your life."

"I won't let you down."

"Don't let yourself down." I glanced at the car. "Are you leaving town?"

"I'm going to New York. My friend is driving me to the bus. I applied online and got a waitress job at the Marriott in Times Square and a room at the Y. I'm not going to screw up."

"I believe you. I think you've got a lot of potential."

Her eyes widened. "You do?"

I smiled. "I do." I set off across the parking lot, heading for the front door. After a few steps, I stopped and looked back at her. "Break a leg."

Dr. Moss drove his rental car straight from the airport, arriving at four thirty, eager to examine the cat sculpture. It took him less than twenty minutes to determine that the seal was not contemporaneous to the sculpture but was itself ancient, probably added during the Late Period of ancient Egyptian history, perhaps in an effort to hide whatever was secreted inside from Alexander the Great's successful conquest of Egypt in 331 BCE. The seal was made of bronze but bore a different patina and had been added by a different, and lesser, craftsman. He said he was willing to open it up but would need cutting tools and an assistant, preferably a master ironworker.

Fred smiled and pointed at his chest. "You're looking at one. I'm a certified welder."

"Good. Let's examine the—"

"Wait," I said, interrupting. "Before you break the seal, I want to get the TV crew up here. I want to memorialize this process—whatever we find inside the cat. I know Cara has you set up at a nice hotel. I'm going to try to get the team up here by tomorrow. Before I call, I need to know if you're willing to have your work recorded for *Josie's Antiques*. I should mention that you'll receive a separate honorarium from the show."

"I'd be delighted," he said.

"Super! I'm going to call Timothy now. If you'd like to work with Fred on how you'll tackle the unsealing, what tools you'll need, etcetera, that's fine. If you'd prefer to wait until morning to hear what's going on, that's fine, too."

He said he was eager to work with Fred.

I went up to my office and placed the call.

"Timothy, you're going to hate me, but then you're going to love me. I need you to get a crew up here now—so we can film in the morning."

"I hate you!"

"Wait till you hear why."

An hour later, as dusk was falling and the moon was rising, the arrangements were complete. Timothy would get the equipment on the road overnight. The crew would fly up in the morning. All the filming would occur at

Prescott's, which was already outfitted with much of what was needed in terms of lighting and wiring. Timothy thought he might be able to use a clip from my video showing the discovery of the objects in the dumbwaiter, so I sent it to him. We agreed that I'd re-create all the steps of my examination of the presentation box. Nate had appeared on previous episodes, so I knew he'd be glad to repeat his work for the camera. Dr. Moss had just agreed to do the same.

I called Maudie to ask if she'd like to appear on camera.

"Heavens, no!" Maudie said. "I'm glad the objects are worth filming, but I don't want to be on TV. Don't use my name, either, please. I don't want to be hounded by people about it."

I agreed that she would only be referred to as the owner.

I ended the call and stared out the window at the gathering twilight. I'd talk about my online research and my conversations with the family, who wished to remain anonymous. The final step—the breaking of the seal—would be filmed on-site, in real time.

The next day, Saturday, with the tag sale in full swing, the TV crew set up their equipment in the warehouse and my office. They were ready by one. Timothy decided to film the redo shots later and to start at the end.

Dr. Moss and Fred began working on breaking the seal. Dr. Moss explained to the camera that laser cutting would require treating the bronze with a graphite spray paint in order to prevent the beam from refracting off the surface, endangering the operator, but since the paint leaves a residue that can alter or damage the object, the preferred method is the one that's been around for thousands of years—sawing.

The two men used a thin handsaw to break through the bronze seal, leaving a scattering of metal shards on the worktable. Once the seal was removed, the opening was shown to be symmetrical, the lip smooth.

Ignoring the cameras as Timothy had taught me years earlier, I proceeded as if I were talking to respected colleagues. I held the light over Ed's head while he used padded tweezers to extract the gold object. Once it was free from the cat, he laid it on a sheet of acid-free paper.

"It's a book," Fred said.

The book was comprised of six pages, bound by two gold rings. Using the tweezers, Dr. Moss turned them, one at a time.

Dr. Moss turned to face me. "This appears to be twenty-four-karat gold." He studied the markings. "The language is probably Middle Egyptian, used from 2000 BCE to 1300 BCE."

"This resembles the Etruscan Gold Book," I said, "you know the one I mean. A construction worker found it in Bulgaria when he was digging a canal. That one dates to 600 BCE and is considered the world's oldest book. You're saying this one is even older? Is that even conceivable?"

"I need to examine the language carefully to be certain, and we'll need to compare the two books. That one is housed in the National History Museum in Sofia—in Bulgaria. To answer your question, given this cat statue's likely provenance, it is definitely possible that this book is even older than the Etruscan one—as much as a thousand years older."

"That's remarkable!" I said, beaming. "You're thinking that someone who cherished the book hid it in the cat as the bad guys—Alexander the Great's troops—were knocking on the city walls."

"I think that's a likely scenario. The book might well have been produced hundreds of years before it was hidden."

"What would you expect the content to include?"

"Probably it's a kind of eulogy, a tribute to someone created when he died."

"Assuming we can verify its authenticity, how much would it sell for? A rough guess?"

Dr. Moss turned to the book, the gold resplendent. "Somewhere between a fortune and priceless."

Timothy called, "Cut!" He turned to me. "You're right! I love you!"

I called Maudie to tell her the news, and she was, no surprise, speechless.

I started describing options for verifying the book—we could take our book to the museum in Sofia, or find scholars who've studied that one to come to us—but she stopped me and said, "Let someone else do it. If I wanted to donate it to a museum, which one is most equipped to take the next steps?"

"The British Museum in London. The Louvre in Paris. The Metropolitan Museum of Art in New York City. The new museum in Cairo, the Grand Egyptian Museum, should be on the list, too."

"Let's keep it in America. Can we ask them to loan it to the Egyptian Museum every once in a while?"

"Yes, assuming they deem it appropriate. They'll need to assess security and so on."

"Good. Arrange it, please."

I had mixed feelings. I thought donating the objects was incredibly generous of her, but I was sad that I wouldn't be able to continue the appraisal. I told myself that everybody won on this one. Dr. Moss, Nate, and all of us at Prescott's got valuable experience and exposure. Maudie learned enough to know that if the objects her beloved sister had given her could talk, the history they'd share would span several millennia. But I wanted to do more. I always wanted to do more.

I walked outside into the hot, humid late afternoon sun and blew a kiss as the caravan carrying Timothy and the crew headed back to New York.

CHAPTER THIRTY-EIGHT

A ugust fifteenth dawned with the promise of high heat and humidity, an ideal day to be on the water.

I arranged for a white stretch limo to drive us to the *Perfect Knot* where it was berthed at a Portsmouth marina. The limo had seating for twelve, so the six of us, Zoë, Ellis, Emma, Jake, Ty, and me, were able to sprawl. I'd brought a thermos of mimosas and plastic cups, and we toasted our way to the yacht.

Captain Ken dropped anchor two miles out. The yacht rocked gently. The midday sun sent diamonds tripping across the water.

We gathered under a canvas canopy. Zoë wore a white sheath and a wreath of lilies of the valley Emma had picked from the meadow earlier in the day, twirling them around a thin wire frame, and carried a bouquet of red gladiolas. Ellis wore a white linen suit with a red rose boutonniere. I couldn't stop crying.

Ty kept his arm around my waist, holding me close.

After the ceremony, Zoë turned her back to toss her bouquet to Emma, but Emma stepped aside, shaking her hands, signaling "no, no, no," and Jake, with the instinct of a baseball player, caught it on the fly. We got a good laugh out of it, and finally I stopped crying.

I rented the local VFW hall for Emma's party. The biggest challenge was arranging all the detailed logistics while maintaining the surprise.

With Cara and Gretchen's help, I was able to arrange for a buffet laden with comfort food, valet parking for the overflow cars at the fairgrounds down the street, and enough bunting to decorate the half-mile stretch between the two lots. Academy Brass would play throughout the evening.

I'd called Lieutenant Commander Silberblatt to invite her and asked that she invite any military parents she knew. I met with the veterans' associations myself to make my pitch—*let's give the new marine the send-off of a lifetime.* I asked Gretchen to organize "military parent" ribbons for the name tags so Zoë could easily recognize her new community. I ordered a hundred small American flags, which would be available for anyone who wanted one at the start of the party.

Ellis and Zoë would tell Emma that they were at the VFW to celebrate longtime VFW member Sergeant Carl Warren's one hundredth birthday.

Five days before the party, Gretchen came into my office.

"We need to buy more flags," she said. "Cara just heard from the head of the ROTC program at Hitchens. They're coming—with past graduates and their families. They expect at least sixty-five people."

I smiled. "This is great, Gretchen. Call around to all the veterans' associations and see if you can get an estimate, then buy more flags."

She smiled. "I'll get Zach to do it."

"Even better."

By the end of the day, we had a solid estimate of 215 partygoers, from students to veterans and their families to Emma's friends—invited by Zoë and Jake and sworn to secrecy. I told Zach to get us 150 additional flags, and we still ran out.

Saturday was sunny but cool and breezy, more autumn than summer. Emma's surprise was revealed as soon as she stepped inside the door. As Emma came into view, Academy Brass struck up a rousing Sousa march, moved into "America the Beautiful," continued with other patriotic songs, and concluded the set with the "Marines' Hymn."

Three hours later, when the party was winding down and the crowds had begun to disperse, Emma hugged me tight, rocking a little.

"Thank you," she whispered, "for everything." She pulled back. "How do you think Mom is doing?"

"Better."

"I love you, Josie."

"You're so special, Emma. So very special. I love you, too."

Emma joined Zoë and hugged her, whispering something in her ear.

Zoë hugged her back, and from where I stood, seeing them both in profile, I had a clear view of Zoë's smile.

Ty and I moved into the Gingerbread House on November nineteenth, the week before Thanksgiving. The place looked bare.

"I didn't realize how big it is," I said, looking around the mostly empty living room. "We have some shopping to do."

"It's hard to know where to start."

"The farm table that was in my kitchen. I was thinking of using it as a craft table in one of the spare bedrooms. How about if we use it as a dining room table on a temporary basis?"

"It's awfully big. Why not just use the small round table for now?"

"Because I think we should host Thanksgiving dinner. We have so much to be thankful for this year."

Ty kissed the top of my head. "I agree."

I went up on tiptoe to kiss him, closing my eyes to memorize the moment, wanting to remember the feeling of acceptance and love forever.

ACKNOWLEDGMENTS

Special thanks go to my literary agent, Cristina Concepcion of Don Congdon Associates, Inc. Thanks also go to Michael Congdon and Cara Bellucci.

Thanks to G. D. Peters, who read early drafts of this novel with care and diligence, and to Academy Brass, a quartet that plays the music of the angels, particularly the low notes.

The Minotaur Books team gets special thanks, too, especially those I work with most closely, including assistant editor Hannah O'Grady, for her many insights, and assistant director of publicity (St. Martin's and Minotaur) Sarah Melnyk, for her guidance and support. Thanks also to director of library marketing and national accounts manager (Macmillan) Talia Ross, the late copy editor India Cooper, cover designer David Baldeosingh Rotstein, and of course, the late executive editor Hope Dellon.

In addition, I want to offer thanks to the selfless souls who volunteer to train service dogs, including Paul DeVito, who helped me understand the process.

To retired USN Lieutenant Commander Cynthia (Cindy) Elaine Barth Silberblatt, who helped me help Zoë, my sincere thanks. To all the members of the United States military—whatever your role, wherever you serve, whether you're on active duty, in the reserves, or retired, thank you for your service.